ANGELS OF LIGHT

ALSO BY JEFF LONG

Outlaw: The True Story of Claude Dallas

ANGELS

OF

LIGHT

JEFF LONG

BTB

BEECH TREE BOOKS
WILLIAM MORROW
New York

Library of Congress Cataloging-in-Publication Data

Long, Jeff.
  Angels of light.

  I. Title.
PS3562.O4943A5   1987   813'.54   86-32155
ISBN 0-688-07251-8

Printed in the United States of America

First Edition

1 2 3 4 5 6 7 8 9 10

BOOK DESIGN BY JAYE ZIMET

The word "book" is said to derive from *boka,* or beech.
The beech tree has been the patron tree of writers since ancient times and
represents the flowering of literature and knowledge.

For Diane

"The existence of some terribly yawning abyss in the mountains ... was frequently described to us by crafty or superstitious Indians. Hence the greater our surprise upon first beholding a fit abode for angels of light."

—LAFAYETTE BUNNELL, member of the Mariposa Battalion, on discovering Yosemite Valley in 1851

ANGELS OF LIGHT

*L*ike that wild boy
who flew too close to the
sun, there was no way the
climber was not going to fall.
The difference was that John's wings
were melting under the moon, and that for
him ascent was not escape but captivity itself. It was too soon for him to admit desperation, though, and so John Coloradas worried
his hands—taped, raw, and smoking with a fresh coating of gymnastic chalk—tighter and higher in the cold
granite crack, grimacing because there was no pain and there
should have been. There would be time enough once (he declined "if") he and Tucker hit flat land to thaw his fingers
and check for frostbite. For now he bit a lungful off the night breeze,
smelling pines so far below you couldn't hear them. Moonlight seared
the wide, stark acres of stone, starving his shadow, beckoning him higher
with its quicksilver. He could taste the chalk powder in the back of his
throat, and from much farther away, perhaps a cave or a stand of timber
on the summit, the scent of moss crossed his tongue, too. And beneath
all the Valley's smells he smelled the storm.

It was going to snow. But not before it rained. And so he kept twisting and fusing his hands and feet into the indifferent stone, wrestling
against the tyranny that hung on him like a monkey in heat. Nasty as it
was, the threat of getting wasted by a Pacific cold front didn't astonish
him. In the pantheistic order of things, it made perfect, dust-to-dust
sense. If he could have spared the motion, he would have shrugged.
Maybe they'd make it, maybe not. Since departing the earth five short

days and long nights ago, the climb had been freighted with miscalculation and fuckups: too little food, too much water, some important pieces of equipment dropped from numb fingers, a half day spent following the wrong crack. Any big-wall climb magnifies such venial errors. A big-wall climb in winter can make them downright carnivorous, and here it was Christmas Eve. The Duracell batteries in their blaster had given up the ghost, robbing them of Talking Heads and the Himalayan climbers' standard Pink Floyd, and John's sole wish was for an end to this combat with gravity, one way or the other. He was, as they say, running on the little red E. When you pull off a close one, climbers call it an epic, as in radical. When you don't, you're stuff, so much meat for the chop shop of mountain lore. Sometimes you can swing in the wind for a full season before they get you down, meaning the superlong telephoto lenses come out of storage for ghoulish trophy shots.

John could feel the continent drifting all around him, and he wondered again about hypothermia. His mane of thick black Apache hair weighed fifty pounds tonight, so it seemed every time he bent his head back scanning for sign of the summit. Summits are elusive things. Ever protean, they shift around, encouraging false hope, defying prediction. Sometimes they leak farther away even as you watch. Other times they suddenly drop away under the tips of your toes. You can fight a mountain almost to your coffin, lose fingers to frostbite, your mind to despair, and finally reach the summit only to find not a damn thing there, just a slag heap without a chin. Or top out with great élan, only to discover the true summit stands across and then up a ten-hour knife ridge. The temptations in mountaineering to cheat—to quit and lie—are abundant; as always in matters of faith, it's between you and yourself. Tonight there was no such temptation. Since sharing a palmful of M&M peanuts for supper while the sun went down and the wind picked up, John and his partner, Tucker, had been stalled on this final stretch of unyielding rock. They'd taken turns failing on it, and now they were out of time for failure. First would come sleet perhaps a few degrees above freezing, then the temperature would show some real downtown hostility. Soaked, they would lose core heat, turn foolish, get sleepy. By morning they'd look like two dragonflies shellacked with superglue. John had begun to hate the summit, which did precisely as much to bridge the gap as loving it

10

would have. The galling thing was that it hung almost within reach. Just a half pitch above—forty, maybe fifty feet more as the rope stretches—the summit was radiant in a spill of moonlight. All that divided John's darkness from safe, flat haven was that silvery line. And all he had to do was touch it. Then he heard the noise. And again, elbows askew, hips dry-humping in close to the rock, he cowered from the monster.

It sounded like bones loosening as a huge, immaculate sheet of ice peeled loose from the summit. Ninety feet long, thirty wide, but only a few inches deep, the glassy slab glinted once in the moonlight as it drifted away. Like a fat man swan-diving, it sucked at the sky for six, then ten heartbeats. The free-fall was downright delicate. Then a corner touched against the girdle of rock three thousand feet lower, and the ice exploded with a roar. Crystalline shrapnel scourged the spidery forest that crowds El Cap's prow, decapitating Jeffrey pines and mangling the manzanita that each spring and summer perfume rock climbers who dot the walls, indistinguishable at a distance from the wild blackberries few tourists dare to eat. The shrapnel would have been a killing rain, but no one and nothing was dying tonight, not yet anyway. Frogs, rodents, and fox bats living and hibernating in the granite cracks were slotted deep and safe; the peregrine falcons that nest on the dawn-facing wall weren't due to arrive for another five months; and what coyote remained in the Valley were off sampling mice in quieter coves. Except for John and Tucker, then, all was well. Ironically, they were in danger for precisely the reason they were momentarily safe, because the headwall upon which they dangled was so severely overhung. The overhang meant that most of the falling ice, particularly the slabs and torso-thick icicles, whirligigged out and away from them. Unfortunately the overhang also meant they could not retreat.

"Fuck," breathed John, a brief anthem of relief. His fingers were blown, and he was tiny, a slight creature willing itself up the hard space and colors that form the vertical boundaries of Yosemite. It didn't matter that no one belongs three thousand feet above the dark soil of California on Christmas Eve in the path of a blizzard any more than it mattered that John *did* belong because he'd chosen to leave the ground in search of dragons or in flight from the common mud or on fire with whatever else it is that propels ascent. He had a soul, he had his reasons, and he was

11

frightened. All that really mattered was the Valley spread below—half a mile wide, half a mile high, gashed deep into the harsh earth by not-so-ancient glaciers. The Valley had its own terms.

"Watch me," he groaned. Frost poured from his mouth. Ten stories below, Tucker couldn't quite hear the command, but he heard the groan and was already watching as best he could, a vigilance more of touch than sight. He was reading the rope's vibrations with his palms, listening to John's desperation. Tucker was scared and his wide white eyes stared blindly toward the summit. It's always worse waiting for disaster than fighting it, but he was patient. He loved John, although he was still too young to realize you could admit that about another man. That he was here on this wall in these circumstances was a testament of that love. John was the only friend he had, and when "the Mosquito" for Christmas had first been mentioned, Tucker accepted the invitation because it was John, not because it was the Mosquito Wall. Agape has its limits, however. Tucker knew that if his partner fell, all their protection, including the belay anchor, would probably rip, dumping them into forever pronto. In a way that only a white suburban American boy can be, Tucker was presently optimistic about their situation. He was optimistic for both of them. Fervently optimistic.

John grappled his weight a body length higher. The hardware slung from his racks tinkled musically, the sound a horse makes shaking its bridle. He stuffed his fist into the rock and cocked the flesh against whatever flakes and crystals might catch it. The hand stuck with satisfactory firmness, and he pulled up against it, releasing with his lower fist so he could jam that, too. The smoothness of the move pleased him. If only the rest of the crack would go this well. He was taking things one inch at a time, and his frown ebbed. Except for the hunger and cold and impending storm, and those two fingernails he'd torn clean away yesterday morning opening a fisherman's knot, and the sapping ache in both knee joints, this was where he loved it most, on the far jagged edge of the world. True, you took more pain up here what with the sun and the wind and the god-awful sheerness picking you bare, but then again where else was everything so obvious? It wasn't so much easier to see—especially for John with his talent for finding the labyrinth in each and every event, even this straightforward, squared-off crack in the rock—as it was just plain easier to do. Up here it was like a Clint Eastwood movie, where the metaphors are always blunt. Physical. Where what you touch—and nothing but—that's what you get.

Over his shoulder, the distant storm was boiling to a soft crescendo. You could see lightning glittering like hungry eels in the snow clouds, but not a sound escaped the roiling violence. Since three o'clock that afternoon, he and Tucker had been monitoring the slow, black tidal wave of clouds that now engulfed half the sky. What had begun as a bud on the west of what an ice climber named Bullseye liked to call Our Video was now bending to flood the moon, his only source of light. In Islam, the new year cannot begin if the moon is covered. So it was for this orphan of the Jesuits. Forty feet more to 1987.

Two ropes were knotted at John's waist. One bellied out into open space, arcing down and then back into the wall where the far end was tied to Tucker. The second rope fed through a series of rusting pitons and nuts fixed into the wall. It was this second rope that was supposed to catch John if he fell.

He pinched a slight granite flake and shifted his weight from the toe of one foot to the other. It was a wintry motion, slow and brittle. The moon, carved white, hung beside his feet. Forty feet more, he coaxed himself. Forty feet into midnight and he'd be up. There he would anchor the ropes and haul their gear up one line while Tucker ascended the other. Forty feet to reentry, to the horizontal planet where trees grew upright and he could stand without clinging, where he could forget the aggravations, the paranoia, the stink of old human shit waiting on the ledges, the community dandruff in his lukewarm Cup-a-Soup.

He'd been here before, muscling against the elements, hugging close to big walls while exhaustion or fear or storms or the mountain itself conspired to dislodge him. He'd always survived, sometimes just barely, but never stupidly. *Sports Illustrated* or *People* or the *Chronicle,* one of those, had made much of this obstinacy after his haunting fiasco in the Andes on the South Face of Aconcagua, attributing his "barbarian survivability" to his aborigine past. "Grandson of a Chiricahua Indian shaman, half Indian and magician himself, Coloradas can stick a finger or toe to almost any surface—granite, brick, or the sandstone of his native desert spires—and it will stick like a spot weld. One of the nation's premier rock climbers, a natural-born mountaineer. . . ." A grim, cold *cuate,* shivered John. Beat, froze, and forty feet short. He eased upward, locking

13

his taped knuckles harder inside the ungiving fissure. The way it felt, the movement it invited, the very smell—all were echoes of a thousand similar cracks. There were other echoes, too, other dimensions as he pulled higher and edged the inner toe of each worn rubber sole against new crystals. Not all were as immediate as the bite of stone against his fist or the urgency rearing high in the cloudbank. Some of the resonance was so old and persistent that it was next to silence. There was, for instance, no ignoring the Chiricahua advice that no one is your friend, not even your brother or father or mother; only your legs are your friends, only your brain, your eyesight, your hair, and your hands. My son, echoed the void gaping under each of John's heels, you must do something with those things.

He fell.

It was that sudden.

As if skinning off a glove, John felt his hand slide from the crack. His toes lost their granite purchase. He gave a reflexive slap to the rock. Then he was off, flying toward the ground far below. Again the wall's exaggerated angle was a blessing, allowing him to drift mute and free, full of fear. He hit nothing. The air was clear. The emptiness seemed to buoy him up. I'm falling, he registered. It was a soft moment, which allowed him thoughts.

Climbers call long falls screamers, but rarely scream when they fall. Their lives don't flash before them. They have no special grip on their fear, no mystical insights into self-control. They drop like quiet ripe fruit, which is not to say they aren't terrified. Their rib cages vapor-lock. Their eyes see. And they hear a voice. Not always, but sometimes. Even among the hard-core, fat-free warrior set—the 5.11 boys with their streamlined lats flaring like vestigial wings, nineteen and twenty years old with tendonitis in their overtaxed knuckles—even among the fanatics, the voice is usually nothing more than adrenaline babble. It's easy for climbers to confuse the wild surge of biochemicals, tape-deck tunes, and naked risk with the song of being. When the abyss sweeps up to devour them they vainly believe themselves tagged by the hand of God, when in fact "flushed" is more like it. But sometimes, rarely, a falling climber really does hear the voice.

He listened. This is what he heard.

Nothing. Absolutely nothing. It said nothing. It sounded like nothing, which, unless you're there dying, may sound like the proverbial one-handed Zen cow patty.

Twisting sideways, then backward, John glimpsed the cadaverous moon rocking all out of kilter. This shoulder, he predicted without question, this hip. They'll hit first. Shit, John, you've done it now. Even so, he wasn't particularly concerned. For one thing, his arms instantly felt as if he'd gone to Cancun on vacation. The lactic acid let go. His lungs quit laboring. He felt great. All his heroic struggling to be elsewhere was suddenly a moot point. Cascading past the glowing stone, John felt like Zeno's arrow, the one forever caught between source and end point. He was at peace.

And then he heard a thin, metallic pop. It was an inconsequential noise, a mere kernel of popcorn exploding. But it was followed by a second pop, and the bottom dropped out of his gallows. John gritted his teeth. Dread deepening, he realized he was unzipping. He had time to think, shit the pins. And then his brain mainlined the fear because he understood his wings had truly been clipped. One by one, the rusting old pitons, the pins that he'd clipped into, were failing. Every time a climber hammers in a piton or wedges a nut into the rock, he customizes and expands his own health insurance policy. The idea is that each piece of protection (or "pro" in the abbreviated surfer-climber patois) is capable of catching your body weight times the velocity of your fall. The size of the pro is less significant than the physics of its placement, but since no one can see inside the crack, no one can state with certainty what will or won't hold. Matters of faith. As John climbed the crack, he had attached his leading rope to seven "fixed" pitons placed on sunnier days by earlier climbers. Because he was in such a hurry, though, he'd neglected to back up the old pro with some of his own setting. Now it was truth or consequences. The weathered old pins were jerking loose from the crack like machine-gun slugs. Pop, pop, pop. It sounded like breakfast cereal. Climbers call it a zipper fall for the way you unzip the pro. Having nothing else to do as he unzipped, he counted the pops.

He passed Tucker. He saw the moonlit teenager as an instant of mercy. Spare me, thought John. Catch me, Tuck. Please. But not a sound passed his lips. It would have done no good anyway. He felt the rope tighten at his waist and counted two more pops. With each pop the rope relaxed again. Gone, he realized. Gone away. The wind poured into his

15

ears and he began to drown in the waves of his inner ocean. Panic began to unpiece him. His graceful, unending breaststroke from here to nowhere began to take on a frenzied, ridiculous tone, which set off a deeper alarm. Climbers still talk about one of their own who erred near a summit and was heard to calmly sigh "Shit" as he sailed past a lower ledge, trying to keep his balance. John was on the verge of losing all balance. He'd lost control of the big picture; now he was losing control of the little one, himself.

And then he heard the voice. It said nothing. Absolutely nothing. It calmed him. The tempest in his ears suddenly abated. His clenched jaw relaxed. The shout in his soul faded. Everything became acceptable.

Just as suddenly, he stopped with a long, dreamlike bounce. The rope stretched elastically, snatching him away from the abyss, and then he was slammed pell-mell into the wall, his shoulder and hip striking first. His lungs emptied with a frosty *whoof.*

Tuck had caught his fall.

He felt pain, but it was a distant, unflowered sensation. John didn't care. Like a supplicant, he reached both hands above his head and grasped the rope, gasping. He touched his forehead to the rough Perlon line. *"Padre nuestro,"* he started the chant, then gave in to his adrenaline and simply sat there. Still clutching the rope, he dangled above the inky forest floor. He raised his head to what stars were left. He heard the abrupt, macho burp of a faraway frog. In a slow, noiseless spin, the world began to accumulate around him again. The same moon was gleaming across the same cold acres of vertical granite, illuminating his long, black hair and the sparse whiskers on his wide jaw. It was like him to watch himself dangling there, tied to a puppet string far too close to God.

At an even six feet he was barrel-chested, with legs that were longer than Apache but slightly bandy all the same. He didn't have to wonder what his vagabond mother had looked like; one glance down his hybrid body told all. Besides these long legs, she'd carried narrow feet and small hands that looked too delicate on him. He was self-conscious about those hands. They seemed so inadequate for all the gripping and grabbing and pinching that climbing demanded. Yet they'd pulled him across land no one had ever touched or seen, and that was something. So many scars had laced their flesh and then sunk under new scars that now and then he forgot their service.

16

Certainly his hands seemed less than true to the desert savagery that was his other half. The Indian in him was prominent: straight hair, black eyes, and huge Mongolian cheekbones. On an expedition to the Chinese flanks of Everest two years before, Tibetans had regularly addressed him in their native tongue, convinced he was one of them. What he most often recognized in the mirror, though, was neither the Anglo nor the Indian. What he saw was the overlay of one culture upon the other, something quieter than intercourse, the mark of history all over his face: smallpox scars. To his eye, the pockmarks ruined his wide, angular cheeks. He saw himself as a bad invention, the product of too fierce a seed or a not quite certain matriarchy. The pitting scars were proof that his mother had vanished into mystery, marooning him and his brother with a dusky, nomadic man who knew roughnecking and bars and a thousand stories of his father's fathers and who could track bobcat from horseback and cut water from cactus and braid rope from yucca and coax crude oil from the barren earth, a man who'd struggled like a hero to be both father and mother to two dusky sons but never quite got it down. His father had forgotten to get John immunized, and·by the time he'd remembered, the disease had finished with his younger son's face. John didn't blame his father. That was part of the fatalism that carried him so brilliantly across the stone walls and kept him a prisoner of the Valley.

He'd even quit blaming himself for the scars he found so ugly. He could look in the mirror these days and touch the pockmarks and accept that he was marred, but that it wasn't his fault. With a sort of reverse vanity that had infuriated his Jesuit high school teachers, he carried everywhere with him a sort of pet humility. *Sports Illustrated* had loved it ("a captivating modesty"). He was reticent in crowds, shy around strangers, and coeds had never quit teasing that he must be retarded or mute. The pockmarks gave him a vigilance. When he looked at people, his dark eyes always saw them looking first, studying his face, his skin, his infallibility. Actually he suspected that the handsomeness is almost never generic, that maybe people were intrigued, not repelled, with his face. That wouldn't be the first admission he'd put off. Too many years had gone into feeling marked. Maybe, he sometimes smiled in the mirror, maybe he carried *penitente* blood in him along with the Chiricahua and Anglo. Maybe he just enjoyed tormenting himself. Sort of like climbing with knees he could scarcely bend some mornings and hands plagued by arthritis. Or hoping for Harvard someday when Berkeley had proved too confining after three short semesters. One thing John had learned was to travel light. Buttoned in the left-hand pocket of his corduroy shirt was a folded Polaroid of Liz, his lover, and a tube of wild cherry Chap Stick for the windburn. Four ounces of luggage, that was it.

Only a few years earlier an American ornithologist on sabbatical had discovered a well-preserved corpse in a Swiss valley. Dressed in tweed clothing and hobnailed boots, the body was lying where it had been disgorged at the mouth of the Zermatt glacier. No one could figure out who it was until the local climbing club laid claim to the young man, identifying him as a certain alpine soloist of the 1880's. Like John, he had been carrying next to nothing in his pockets: a round-trip train ticket only half used, some sprigs of edelweiss, three coins. There's something about human beings in the mountains, they seem to care less about the anchors that other folk require. The result is that they take on a curious lightness. How else to explain, for instance, the middle-aged Spaniard strapped in fourteenth-century armor who was similarly resurrected at the foot of a pass in the Pyrenees in 1937. Climbers had a way of eluding gravity, even climbing out of their graves. John wasn't there, but two summers past at a base camp in the Patagonian range, near the fang called Cerro Torre, a party of Yosemite climbers had recovered another such Lazarus or at least part of him. To everyone's horror and titillation, one Matthew Kresinski had shaken hands with the desiccated arm extending from a flank of ice, then snapped the entire arm loose to use as a backscratch.

The moon floated perilously close to the billowing storm clouds. Frost poured from John's nostrils. He suddenly felt like taking a nap, just a short one.

"John?" Tucker's voice fluttered down and prodded him. John looked up toward the paltry cobweb of nylon slings and ropes that anchored both their lives to El Cap. For the moment he didn't bother to answer. Somewhere in that mess of ropes hung the silhouette of the world's best climber, at least for the past six months. Tucker was up there somewhere, stoically holding John's hundred and eighty pounds through what amounted to a makeshift pulley system. The boy had been stationary for the last two hours, dangling from the rock while feeding out rope as John deciphered the crack. Belaying could be very cold work. It could also be punishing, especially when your partner took a screamer the length of a football field. Belayers had been known to lose teeth, break bones, and burn their hands to the ivory catching falls half that distance. All the same, John luxuriated in the glory of his own survival for a moment longer.

"John?" Tucker repeated, more urgently. John was tempted to let him wonder a bit longer, not because he was sadistic but because he could. He'd earned a minute's rest down at the end of the rope. But he roused himself.

"You okay?" John called up, stealing the initiative. His voice quavered a little, which annoyed him. It annoyed him, too, that he would be annoyed. Machismo was not one of his ambitions.

"Yeah." He could hear the boy's relief, and then a philosophical "Wow."

"Nice catch, Tuck." The wind spun John in tiny circles, back and forth.

"What?"

"You caught my ass."

"What?" Climbers use a small but efficient vocabulary of monosyllables for communicating in wind and around corners. None of John's compliments were making much sense to Tucker.

"Merry Christmas, Tiny Tim," John tried again.

Though it didn't belong in the vocabulary either, Tucker understood this time. They'd been kicking that old dog all climb long. Merry Christmas Tiny Tim to the last of their red and yellow M&Ms. Merry Christmas Tiny Tim to each other's penis during the morning pee, to an unsafe belay anchor on the fourteenth pitch, to the end of their good weather.

"Yeah." Tucker was no longer amused. Nor was John.

It was cold, he was exhausted, and the summit was a whole lot more than forty feet away now. He'd have to climb the pitch all over again. Glittering overhead, liquid in the moonlight, hung the icy summit. The holy fucking grail. He sighed. He had memorized most of the moves up to where the rock had spat him out, but even so it would take another hour to get to the top, maybe two or three. He doubted the storm would wait that long. John moved his limbs one by one, checking his shoulder and hip for damage. Bruised, he knew. He studied his taped hands as if they were traitors. He felt old. Ten months into his twenty-eighth year, he *was* old, at least by Valley standards. It was high time to quit climbing but difficult to let go. More than the life-style of a rock jock tiptoed in the balance; it was also a heritage, a full-blown past rooted in centuries of simple lust for the mountains. On both sides of his family, Anglo and skin, ancestors had loved and coveted their abrupt landscapes. At least he liked to think so. More than anything else, the defiance of gravity guided his thoughts about heritage and gave him license to think of himself as a mountain man. The thought of leaving these walls and mountains caused him pain—pain, he sometimes rhapsodized, like the fur trapper Hugh Glass must have felt, grizzly-scarred and lame, bidding adios to his people at the 1824 rendezvous in Jackson Hole . . . like Maurice Herzog, the great French alpinist, must have felt as he watched the doctor snip off frostbitten joints in the jungles below Annapurna. Echoes. The thought of turning his back on the mountains and never returning was as terrible to him as it was romanticized. That was all part of it, though. The over-blown melancholy. The power and the glory.

"You got me?" he shouted. The wind opened a window for his words. Tucker heard.

"Take your time." Tucker didn't really mean it. He sounded weary and frozen.

John let Tucker wait just a little longer. He knew this wasn't the time and place, but he wanted to rest and digest the adrenaline, draw in the moment all the same. Once the climb was over, he'd forget these thoughts about aging or, better yet, fish the thick spiral notebook out of his gear box down in Camp Four and jot down his confessions under the heading "Mosquito Wall." The notebook was dense with similar ram-blings filed under such names as Muir Wall, North America Wall, the Shield, Bonatti Pillar, Super-Couloir, Walker Spur, Everest-North Face, Ama Dablam, and all the other major routes he'd done or attempted. Finger paintings, Liz called the journal, the stuff of his never-ending childhood. His eyes followed a lone set of headlights creeping along the valley floor. An orange satellite cruised up beside Taurus, then sank into storm clouds.

And then, for just two or three moments, between wisps of sharp breeze, John heard something new and separate. It was a faint, irrelevant buzz, like the drone of a gnat. Just as suddenly it was gone, next to imaginary. The noise was an airplane, off course and sliding to its doom. Though John didn't give it a second thought, he would remember this moment several months later. He sniffed the air and wondered how Tucker had put up with his stink for so many days. He smiled, just barely, then grabbed the rope. Up, he commanded. Up so you can go down. Up. Down. The no-exit, alpine circle game. Sisyphus never had it so good. He pulled hard.

"Fly or die, Tuck."

The salute came right back down at him. "What?"

"Fuck this whale."

"Yeah, John. Fuck it."

John started all over again.

2

*O*n the night be-
fore Christmas the Sierra
Nevada set in motion colum-
nar inversions over lakes that
served as constant temperature sources.
Through such whirlpools of air, an aging
Lockheed Lodestar, off course, tried to thread
the mountain range. Near the crest a
fierce and sudden battle of physics ensued, during
which the aircraft sacrificed its right wing in order to
maintain the temporary equilibrium of its whole. Minutes later the greater part of the plane came to rest at the bottom of Snake Lake, an oval tarn so named for neither its shape
nor the presence of serpents thereabouts. It was one of those
elapsed and dusty facts that a trapper with Jedediah Smith's expedition
in the early nineteenth century had so christened the lake after his favored Hawken buffalo gun, which had a way of snaking its lead balls
around barriers and into the heart of things. Nomenclator forgotten,
there it lay, an insignificant body of water coiled upon itself just below
the tree line at ten thousand feet. There was nothing spectacular about
the lake, which made it doubly irrelevant in this spectacular geography.
Bullseye once argued (on mushrooms) that God must have been in His
SoHo phase while creating Yosemite and the higher Sierras, how else to
explain the weird domes among dinosaur forests, the rioting colors and
slashed, sculptured valleys? The area was wild with an egotist's vision.
Towering above Snake Lake was just such a sculpture, the East Face of
Bowie Peak, a study in tan-and-black severity, all sharp right angles and
cut-up space. If Bullseye was correct, then Snake Lake—so mild with its

23

stooped basin and quiet blue gentian that even people who'd been here could never quite place it—was an act of divine omission on the psychedelic blueprint. Had the access been shorter and more sober, elderly couples might have enjoyed picnicking by the docile waters.

The dismembered plane struck at 210 miles per hour, hanging a geyser beneath the stars that lasted all of a few seconds. As if closing one contented eye, the lake slowly froze over in the following weeks, covering the dead machine with a thick sheath of ice, snow, and pine needles. The cold sediments would have kept the secret perfectly except for one item: Seven telltale feet of the tail section jutted above the lake's surface.

On February 28, more than two months after the crash, a party of snowshoers discovered an airplane wing with the obituary N8106R emblazoned on its metal skin. On their way back out of the forests high above Yosemite Valley, they forgot exactly where they'd found the wing, but that was all right. For the time being, the call letters were quite sufficient. The Federal Aviation Administration was first. Contacted by one of the snowshoers, it pieced together a background report on the plane. N8106R was a Lockheed Lodestar with a five-thousand-pound load capacity, registered to a fictitious person in Albuquerque and purchased with cash in Bartlesville, Oklahoma. Beyond that there seemed to be little information: No flight plan had been filed, no distraught relatives had called for help. The news of an unknown plane crash puzzled the FAA only mildly. The existence of a flight over the Sierra in a snowstorm at night was odd, but not so odd that the plane's purpose was a complete mystery. Smugglers rarely file flight plans.

The FAA contacted Customs. The presumption that drugs were involved was automatic; therefore Customs contacted the Drug Enforcement Agency. What exactly was being smuggled, how much, and where it was at present remained unanswered questions. But three agencies were now involved, and that, the respective authorities felt, was a good start. Had the crash occurred in warmer weather and closer to the highway, representatives of the three agencies no doubt would have examined the site themselves. But given the fifteen-foot backcountry snows, it was deemed wise to contact the National Park Service, which was essentially in deep hibernation until the tourist season kicked off on Memorial Day. Seldom is the NPS called upon to bolster national security, and provided with this twenty-four-carat opportunity, it was not found wanting. With what amounted to a snappy bureauwide salute, the Park Service jumped to life, and on March 10 ten rangers on its Yosemite winter staff were dispatched to pinpoint the wreckage. The rangers were rebuffed once, then twice, by blizzards. Finally, on March 27, a young ranger by the name of Elizabeth Jenkins unlocked the mystery of N8106R.

A bright, large-boned girl from a southeastern Oregon cattle ranch, and a graduate of the University of Washington's forestry program, Liz Jenkins was the sole woman in the company of nine men, most of whom were taciturn about having her along. Equal opportunity was not exactly an unknown trespass in the Park Service; nonetheless, Liz had discovered, the bureau preferred to digest fads at its own bucolic rate. Female rangers were all right, make no mistake, but the feeling was they might better feather into the job by guiding nature walks or policing campgrounds during the summer season. Over coffee, two of the men present had gone so far as to hazard the belief that menstruating women lure bears and put them in a mauling frame of mind.

Luckily, Liz had not been present for this airing of superstitions. As much as the more progressive rangers loved baiting the old fogies about their outlandish demagoguery, even they were less than enthusiastic to have a woman along. It wasn't Liz, certainly—she was a sturdy enough *femme*, if a bit acid and quick on the draw. Rather they shared the opinion harbored in firehouses and police departments from the Florida Keys to Port Angeles, Washington, that out yonder on the firing line muscle makes the difference. Bust a leg up in the backcountry and if your partner's a lightweight, that's all she wrote. Liz herself rankled them less than the idea of her did. She'd been hired solely to satisfy a trend, that's how most of them lived with it. For them, her rationale was simple: She was on a husband hunt. It made blunt sense. Where better to gold-dig than in the Valley midwinter among handpicked hot-blooded rangers? But here, too, Liz had proven troublesome, especially—though not exclusively—in the minds of the men actually eligible for her exploitation. For somewhere along the line she'd taken a wrong turn and parked her ass with the climber crowd, a seedy crew devoted to hedonism and multiple abuses of the system. Ignoring discretion altogether, she'd taken as a lover one of the Park Service's more dedicated headaches, Matt Kresinski. As if that weren't grievous enough, upon dumping Kresinski, she'd taken on John Coloradas, another of the Park's problem boys. Hardly boys, these two, more like ex-cons among the impressionable juvenile delinquents in Camp Four, climbers' camp.

So it was, as they poured their coffee into the snow and prepared to slog on, that nine rangers tried to ignore Liz's golden rope of hair as they crept higher and deeper into the mountains east of Yosemite. No one knew exactly where they might find the downed plane, or if they ever would. They had probed every likely-looking hump of snow and studied miles of the surrounding forest for signs of sudden trauma: broken tree-tops, torn metal, bodies. After forty-three kick-ass miles loaded with sup-plies and gear, the general feeling was that if they hadn't yet skied ten feet above the buried wreckage, then they soon would and would never know it. They had found the wing, but that was three days ago, and the airplane could be anywhere. Another commonly held opinion was that an airplane filled with dope and missing a wing would not be going any-where until the spring thaw, at which time two hippies on a leash could locate it with minimal effort. Turn one of those climbers loose up here and you could have the plane tomorrow morning by breakfast. With lit-tle enthusiasm, the cold and grouchy expedition finally stopped for yet another night out and started making camp.

By eighteen-hundred most of the rangers were neatly burrowed in snow caves and tents, snug and drowsy. Liz was not. She wanted that plane. Telling herself this was just a chance to spend an extra half hour with the slow red alpenglow that was soaking the frozen peaks, she re-fused to admit she might also be trying to prove herself to these men. John called this tendency of hers "punching out the guys," which pissed her off. She wasn't that way. All she wanted this freshman year as a full-time ranger was to make it through without having to grow testicles. Why she should care about getting through the winter, though, was a mystery, because she was resigning in just a few months anyway. It was unpleasant for a ranch girl and athlete to confess, but she disliked the wilderness, this wilderness anyway. Once the summer closed out—or that job with the Bureau of Land Management's Wild Horse program opened up—she was history. The Valley could do without her.

She headed for the crest of a nearby ridge. She was a methodical, Nordic skier, neatly attuned to her own pace. Few of the rangers knew, certainly none from watching her serviceable technique on touring skis, but Liz had put herself through college on a racing scholarship. Besides the degree and an alpine ski racer's heavily muscled butt, the racing had gained for her little more than the incentive to quit chewing Red Man. No Olympics. No berth on the USSA National Team. Too few trophies to even clear a shelf for. Not even an injury to brag about to her brothers. Competition was a dirty word. "Punching out the guys" sounded ugly to her. Like other large women, she was confounded by her size and strength. Over the years she had shortened her cowgirl stride, softened her voice, and mastered other such physical diminutions. The few men she'd cherished had always been larger than life. Matthew, for instance: a god in size elevens. Talk about backfires. He was the one who'd coined "the Amazon" for her. Somehow with Matthew she'd always felt like public property, a six-foot-tall Playmate who'd strayed into the wrong locker room. Until John came along she hadn't realized how destructive Matthew really was. Not that John came trouble-free. He had a fierce, but oddly distracted determination. In that respect, they were almost too alike. Vigorous but not definite. Watching him among his Camp Four people or asleep beside her, Liz could detect a beautifully tended fire grown cold. It made her sorry not to have been there a few years earlier, before South America ruined him. She'd been cramming for finals in Upper Sonoran to Arctic-Alpine Life Zones the year he was down on some mountain, losing a climbing partner, building a scandal. And yet no one, not John, not other climbers, not even Matthew, who stopped just short of calling whatever had happened murder, would talk about it. Even John's close friend Bullseye was quiet about the dark incident except to say, "After Peru some of his dogs quit barkin'."

"The altitude affected him?"

"Come on, Liz. I mean he quit smilin'. I mean he got *atmospheric*. Like the Cheshire cat. Sometimes he's here, then poof, he's not."

"Meaning?" One was always asking Bullseye to clarify.

"Meaning there's no such thing as a happy ending. Happy middles, maybe. But no happy endings. It's rationally absurd."

"I don't believe that."

"No shit, Lizzie."

Bullseye was half right anyway, she was unabashed about her quest. So why keep on with a man who made plain, simple joy feel like an open zipper in church? How much plainer and simpler could you get than a climber? Weren't they supposed to have the stuff of life lodged under every fingernail? The Valley was making a fool of her. First Matthew, wild, nuts, and crude as hell. Then John with his pilgrim melancholy. Climbers. Damn climbers. The slope steepened. Spreading into a quick herringbone, she mounted the rounded top.

The ridge was bare on both sides of the crest, its vegetation long ago slaughtered by the wind. At the north end of the ridge a gentle decline swept out through a miniature forest of stunted, twisted pines and introduced Snake Lake. Visibility was marginal. Curtains of gauzy spindrift closed away the horizon, though now and then they parted to show the ghost of a mountain drifting high overhead. A single gigantic slab reared above the lake like a gray tombstone, then blowing snow cut her sight. Perched on the tip of the ridge, Liz caught another frigid burst of wind and felt cold for the first time all day. The far peaks were taking some weather, too, and the alpenglow had gone dull and pewter. Not much sun left. Time to head back down to the encampment before John's bronchitis flared up in her lungs again. He'd brought the virus down from his crazy Mosquito Wall escapade and it had taken them both a month to recover, a period marked as much by claustrophobia as hoarseness. Bronchitis aside, winters in the Valley were famous for inflicting cabin fever. The cabin was king-size, but so was the fever.

As she turned her back to the wind and prepared to skate back down the ridge to her tent, Liz began thinking of Reno again, a reliable counterpoint to this grunt work. She was bound for the bright lights as soon as they located the wreck, because Reno was where the BLM had its regional headquarters. That's what she told people. In fact, she was taking a half-month's pay, five days of paid vacation, and her man, and she meant to lose herself in grossly civilized decadence. No art museums or foreign films or Japanese teahouses. Nothing fancy this trip. The best part was how when she'd asked, John had said sure, anywhere you want. However brief the jaunt, they were going to leave the Valley together. The way tourists visit Yosemite, they were going to descend into the outside world. Tucker was tagging along, but that was okay, he was like a kid brother to both of them. From where she stood hunched against the wind, Reno was less than a hundred crow miles away. With Tioga Pass shut down for the winter and spring, it would take a half-day's driving, though. Another blast of wind hit the mountainside, punching the *cagoule* hood against her wool cap. Reno was one more reason to hurry up and find this damn plane. The plane had taken on shades of the Lost Dutchman Mine, always elsewhere. Because she figured they'd expect her to, Liz alone in the group hadn't bitched about their open-ended mission. There was no way for her to know it, but her stoicism had become one further source of resentment. It would have delighted her. She cast a final glance down at the lake's snowy flats, and the ghostly mountain hovered between veils of white. The sun was finished. She planted a pole to shove off, then ducked her head forward and squinted. And like that she found the object of their desire.

Perhaps a hundred feet from the drift-covered shore, she saw the up-right tail section of an airplane. It jutted like an invincible erection, the sole clue that something larger and more stimulating lay locked beneath the ice. Liz nearly reached under her *cagoule* for the walkie-talkie on her hip. The thought hit her, though, that this could be nothing more than illusion. It sure as hell looked like a plane's tail, but if she dragged the gang out of their toasty sleeping bags for a mirage, there'd be no end to their cackling. Could be a tree or a rock . . . she wiped at the snowflakes clustering on her thick eyelashes. Whatever it was, she resolved to touch it first.

The day had been long and the company annoying. Add to that her excitement and a flagging blood-sugar content, and Liz's glide was a trifle more aggressive than it should have been. She kicked off, then kicked again to exploit her momentum. Her speed picked up on the crusted snow, and it looked like a straight, clean glide onto the flats. Until a suitcase-size mound loomed in her immediate path, she gave no thought at all to braking or turning. Then suddenly there it was, just big enough to snap her wooden ski tips if she hit it. She tried to telemark, then stem, but the crust suddenly dropped off into deep powder, trapping her full speed ahead. With a futile last-minute twist she tried to ram the object broadside instead of tips first. Her tips drove straight into the object. For a moment Liz managed to stay upright, furiously stabbing at the snow all around her to find solid ground. She toppled ignobly.

"Bastard," she muttered. "Son of a bitch." She rose up from the snow. Carefully brushing the telltale snow off her clothing, she checked her skis and poles for fractures and with great relief found none. Her pride and equipment accounted for, Liz stabbed at the offending lump with one pole. It looked like the winter kills they used to find on her family's ranch. Her dad and brothers and all the other ranchers always cussed the coyotes and ignored the obvious starvation, which is to say they blamed the Devil, not their own poor foresight. Pride. A family trait. She expected the tip of her pole to glance off a rock or an iron-hard tree stump. Instead the tip penetrated whatever lay underneath. With a jerk, she pulled the ski pole free and stabbed experimentally at the lump again. Within its coating of snow, the surface resisted, then gave under the tip. Not so different, she thought, from cow flesh. But what could it be? She popped the pole loose and prodded the lump for an answer. An old buck doe, maybe, or a bighorn? Too bulky to be a marmot. Too small to be a bear. She pressed on the pole's strap and slid the tip in. Right then it struck her what was lying under the snow.

"Oh, my God." She yanked at her pole, but now it wouldn't come loose. That or the strings in her arm weren't working. They'd warned her, warned all of them. "Gentlemen." The echo. "And lady." And it had been for her benefit, much of it, even though she'd been on body evacs before. "Chances are you won't find the pilot and his buddies neatly buckled in their seats awaiting our assistance. More likely they'll be scattered to kingdom come over the mountain range. They aren't a priority anyhow. The plane is. So if and when you encounter any remains, just bag 'em and tag 'em. They will be choppered out at first opportunity. My hunch is, between the weather and the animals, none of those jockos will be seen again. Ever." She pulled at the pole but with more repulsion than zest, then gave up on it and yanked her hand free of the strap.

Liz was much too down to earth to believe in ghosts. Still, the wind and encroaching darkness were taking their toll. There was a dead man lying across the top of her skis. She was stuck here. Stuck. The sky's monochrome kept slurring into a thicker and thicker gray, and her imagination began taking over, no help at all. Watching the lump of snow for supernatural shrugs and shudders, chiding herself for being superstitious, she tried to slide backward. It doesn't take long for a layer of ice to stud the base of a cross-country ski; so it was that with the skis jammed against the corpse in front and too beaded with ice to slide backward, all Liz could get to move were her heels in the bindings, up and down, nowhere. A deepening revulsion seized her, and the sensation of flesh yielding to her pole's metal tip crept up her right arm all over again. With all the calm she could muster, Liz tried without luck to slide forward and away from this mistake. Her brashness was a curse. The word "don't" usually served to punch on her overdrive.

"Idiot," she whispered to herself. The search for glory could have waited until tomorrow morning. It could have been done the right way. To begin with, she didn't belong out alone, particularly after dark. "Stupid, stupid," she cursed. Now there were holes in the body, she didn't want to think where, his head or his arm, and she was smack up against it, trapped. If she could just get a little distance, a minute to breathe, the shock would settle out. Procedure. That was always the saving grace. She'd seen dead and injured before, but rescue work was not her strong card. Anticipating a job with the Park Service, she'd put in a couple of semesters as an emergency medic with a Seattle ambulance service, just enough to pick up some skills and spoil forever the popcorn joy of horror flicks. They tell you it gets better, but for Liz it never had, that dread before arriving at an accident scene. The hand reaching out through the shattered windshield. It was one thing when the bits and pieces were calf nuts or the notch sliced off a beef's ear at branding or deer or elk offal. But to her the human animal was sacrosanct. It belonged all in one piece. Just last August, there'd been that New York boy killed when his—or someone else's—rope broke near the summit of Washington's Column, nine hundred feet to the deck. Thank God it wasn't her who'd first found what was left. Worse than what sharks do to you, they said, at least sharks cut clean. Under the Column it was just tufts of hair, some bone, and meat. That distant afternoon still gave her nightmares, right down to the solitary Steller's jay that had challenged them, blue feathers against the blue sky. When they looked up, way up, there perched on the highest limb of a tall tree was one of the boy's climbing shoes, laces still tied in a bow, toe balanced on a bunch of needles as if its owner had gingerly stepped right into the sky and vanished.

Fighting desperation, she tried again to shuffle her skis in place and shuck the ice. No luck. Even as she watched, the lump under the snow seemed to be moving. Just the wind bending the snow's shape, she knew. But it was getting harder to convince herself the lump was not going to rise up from the drift, holes and all. Liz pawed at the drawstring on the bottom edge of her *cagoule* to get at the walkie-talkie. "Come on," she muttered at the *cagoule,* eyes fixed on the lump. Her mittens were suddenly too thick, and she was uncertain her jaw would work anyway. She

31

gave up on the radio. The way things were going, she'd drop it in the snow or the batteries would be dead. Even if they weren't, the ridge would probably block transmission. She was getting scared. Night was near, and here she couldn't move, wed to this bent, broken thing. No one could hear her. They probably didn't even know she was gone. She considered releasing her toe clamps and postholing the mile back to camp, but the drifts could easily be twice her height in places. The only other thing was to unbury the body and pull her skis from its grasp. Whatever she decided, it had to be done and now. She flapped her arms across her chest to work up some warmth. Her breasts were tender from her monthly water, but she commanded herself to ignore that and concentrate. You got calluses, her grandpa, the dour old homesteader, used to say. Use 'em. "Use 'em," she said out loud. She was whistling in the dark, searching for resolve. There was only one thing left to do. Dreading what was to come, she bent forward to work on the snow.

The wind had not quit blowing, meaning the lump had been subtly changing its contours the whole time Liz was standing beside it, shifting and redrifting into new shapes. A drift, like a sand dune, can be many things even while it is none of them. There is no better evidence that the mind is its own animal, perceiving secrets where there are none, scorning logic, flying off with no hint of return. What had originally presented itself as a body now took on new dimensions, but Liz couldn't see the change yet. All she could see was a dead man. Tentatively she scooped away some snow. Encountering nothing but more snow, she set one knee down upon a ski and leaned closer. With greater zest now but no less dread, she began shoveling snow right and left. Once committed to the task, she took little time to expose what lay beneath. Through the rest of her life, she would never forget her amazement.

A foot down, her fingers brushed a hard object, and she rocked back onto one heel with second thoughts. She had no choice, though, and knew it. She forced herself to reach back into the carved-out cavity and dig away the remaining snow. The surface was burlap, tan and utilitarian. She presumed it was clothing or a makeshift blanket, or maybe a rough shroud wrapped around the body by some temporary survivor. She was wrong. She was so wrong she forgot to be relieved. Steeling herself, she swiped away the entire side of the lump. The burlap was stretched taut and flat. Under the burlap, showing through a gash in the corner, a sec-

32

tion of plastic showed yellow. She plunged her arms to the shoulder into the snow and pulled to one side a big, crusted chunk, enough to uncover bold black lettering stenciled onto the burlap.

Slow as a dream, the wind finished uncovering the word "ESPECIAL." Her mitten slapped away more snow. Across the line beneath marched three red X's.

And beneath that was an ostentatious, hand-size outline of a marijuana leaf, its five toothy fingers splayed like a partial sunburst. To Liz they were as fabulous and remote as hieroglyphics, but DEA and FBI agents would soon recognize the marks as a signature. The way a consumer can savor a product's background from the label on a jar of imported olives, federal officials would understand which part of which Mexican state the crop had been grown in and by which ranchero, who the middlemen were, when the vegetation had been bundled and when sold, what portion of the year's harvest this cargo represented, and even which group of *federales* were on the take. To the layman, branding your bales of marijuana this way might seem foolish. But real risk generally lies beyond or before what is directly perceived, in what is not seen rather than what is. Federal agents would appreciate the stenciling for what it was, the signature of gamblers, an act of style.

If not for the cold, Liz might have stood there marveling even longer. Instead, with darkness colonizing, she forced herself to continue tunneling around her skis and the bale of marijuana. It was awkward work and the altitude was almost eleven thousand feet, but she didn't stop to rest, knowing that until the tent safely enclosed her she'd have to continue moving or freeze. On the butt end of the bale were painted the numerals "23." Twenty-three pounds, she wondered as she kept digging, or the twenty-third bale? Or more likely, twenty-three kilos. Fifty pounds of pot? Sweat tickled the hollow of her spine. She was overjoyed. A bale of marijuana! The thought of secreting it somewhere and returning some other time never even occurred to her. Its political value far outstripped its street value. The big little Amazon had scored a coup first. The girl. The mizz is it or miss or missus? There was going to be some heartburn and godfuckingdamns in the other tents tonight. High fucking time, too. God, she was going to have fun with this, and not only with the other rangers. What would John say when she told him? And her family, they'd bust, stuff this exotic only happened on their satellite dish. And if she hadn't stayed out the extra bit bounty-hunting on her own, someone else would have found it and maybe no one. Maybe the plane would have remained a mystery, probably not, but at any rate this was her bale.

Ten minutes later, puffing and sweaty, she freed the first of her ski tips from beneath the squat rectangular bale. Her second tip took only a little more digging. One by one, quickly now, she released each ski while balancing on the other, scraped the ice from the bottoms, then repinned her toes. Sliding her skis back and forth to keep the bottoms clean, she took a final survey of her victory. She invested a moment and a grunt shoving the bale upright for maximum dramatic effect next morning when they all came skiing over the ridge. One last shake to loosen clots of snow from the burlap and she was ready to leave. Her grandkids would clamor to hear about that time, that airplane in the lake, that bale. It felt good. It felt great.

With a broad white smile, she lifted her eyes from the bale and swept her skis up and around, reversing direction for the climb uphill. Only then did she notice that on every side, upslope and all the way down to the lake, she was surrounded by lumps of snow, a whole buried herd of them, each no different from this one.

*T*ake cowboys. Un-
til the dime novelists and
showmen came along to
spruce them up, wipe the spit off
their whiskers, and altogether lift them
out of context, cowboys were just unwashed proles on horseback, and still you
had to close your eyes and pinch your
nose to imagine them as sombreroed cavaliers circling endlessly in a sagebrush paradise, dodging the
Devil's whispers. Bullseye's point would have been
that the same goes for what an Italian mountaineer once
labeled "conquistadores of the useless," your pungent, garden-
variety climbers. It was one thing to see them spidering up
burnished crags on a Saturday afternoon sports special or advertising
razor blades ("Take it from a master of close shaves"), something else
entirely to be smelling and hearing them when you've sustained a sec-
ond-degree sunburn on the back of your neck and arms, sprained one or
both ankles on the quarter-mile hike to Yosemite Falls, locked the keys
in your car, lost your traveler's checks, and otherwise earned yourself a
very quiet dinner at the Four Seasons Restaurant. A sort of Ho Jo's of the
wilderness, the Four Seasons specialized in catering to precisely that kind
of survivor. Climbers did not. The way the night belonged to the Viet-
cong, the Valley was owned by the hard-core, high-voltage subculture
that lived on the dirt of a campground tucked behind the Conoco gas
station across from Yosemite Lodge. The winter had been long and dis-
tressing for most of them, too wet to climb rock and just warm enough
so that the waterfalls never properly froze or "shaped up." Consequently,

35

on this early evening in late March the conquistadores were showing no mercy at all.

They were expatriate rabble with their hair in leonine disarray and their clothing either unwashed or so old and patchy that washing was a questionable expense. A dozen or so of them were lording it over two tables shoved together in the middle of the restaurant. Some wore tennis shoes with the soles taped to the toes; others sat bundled in lifeless parkas devoid of down feathers and repaired with crude X's of white adhesive tape. Legwear ranged from angle-length knickers to navy-surplus wool pants, blue jeans, and fluorescent lime or pink Lycra tights with racing stripes; on their heads were caps, wool balaclavas, and one or two bandannas wrapped pirate-style. What little money they had came from misused student loans, odd jobs in the park, and the dumpsters, which yielded aluminum cans worth a nickel apiece at the local grocery. Between a young man wearing a peasant shirt hand-embroidered with crude marigolds and his much younger girlfriend, for instance, lay a shiny plastic garbage bag filled with just such loot. This would keep them in beans, and therefore on the rock, for another week, after which they would forage again. "They were typical mountaineers," some observer remarked a century ago of another species of Rocky Mountain man, "outcasts from society, discontented with the world, comforting themselves in the solitude of nature by the occasional bearfight."

As usual when collected together, they were too loud tonight, radiating the sort of vulgarity beatniks and Left Bank artistes used to, their behavior so outrageous it set the jaws of the family men, mothers, and honeymooning couples straining to enjoy a civilized meal at the surrounding tables. Known to the park rangers as C4Bs for Camp Four Bums, they weren't a gang, and many weren't even friends. If anything, the label designated a life-style, a willingness to live in a tent or cave year-round, to subsist in order to climb. They put ordinary hippies to shame with their hard-core devotion to the rock, with their biceps, poverty, and voyageur ways. As tedious as they too often proved, they were in effect John's extended family. Sitting among them, there was no need to say anything. The vortex just swept him up and around and around. He closed his eyes.

"*Dominus vobiscum,*" entoned a rich, mock baritone.

"Lay off," a second voice quietly menaced.

"Kyrie eleison, kyrie eleison." Bullseye kept right on. It took concentration to properly transmogrify one's hamburger and Bud into the body and blood. Nobody was paying much attention to the rite except for the one man his irreverence was meant to sting, Burt Tavini, a muscle-bound Born Again of questionable morality, the perfect Christian soldier. Under Kresinski's tutelage, it was Tavini who'd begun booby-trapping his fixed ropes so that outsiders like that New Yorker would quit stealing equipment. It was simple. You hang your gear from a couple of very tenuous pitons, just enough to support the weight of the gear. Tie a rope to the false anchor, make it look real. And then you down-climb the crack for the night. Any thief happening along will start to ascend the rope, get about halfway, and, hey, the pins pull. Swift blind justice. Given that a climber's life-style depends on his gear, and further given that most Valley rats equate life-style with life, what Tavini had practiced was the old eye for an eye. Until last August it had been just a glint in Tavini's eye, and the booby traps had never been triggered. Since then none had been set. The thief's death had shocked them all, almost enough to report the real circumstances to the rangers. But no one had.

"Christe eleison." Bullseye passed an air cross over the hamburger cupped in his hand.

"I said stop it, Bullseye." Tavini liked people to believe he was a soft-spoken man, someone deeply contemplative like Billy Jack or Chuck Norris.

"Et cum spiritu tuo."

"You dickhead," Tavini finally erupted. John smiled. Score again for Bullseye. At Tavini's choleric outburst the two tables of climbers momentarily noticed the fool and his Antichrist.

"Hose him, Bullseye," came a shout.

"You dickhead," someone mimed with glee.

"Infidels," Bullseye excoriated them. He crossed his fingers as if warding off vampires.

"Your mama."

"Eat yourself, man."

"Yeah. Raw."

Like clockwork, whenever the weather turned nasty, a glut of C4Bs could be expected to show up here in the restaurant, in the adjacent bar, or in the lounge next door. To the few tourists who actually analyzed the source of their indigestion, the climbers' nonchalance was appalling. They were so ruthlessly, generally nonchalant, it seemed, about everything; indifferent about their golliwog appearance, their forest odor, their machismo, their awkward, narcissistic shuffling about, above all indifferent about their lives and limbs. They seemed indifferent to everything but that vertical frontier hugging Yosemite. They were backwoodsmen down from the walls, Natty Bumpos slung with Perlon rope and sporting a disdain for Winnebagos, yuppies, and the Sierra Club.

"Why *do* you climb?" Flatlanders always asked it that way, emphasis on the "do" as if trying to seduce a Mason into revealing his secret handshake. Even the legendary British Everester George Leigh Mallory, ever courteous, got fed up with the question. His famous reply—"because it's there"—had been a stroke of genius, so much dumber than the question that it had taken people's breath away and reduced them to silence. Had anyone dared to ask the climbers tonight, the answer would have been a whole lot dumber and ruder. Nobody was asking.

At the head of the two tables sat Matthew Kresinski, self-delegated liaison between the C4B banquet and Connie, a gland-rich waitress who had worked in the Valley for years. Kresinski had arms the size of calf flanks and a nose as straight as an old English war helmet, with a temper to match. Just now he was happy, smooth as bourbon. Each time a tray arrived heavy with beer and California wine, Kresinski hugged Connie close and got a big handful of ass. She was getting no younger, and Kreski was good at what he did. So the climbers knew, was she. Kreski was like that, a beneficent tyrant who believed in share and share alike. Graphic information was his version of the trickle-down theory. Connie flexed her glutes for his benefit, then, murmuring as she passed drinks over his shoulder, tried to complain about his lack of discretion.

"Don't, Matt."

"But you got such a nice butt."

Mornings, she woke early and jogged just to keep it up. She brushed his hand away. "The manager told me, you guys have to keep it down."

"I do what I can, Connie. They're fucking savages is all."

"Well, just try and control them tonight, please."

"We got money tonight."

"You better."

"We do. Sammy scored some cans in the Conoco dumpster."

Connie looked down-table at a jolly beanpole of a boy with bright red hair. She was starting to pick up the names and a jaundiced background to go with each. There was John Coloradas with his mustang looks and white T-shirts, always brooding, a killer and a liar, Matt said. And Cortland "Bullseye" Broomis, just starting to show some forehead with age, overeducated and, said Matt, overestimated. "He's okay on ice. But put him on a piece of rock and he moves like a turd in the sun." Katie, the petite Hawaiian girl with crack scars from fingertip to wrist on both hands, was "our little gook whore." In his eyes nobody was whole. The rot was on them all, all but him. Physically, anyway, he *was* perfect. Plus some. When he tossed in this or that nasty tidbit, Connie kept her mouth shut. She'd learned from a bad divorce that you stick by your man or lose him. Even when he slandered Tucker, she kept it zipped. Tucker was her favorite, what little she knew about him. He was everybody's favorite, it seemed, the wild child of any gathering because of his naïveté and gullibility. Thin, with wide shoulders, a grown-in Mohawk of black hair, and acid-green eyes, he stuttered every time she tried to talk to him. That was because Tuck hailed from Norman, Oklahoma. "Normal, Oklahoma," he would sadly confess if you asked. "Nothin' there but the football stadium." His hair was clipped into a shaggy Mohawk and he wore Ray Charles-style sunglasses in a semi-Terminator look. "The Boz," he'd identify the look, mystified that no one out here seemed to know him. "You know, Brian Bosworth. Middle linebacker? Oklahoma U?" Word was that Tucker had the hottest streak going in the Valley, at least during the past climbing season. Word also had it he was a virgin. And he never failed to call Connie "ma'am."

"Must have been a lot of cans." Connie knew Matt was lying. Either they were next to penniless, or else someone had stolen something and pawned it down in Fresno or the Bay Area.

"Some fucking turkey threw his brand-new Nikon out with the Pepsi cans, too." Pawn money. A sweet, wolfish grin stole across Kresinski's face. He cared not one bit if she believed him, and she knew it. Around Matt, she was learning, one could never think of oneself too much.

"Does that mean I get tipped tonight?"

"I could have sworn you got tipped last night." He reached for her butt again. "You go for tip, don't you?"

"Matt . . ." She looked around. No one was listening.

"More burgers, three more burgers," a voice demanded from the row of faces.

"*Cheese*burgers," a neighbor amended.

"And beaucoup fries, man."

"Sammy's paying for all of you?" Connie asked Kresinski.

"Don't know. Ask him."

She sighed. By evening's end they'd be lucky to have money for half the bill. That wasn't her problem, though the manager knew she knew these people and had taken to haranguing her. Drinks delivered, she backed away from the table and headed for the kitchen.

"Lots of ketchup," trailed a shout. "And hot water."

The hot water was for the ketchup, which was for the few with no money at all. An old trick. Tomato soup with free table crackers.

John plucked a fry from his plate, tuning in and out of the disparate frequencies pounding in from every side. A group of surfer types had colonized one end of the table and begun heaving product names at one another in a hectic battle of mix and match. "Maytag." "Pillsbury, man. Pecan Frosting." "Serta Perfect Sleeper." "Frigidaire." "Veg-o-Matic." "A T and T. All of it." They shouted as if there were rules to their frenzy. Last time they'd spent four and a half hours singing commercial jingles. Across from him Tucker was being roasted by a pickup partner for the day. Tavini was still glaring at Bullseye, both of them gnashing away at their burgers, meaning everyone would be getting an earful about the evils of red meat over the next few days because meat plugged Tavini's bowels like Portland cement. Tavini's mainstay was organic peanut butter spooned straight from the jar. In a perpetual state of what body-builders call "ripped," his muscles showed spectacularly through his cellophane-thick skin, not a drop of lard to be seen. When asked why the diet, his bullshit answer was always "Strength-to-weight ratio." No one was fooled. Tavini was the only one who didn't seem to know that he was a latent.

Tucker, too, was ripped, but without the vanity. Honed, in rock-speak. Buffed and polished. No beer, no wine, no California Coolers, no Wild Turkey, booze, or pot, not even milk or soft drinks. He was, for one thing, trying to drive his weight down to 140 for an upcoming climb. Teetotaling was a matter of principle, too. He would no sooner insult his brain cells, liver, and muscle tissue with alcohol or drugs than other people at this table would step on a $120 rope. For a young man who carried a firmly bristled toothbrush in his shirt pocket everywhere, this was a perfectly reasonable concern. He'd seen too many big-wall men with the gaping tooth line of a Third World beggar. The one great hazard in his world was Oreo cookies, one of which he was secretly prying apart under the table. His inability to resist an Oreo disappointed him. There were even nights when he couldn't sleep while pondering this chink in his armor-clad discipline. For Tuck the world was Yosemite, and Yosemite the world, he took meaning that simply. So simply, in fact, that when Bullseye once asked him if it were that simple, Tuck denied it, thinking the concept somehow complicated. "The world's round," he'd actually retorted. His sincerity had silenced Bullseye for a full half hour.

"So the gumby's up there fifteen minutes now," Eddie Delwood was relating with exaggerated animation. One hand was cocked high overhead, fingers just so. The other arm was stretched off to one side just inches from Katie's face. She was staring at the hair on his knuckles in disbelief and would have said something, but tomorrow was her turn to go climbing with him and she'd probably be giving him a hand job on the top ledge because he paid good coin. Indisputably the worst climber in Camp Four—some insisted in all America—Delwood was a trust-fund baby, a TFer in the lingo. He had the largest, newest, and finest collection of gear, bar none, and consequently never lacked for partners. He rarely returned from a climb with all his gear; as long as he tolerated the petty thefts, he was in turn tolerated. Today's climb with Tucker was a notable exception—nothing had been stolen—and Delwood was ebullient because he believed it might signal a new opinion of him, an acceptance into the club. In fact, Tucker had never stolen a thing in his life and the thought had simply never occurred to him that Delwood was easy pickings. Just a jerk.

"He's out there. I mean *out* there," boomed Delwood with his foreign accent. He was from New Jersey. He'd finally given up claiming he was from Asbury Park, which was a lie at any rate, when it became evident no one gave a shit about the Boss. "He's not movin', just like stuck onto this piece of 5.12 lichen with a foxhead for pro. Micro-pro. Sixty feet out. Man, we're dead fucking baloney if he falls. . . ." Across the table Tucker held his saliva, afraid to swallow, excruciatingly aware of the blush under his windburn. Nothing would grant him the dignity he

41

yearned for, not this night with these people anyway. They wanted their little babe-in-the-woods Tuck, their hayseed Kid. He was so tired of being the Kid. Maybe Delwood would choke on his beer and die. Maybe Katie would bite his wrist and bleed him dry. Bold as she was, and Katie had once brewed and drunk a poison ivy soup as preventive medicine, she wasn't *that* daffy. Maybe an earthquake . . . But Delwood wasn't dying and Tucker wasn't going anywhere. The rush of eyes had him tight, and his corduroy pants felt stapled to the chair.

"So he's up there, like paralyzed . . ."

Was not, Tucker tried to interject. Nothing came out.

"And then I see doom." Delwood tapped at the mild tracery of veins on his thin forearms. "Tuck's veins were turnin' green! Green, man! The strain!"

John watched Tucker's agony from across the riot of soggy buns, scattered fries, and empties. From the way Tucker's hands were moving under the table, he suspected the Oreo down by the boy's knees. His shyness was as much a part of the portrait as his finger strength and Lancelot purity. Tucker looked at John, eyes pleading. Because there was nothing else to do, John winked.

"We were goners. I knew it then. He was gonna peel and we were gonna die. I got all shaky like a big titty."

"Shut up, Delwood," sounded a voice at the far corner of the table. Tuck took the opportunity to swallow hard. People had finally had enough of Delwood.

"You *are* a big titty, Eddie," followed another voice.

Delwood's hands dropped to the table. He looked suddenly crestfallen. "Yeah." He wrapped it up in a leaden voice. "Well, anyway, he flashed it."

"Is Edward finished now?"

"Edward. . . ." The peanut gallery was taking over.

"Neato, Tuck." People quieted. It was Kreski. The King. "Another first ascent. I gotta start eatin' my Cap'n Crunch."

"Yeah," Tucker managed. He looked at Kresinski. Alive beneath their bony shelf, Kreski's two vapor-blue eyes were measuring him, deciding things. Because Kresinski wore Ray Bans even on a cloudy day—"It's the UV factor, man, you guys are startin' to look all wrinkled like scrotums"—his face carried a deeply tanned mask with two pale moons under the thick brow. The dark glasses served to hide his thoughts, of course, but more, when he took them off it was like the unveiling of weaponry. There was a singular edge in that blue stare, and he never tired of stropping it sharper on the skin of his herd, these rock and rollers. Tucker discounted the fine wide smile, not a caffeine stain in it, then dropped his gaze. You always did with the King. At least he always did.

"You got a name for it?" Katie asked Tucker. To the victor the spoils. He could call it anything he wanted. It's ancient wisdom that a thing has no value until it has a name, and the climbers obeyed the call with a poetry Bob Dylan would have envied. John was the informal scribe, Bullseye the informal librarian. In his van Bullseye kept John's ring-bound notebooks filled with sketches of every wall and slab in the Valley, page after page of lines and dashes and notations that brought to mind the yellowed, forbidding maps of antiquity. Cartographic warnings such as "Lions" or "Here Be Dragons" had their counterpart in John's Spooky, Rotten Band, Very Sustained, and Weird. Each line represented a route, each bore a name. Some were plain, like Jamcrack Route or Mid-wall. Others testified to a marvelous whimsy. Side by side down on Arch Rock, a crack named Application rose beside Supplication, Anticipation, and, hardest of the four, Constipation. Some routes took themselves seriously, like Adrenaline or Trial by Fire; some came with a smile, like Pigs in Space. Pinkie Paralysis was a digit killer in the Fingerlickin' Area, and Meat Grinder over on Cookie Cliff could turn your knuckles into hamburger. Sherrie's Crack led to Knob Job, a scattering of "chicken heads" or stone knobs. There was a Hand Job, a Whack and Dangle, and a Squeeze-n-Tease. There was Flatus, Black Heads, Bulging Puke, Pot Belly, and a Fecophilia on Manure Pile Buttress, named for the corral where horses were once kept for the early tourists. Some routes bore testimony to the psychedelic era such as Cosmos, Mescalito, Tales of Power, Separate Reality, Magic Mushroom Wall, and Reefer Madness. El Cap's North America Wall, so christened for the vast dark blemish shaped like that continent, carried a Pacific Ocean Wall off its west coast. In Church Bowl you could climb Bishop's Terrace to Bishop's Balcony, and descend to Fire and Brimstone. On Higher Cathedral Rock, Mary's Tears hung beneath Crucifix. To the layman thumbing through John's notebook, it looked like a map of constellations—connect the stars, apply the legend of terrain symbols, add route names and number ratings, and you had created an elemental creature, a climbing route. It fell to the party who first ascended a route, however short or long, to name it. Once named, the route became part of the "Bible," which any and all could peruse at any time, for Bullseye's van was never locked.

"I don't know," Tucker hedged. Originally he'd thought of calling the smooth, slick white crack Ivory Dreams, but yesterday had been smitten by a photograph that changed his mind. However, he suspected that here and now was not the place to reveal the title.

"Come on, Tuck," Sammy badgered him. The surfers broke off from a two-against-two chanting of a beer commercial.

"We need the Word," said Bullseye.

"I don't know," murmured Tucker, and his voice dipped to a near whisper. "Somethin' . . ."

"Somethin' like what?"

The halt was crushing. "Like, I don't know. Maybe, like . . . Whitney."

As if holding aloft a dripping scalp, one of the surfers shouted, "Whitney."

"Oh, whoa," joined a buddy. "Whitney *Houston?*"

Everyone else joined in the gang bang. "You like her eyes?"

"Or those lips, God."

"She give you a *boner,* Tuck?" Tucker's misery soared. He was utterly speechless.

"What's it rated?" Katie tried to rescue him. She desired Tucker with a Victorian hopelessness, resigned to being just a buddy. This onslaught of catcalls and teasing hurt her because it hurt him. He was beyond rescue, though. They had their teeth in tonight.

"Tuck don't rate things," someone said. It was true. He viewed the ratings game as a compromise of the art.

"He just climbs for the purity of it all," Kresinski edged in. The way he said it made Tucker's aesthetics seem silly. John looked over, annoyed by the man's undisguised envy. Kresinski noticed and marked him, too, with a grin.

Caught up in the furor, Delwood reemerged from exile. "It's a 12, I tell ya, a 12 C," he gushed. "Maybe even a 13." The way Ansel Adams interpreted the Valley in terms of light, and geologists in terms of the El

44

Portal and Wisconsin glacial stages, climbers saw the physical forces in their own way, using a system of numbers ranging from 5.0 to 5.13. The 5 signified fifth-class or "free" climbing, in which you used hands and feet alone in the actual ascent. The number following the decimal point indicated how hard, on a scale 0 to 13, the most difficult climbing move along the route was. More than a quick thumbnail sketch of a route, the numbers comprised a sort of gunslinger language, a method for communicating one's latest kill.

"No disrespect, Ed," said Kresinski. "But how the fuck would you know a 12 C? Or even an 11?"

Rebuffed for a second time, Delwood lost all spirit.

"It's just practice anyway," Tucker said. Calling "practice" a route so severe that few if any other climbers in the world could touch it brought Kresinski to the corner of his chronic anger. John watched Kresinski sit back in his chair, quiet, crouched for an opening.

"What's a 12 C 'practice' for?" Tavini asked in disbelief.

"The Visor. Me and John. We're gonna do it." So tonight's the night, thought John. Until now the Visor had been held top secret. Only three people had known about Tucker's designs upon it.

"The what?"

"The Visor," said Bullseye, the third of the three. It was time to share the bold idea. "On Half Dome."

"That roof at the top?" said one of the surfers. "That Visor? Forget it."

"*That* Visor," Bullseye affirmed. "Call it Tuck's sainted quest."

"His what?"

"Yeah," Kresinski leaned forward, smelling blood. "The Kid wants to prove he grew some nuts for his eighteenth birthday. Or was it your seventeenth?"

"You had a birthday?" Katie tried to digress.

Tucker hated being called the Kid. It was yet another of Kresinski's inventions. Tucker sat in his seat, staring at the saturated tablecloth. There was nothing to say. There never was.

Then a new voice broke in. "You worried, old man?"

The voice had a New Mexican clip to it and people knew right away where to look, to John Coloradas. John leaned forward into the thick of it. He'd had a bellyful. Drunk or getting there or just plain looking for some return fire, Kresinski pushed too hard. Fuck him, thought John, but he didn't bother flashing his wild-mestizo look, it wasn't worth backing Kresinski all the way down. It would be enough just to get the bull off Tucker's back. Even those pretending not to were looking now. There was an uneasy titillation, no one quite sure if there was humor or not. The Apache versus the King: august figures.

"I'm gonna live forever, sport," Kresinski snapped back. "How about you?"

"Here I am," said John.

The two men didn't waste time glaring at each other. They'd locked horns often enough to do this in the dark without words. Each saw the other as corrupt. They'd lived with that mutual contempt for so long it had built into a source of pride. Where other men with this kind of hatred would have pulped each other in a one-on-one and finished the feud off, John and Kresinski held off. By not physically striking out, they reminded themselves of what they were not, that other. Call it style, which climbers value above almost everything. They'd lived in the Valley in the same camp for going on a decade now, never a blow struck. Even so, when they circled like this, everyone else got scared. It's one thing watching a couple guys sissy-box. If John and Kreski ever decided to really rodeo, though, there was going to be destruction. It would tear the Valley asunder, wreck their encampment, lay waste to their idea that ascent was all.

With his thumbnail, Kresinski started peeling the label from his beer bottle. "Don't you know you can get arrested for climbing with jailbait like Tuck?" No one laughed. A black hole gaped in their bonhomie. Everyone felt it and was confused. This was group. The King was king. Coloradas was a loner, remote and yet right in the middle. And the rest of them, they were quiet. Pawns were pawns, that was part of it. For a bad moment they saw how trite the construct was and how servile they were to it. "Ah," Kresinski expelled, seeming to drop it after all. "Who the hell cares if John climbs with the cupcakes?" He was getting somewhere else, though, and people let him get there. "Hell, who cares even if he comes home empty?"

There it was. The Andes. Tony Schaller. The storm.

"My advice, Tuck. When you're up with your friend there, make sure you can get yourself down. If it starts lookin' hairy, bail out. Come down. Better safe than fucking dead."

The insult to John outraged Tucker. "You know what?" he revealed. "Tony thought you were a jerk. He told me so." In fact Tucker had barely known the big-boned man before his death on the South Face of Aconcagua. They'd done a few hard climbs together here in the Valley, not much but enough for Schaller to have confided exactly the sentiment Tucker was now sharing.

"Save it, Tuck." Kresinski smiled patiently at the furious boy. "Wait 'til you've sprouted a few pubes. If you last that long."

"You're a jerk," Tucker repeated. It was the worst word in his tightly limited vocabulary, and because of that it had a peculiar sting. Kresinski flushed, and his trophy-hunter eyes bleached bluer. He was about to hit back when Bullseye jumped in.

"Look," he said. "Remember Perry Watts? What, '79? August, Malibu, right?"

"Oh, grody," recognized one of the climbers, an ex-surfer. "Listen to this one. What that great white did to him."

"It was this day of perfect waves," related Bullseye. "Eight-foot lefts and ten-foot rights, beach breaks and boneyards. Classic overhead glass all day long. But around five, where's Perry? Gone. He's just gone. Everybody's bummed. And next morning his board's lyin' there on the beach with a twenty-inch bite out of the edge. And before the sun goes down, old Perry finally makes it back to shore. He was missing the same twenty inches that his board was. One clean bite."

"A nightmare of fucking terror," said another of the surfer-climbers.

"So, man?" slurred a foggy voice. "What's the connection with Tony?"

"Damage," said Bullseye. "You run risks, you take damage sometimes. Sharks. Gravity. Loose rock. Hard wind. Avalanche." He paused, and most everyone filled in the blanks with their own private close calls. There was truth in his words. Bullseye's eyes were bright. "That's what happened to Tony."

"Bullshit," snapped Kresinski. "The one risk you shouldn't ever have to run is a partner who ditches you."

"Leave it," advised Bullseye. "It's history."

"Oh?" Kresinski's monotone radiated old amusement. "As usual.

47

Our in-house fry-head knows something the rest of us don't." A few uncertain chuckles fed into the stew, hopeful noises. But the showdown wasn't over yet.

Bullseye climbed to his feet, once again boiling mad at this mutation people dignified with a human name. Kresinski. An animal. Frankenstein couldn't have done worse. Or better. On the outside you had Michelangelo's David, a slimmed-down Schwarzenegger with tendons even that rippled. When he moved, it was like this glorious call to the sun to reach down and touch him, a walking hosanna. Yes, beautiful. But inside . . . all Bullseye could picture was a pithed frog, cold, amphibious, dead. The joy and tragedy of life had been aborted. Instead of Beethoven or Joan Armatrading or a solitary hawk keening over wide space, all Bullseye heard when he looked at Kresinski was vicious noise, the sound of scavengers fighting over a road kill.

"Sit down," Kresinski said.

With an effort, Bullseye straightened. "No."

Kresinski was running his fingertip in a delicate circle around the top of someone's empty wineglass. The glass didn't sing. He quit and looked up at the tall drunk. "Sit down anyway."

"The petty tyrant," Bullseye hectored. "No one wants your fucking psycho-trauma."

"My fucking *psycho*-trauma?" Kresinski sneered. Now people did laugh because it was just Bullseye, and you could take him either way.

"The Visor?" A reedy, new voice cut through the hurly-burly. It was Pete Summers. Pete the Feet. Climbers catalog their rock moves according to type: crack, face, friction. Friction climbing takes steady feet and a steady head. Pete knew a thing or two about friction, and applied it now. "The Visor's all manky and thin. There's nobody can climb the Visor."

That quickly, the squall blew over. "Wah," confirmed another voice. "I checked the Visor out once, dude. It's way gnarly."

"Way way gnarly," someone else plugged in. More voices attached, Valley talk that had little meaning but clearly begged for a cease-fire. Bad vibes hurt their ears. "It's 5.14, that's what it is, man."

"Oh, man, get out. There's no such thing."

"There's a crack," said Tucker, fastening onto the new debate with sullen relief. "I know it'll go."

"No way." But it was friendly.

"Okay." Tucker retired from their skepticism. That in itself was plenty. Fly or die. He didn't care what they thought.

"I want to see this, man. When you goin' up?"

Bullseye sat down, also relieved. His head was spinning.

"After Reno," said Tucker. He'd never seen Reno.

"You ready?"

"Look at him. He's tuned and dialed."

"You amped, dude?"

Tucker resumed his embarrassment.

"Where's my damn burger," one of the surfers shouted. They were back on track. As if listening to an interior music, Kresinski nodded his head rhythmically and stared at John, who shook his head slightly. *Que jodón*, he thought. What bullshit. He sat back in his chair. Menopause. That was the problem. We're getting old, but Kreski's getting old and mean. Bad enough to lose your only friend—and Schaller had been lost to Kresinski long before his death on Aconcagua—now menopause was on him, too. At an age when triathletes have barely started serious training, John and Kresinski and Bullseye were eyeball to eyeball with Happy Trails. This year it was Tucker. Next year, who knew what youngster would appear and polish off the state-of-the-art test pieces. Bit by bit, the new generation would chew its way through routes that old-timers had struggled and died upon to create. Climbers call it flashing when a hot-shot powers up a difficult route with no apparent difficulty. Tucker had accidentally flashed one of Kresinski's proudest accomplishments, Black Soap, so named for the color and slickness of the rock. Like the four-minute mile, it was supposed to have stood for years to come, un-touched. Worse than his casual ascent, Tucker had done Black Soap without a rope or partner, mistaking it for an easier climb to the left. Upon learning his error, he made the mistake of downgrading the crack from 5.12 to easy 5.11, and when challenged had climbed it again, again without a rope. Kresinski hated him for that. It was no excuse for the malice, though.

Then someone new and female arrived behind John.

"You guys think this is Beirut?" The voice was bass and smoky, Lauren Bacall in silk. John didn't need to turn, he just read the expres-sions across the table. Several pairs of eyes walked up and down, from face to chest to hips and back again. Bullseye quit scowling. Tucker lit up.

Liz had finally arrived. He'd heard the expedition had returned that afternoon. He'd heard other things, too. They all had. "You can hear the fireworks clear over at headquarters," she scolded them. John couldn't resist twisting around. She had cleaned up and changed, and her blond hair was still wet from the shower. A park ranger shirt was tucked into clean but frayed blue jeans. Her face was deeply colored by the wind and sun. John saw her beauty all over again. It had been a solid fortnight since they'd slept together.

"Lizzie," called out Bullseye, always delighted to see her. "Back from the wars." Already Kresinski was a forgotten fly in his ointment. Bullseye's voice put a smile on Liz's face. John kept watching her, waiting for a glance, knowing she was playing with him. "Come 'ere, come 'ere," Bullseye invited with an outstretched arm behind the circle of chairs. "Your harem boys await."

Liz began moving in a leisurely circuit around the entire table. She could have squeezed behind two climbers and reached John. Instead she drew out the pleasure of their first touch. Not that they could do much touching here in front of the world, but that, too, was part of the game. The very idea of privacy was titillating, which made their trip to Reno that much more enticing. She'd reach him in her own sweet time.

"Boys is right," Liz mocked them. She let Bullseye hug her and moved on.

"We heard you were back."

"We heard you brought us a present."

"A present?" She tousled Tucker's black mop.

"Yeah, you know, it goes in your lungs and makes you happy."

It was only a shadow, the momentary look of confusion and then distrust that passed over Liz's eyes. Then she was smiling again. "Sorry," she said. "Just me."

Over beside Kresinski, Tavini stood up without bidding to make room for Kreski's Amazon, the place of honor. It was an old habit from a bygone time. Liz placed her hand on Kresinski's shoulder, a familiar but distant gesture; Kresinski reached up to trap her hand. She was faster, though, leaving him with a handful of his own empty shoulder. He scratched at his shirt to mask the rejection. Tavini cleared his throat at his own stupid blunder and sat down again as Liz moved on toward John. She met his eyes and bit the corner of her lip, but kept it slow anyway. They were dancing. It was just them now. He slid one cheek off his chair, opening a space for her to sit.

"We still on for Reno?" she demanded. It was just for him, and the few who could hear tried not to. Bullseye was cranking up again, something about dragons and yeti and mountains on other planets, and people flung their attention toward his bankable goodwill.

"Maybe."

"Better be," she warned. Her hip nestled down beside him. She was warm and smelled like coconut shampoo. John circled his arm around her to give a hug and she held his hand. They didn't kiss, though. She didn't like to, not in front of this crowd. Kreski had taken care of that for her. She and Matthew had been lovers for less than a month, long enough for her to learn the hard way. It still hadn't occurred to her that everyone present knew she gave great head. Leaks, Kresinski called his little tales to the gang. Deep background. Since John and Liz had gotten serious, no one dared to repeat the anecdotes except their author.

"Me," Bullseye was bragging. "I'll say it out loud. I'm the guy. Okay? I voted for Ronald Reagan. And while you were still peeling Elmer's glue off the kindergarten floor, I was votin' for Richard Milhouse, too. Yeah."

"No, you weren't," a wasted surfer sputtered, uncertain if he was being goofed on.

"Yep." Like a Baptist preacher, he netted them in. "Ever hear of the pucker factor?" Among climbers, the pucker factor is that degree to which one's anus squeezes shut on horrific rock moves. "Well, that's what it was. Sometimes you have to go with your instincts, and my instincts said, vote Dick. I won't say I knew about, you know, Watergate or, hell, Cambodia or that guff. But I will say, damn it, I smelled absurdity. And in absurd times like that . . . like these . . . you gotta go for the absurd. Absurdity cancels itself out."

"What?" yelled a defiant surfer.

"Look," Bullseye explained. "Follow me on this. If God can create anything, can He create a set of barbells so heavy He can't lift it?" That was one of his standard paradoxes, guaranteed to discompose the mellowest West Coast child. Bullseye was back in the saddle.

"What?"

"You want a beer?" asked John. He had his lips by Liz's ear.

"I don't know. I'm pretty beat." Ordinarily that was code for sex, affection, and sleep, in repeating order. This time she meant it, though, John could see the exhaustion under her tan. There'd be time for all the extras in Reno. What he really wanted was to hold her close and wake up to the distant roar of the Valley's falls. On very quiet mornings before traffic started up, you could hear the thunder of Yosemite Falls syncopated with Bridalveil Falls' lighter pitch. By walking in different directions, you could tune the instruments and find that exact place where they made music.

"Are we still going in the morning?" Tucker asked across the table. He sounded groggy, overdosed on the bedlam.

John turned to Liz. "Crack of dawn?"

"That's what I came hoping to hear."

"Wait a minute. The Kid's going along on your honeymoon?" Kresinski broke in. "Hey, leave him with me. I'll baby-sit for you." John closed his eyes. Long ago they'd decided Kreski must have been a kamikaze in his past life. His talent for destruction was matched only by his charisma.

"Oh, now, Matthew," Liz addressed him. "Don't be a pill."

"I'm goin'." Tucker stood up. He fingered his toothbrush.

"We'll wake you up," said Liz.

"Night, Tuck." The tequila had ruined what discretion Kresinski occasionally let show. It was definitely time to leave the restaurant, John decided, before Kreski got unbearable.

Making good his escape, Tucker stepped high and around a tangle of legs and chairs. He muttered to pave his exit and pulled on his rust-colored Gore-Tex parka. It bore four Gore-Tex patches, each blue, each impeccably stitched on. No rural carpenter took better care of his tools than Tucker did of his few possessions. His crampons were sharp as cats' teeth, his ropes received frequent checks for weak or frayed spots, his climbing shoes had leather panels painstakingly hand-sewn to the canvas.

"You baggin' it?"

"The Kid's takin' off."

"Watch out you don't dream about Whitney, man. Get your boxers all gooey."

"G'night, Tucker," Katie breathed to herself in the far corner.

Tucker would have traded anything for invisibility, even his collection of old Silver Surfer comics. Not at all resigned to his high-profile send-off, he made for the door. He tripped and bumped a dinner table. Tourists were spurning him, too, heads turning at his awkward passage. The catcalls trailed behind like a string of tin cans. Just as he reached the green exit sign, a breadball bounced off his head and more laughter ejected him into cold black freedom.

"So how'd it go?" Bullseye asked Liz.

"It was a long haul," she said. "Deep snow and storms." Evasion. If not for the rumors flooding Camp Four, the climbers might have respected her brevity. They had to know, though.

"Come on, Liz," Pete coaxed. "You find the airplane or didn't you?" John felt her tense up.

"We found a wing. Even saw the tail. But everything's locked in solid ice." She paused. "There were no survivors, we know that now."

"What kind of plane?" They were persistent.

"A small one. Twin propeller. A Lodestar, I think." She didn't know they already knew that much and more.

"Any of your bozos freeze?" Kresinski changed tactics.

Liz decided to take offense. "You know, Matt, there's rangers who'd bury you for that remark."

"Bring 'em on, Liz."

"So you never found out what they were carrying?" Sammy probed.

"Negative." She was lying. Everyone knew it. "I guess we'll find out in early summer when the lake thaws out."

"What about those bales of high-grade sinsemilla?" Kresinski asked. A conspiratorial sobriety dropped squarely upon the two tables. For the first time all evening, the other diners enjoyed silence.

"What?" Her voice was small.

Kresinski trained his eyes on her. There was not a thing John could do. Besides, like the others, he felt the Valley belonged to them. The Valley and the mountains surrounding it. "The weed, Liz."

She didn't answer.

"You're so cute when you're modest." Kresinski paused. "Liz, we know."

Liz sat in total stillness. Suddenly everything felt much too close.

"You found the first of twenty-one bales. They were airlifted by a navy helicopter in two sling-carried loads. The rest lies at the bottom of a lake. Why cut a high mountain lake open if you can just wait until spring thaw?"

All she could manage was, "Who told you?"

Kresinski's eyes moved from her face to her breasts. "You did."

"What?"

"Which lake?" Kresinski demanded.

"I didn't tell you anything. I just got down."

"And here we all are. One happy tribe."

Finally, Liz caught her breath. "You can quit flexing now, Matt."

"No big deal, Lizzie," Bullseye assured her. "We're just citizens. We'd like to help the Park Service and related agencies clean up, you know, an eyesore." He was offering her a bridge out of the ugliness, bless him, and she took it.

"I bet you would." She tried to laugh.

Connie arrived with another trayful. Kresinski cheerfully snaked one big arm around her waist and nuzzled the side of her bosom. "When you got mammaries in a uniform," Bullseye once expounded for their benefit, "any uniform ... they're called a bosom." Connie tsk'ed her suitor, not unhappy with the flirtation. Then she saw Liz and understood. "Stop it," she said.

"I'm just glad to see you," Kresinski said. "You were gone so long."

Only the goofy and stoned missed the point of his satire. Liz blushed. "You want to get your hands off me, Matt?" Connie said.

Kresinski looked up and kissed the underside of one breast. She pushed his head away.

"Jesus," Liz softly cursed. "Why does there have to be only one restaurant in this valley?"

"Ignore him," said John.

"Yeah. Right."

"Well, let's go then."

"No. Damn it, I've been thinking of a hot meal for thirteen days."

"All right," John soothed her. "I see an empty table over by the door."

"No. I'm eating my supper in this restaurant." She set her palm flat by a beer stain. "At this table."

Kresinski wouldn't let Connie go, not without a scene she didn't want. The climbers had seen Kresinski's women come and go, and occupied themselves with small talk and setting appointments with each other to climb this or that tomorrow morning once the sun had heated the south-facing slabs. "Leave me alone, Matt." Kresinski's arm stayed bunched around her hips. Kresinski didn't just burn his bridges, he demolished them beyond recognition. Connie pinched his hand, which only inspired a cold smile. "I mean it," she warned, near tears. "Come on, Matt," she pleaded softly. At times like this, in the gentle moments gone brutal, the Camp Four clan saw Kresinski's craziness and wondered about their own parts in the puzzle. For most of them, big walls and multicolored granite were the only things worth climbing on twice, and Yosemite was a sort of world capital. Kresinski confirmed that over and over with his unfailing returns from far-flung mountains in places most people only see in *National Geographic*. Other locals, most notably John, had climbed throughout the planet's cordilleras, but none returned so loudly or brazenly as Kreski did, nor did anyone have his heavy-metal gift for wrapping a mountain or wall or even a mere forty-foot crack in such hairy-assed terms. They liked that about the King because he was diplomatically generous in making them feel bold and separate and superior, too. They were mainly white, middle-class boys on the lam from white, middle-class duties: school, marriage, jobs. But with Kresinski they could perceive themselves as more rarefied beings: electric drifters cruising the high, bare angles, navigating the brute, psychedelic canyons. There was a price, though. To share with the man, you had to be with the man. Watching him with Connie embarrassed them, but not enough to break with the code. Had he been here, Tucker would have said something, and John should have but didn't. Nor did Bullseye speak up. Katie almost did, but then figured it would come off as sisterhood, *semper fidelis*.

Finally Kresinski was done with her. Releasing his biceps, he opened the cage and turned her loose. Connie stumbled backward, then wove her way back to the kitchen.

"Lord of the flies?" Liz asked him. "Or just Attila the Hun?"

"Anything you want." Kresinski smiled. Then he got Sammy's and Tavini's attention, and no one had to wonder anymore why he'd turned Connie out here and now. "Man, she's moody," he said. "But I'll tell you. The squeeze box on her forgives all sins." In publicly junking Connie, he'd also junked Liz, even though it was Liz who'd left him. Publicly.

And again, as before, he put it into them all that they wanted what he'd already had. Because he could do that, they feared him more. Even John.

4

"Remember
The Misfits?" Liz suddenly
spoke up as John eased them
down over Donner Pass. Even at
ten miles per hour, it was all he could
do to keep the little Japanese pickup from
fishtailing. They didn't belong up here with
a blizzard on the outside and that helicopter music from *Apocalypse Now* blasting away on the
inside. The chain law was in effect, and if not for a set of
cheap plastic fakes John kept under the seat, they'd
still be waiting in the California sun for the all-clear, and that
could have been days. The plastic cleats had disintegrated just
past the state trooper's checkpoint, so they were down to a
crawl now, sandwiched between cautious eighteen-wheelers. Liz wondered how many nervous mothers in the cars passing them were telling
their kids in the backseat about the Donner party. It was the first fable
she could remember her own mother telling her, and she'd taken its lessons to heart. As she grew older, she'd found that the same basic lessons
recycle. No free lunch. The grass is greener on the other side. And in danger as in love, life is one big fuck: you insert, you extract. Bullseye held
the copyright on that one.

She rubbed the edge of her bare hand against the crystallized side
window. It felt like she was passing through a veil from one world to
another. It always felt like that when she left the Valley, but especially so
today. Somewhere out beyond the swarming inch-fat snowflakes, a ruby
was glittering on her bold high desert, a chance for a different beginning.
They would descend from these Nietzschean heights, escape the snowy,

craggy fastness, and there would sit Oz in the land of brute mustangers and underworld miners. With its ethereal towers and pulsing rainbows of lights, Reno had always reminded her of the city at the end of the yellow brick road, or at least of I-80. People were perpetually happy there, money was free, the casino workers dressed like Munchkins. Throughout her childhood, Reno had meant feed and seed stores, the doctor and the dentist, but it had also meant Target and new clothes and a lunch pail with cartoon characters on it for school and the boot and saddle shops where common everyday things were so gussied up with turquoise and tooled leather your mouth fell open. Reno was where she'd bought her first comic book, her first box of tampons, and, in great fascinated secrecy, her first *Playboy* magazine. It was where she'd seen her first real lobster and where she and her older brothers Ken and Steve had spent their first real paychecks, two hundred dollars each for the summer haying, on custom-made silver-mounted bridles with their initials stamped deep. The bridle was the one piece of her rig she'd brought to college and later Yosemite, practically an artifact.

"*The Misfits* was a Walt Disney movie," Tucker expertly recalled from the backseat. Liz turned. Jackknifed sideways in what passed for a seat in the rear of the king cab, Tucker would have looked ill if not for the shock of black hair erect on his head.

"No," she said. "It was about mustangers. Remember? It had Clark Gable. And Marilyn Monroe." Before Tuck's time. But in Burns, Oregon, that had been the Saturday afternoon fare, probably still was. John Wayne and Randolph Scott and Clint Eastwood. Stuff the cattlemen's kids could hoot at and aspire to. After the movie, she'd bought a checkered blouse just like Marilyn's and quit minding about the dust in her hair. You could be beautiful even with dirt on you. "And there was that other actor. A young guy. Nice and smoky and alone. A James Dean clone, what was his name?" And all those noble horses.

"Oh," faded Tucker. The music swelled. Wagner. The Furies were descending. It was his choice from the small library of classical tapes he presided over, part of a self-education program he'd started for himself. Nights he always tried to read a page or two of the dictionary; according to John, he'd almost made it to the letter B before switching to random pages. A true rustic, Tucker could tell you the meaning of polysyllables he'd never heard pronounced. Wagner came out with a twang, Wag not Vog, and Beethoven's first name sounded like a gross insect. Part of the reason Liz loved John was this awkward, graceful boy; anyone who looked after Tucker the way John did had to be worthy. "Guess I never heard of a mustanger," the boy finally confessed.

"They round up wild horses and chicken-feed them."

"Oh." Still in the dark.

"Dog food and glue and chicken feed."

"Oh."

"I was a mustanger once." She couldn't tell from his expression how the admission sounded to him. All that showed was his innocence. Never change, she begged silently. Just stay the way you are.

"You kill the horses yourself?" His question carried no judgment.

"No. I just stood on one point of the gully and flapped a blanket. The horses went right into a portable corral and a semi came along and that was it." That was it anyway until Kenny came in late with a troubled look and trailing a colt. Until then she'd had no idea. Her brother had been late because he'd traced back along the path and shot all the horses that had broken their legs on the run in. She could trace the end of her childhood to that moment, when her teenage brother became father to an orphan colt. From then on she'd made a point of understanding the world. Ignorance was no excuse for giving away your choices. Mustanging was ugly work. Grimy, cynical, or just plain making the range work for them instead of them for it, mustangers would agree it was ugly but would also insist it was necessary work. "Overgrown rats," mustangers cussed the wild horses. You'd call liar on them to see a wild stallion moving across the earth, floating on his bed of glossy muscle. But when the environmentalists came along, the mustangers got proved right. The environmentalists passed laws. They put a halt to the plundering of herds. And the wild-horse population ran amok. Ranchers, once proud to have a few of yesteryear's chargers haunting their range, took to shooting the beasts on sight despite a hefty thousand-dollar fine. On her summer and Christmas breaks from college, Liz would come home and listen in on the growing anger. Year after year, the Jenkinses were forced to ante up to the feds a penalty fee for overgrazing that was caused not by domestic stock but by "their" wild horses. And madly

59

breeding right alongside the horses were the federal regulations, each year another four or five pounds of paper to deal with. People complained, but then stockmen always do, that's how Liz looked at it. Then one afternoon while the Super Bowl was coming over their satellite dish, she heard colt-loving Kenny say maybe the mustangers had had something, maybe the horses *were* overgrown vermin. Damn those horses. And damn those feds.

Naturally nobody cheered when she became a fed herself. Nobody was going to cheer if she got this job with the Bureau of Land Management. But Liz was Liz. They were real philosophical about that, always had been. Nobody agreed with her. Nobody argued with her. She was just there. All her life she'd felt like a starving trespasser, a ghost. More than anything, she wanted substance. She wanted to have an effect on someone. It was close to that with John. She scared him, that was obvious to her, and that was a hell of a thing to see in your lover. But their garden was growing. He knew she wanted to be reached for, and so he was reaching. He was reaching further than anyone ever had. It felt good. Their journey was just beginning. She had no idea where it was going to take them. Right now she didn't care. John had the makings of a companion. Daydreaming, Liz fell asleep.

Somewhere between the Wagner and piano concertos she didn't recognize, John said, "Reno." Liz opened her eyes. The snow had stopped, disappeared in fact. The highway was dry. The hillside showed brown with patches of bluish sagebrush. The heater and window wipers were turned off, and as advertised, there lay Reno. It looked plain in the daylight. Downright sorry. "I must have slept," she said.

"Good. You need it." He didn't say it in the past tense, which probably meant she looked like hell in the present tense. He wasn't mean, though. He never was.

"Montgomery Clift," Tucker greeted her.

"Hmm?" Her eyelids weighed heavy. She rolled down the window to draw fresh air.

"The guy in the movie."

"Movie?" It took a minute. "Oh. Right, you're right. I thought you hadn't seen it."

"I didn't." No explanation.

"Next five exits," John read off.

"Let's just try downtown," said Liz.

"Downtown," John repeated. "You bring your nickels, Tuck?"

"I don't gamble."

"I thought you'd never been in Nevada," Liz said.

"I haven't."

John looked at Liz. "I'll sell him to you"—he nodded at the rear—"cheap."

"What would I do with him, though?"

"Succulent young vegetable like him? You'll figure something out."

Tucker couldn't think of any way to play along, so he blushed, which was just as good except he hated blushing. "Hope we don't get soft here," he interposed. It wasn't going to work, though. His concerns about losing finger strength during the holiday had already been voiced too frequently.

"That's the attitude I like my men to have," said Liz. "I'll buy him."

Tucker wanted to banter. He wanted to stick his tongue in her ear and shock her the way she shocked and excited him. Sammy and Bullseye had once offered to coach him, but he'd told them it was stupid. There was no mistaking Tucker's infatuation with Liz; John saw it, Liz felt it. She encouraged it with innocent little touches—mussing his hair, an arm thrown around his shoulder, and with impossible invitations like this, always public.

"Downtown," John announced, arcing off I-80 onto the exit ramp. "Should we find the BLM office first?"

"Tomorrow," said Liz. "Right now I want a margarita. Let's get the fiesta in gear."

"How's Motel Six?"

"No way, John. I made reservations at the Sahara. Everything's ready. A really sleazy room with red curtains and HBO. Room service. Complimentary drinks with little umbrellas in them. The works. And I told them no mountains. If we look out the window and there's mountains, we sue. No mountains." Tucker stared at his folded hands. He'd never heard Liz talk like this before.

"Sound okay to you, Tuck?" John's voice said it sounded okay to him.

"I'll just sleep in the truck," said Tucker. They'd been all through this.

"You're sleeping with us," Liz said firmly. "You're in a city now, Tuck. If the muggers don't get you, the cops will. That's that."

"The desert," Tucker mumbled. They'd been through that, too.

"Should have let me teach you how to drive a stick," John said. "You're marooned, amigo. The Sahara Hotel. It could be worse."

"Besides," Liz concluded, "you need some practice living like a human being. Save the caveman stuff for Camp Four."

Tucker suddenly wondered if they were punishing him for tagging along. All he'd wanted was to see Sodom and Gomorrah, not participate in it. He should have known better.

"I didn't mean it to be this way," he tried.

"Tucker . . ." sighed Liz.

"The secret to a place like Reno," John took over, "is nickels. Don't play quarters. And stay away from those big silver-dollar machines. Nickel slots. You can play forever."

"We'll get fat," Tucker muttered. He had his weight almost precisely on schedule, down to where pinching the flesh on his belly yielded as much fat as the back of his hand. He'd even cut down on his regimen of five hundred pull-ups a day and endless laps on the rope ladder, figuring he needed the weightlessness more than the lat strength. The Visor was almost right there upon his fingertips, if only he could keep off the lard of civilization.

"We'll find you a Nautilus," John said at the rearview mirror.

"There's got to be aerobics classes in a town this big," Liz added with a straight face. Tucker couldn't believe they were saying those things to him. The only way you get in shape to climb is by climbing. He was deep into the country where mistakes cost you dearly. A child of the suburbs, such instincts didn't come naturally to him. Common sense was something he'd had to pretend to ever since entering the Valley. For that reason, once he put two and two together, four became law. You tie off your knots and flip your biners gate-out, or you eat it. You dissect your fear or it devours you. He'd learned how to learn. Lesson one: Shut up. See. Listen. That and a few other homemade axioms kept him good and sober.

The Sahara loomed ahead. In the rearview mirror John saw the edge of his face eclipsing the edge of Tucker's profile. "We'll survive," he said. He didn't belong here, either. Reno was going to remind him of who he wasn't. Cities did that to him, stole his flesh and bones. They made him feel amorphous. Even the parking lot attendants had shape in this glittering exterior world, but John . . . out here he was just a fiction. Only a fiction could inhabit cliffs in a place that had struck frontier painters as a gothic dream. He threw a fast glance at the mirror. There were crow's-feet around those eyes, his, not Tuck's, not yet. A whole lot of hand-to-hand combat with his own shadow on vertical rocks beneath the white sun was starting to show. Time's march was on. You only get your first thirty years to pretend it's not, then the masterpiece loosens into fissures and peeling paint. Reno was going to be a broken mirror. Everywhere he turned, pieces of himself would be reflected back. John grinned at the scars crisscrossing the backs of his hands. Only a world-class athlete in a sport bare of cash or public recognition would believe how alone and old and foolish he felt on the eve of his retirement. All he could seem to communicate to Liz, who didn't or wouldn't understand, was that he felt sorry for himself. I know you, Tucker, he was thinking. Look at the future, bud. I'm it.

"HBO!" Liz gushed, catching sight of the hotel marquis. She sensed John's and Tucker's flagging spirits. They were like brothers sometimes. When one was down, the other was, too. This trip being her idea, she drew on what hostess skills her mother had imparted and treated them both like children. "First we get our room. Then we clean up. Then dinner. Mexican food, how's Mex sound, Tuck? And then on our way to the movies we'll go find an ice cream store—"

"Ice cream," Tucker groaned. A desert monk couldn't have sounded less enthusiastic. Liz steadied herself with a big breath.

"Let's make a deal," she said. "I promise to go easy on the sensuality if you'll go easy on the asceticism."

"Asceticism," Tucker repeated to himself. It was apparently one of those words he'd never heard aloud.

"You're asking the impossible," John told her.

"Maybe from Tucker here." She reached around and lassoed the boy's head with her arm and stamped a heartfelt kiss near his eye. She held on, too, and felt Tucker's shoulder close into her hand. "But not you, John. You're already ruined. And there's no going back."

John looked over. In the fading light, every contour of her face was exact and perfect. Her gray eyes were alive, lower lip seductively trapped in her teeth. "Maybe," he said.

"Uh-uh, John. I've got you by the balls. And you know it." She heard Tucker swallow hard, caught beyond his abilities.

"Yeah?" John was beaming.

For a moment they watched each other. Then Liz looked out the window. "I guess we're just about there," she said.

In the middle of their third and final night together Tucker tried to escape through the window of the hotel room, which was neither sleazy nor red but definitely luxurious beyond anyone's need. John was lying with Liz curled against his chest when he heard a mechanical thump and opened his eyes. The city lights were breaking and splashing across the room's walls as the curtains shook violently. There was no wind, though, just air-conditioning and Tucker. John lifted his head from the pillow. Highlighted against the glass, Tucker was stark naked with one bare leg over the top of the opened window. A half minute more of tight snaking and he'd have the rest of his body out, and then it would be a cold, quick drop through twenty-three floors of air.

"Tuck?" John gently called. This was nothing new. Everyone had heard the tales of Tucker's nightmares—how he'd torn his tent to shreds one night, and put his hand through a bedroom window another, how he'd sleepwalked off a bivouac ledge on the South Face of Mount Watkins (with a rope attached, luckily), or how if you woke him up sometimes he'd start whistling as if it were all just a joke. Everyone had opinions about Tucker's affliction, none of much use except for Bullseye's, which was naturally the most exotic. "Simple," Bullseye cheerfully theorized. "He signed a deal with the Devil." It was an argument that patently frightened Tavini, who was in constant horror of his own darker urges, but in a way it made sense. How else could a person climb the things Tucker climbed short of enlisting supernatural help? On the other hand, if it were that simple, every climber including Tavini would have signed his soul away long since.

"Hmm?" Liz stirred. She rubbed her warm back against his chest. Under the cigarette and casino odors her hair smelled like Liz, a rich

Scandinavian smell that was more a function of her toilet than her Norwegian roots.

Louder this time, John said, "Tucker." Liz was having her own dream. She began stroking his upper buttock, then scratching it. Visions of sex. Or insect bites. The window was not designed to be climbed through, and Tucker was finding it difficult to get his shoulder into the outdoors. The urgency faded.

"Tucker," he whispered. Liz suddenly grabbed a handful of muscle and pulled his body tight against her. Her face turned into the pillow, muffling a slight groan. Just then Tucker whipped his head around. "What?" he demanded. There was fear in his voice.

"Tuck, wake up."

"What?"

"It's John."

"John?"

"We're okay."

"John?"

Tucker took a moment to digest the greater reality. "Oh," he finally said. "Yeah." As if wrestling oneself buck naked out through a skyscraper window were perfectly natural, he casually stepped back into the room. "Air. I just wanted some air."

"I know," whispered John. Liz had finished with him. She released his buttock and with a sigh cradled neatly into his arms.

"Sorry," Tucker whispered back.

"No problem."

"I did it again." He worried about himself. They said he'd fried his synapses. Too many days sailing too far beyond charted waters. Visions, Bullseye called them. Dead-of-night, singsong visions of the godhead. In Technicolor. Calling him home or into the On High. You watch, someday Tuck's going to lift right off the valley floor and not even the *National Enquirer*'s going to believe it. In the old days they used to name stars after people like Tuck. We'll name a star after you. A whole fucking constellation. Tucker hated that talk. It scared him, everyone waiting for him to crash and burn. It was troublesome. Death or serious injury he could handle, but not the loneliness and exaggerations. There was a way out of the nightmares, he knew there was. The journey free was going to

65

be intricate and harrowing, that was a given, no problem. And it would be costly. It might cost him everyone and everything, but that was better than someday mismanaging a toehold on a plastering of wet lichen near the wrong end of a 5.13, no pro. Or turning into an ice cube on the Mosquito or who knew where or when it might catch up with him. All of eighteen years old and his life was already too short. If it were as simple as selling his ropes and gear, man they'd already belong to someone else. He'd give them away. But true odysseys never let you loose until the end, and he was still somewhere in the middle. Thorns and vultures all around. Temptations and dangers. He'd find his way through, though. It was all very physical. First the Visor had to let him pass. Then Makalu, that monster. Then he could be done with the verticality altogether maybe. Maybe.

"Go to sleep, bud."

Next morning John woke at seven-thirty, late for him, and reached for Liz. She was already in the shower, and Tucker was gone, his sleeping bag neatly stowed in a clean, bright yellow stuff sack. There was a bed for Tucker, but that was going too far, and so the boy had quartered himself on the floor. He kept all his possessions stored in stuff sacks made of waterproof, rip-stop nylon, which made his little world ultimately portable. Literally everything the boy owned fit into an expedition-size backpack, with room to spare for an extra gallon or two of water. Only in the last few years had John seen the charm in that sort of dedicated poverty, because he'd been embedded full-time in it himself. Now, having followed his dad's clay footsteps as a bohemian roughneck for a few seasons, he at least had a truck and six hundred dollars in a money market account. Another year or two, he might actually vote. Never far away was the memory of crossing Berkeley campus on his way to another weekend in the Valley. He had been Tuck's age, loaded down with ropes, and the hardware was ringing musically with each step, when suddenly a news camera crew swooped down for a man-on-the-street interview. American troops had just invaded Cambodia. The news crew wanted to know what was his reaction? They'd been filming hippies and Marxist radicals all afternoon; now here was someone out of the ordinary. The microphone hovered in front of his nose. The newscaster, a remarkably thin and fiery woman, hung on his silence as if his first words might open new

66

worlds. Cambodia? he finally asked. The sound man had looked at the cameraman. The truth was, he'd had no idea where Cambodia even was. The war in Vietnam meant student strikes, and strikes meant free time for the Valley. His geography consisted entirely of the world's cordilleras, the mountains he'd seen and the ranges he hoped to. "Kill the mike," she'd said. The shame of that afternoon could still rouse a "you dumb fuck" shake of his head. Any Jesuit worth his salt would have punched him out for the intellectual lapse. He looked at his bare toes sticking out from the bottom of the sheets. Some things never change. He was still in the Valley, still lost and lapsing.

Liz emerged from the bathroom stripping the water from her waist-length hair with a red comb. "You're up. Sleep well?" Her long body was a marvel.

"Yeah, minus one of Tucker's spells." He stretched and kicked the covers loose. Now he was naked, too. He watched Liz's eyes, then worked down her body again. Their bodies were taking over.

"More dreams? Poor Tuck." She moved close to the bed. Her dark golden pubis hunted nearer his face. She was talking to him from high above where she looked down. Her nipples looked enormous atop her rib cage. With a long even stroke she pulled more droplets from the heavy hank of hair and let them sprinkle down.

"So did you."

"So did I what?"

"Dream." He ran his fingers down the edge of her saddle. She pushed in closer. Her mouth came open from the sensation, but she started the comb down from her head again with forced deliberation.

"How do you know?"

He told her. "Sort of wondered what were you dreaming about," he said.

She stepped across his chest, spreading herself. "Breakfast?" she pondered and brushed his lips with one fingertip. The red comb fell onto the far pillow.

"Where's Tuck?"

"He went for a run." That gave them anywhere between two and three hours. With the lungs of a Sherpa, it took a lot to max him out. Balanced with both hands on the wall, Liz began lowering herself.

"Tell me about that lake, Liz. The airplane." It was already a game between them. The interrogation and evasion could go on for a very long time.

"What lake?" She was kneeling over his arms. All she could see was his beautiful face.

"Cocaine. Diamonds. Gold." He reached up with his tongue. The first touch arched her back like an electric shock. He did it again.

"John . . ."

"Gold." He found the crest and her breath emptied.

"You talk too much," she said, and that was the end of their playing.

Afterward they descended to the hotel restaurant to await Tucker. Slot machines cranked away in the background, otherwise breakfast was as Liz wanted it, quiet and elegant and just expensive enough. At nine-thirty, halfway through John's second cup of Earl Grey, Liz announced, "We've got to go."

"Right."

"Where is he?"

"Don't worry. He probably turned his jog into a marathon."

"You don't think he's hitching back to the Valley, do you?"

"Nah. Probably embarrassed about his midnight stalking is all."

"I feel terrible leaving him like this."

"He'll find something to do until we get back. There's always MTV." Like Tucker, John had found the rock videos irresistible and even alien. Some of the cultural references woven into the videos were so contemporary, he could only squint at the screen. Newspapers had the same effect. He was out of touch.

"I just hope some hooker doesn't get hold of him. You remember that cocktail waitress yesterday." Lots of cleavage and eyeliner. Lots of attention to their silent minority, Tucker. That was nothing new—John had long ago observed women's passion for the shy Billy Budd types— nor was Liz's maternal jealousy.

"Tucker?" he said. "You really do believe in charity."

"What's that supposed to mean?"

John heard the irritation and looked at her with surprise. "Nothing. Just he doesn't have any money. A hell of a customer."

She looked at her watch and stood up. "We can't wait anymore. The secretary said ten-thirty. Sharp. She said this may be Nevada, but they run their offices on federal taxpayers' money and federal taxpayers' time. If I'm late, forget it."

"Maybe we ought to be late then."

She refused the humor. "I want this job, John."

"They're going to fire you before they hire you because their clocks say ten-thirty-two? Whatever happened to good old mañana?" There was no repartee. Ever since the eggs Benedict had arrived undercooked, Liz's fuse had been burning. It wasn't the eggs, of course. It was the interview. The escape hatch. "Not that I have a wristwatch. Or pay taxes," he tried mocking himself. "Hell, I don't even have an address." He paused in the clowning, figuring a small litany was equal to a big one. Either she was going to lighten up or she wasn't. He should have known, though. If their sex wasn't going to do it, probably nothing was.

"Nothing I'd brag about," she curtly dismissed and kept right on staring at the bill.

"Let's boogie then." He tossed it off nice and airy to contrast her bitchiness. She flicked a glance at him and grimaced.

"Just give me a break, John. Today's a big day."

"I'm right here. I'm with you."

"I know."

They slid from the booth, paid up, and left behind the chugging, ringing slots. Out on the sidewalk, his Nikes gave him an extra inch on her, and even then he wasn't looking over her head. He loved walking beside her. People looked. He felt special. Not special like when you descend from a big-wall cut and gaunt and fried to a crisp, tentative and weird from the thirst and solitude, and the tourists give you wide berth and whisper "rock climber" as in Hell's Angel or speed freak. With Liz there was an elegance. Just the way her loose, heavy hair hung, people looked. But more. When she draped one long arm around his shoulders, she was announcing her equalness. Her blond against his dark, both whip strong in their blue jeans, they looked born for each other.

It was a good half hour out to the Palomino Valley corrals through country wide open enough to make John feel like his soul had dropped loose and bolted for the long and far away. Part of it was that this was much the same as the desert of his boyhood, stark with the same Sonoran vegetation that washes against oil rigs from Wyoming to the Mexican border. Rabbitbrush was budding yellow and sage hung rich in the air.

The winter had not quite digested all the tumbleweed stuffed tight against the barbed-wire fences, and the speed signs and open-range signs were all aerated with bullet holes. This was terrain he'd fled from once before, and now she wanted him to come back. He wondered if other refugees suffer the same vertigo he was feeling in this reminder of a bygone homeland. At the same time, he felt relief. Rounded old volcanoes crouched with their spills of lava rock, dinosaur country. Not all bad memories. There's things inside other things, his father used to cough out. Some Indians do that, cough their words as if language itself were a humiliation. John and his brother would stand stock-still in his cool shadow beneath the infinite sun. Sidelong like a flimflam man or shaman he'd spit some Red Man, no joke, and heft a palm-size slab of dull gray limestone picked off the ground at random. You got to look for those secret things, he'd say, otherwise what's the use of being a human being? And so saying, would crack his geologist's pick against the rock. He'd pry apart the two halves, and in there carved on the dark brown walls would lie a fossil leaf. Or an animal print. Or a seashell. You'd marvel at the oldness, smell the rock, cup the fossils to your ear and listen to reptiles rustling through giant trees that weren't there anymore. Within this world of illusion lay another. That was a valuable lesson, especially when the chain on a pipe changer ate half their dad's right hand one night and he turned into a poor illusion of their magical father. After that the old man lost his enchantment with the earth and took to bad-mouthing the bosses and sluts and goddamn machines, everything, even his two pups. But they stuck by him because inside things are other things. Somewhere inside that bastard with bony fists dwelled their father. So John and Joe busted their young asses roughnecking, risked their fingers on the same pipe changers and kelly rigging, cussed the same bosses, the same machines. They didn't have to, but they turned over half their paychecks to the old man. The Jesuits told them not to, their dad would only drink it away. The boys gave him money anyhow. He drank it away. He died. That simple. And John fled.

"Turn down here," Liz said at a dirt road. Fire-blackened land swelled and dipped on the surrounding hills, rushing right down to the wood and steel corral posts of the wild-horse center.

"Ten-twenty-three," he said, looping into the dusty parking lot. "Sharp." He heard his own bitchiness this time. He pulled in front of a one-story building with pitted aluminum siding and turned off the engine.

"Please, John. This is for us." She squeezed his hand.

He squeezed back. "Well, good luck. I'll wait out here. Over there. By the corral."

There was another pickup in the parking lot, a real one, not a Japanese dwarf like his, and it bore the inevitable bumper sticker promoting guns. That and the sound of horses running spontaneous circles in the far enclosure was it. Liz didn't get out quite yet, though, didn't even look at her watch to check the correct time. "I don't want to waitress, that's all."

"I don't want you to."

"And I don't have any other skills. I know trees and I know horses."

She was earnestly trying to be nice, but her words made him feel foolish. "I know rocks" was all he could say. Oil rigs and rocks. His earlier elation about being partner to her was sinking fast. A fine pair they'd make, a prole and a bureaucrat.

"I just can't stay in the Valley anymore," she said. There it was. "And you can't either." There it was in deuces. But then he'd come to Reno and Palomino Valley for this very reason. Liz had to say leave and he had to say I'll think about it. "It doesn't have to be here. It doesn't have to be horses. We just need to leave the Valley, John. We can go anywhere. We can do anything."

He looked down at her hand. The first time he'd held this hand, it wasn't her long fingers or strength that astonished him so much as the thick ridges of callus on her palms. They weren't the horny pads you find on the climber's fingertips, just old-fashioned working calluses in the meat of her grip. It was the hand of Eve.

"I'll think about it."

"I know."

"But the train's leaving?"

"The train's leaving."

In the tradition of
boxers who pickle the skin
on their knuckles in brine
and urine, of alpinists on the
streets of northern European cities who
carry balled snow in their bare hands as a
prophylactic against colder, steeper walks, of
cyclists, kayakers, and football players
who endure freezing showers and ice baths for the
sake of improving themselves—Tucker had a theory. It
reduced to one word. The word was Suffer. That was
it. It was that fundamental. Suffer. Suffer enough and you reach
an end to the suffering. Suffer enough and you get transformed.
There's something to it, of course, the idea that by humiliat-
ing the flesh you lift yourself closer to God. Not that Tucker had in
mind the intellectual history of self-mortification, from early Christian
martyrs and Blackfoot warriors to flagellants in the streets of modern-day
Tehran. He simply kneeled face forward in the bed of John's pickup
truck and kept his teeth clenched against the early-morning bugs. Like
that, all the way from Reno to Sacramento and then to Yosemite, he let
the various winds pour over him, steeling himself for the day he would
rise upon the West Face of Makalu in Nepal and be baptized in the jet
stream dividing earth from heaven. His knees ached from the corrugated
sheet metal, and passengers in passing cars probably thought he was a fraternity pledge. But he could feel his skin toughening. His blood thick-
ening. He forced himself to peek through what would one day be the
hurricane-force winds of high-altitude mountaineering. He pondered: to
let his hair grow out for the big mountain or to keep it short like a Ma-

73

rine Corps AWOLs? Longer hair might trap heat, maybe it wouldn't. That was a pertinent question to ask John, who'd been high, eight thousand meters and higher. Like that, with Tucker in the rear of the truck shoving back at the world with wild fantasies while he "caught wind," they arrived back in the Valley on Thursday morning to find the early sun casting rays bright as canaries.

"Home," John announced as he swung right at the Conoco gas station opposite Yosemite Lodge. Behind the gas station and its rustproof, bearproof dumpster, with a much-despised wooden National Parks marker reading "Sunnyside Campgrounds," lay the teeming, ground-level slum to which any climber worth his beans, even the Eastern Bloc lads, will make at least one pilgrimage in his active lifetime.

"Home," Liz dully echoed. The Valley was no more home than Reno was Oz. She was thinking that if only there'd been the time and money, they could have flown to Mexico, a beach, a village, a boat, anywhere. At least they could have pretended to be pioneering new land. Circle the wagons. Unhitch the oxen. Taste the river. Work on a tan line, something sweet and salty to accent their nights. Spend some time. Warm time. She stared off into the woods. Screw the BLM. Screw the Valley. And if John couldn't rise to the occasion, screw him. She'd be so much dust on his narrow, pinched little horizon.

It suddenly seemed like they'd been gone a very long time. When they'd left, the Valley's furniture—its conifers and ponderosas and massive, upright planes and the waterfalls that had paused blue in midflight for the winter—all had stood still. Now everything was in motion. Bluejays threaded the trees, the Merced was thawing. Yosemite Falls was frothing white with early runoff and the meadows were promising wildflowers soon. They'd left in winter and here it was spring. She groped for the date. She groped for the headline of the Reno *Gazette* she'd purchased yesterday with the last quarter scored off a slot machine. Nothing came. Already the time warp had taken effect.

"What in hell . . . ?" John muttered.

Only then did Liz take notice.

The parking lot was skeletal. An old Buick with British Canadian plates, two Chevys from the Beach Boys era, and a much-cannibalized orange Saab rumored to be hot sat at scattered points, sad carcasses in some flatland junkyard, any flatland, all flatland being junkyard. Otherwise it was barren, not a soul to be seen. The engine idled as they gaped at the emptiness. The resurrection of John Lennon couldn't have stunned them more. Liz reached forward and punched off the tape deck, leaving them blank, no theme music, no idea what was what. Back in the bed, Tucker got off his knees and stood in place, two unmoving stovepipes of faded denim in the rear window. There wasn't even a game of Hacky Sack going on. No one slouching about spooning peanut butter from the jar, not a wave of greeting, not a sound. Even on slow days the Camp Four parking lot brought to mind the bazaars of Bombay with their scarves of motion and gossip and color fluttering everywhere. This morning it looked like a neutron bomb scare. But even then someone would have stuck around to see what a neutron bomb blast was *really* like. This was different. Camp Four was empty, and Camp Four is never empty. John switched off the truck. No one moved. Tucker's legs kept on blocking the rearview mirror. Liz waited for an explanation. It was eerie, well re-hearsed but not too interesting, sort of like the opening of your better Steven Spielberg movies. The whole thing was a joke, of course. "Rang-ers must have booted everybody out," she said.

Tucker nimbly hopped out of the bed. "Weird," he pronounced and headed for the pathway leading into camp.

"Let's see what's up," said John, and he and Liz followed Tucker past the bulletin board tacked and taped full of scribbled messages. "For sale 1 pr. unused EBs size 43. $20. Site 16"; "Wanted, climbing partner. I lead 5.11. Joyce. #3"; "Final descent. Selling out, going to Hawaii. All gear at bargain rates. #22"; and a "Joe meet Henry" dated 7/15/75, an artifact of the remote past. The pieces of paper flapped their butterfly wings as John and Liz breezed on without a glance.

In deeper, past the thirty-foot-high Columbia boulder spotted with chalky handprints like petroglyphs and smudged with shoe rubber, John slowed down and began to wonder. There were no people in here, either. But neither were there many tents. That was odd. A joke was one thing. Pulling up your tent stakes, unjointing the poles, and packing out all your gear took the practical out of practical joke. He doubted if even Bullseye could have orchestrated such a mass prank. There were better things to do with one's time than break camp and then remake it. Bulls-eye was eliminated from suspicion when they passed Kresinski's campsite and saw no tent there, either. Kresinski would never have played along with Bullseye. It was starting to look as if people had actually left. More ominous still, the few tents that remained were in unnerving disarray. The spines of some had relaxed and bowed, leaving the tent walls limp. Some had collapsed altogether. In their short absence the camp had been utterly depopulated.

"What's going on?" said Liz.

John lifted and dropped a hand. "New regulations?" he tried. During the reign of James Watt as secretary of the interior, the rangers had exercised a heavier hand. They'd threatened to muscle the climbers out time and again. Maybe they'd finally carried through with it.

"Impossible," Liz said. "Not in three days' time. I'd have known about it before." She wasn't so sure, though. She was, after all, mistress to the Camp Four monarchs, first Matthew, now John. If a resettlement of Camp Four had really been in the works, it would make a certain kind of sense not to have told her. She'd always kept her professional life distinct from her love life, even despite heavy pressure by Kresinski to "help me boys" when ten C4Bs pulled a fire alarm at the grocery store and went on a cash-free shopping spree up the empty aisles. Naturally they'd gotten caught. The case was finally dismissed, but ever after that Kresinski seemed more fascinated by her refusal to "lose" the park's investigation report than by her magical hair or cloistered heart. When she finally realized that what Kreski was bent on seducing was really her loyalty, Liz dumped him. She was still trying to figure out if the last straw had been the assault on her morals or her pride.

"It's like the end of the world," said John.

"Or the beginning," Liz corrected him. This was how it should be. The forest empty of chattering, arrogant people. A fresh start on clean ground. John cut off the trail with the odd caprice of a bird dog searching for a nest. Liz followed, not entirely cynical. It could be fun walking with him. He had a true gift for finding the most remarkable stories imprinted in the earth, reading how many of what species had gone where. Footprints, broken twigs, depressed moss—it was all signatory. Man or animal, they had a contract with the world, all you had to know was how to read it. Beyond that, however, John could look at a sign invisible to everyone else and tell you what its maker had been thinking. Rabbits, snakes, deer, tourists. They all reduced to the same desires and whims when John read their tracks. All were in need of the earth.

The emptiness was mystifying. The farther they hurried on, the more inscrutable the camp's evidence became. It had the feel of those mysteries you learn about in junior high school: the sudden departure of the Mayans, the unexplained evacuation of Mesa Verde, the disappearance of Atlantis. Compressed rectangles clearly showed in the pine needles where tents had been uprooted. Pulley systems used to dangle food sacks high off the ground where animals couldn't reach dangled from tree limbs like emptied nooses.

"John," Tucker called over from a distant site, "your stuff's all gone. And my tent, my gear, it's all gone." He sounded heartbroken.

"I don't know," John muttered to himself. Liz hung back, waiting for the verdict. All she had to do was check in at headquarters to get the answer, but it pleased her to watch John exercising his Apache arts. He was like this on rock, too, masterful, confident, self-conscious, in his element. Maybe that was why she hated to watch him climb, because one glance told her he belonged up there, reading the granite with his fingertips. John paused by a fire pit, apparently picked at random. Just like a Hollywood injun, he touched one knee to the dirt and felt the ashes for a trace of heat. Still obedient to the cliché, he let a palmful of ashes sift through his fingers, then stood up and declared his findings. "Three days," he said.

Tucker came loping over from the far end of camp, all leg. Naturally he wasn't out of breath. "It's like a ghost town."

"Whatever happened," said John, "we just missed it. They left the morning after we split for Reno."

"I don't understand," Tucker let them know. He was a top-of-the-line man, meaning the loss of his gear was going to cost him more dearly than anyone else. Where a hundred-fifty-dollar tent might suffice for his neighbors, Tucker believed in buying only the best. Now his beautiful cantaloupe-color dome tent that turned the sunlight into a soft orange glow on the inside was gone. His rattlesnake-checkered red-and-black Blue Water rope with only one moderate leader fall on it, no retirement in sight, had vanished. Everything was gone, even his collection of Beethoven, Bach, and Miles Davis. Even his photo of the seldom-seen West Face of Makalu. He'd have to write off to the Japanese Alpine Association and try to pry another photo loose of them. Then he remembered that his address book was gone, too. It was bad. They'd cleaned him out, except for his sleeping bag. And his Sony Walkman and three tapes. And the parka he was wearing. And luckily he'd taken his new pair of Spanish Fire climbing shoes with the sticky rubber soles with him to Reno, along with his chalk bag. Suddenly he wasn't so bad off after all. An afternoon spent prowling the dumpsters and the aluminum cans would provide him money for food. Winter was over, so he could sleep under a picnic table or in the open. If it rained, there was always the log-cabin bathroom floor. Above all, he could continue climbing. Whoever it was hadn't stolen that from him.

"Why don't I go call in?" said Liz. "Unless a spaceship came and kidnapped all the happy campers, they'll know where everybody went." There was a ghetto-style telephone booth back by the parking lot with spray-painted graffiti and a shredded telephone book. John watched her walk toward it, and with a backward glance she caught him watching and tsk'ed at him self-consciously. Her walk embarrassed her, half man, half woman. She'd compensated for her size so many different ways that it was hard to tell what was her original Oregon stride and what was affected. He'd seen game animals transplanted to new territory walk like that, testing out the terrain as if they'd lost their bodies and didn't belong anywhere.

"Pretty dang weird, huh?" Tucker observed.

Suddenly John had an idea. He turned to the west and filled his lungs. "Hey, Bullseye," he called through cupped hands. There was no echo. No reply. He tried again. The second time they heard a faint yodel, authentic Tyrolean, vintage 1974, the year Bullseye had spent teaching American GIs mountaineering above Garmisch, Germany.

"Should have tried there in the first place," said John. Side by side, he and Tucker set off at a rapid pace. Bullseye would know what was going on.

"Yeah," said Tucker. "Now we'll get this thing squared around."

They followed the trail to its end and on past the "NO CAMPING PERMITTED BEYOND THIS SIGN" sign. Pine needles crunched underfoot. The park-sanctioned border of Camp Four fell behind and they entered a denser wood with underbrush intact and a riot of squarish rocks lying where a landslide had tumbled them. Not one, but two big deformed trees carried gashes from old lightning strikes. Animals stirred in the thicker distance. It always struck John this way. A few steps from Camp

Four and you were beyond the sanitary park with neatly managed campsites. Here in this topsy-turvy swatch of wilderness halfway to Bullseye's sanctuary you were partway back in time. Here, mimicking the aborigines, John had even harvested hazel and piñon nuts. Not many people came this way. There was no scenery for the tourists, no rocks for the climbers. The still mediocrity of the place made it a perfect barrier to trespass, which was the whole point. Bullseye liked his privacy. And yet, John saw, a lot of people had recently come this way. The prints were clear and showed lighter on their exit than their entrance. That could mean only one thing. Heavy loads in, light or no loads out. Camp Four had made its exodus through here. But why?

"Something's up," he told Tucker.

"Yeah?"

They pressed through a screen of willows and brambles, and suddenly the forest opened onto a circular clearing with a thick shaft of sunlight angling in. In the middle of the clearing, lodged tight against a fat young oak, stood a '69 VW bus. It was so intricately camouflaged with forest green, tan, and gray paint and so overgrown with ivy and moss and ferns that the occasional "civilian" hiker saw here nothing but a squat, featureless gob of granite. "Low profile" was so dominant in this blueprint that while rangers knew of the van's existence, few ever visited because it was so easy to miss. Besides, rules need the rare exception, and Bullseye was nothing if not rare. The van had no wheels or engine. It was the perfect vehicle for Bullseye because it hadn't moved in over nine years and probably never would. Legend had it that he'd talked a gang of San Diego bikers into carrying the van through half a mile of woods in the dead of night in exchange for information he didn't have about some rival gang. By the time the hoodwink was discovered, the bikers had forgotten where they'd deposited the van, leaving Bullseye to make his slow last stand against nothing in particular. There were theories about why he lived out here alone, the most prevalent revolving around his allegedly eternal love for Janis Joplin. It was said that he'd once dipped his stinger in the Bayou Queen under a whiskey moon outside Atlanta, Georgia, or somewhere south, and that afterward no other woman would do. True or not, there had been no woman in Bullseye's life for years now. Kresinski made much of it, calling him a capon at best, a "brown-eye" at worst. Climbers new to the Valley, and therefore new to Kresinski's venom, were careful to avoid climbing with the Faggot Hermit. Everyone else knew better. Climbing with Bullseye was like a trip to the museum. Steeped in the practices and reliquiae of the late sixties, he nested among piles of Zap and Bayou comic books and SDS manifestos on yellowing paper and old Leadbelly and Yardbirds records and a black Peace armband still smelling of tear gas. People figured his clock had stopped, that was all. He was rumored to know more about the night sky and planetary paths than even Carl Sagan, and if you asked and he trusted you, he'd allow that his greatest ambition was to climb the outside of the Ice Palace in St. Paul, Minnesota, the next time they built it. No one swallowed that one, though. For while the rest of them left the Valley to attend random semesters of college or headed south to Baja or the desert rock at Joshua Tree or took off to work or go on expeditions or just get out, even if getting out meant just driving a few hours westward for nothing more than the closest drive-in and McDonald's, Bullseye never did. It had been so long since he'd stepped foot outside the Valley that people knew he never would. Here was one child the Valley would turn into bones before it let him go.

He was sitting on the front passenger's seat tending a row of pine seedlings in Styrofoam cups when John and Tucker broke through the thicket. Everything was calm, Bullseye most of all. "You guys." He smiled. John recognized the mellow alert, one of Bullseye's leftover specialties. The mellower he showed, the more excited he was. A tawny mutt named Ernie lay sprawled by the rear axle gorging on the warm sunlight. At John's approach the dog flapped its tail up and down a few times, then drifted off. Ernie, too, was an outlaw legend. Reported sightings had described him as a coyote, a rogue wolf, a bear cub, a raccoon, a mountain lion, a werewolf, and a naked lunatic. Few rangers had ever seen him. None, except for Liz, knew to associate him with this other outcast.

"What's cooking?" said John.

"Beg pardon?" Bullseye coyly grunted.

"Come on."

Bullseye stopped what he was doing. "I been waiting for you guys." He looked right and left, fighting down a huge grin. If there was one thing he loved, it was a conspiracy. "There's big doings," he confided. "Big." His excitement started to show, but he managed to rein it in and finished tamping peat and soil around the base of a luminous green seedling. Having nothing to do with his hands, Tucker slotted them in the top of his front pockets and let John do the talking.

"You got our stuff?" John asked. He'd already guessed Bullseye did, but hadn't voiced the thought to Tucker in case thieves really had struck.

"Yeah."

"You do?" Tucker was overjoyed.

"You hit any jackpots in Reno?"

John sighed, making room for the punch line.

Bullseye rubbed his hands gleefully. "Because we hit the jackpot here, boyos."

"But where's our stuff?" said Tucker. From the corner of his eye, Bullseye tried to measure the pair's curiosity, and finally his excitement broke loose. He kicked his feet loose of a pile of paperbacks under the dashboard and swung from the seat.

"I'm the only one that stayed," said Bullseye. "Me and this." And with a natty arc, he slid open the van door. There, folded, stuffed, tied, and stacked from carpet to ceiling, lay all the possessions of Camp Four. Miles and miles of rope bearing every color of the rainbow were piled in neat, limp coils. Tents, shoes, chains of silvery carabiners and high-tech hardware, three acoustic guitars, gas stoves, dirty clothes knotted with twine, a typewriter, and even an IBM PC jr. all inhabited the dark cavity of the van. It smelled of mildew and wood smoke and old sweat.

"Yeah" reveled Tucker. "Cool."

"You going to tell us or not?" said John.

"You guys ready for a little walk?"

"Jesus, do I have to pull it out with pliers?"

"The lake, men. The lake."

Just then Ernie snapped his head up off the ground, snout pointing toward the eastern willow break. "Someone's coming," said Bullseye. The dog vanished. A minute later they heard Liz calling, "Hello, hello."

"In here," John shouted.

"Boy, I don't think Delta Force One is going to be her kind of outfit."

"Delta Force One?" Tucker asked. He'd spotted his rattlesnake-checkered rope and was trying to extricate it from the pile.

"There you are," Liz said from the thicket. She shouldered through

81

the brush and joined them at the van. "No one knows a thing at head-quarters. It's a big mystery. In fact they instructed me to report *my* find-ings."

"I missed you, Lizzie," Bullseye interrupted.

"God, look at all that gear," said Liz, just noticing. "Where'd every-body go?"

Bullseye hesitated. "There's been some developments. Some group investigation of, uh, rumors." Unable to get his coil loose, Tucker untied its knot and began pulling the rope out in a single strand onto the top of his Adidas.

"Fuck," John whispered. The lake.

Liz understood, too. The little half grin stayed on her face for another few seconds, then guttered away. Suddenly she looked very sick. "Oh, no," she groaned. "Bullseye, tell me this isn't true."

"What?" said Tucker.

"Too good to be true, Liz. What did you expect?"

"Hang on," said John. He was feeling weak in the knees, too. "You mean Kreski talked the whole camp into going—"

"It wasn't exactly the Children's Crusade," said Bullseye. "People know what they're in for. They've been goin' up in waves. A few of the animals have come down and gone back up already—you know, like twenty-five-hour days. It takes two days in. And loaded up, about two days down. I'd say Camp Four should start filling up tomorrow in the P.M." Rope scattered across his feet, Tucker still didn't comprehend the news.

"Stop," Liz commanded. "I don't want to hear it. I didn't hear you." She turned around and faced the willows. "I didn't see you. Damn it, don't you understand—"

"Don't blame me," Bullseye said. "I'm here. They're up there."

"But . . ." She stopped. "It's crazy."

"Yeah." He said it with relish.

"Don't you know what kind of trouble . . ." She couldn't seem to finish a thought.

"Kreski's just a daring kind of guy," Bullseye observed. "Aren't we all."

Liz turned, anger crabbing her brow. "I'm serious, Bullseye. And John. I was never here. Damn it. You people . . ." She didn't wait for refutation, just hauled off into the forest. John followed her. With each passing second, the implications of "the lake" were becoming clearer.

"Liz, wait a minute," he said. "You have nothing to do with it."

"You people." She stormed ahead.

"Would you just slow down a minute—"

"No."

"Slow down."

She stopped. "Are you going up?"

John hesitated.

"I don't want to know you." She yanked her sleeve from his grip.

"Would you just—"

"Just leave me alone, John." Whirling around, she punched him hard on his chest. "I should have known better."

"Yeah? Well hit me again. That'll make it all go away."

"I'm done with you."

"And you're a cunt." He said it just like his dad would say it, slapping her hard with the word. He'd never called her that. Then again, she'd never hit him. She hit him again, catching him on the ear this time.

"Damn it," he said, touching the ear with his fingertips.

Glaring to keep him at bay, Liz backed away and stalked off through the trees. "Run away from it, Liz," John called after her. Then he wished he hadn't said anything. He slapped at a dead twig and sent it flying. Words. Fists. Fuck it all. A rustling to his right made him stop. There was indistinct movement, then a dirty yellow shape burst from the brush. It was Ernie. The dog cranked its lips back in a ghastly smile and wagged its tail thick with brambles. Together they returned to the clearing.

Bullseye and Tucker were kneeling beside a USGS topo sheet spread out on the ground. Both looked up when John reappeared. "Snake Lake," Tucker said to John. "I never heard of it."

"But it's there, Tuck." Bullseye touched the map precisely.

"And everyone else is, too," said John.

"Everyone," Bullseye emphasized.

"And there's drugs."

"Beaucoup drugs." Bullseye rocked onto his heels, stood, and reached into the van. He pulled a ten-gallon plastic garbage bag from behind the front seat and opened it. "Reach your hand in there, Tuck."

Tucker hesitated. "What's in there?" But it was obvious he was pretending. He knew, too.

"Gold."

Tucker dipped his arm deep and extracted a handful of dark green and red vegetation. It was wet and stuck together. "That's like a fraction of what Sammy brought down. He said take it all. There's more. Tons more."

John stepped up and took a pinch. He smelled it. "Jesus, it's soaked with gasoline."

"Airplane fuel. No problem. You should see it burn. Pure, smooth. Sinsemilla. Not a bud in the whole crop. It creeps down your spine and takes you on a tour. It's like '69 all over again." Sixty-nine was Bullseye's touchstone, the height of civilization as he knew it.

"I don't believe this."

"It's true. The plane hit square in the lake. What blew onto shore is what the rangers snatched. The rest of it . . . all we can figure is they decided to wait for the spring thaw to do their work for them. They're lazy. We're not. We're fucking hungry. You hungry, Tuck?"

Tucker swallowed and dropped the pot back into the garbage bag. "But what if they decide to bust us?"

"They can't bust all of us. Besides, they're sleeping. By the time they wake up, we'll be millionaires."

"Snake Lake," said John. "That's a long ways up and in."

"Two haul-ass days. But I got us a shortcut figured out." Bullseye pulled his fingertip across the topo, tracing a strenuous trek up and down the altitude lines. "We need skis," he commented. "But if we leave this morning we can make it tomorrow morning."

John pointed at a parallel set of lines that showed slopes that were steep, but not steep enough. "That looks like avalanche country." South America had taught him well.

"A regular Valley of Death." Bullseye shrugged. "There's always the long route."

Tucker watched the negotiations, accumulating the behavior of grown men.

"And this here," John said, stabbing at a tightly bunched set of lines. "That's real climbing."

"Climbing?" Tucker parked up.

"Ice," grinned Bullseye. "Two hundred feet of sweet blue ice. Sammy said forget it, no one could ever climb it clean." To Bullseye, the Iceman, that constituted the ultimate challenge.

John bought in. "Okay," he said. If nothing else it would put him beyond Liz's reach for a few days and get him up into the backcountry. And it was always a pleasure to watch Bullseye strut his stuff on steep ice.

"What do you say, Tuck?"

"What about the Visor?" the boy wanted to know. "We're honed. We're ready."

"Yeah, but it's not ready for us." From where they stood the upper reaches of Half Dome swelled above the treetops. The Visor jutted out at the very apex of the wall, blue and cold. Because it faced north, away from the sun, it would be winter up there for some time to come.

"Besides, the Visor's not going anywhere, Tuck," Bullseye popped in. "Hell, after this you can go and *buy* the Visor. After this one we're going to own the whole almighty Valley."

6

*O*n three-pin back-
country skis, the three of
them whispered up the
snows of Bullseye's Valley of
Death toward Snake Lake. They were
on cruise control, lightweight and streamlined, packs empty except for sleeping bags,
some ice and rock-climbing gear, a couple
pounds of trail food, and a gas stove to melt snow.
Casting fretful glances up at the fattened slopes on
either side of them, they saw what John had foreseen
with one scan of the map, that the avalanche factor was radical.
They were so quiet infiltrating the narrow valley and the air was
so thin that each felt like his ears were packed with cotton.
There are places like that in the mountains, the glacial fields of Denali,
for instance, or the plateau above the Khumbu Icefield on Mount
Everest, where sound almost ceases to exist. You feel endangered, as if
your next footstep might turn to stone or this veil of earthly illusions
might suddenly evaporate and leave you nowhere and nothing. Bullseye
tried whistling through his teeth, then quit. Tucker felt an urgent need
to practice aloud what he would say when the feds arrested him for this
caper, but took his cue from John and held on to his words. In early days,
mountain folk believed that a sound even as slight as the beating of a
swallow's wings could trigger an avalanche. Burdened with superstitions
of their own, the trio slid between the deadly slopes with the timidity of
thieves. Just in case the slopes avalanched, they kept fifty yards or so between them. Sunlight ricocheted off the diamond-bright snow, and when
they stopped for night all three were suffering sunburn on the rims of

their nostrils. John found a large rock shelf that would brunt any nocturnal slides. With a slice of new moon dangling in the east, they crawled under one by one. The day had sapped them all, but they were too excited to fall asleep right away. Bullseye tried to engage their attention by telling them, in a stage whisper, about a New York intellectual's film analysis in which she correlated fascism with the love of mountains, but only succeeded in dumbfounding Tucker. Bullseye sensed the lack of interest and quickly detoured.

"I haven't whispered like this since me and my friends watched all the girls at my big sister's slumber party," he said.

"The avalanches," Tucker somberly whispered back.

"I know," answered Bullseye. "The old Lightnin' Man." The Lightning Man was an in joke. Once upon a time, Satchel Paige stole two bases and home plate during a fierce thunderstorm. When asked where the burst of energy had come from, he explained it was because of the Lightning Man coming to get him. Pete had imported that little anecdote to Camp Four, where it instantly entered the language. Climbers divided their risks between objective and subjective hazards. The subjective hazards were those you created yourself, the ones you imposed upon the rock. Trembling knees, sweaty fingertips, a foolish move: Those and other symptoms of fear or pride could cause you to fall on a perfectly safe rock. Add some rain to slicken the rock, however, and the hazards became objective. The risk became exterior. It became the Lightning Man. Rockfall, avalanche, deep cold, rotten rock, bad ice, storm. The Lightning Man. Usually subjective hazards just made a fool of you. But when the Lightning Man beat you, you were dead. Tucker knew all about the Lightning Man. "It reminds me of when I was a boy," whispered John. "My father took me and my brother into the Superstition Mountains looking for the Lost Dutchman Mine. We went into a sacred area the Apaches call *zhich-do-banajegahi*. The taboo mountain. The Apaches say that gods live there, and that men's spirits pass through on their way to beyond. They say that a race of little people has its home there. And that it holds a window to the past. We got there at dark and we whispered all night long. We were too afraid to build a fire because of what we might see. And if we talked out loud, the spirits might find us."

"You find the Lost Dutchman?" asked Bullseye.

"No. Next morning my father remembered that the mountains could change their shape. Trespassers die because they can't find their way out. And we were definitely trespassers. So we hauled out of there. *Rápidamente.*"

"What was the rock like?" Tucker couldn't keep from asking.

"Go to sleep, Beanie," said Bullseye.

Before dawn next morning, John wiggled out of his sleeping bag and waxed all three pair of skis with a hard green klister for the cold April snow. Tucker didn't move in his bag until Bullseye nudged him awake and handed in a mugful of lukewarm chocolate.

"Two more miles," John softly informed them, map in hand.

"To the lake," asked Tucker, "or the ice?" There was a difference. He was secretly praying that Sammy would prove correct and the icefall would be too difficult to climb. In his opinion this lark up to Snake Lake was a costly digression from more important issues, mainly the Visor. The sooner they returned to the Valley, the better. It was a matter of minutes to work their sleeping bags into stuff sacks, chew a handful each of generic beer nuts, and step into their ski bindings. They glided off blowing frost like high-strung racehorses, quickly awake, skating neatly across the hard crust. As they gained altitude, the trees turned into dwarfs, crumpled and mangled by chronic storm winds. This morning, however, there wasn't a puff of air. Snowflakes that had descended overnight balanced on pine boughs like fine white gold dust. Soon the drainage took a sharp left-hand turn, then a sharp right. The lazy slopes turned into jutting maze walls a hundred, then two hundred feet high on either side.

"Finally," beamed Bullseye. For now the walls were too steep to hold snow. They'd survived the avalanche channel. Another bend in the twisting drainage and there it stood smack in the middle of the cold shadows, a hundred-and-fifty-foot-tall ribbon of blue ice dangling from a concave scoop of rock. It was a spillover from the lake, or so the map indicated.

"Your mama," swore Bullseye. He didn't punch his pole tip against the binding release and dive for the gear in his pack. Instead he just stood there, and you could tell the thin column of ice looked insurmountable, even to him. Tucker was relieved and thrilled at the same time, glad because now they could retreat to Camp Four, but excited because first Bullseye would try his hand at the glassy barrier. He wasn't going to get far. But he was going to try. And the thing about ice is that it's not rock. And the thing about rock is that you can second-guess it usually, ice never.

"Doesn't look like it's in very good shape," John appraised. He was giving Bullseye an out if he wanted one. In fact much of the ice looked primo, nice and plastic, not too brittle, not too soft, and Bullseye knew it.

"It'll go. A bit thin," he conceded. "But I think she'll go." What Bullseye was talking about was ice so scarce in places that it hardly glazed the underlying rock. Near the top the column seemed to be attached to the rock by little more than a smear of frozen water, a condition alpinists call verglas. It was amazing that all those tons of inverted dagger could be held upright like this, more amazing still that Bullseye was willing to commit his body weight to it.

"Maybe we ought to see what the sun does to it," Tucker suggested.

"Nothin' good," said Bullseye. "Might as well give it a shot before the whole thing comes loose and falls on us."

"Whatever," John consented. He could hear the faltering in Bullseye's tone and wanted the man to know they were behind him no matter what. "No big deal if we backtrack and take the regular trail around."

"No big deal," said Tucker.

"Yeah," Bullseye said to himself. He had his hand up by his face and was sighting along his index finger at each section of the column, linking the possibilities visible from the ground. "There," he muttered, "over to there. And there."

John and Tucker skated over to a flat table of rock and took off their skis. It was best to leave the sorcerer to his divinations. Bullseye was reaching for that calm part of the pond where all the circles open up, where Heidegger and Nabokov and Picasso and others like them say yes. Here. Now. Closer up now, while he unfurled the one coil of rope they'd brought in, John examined the ice. It was so intricately fluted that it looked like stale, filigreed gingerbread, and promised about the same solidity. It was going to be like climbing on Wheat Thins up there, provided Bullseye even got off the ground. The pointed bottom of the ice hung eight or nine feet above the ground. Bullseye was going to have to stretch on his tiptoes just to get a tool in. From there, if the whole thick spear of ice didn't detach and impale him, he'd have an opportunity to decipher thousands of false and true codes frozen in the water. Ice is strange stuff. It can look like shit plastered on stone and yet feel like a million bucks. Or a nice fat curtain of perfect turquoise glass can suddenly delaminate and there you go, down among the plate-glass shards. With ice you take your chances. Ice screws aren't like ordinary rock protection; like ice itself, screws seem to have a mind of their own. Indeed, technology is the crux of the problem with ice climbing. On rock you can feel your relationship with the wall through your fingertips. If a fall is imminent, usually you know it before the fall. On ice, each hand holds an ax or a hammer, each boot is encumbered with a crampon. You're climbing on, at best, a half inch of sharpened metal at each point of contact. If the tools fail, you fail.

Bullseye joined them and took off his skis. From his pack he pulled a pair of black Chouinard crampons with wine corks stuck onto each sharp tip, twenty-four in all. He unstrapped a fifty-five-centimeter-long French ice ax from the rear of his pack and reached inside for a wicked-looking hammer called a Hummingbird. Side by side on the table of rock, the tools gleamed. Like Tucker, when he bought, he bought the finest. For protection, he drew from the pack three hollow ice screws, plus a handful of knotted slings. Tucker watched in awe. He'd never climbed ice with Bullseye, though everyone said you hadn't lived until you did, and so every move, every tool, every piece of pro was a part of this graduate course in extremism. He waited for Bullseye to extract more protection. Bullseye didn't.

"Did you bring the rest of the pro?" he asked John.

Bullseye looked blankly at him. "John brought more?" he said.

"I was supposed to bring something else in?" asked John.

"I just thought . . ."

John looked at Tucker, then at what the boy was staring at. He remembered the first time he'd climbed with Bullseye, too. "Oh. The pro. No, we're talking skinny here. Skinny means happy, right?"

"Right," said Bullseye. He wasn't smiling, though. The ice had him spooked. With the authority of Shane loading his handguns, Bullseye methodically pulled the wine corks from each tip on his crampons, exposing much-sharpened and resharpened points. He strapped them on to the bottoms of his boots, flexed his foot up and down, and tightened the straps some more. Instantly Bullseye seemed different to Tucker, dangerous instead of frivolous. With the crampons on his feet and an ice tool in each hand, he *was* dangerous. When ice climbers fall they're the proverbial loose cannon, everyone's worst nightmare including their own. Every flailing limb turns into an uncontrollable weapon, and the belayer can end up looking like a sawmill disaster. On rock you get abrasions. On ice, lacerations. It's the difference between sandpaper and surgical knives. Sitting among the shadows blue as Dresden chinaware, Bullseye grimaced at the high blue column. Already he was in love with it. He tied one end of the rope to his harness and stood up. He hyperventilated, then exhaled altogether and flapped his arms. He loosened his knees with a deep bend and tossed his head from one shoulder to the other.

"Want me to belay?" asked Tucker. In truth he didn't want to. He wanted to watch the unfolding masterpiece.

"Better let John," said Bullseye. "He weighs more." To a climber the remark was succinct; if he fell, he expected to fall far and hard. The heavier your belayer, the greater your chance of getting caught. Borrowing one of the three-foot circles of sling, John lassoed a rock and clipped himself to it. Tucker noted that John had positioned his belay spot well away from the fall line, that imaginary path straight down from up. Bullseye reached into his pack one last time and brought out his trademark, a badly scratched fiberglass helmet with a red and white bull's-eye painted on the very crown. As a general rule Valley climbers disdained helmets as pussy ware. Only Bullseye got away with a helmet, and only on ice. His brain meant a lot to him, though not to the exclusion of his pride. On rock he was like everyone else, gray matter vulnerable to the tides of war. He tightened the strap under his jaw and worried on his fingerless gloves, and finally put a hand through the strap of his ax and hammer. He looked at John, who nodded his readiness, and delicately stepped across a scattering of rocks sticking up from the river ice. No more wisecracks. Tucker didn't wish him luck: too bush. Not a cloud in the sky, it was a good day for hanging out your balls.

With all that metal on, Bullseye sounded like a robot. His crampon points squeaked on the flat river ice, his ice screws clinked. Eyes high, he walked around the hanging tip of the column and studied the odds of getting off the ground and staying off. With the blunt end of his ice hammer he tapped at the column to sound its firmness. It sounded just like it looked. Like a very fragile, elongated chandelier that didn't want to be climbed. He didn't dare hit it again. Best save any concussions for real tool strikes. At last he found a piece of the column that, to Tucker, was indistinguishable from any other piece. On his toes Bullseye reached high and swung his hammer, this time its sharp tubular pick end, against the ice. Immediately the bottom twelve inches of the column fractured straight across and dropped to Bullseye's feet with a thud, then scuttered away down the frozen river. "Hmm," he appraised.

He stretched high again and, because his hammer would no longer reach, tried the ax pick. With a flick of his wrist he tossed the pick against the ice, and perhaps a quarter of an inch stuck with a dull tick. Bullseye cautiously lowered his body weight onto that arm and it held. He exhaled once more and then slowly pulled himself up with one arm, no feet. His crampons dangled down, his opposite hand poised in space. All he was holding on to was the vertical handle of his ax, and all that held his ax was a dime's edge of frozen water. As soon as he rose within striking distance, Bullseye wasted no time and coolly flicked his other tool, the hammer, into the plastic surface of ice. Now able to employ both arms, he pulled himself still higher and then did what gymnasts call a lock-off, holding himself chin-high to one hand while letting go with the other. He locked off on his hammer hand, and that allowed him to quickly, but carefully, pry loose his ax. Just as quickly he clapped the ax pick back into the ice, only this time another full arms' length overhead. He pulled up on that, locked off, and then repeated the same process with his hammer.

His technique was fluid, perfectly suited to the medium. He'd been climbing ice for so long that the mechanics had all been smoothed out, leaving John and Tucker with a clean, virtuoso performance that had no seams. Repeating his trick with the one-arm pull-ups and lock-offs four more times, all within the span of maybe two minutes, Bullseye reached the level where his feet touched the bottom of the ice. He held on to both tools and gingerly kicked one of the two bucktoothed crampon points into the ice. It was less a kick actually, than a nestle. With the toe of his boot he slid the filed point into an air bubble beneath the surface that he'd committed to memory while passing upward. His toe stuck. A bit higher and to the side, he copied the motion with his other foot. Now he was really in heat. He eased his body weight down onto his feet and rested first one arm, then the other.

"Niiice," he breathed to himself, and down on the ground they heard him distinctly. Tucker watched the red and white bumblebee crown of Bullseye's helmet as the climber plotted his next series of moves. The rope looped down into John's hands, a thoroughly useless appendage until Bullseye decided to place an ice screw. He didn't because it was much too soon. There were only three screws, for one thing, and besides he didn't trust the little bastards. He had no reason to. It wasn't that he didn't believe in protection. He'd gone through such motions of faith thousands of times, placed more screws in his career than any man alive. But he'd never fallen and hoped he never would. In his opinion, a tube of threaded airplane metal was about as useful on long screamers as a puppy treat with rabid dogs. If you were going to get bit, you were going to get bit.

The next fifty feet went quick and easy for him. Anyone else would have balked bug-eyed at the hazards, but Bullseye scarcely even looked to see that his tools were sticking. All Tucker could figure out was that he climbed by touch. Like listening to a tuning fork, maybe, Bullseye must have felt the vibrations of metal in ice and known which to go with. "Interesting," Bullseye commented at one stage, though it didn't look interesting to Tucker at all. Gripping and manky was more like it. As ice will do, the column changed character partway up, spreading into brittle honeycombs that looked good for three pounds max. Bullseye just slotted his ax and hammer points in the fragile pockets and kept on trucking. Now and then bits and pieces of his progress came raining down, tinkling like fragments of a broken champagne glass. And still he didn't place an ice screw.

"Thin?" John hinted up to him, hoping he might place a screw.

"A little."

"Feel good?"

"Uh," grunted Bullseye, concentrating. That was that. You don't tell climbers how to climb, particularly high priests of the art like Bullseye. He reached an overhanging ceiling loaded with foot-long icicles. Instead of clearing them away with a sweep of his ax, Bullseye maneuvered over and around them. Not one of the icicles came loose.

Where the ice thinned down to a scanty plastering of clear lacquer on rock, Bullseye paused. He'd reached the verglas and there was no place to

94

screw in pro even if he'd wanted. The sun was coming, the ice would warm. What little covering the rock had up there would melt away. He had to move. Had to move.

He started to move, then balked. His hand tightened on the hammer handle. "Golly," he said, reaching for something deep inside. There wasn't a thing Tucker could do except watch, and only one thing more that John could do and he did it. He let go of the rope and very quietly unclipped from the belay anchor, then backed away to where Tucker was sitting. Tucker understood. With no protection between himself and the ground, Bullseye was unbelayed anyway. By sitting any closer to the column than he was now, John would simply be a target. He wasn't abandoning ship, because Bullseye hadn't constructed one to abandon.

Bullseye's hand tightened on the rubber handle again and then loosened the hammer tip from its icy seat. He had second thoughts again, though, and pocketed the tip back in. His left leg quivered ever so slightly, betraying muscle fatigue and a crack in his mental armor. Sewing machine leg, it's called. Bullseye straightened his legs and locked the knee back. The quivering stopped. John and Tucker heard him hyperventilate with three fast bursts. Bullseye was going to go for it.

He freed the hammer from its bite and, scrutinizing the surface higher up, set the tip against a patch of verglas. With the softest of hits, he tapped at the patch. But instead of sticking, the hammer bounced off the rock and the verglas fell into pieces. His leg quivered. He straightened it out. He found another patch farther right. This time he didn't strike with the hammer. Using it like a carving knife, he whittled a minute notch in the verglas with the hammer's pick. Then he set a pencil point's worth of pick on the notch and pulled down on it. It held. Like a curator brushing dust from a pre-Columbian pot, Bullseye exacted an equally tiny hold from another patch of verglas with his ax. Between patches, the granite was slick and bare. Tucker had begun shaking. He was transfixed, face empty, and seemed unaware that his whole body was trembling. It wasn't the cold. John turned his attention back to Bullseye. Every climber carries with him the memory of certain special climbs. They aren't necessarily the most difficult, but for one reason or another they speak to the climber with an unusual accent. Each move is there to be revisited: the smell of the rock, the type of rock, the stretch of your limbs, where the pro set, where the sun hung . . . all of it echoes. This climb was one of those for Tucker, John could tell. Tucker wasn't down here, he was up there. Bullseye was his wings.

A New Wave splash of sunlight suddenly lit up across the highest reaches of the column and stone. Bullseye's helmet bent back. He saw the sunlight and returned to the business at hand. There was nothing to do but climb. He went on shaving little niches for his tools and crampon points. A patch of verglas near the very top let go in the warm sunlight, broke up, and tinkled into the deep. Pieces of ice sparkled on Bullseye's shoulder. He kept on going. Another dish of verglas peeled off, victim of the gathering heat. First Bullseye's hand, then Bullseye himself emerged into the sunlight. Time was fast unfreezing. Twenty feet more, all glistening with light, and Bullseye would be home free. He worked his tools and kept his nerve. He was no longer climbing just an object; he was climbing on the surface of time itself. Twenty feet translated into twenty minutes at this rate. At this rate twenty minutes was too long. He kept on climbing.

John and Tucker quietly recalculated the fall line and moved back farther. From where they sat it looked like Bullseye was climbing on wet rock. But finally he made it. His ax disappeared over the top edge, then his hammer. He'd reached the upper streambed. Too tired to say anything, Bullseye pulled up and over and off the face, and that was it. He was gone from sight.

Tucker quit shaking. He was safe.

"There you go. Bullseye on ice." Even as John said it, he knew he'd be seeing this same bravura performance again and soon. Only next time it wouldn't be Bullseye sculpting his way up ice, it would be Tucker remembering on the far ragged edges of the Visor, climbing the way mythical heroes climb.

"Intense."

"Olly olly oxen free," rattled down a shout. They looked up and there was Bullseye, legs cocked wide like a sailor's, leaning out over the edge. "I'm off." The tools were gone from his hands, replaced by a firm grip on the rope, which was tied off somewhere behind him. By off, he meant off belay. John could quit tending the rope.

"You were never on," John confessed with a shout.

"I know," said Bullseye. "Wild."

"You want to haul the packs up?"

They weighed practically nothing. Five minutes later all three packs and the skis and poles were up with Bullseye. "See anybody?" called John.

"Not a fucking soul."

"How about the lake?"

"It's foggy up here. Come on up. I'm gonna look-see." Bullseye's head popped out of view. End of communication.

"You want to go first, or me?"

"Go ahead," said Tucker. The final barrier had fallen and they were committed to the lake now. He had to arrange his bravado.

"Don't worry," said John. He clipped a pair of jumar ascending devices onto the rope and wiggled sling stirrups over the toes of his boots. "The feds aren't coming. I doubt if there's anybody even left. We'll see the lake, ski out, and be home by dark." He slid his right jumar up the rope. Small teeth in the spring-loaded jaw jammed on the downstroke and the jumar held tight. John stood on the stirrup attached to that jumar, then did the same with his left jumar and foot. He stuck his hands through the jumar handles and, rhythmically raising right hand and foot, left hand and foot, walked up or "jugged" the rope.

"No problem," murmured Tucker.

Nearing the top, John entered the sunlight and started sweating. The difference in air temperature was so emphatic it took him by surprise. He finished off the remainder of the pitch, a matter of two or three more minutes. The patches of verglas had already melted or fallen away. For the final thirty-five feet his boots scraped over wet rock. Had Bullseye paused any longer, the column would have foiled them. The gateway would have remained locked, at least until another cold night had frozen the melt and given Bullseye a second chance on new verglas. As he jugged the rope, John investigated Bullseye's route, trying to extrapolate from this wet trickle of water and that button of stone where the climb had unfolded. But already the climb had vanished. The ice had changed. Metamorphosis had hijacked them. The past and present were nothing more than liquids on the hard rock of the world. You go. You do. No poetry to that, thought John. He shook the sweat from his long black hair. Why can't she just let it be, he started thinking. Then his jumars hit the top edge and he didn't have to think anymore. The first thing he saw was the mountain.

Shaped like a giant isosceles triangle, the East Face was a blinding golden sun-scoop above the thinning mist. The brilliance hurt his eyes for a minute. Bowie Peak, said the map. Twelve thousand forty-four feet at the summit, minus ten thousand eight sixty-five for the lake: that made the radiant face eleven hundred feet high, give or take some, by Valley standards, a day climb. But still. Eyes pinched, John tried to penetrate the glare and figure out the technical value of this glittering plum. Much of the face's charm turned out to be a function of the light, though. It wasn't nearly as steep as he first thought, and there was a chimney of ivory snow indenting the entire center line. It led up to a wide ledge. Factor out the whitewash of sunlight and it was nothing spectacular, just a thousand-foot turkey shoot. Moderate, real moderate. Like kissing your sister. Or watching ice melt. He swiveled on the flat glassy streambed and looked below. Tucker was sitting on a rock. He was small. Everything was dressed in blue. There was no complexity. It looked starved down there. Two-dimensional. Like a black-and-white TV. "I'm off," he called down. Tucker waved a hand and hopped off his rock.

Bullseye's pack and skis were gone, John saw, and his tracks showed where he'd removed his crampons and then headed over a ridge into the mist. The snow was crusted hard and his boot prints stood on top. In the distance other peaks showed as islands drifting on a lake of tangerine fog. Another fifteen minutes, maybe, and the spectacle would burn off. Mountains would simply be mountains. John shucked his jacket and sat down to wait for Tucker. Simply, unabashedly, he drew in the serenity. Straight from Reno to this, now that was culture shock. He loved silence and color, but like many climbers didn't talk much about such appreciations. Too often they come out sounding like Yoko Ono on a poppy binge. The sublime: It conjured images of green Jell-O. And of Jesuits, them and their twenty-two-cent Thomist propaganda—the Good, the True, and the Beautiful. No, among the tribe, certain things like the sacred and profane could be taken for granted, and you didn't have to flap your gums about it. Not one among them hadn't seen night mountains getting harrowed with lightning bolts and otherworldly cloud formations folding on summits and pits so deep there was no bottom, none at all. They'd tasted milky-white glacier water and listened to satellites creeping across the moon. They'd eaten canned pudding using pitons for spoons and sucked the blood off their cuts for the salt. They'd smelled bears shitting in the woods. There was your sublime. There was your go and do. It went far beyond peace-love, brother. That was hippie hooey. This here was dead center of the celestial harmony, but all words did was cheapen it and so climbers mostly just told sex and death jokes. John basked in the quiet, not even a jet raping the sky, and then Tucker joined him.

"You want me to pull up the rope?" Tucker asked.

"Nah," said John. "Leave it fixed. Might as well leave the skis here, too. All the hard work's done. Might as well go out on the tracks we cut coming in."

Tucker dropped the slack rope in his hands. The rope slapped against the ice as it came tight down below. "I don't see any lake."

"Shouldn't be too hard to find if it's here. You up for some exploring?"

Tucker wasn't. Nevertheless he slipped on his big, empty pack and they padded up the rounded drifts aiming in general for Bowie Peak, first ascended by two cowboy-gold miners in 1872. It took its name, according to the stories, from the knife they'd jabbed into a crack and used for a foothold. Back then anything went, even lassos. As John and Tucker topped the ridge, the face got bigger and bigger. At the base of the face, they discovered, three-hundred-foot-high cliffs formed a cirque, or ring. The center of the cirque was filled with fog, but down there, John guessed, was their lake.

Abruptly the air ripped open with an ugly noise. John flinched. The mist on the lake parted. And there stood Kresinski with an enormous timber cutter's chain saw in his hands. The mist opened further. The lake was frozen over and he was standing twenty yards from shore on the ice dressed in a tight white T-shirt and even tighter purple Lycra tights, surrounded by a small herd of figures keeping their distance from the machine's long snarling snout.

"Kreski!" said Tucker. Even from this distance you could see the man's big arm muscles wrapped with veins and shivering from the chain saw's vibration. John knew the underside of the carriage would bear the stenciled legend U.S. PARK SERVICE. He recognized the make from a firefight the rangers had used him for in late summer 1976. They'd tried to hire him on as a seasonal after that, too, but the tourist season was also the climbing season. That, in fact, had been the topic of his first conversation ever with Liz. You ranger, me climber.

The mist suddenly lost its glue and came apart altogether. The whole lake appeared before John and Tucker. Like Liz and Bullseye and no doubt everyone else in between who'd visited, they were utterly astounded. Jutting from the ice like a red, white, and blue leg bone stuck the truncated remains of the airplane's tail section. Five feet tall, it stood eighty degrees vertical. Another two feet of the tail lay on the ice. Someone—the authorities or Kresinski with his chain saw—had lopped off the very top of the tail in order to look down inside the submerged plane. The surface of the lake was fused with snow that had seen whiter days. Everywhere footsteps and ski tracks mutilated the snow, and out toward the middle a helicopter's skidmarks were still melting. There were pink stains from spilled kerosene and gas, black stains from oil, yellow stains from urine, orange stains from the vitamin freaks on B complex, and bright orange and pink X's that looked like swatches of Day-Glo spray paint. Bottles and food wrappers littered the lake. A balding stand of pines on the north shore had become the repository for pieces of plane metal torn away in the crash. Twisted aluminum glinted like Christmas tinsel in the upper bones of thin trees, and the entire right wing of the plane lay where it had been ripped loose. A good thirty strong, all of Camp Four was out on the lake laboring at the ice with the meticulous frenzy of a cargo cult. A dozen holes had been cut down to the water level, and these were marked by waterlogged vegetation and discarded burlap and yellow plastic. Above the racket of Kresinski's stolen chain saw, somebody rebel-yelled.

"*Carpe diem,*" John breathed out.

"Sorry?"

"Seize the day. They've gone and seized the day."

Tucker didn't know what to make of that and stored it for later. One thing he did know was that any minute a whole hornet's nest of helicopters could come stabbing hot and bristling from below the near horizon and that luck alone would allow a few people to escape. The feds would be armed and ready. Bullseye was wrong. If they wanted to, the feds could bust every mother's son's fanny. He searched for the word, eminently mispronounceable, found, and excavated it. Abattoir. A place of slaughter. Snake Lake. The feds would slaughter Camp Four.

"Amazing," said John.

"I guess Liz was right."

John looked at the boy. "Right about what?"

"That there was a whole lot more under the lake than on it."

"She told you that?"

"Yeah, we talked about it in Reno."

She'd told John nothing at all. John was amused. Deprived of taking Tucker's virginity, she'd taken his confidence. "How come you didn't tell me?"

"Liz said don't."

John punched Tucker on the arm. "Let's go check it out."

As if carrying a heavy weight, Tucker shifted the pack on his back and adjusted the shoulder straps. He was torn between descending to the lake and telling John forget it. But "forget it" was perilously close to abandonment, and you never ditch your partner. Never. Tucker was an open book, his reluctance apparent.

Just then a small party of four departed from the pine stand and slowly plodded down-valley. For the first time John noticed a trail beaten in the snow, the long cut. A stampede of cattle would have been harder to track. None of the slow figures looked up from the trail. They moved with the kind of burdened walk you see in the Third World, human beings harnessed to their labor. They could have been Thamang or Balti porters in the Himalayas and were obviously heavily laden.

"Isn't that Katie?" said John. Louder he called, "Katie," and the caravan halted. Two people tried to lift their heads, but the packs kept them bent over. John and Tucker slid and cantered down-slope to the trail.

"Johnny!" chirped Katie. She was even happier to see Tucker. "Tuck!" Bent beside and behind her, Tavini, Pete, and some stranger with a beard and stomach muscles each grunted hey's. Their faces were haggard but luminous. Each was wearing a dazed, Mona Lisa grin. Tavini and the bearded stranger moved around and continued down. "Later," Tavini said gruffly. John wondered if he was going to tithe any of the loot over to Jerry Falwell or whoever his guiding light was. One thing was sure: Bullseye was going to have fun with Tavini next time they all met for dinner. The stranger wagged his eyebrows at John and then they were gone.

"Help me out of this," said Katie. John staggered under the weight of her pack. There were at least ninety pounds in there, and not much more than ninety carrying it. She straightened up. "Dump it, Pete," she ordered. "Let's take five."

Tucker helped Pete flop backward onto his enormous, dripping pack and unstrap. Katie's T-shirt, one of twenty she maintained, trumpeted "This Ain't No *#*&!!! Wienie Roast." "Cool, huh?" she said.

"Hey, you animals got any food?" said Pete, lying on top of his pack. "Or vitamins. Man, I'm starvin'."

"We been here since yesterday," Katie explained. "Dug all day, all night, all today."

"Kreski said fuck the eats, man. He didn't say it was two days in and two days out, though."

Katie shook her head sadly. "And so doo-dah here didn't bring in any food."

"Or vitamins," added John.

"Half the people up here came empty. Milk and honey, Kreski said. Shit. We're gonna look like Ethiopia in another day. Lucky thing we got the weather on our side."

"Yeah, but check the booty," said Pete. He squirreled a hand into the top of his pack and brought out a fistful of familiar-looking weed. "Huh?" he challenged. "And if I don't blow my knees out on this load, I'm comin' back for more. Only I'm bringin' food next time."

"Gold fever," said Katie.

"Kreski even got a pipeline set up to turn the stuff down in the Bay area. All we got to do is get it to the trailhead. Twenty-five bucks an ounce. A *wet* ounce, man. But fuck, I'm beat out already."

"Squeeze Tuck," said John. "He's got the Oreos." Tucker flinched.

"Oreos!" barked Pete. "You give me ten Oreos, I'll pay you twenty bucks, man." Tucker sidestepped him like he was yesterday's bad news. "Fifty bucks, Tuck. That's five bucks per unit. Come on." Tucker's face thawed. In the background you could hear people laughing and yelling, propelled by the moment. And Pete's shenanigans were contagious.

Tucker's spirits visibly lifted. He let Pete trail after him bargaining furiously.

"I'm wiped," Katie said to John. She kept her eyes on Tucker, though. "But what a kick."

"It's going to be hard to beat this one," John agreed.

"Tell me about it. Last night we must have smoked a pound of this stuff. In five minutes flat the crew was all seeing ghosts. Ask him." She jerked her thumb at Pete. "He started the one about seeing a green light shining up from the lake floor, and pretty soon everyone was steering clear of the lake. You wouldn't believe the bullshit. There's talk about gold bullion down there. Cocaine, M16s, diamonds. I'll bet the secret of who killed Bruce Lee's down there, too."

"Five Oreos, man." Pete raised his voice. "A hundred bucks and I'll tell you where there's a parachute. I seen it but I didn't go up there. Dead man's up there, I know it."

"Where?" Tucker suddenly demanded. A parachute? A dead man? He liked mysteries. It would give him a project, and better yet, an excuse for not being on the lake. Maybe when the helicopters arrived, they wouldn't see him.

"Up there behind that shoulder of rock." Tucker fixed him with a withering hanging judge's glare. Liars repulsed him, and everyone knew it. "I'm not shittin' ya," Pete swore. "Come on. All I want's some food." Tucker took a moment to make up his mind, then unthreaded the top flap straps and flipped open his pack. "It's there," Pete promised again. Tucker sucked on his teeth and none too quickly dipped his arm into the pack to remove a rectangular, gallon-size Tupperware container that was the last of his family reliquiae. He vividly remembered standing in his mom's Colonial-style kitchen with copper Revere Ware hanging by the microwave and deciding he was stuck, adrift, marooned, and taking a deep breath and looting the bottom cupboard for souvenirs of his childhood. Neatly arranged inside the Tupperware tub, padded with Park Service industrial-strength toilet paper, lay three dozen Oreos, not a one broken.

"Here," he said, handing over the five required by contract. Being Tucker, he gave Pete an extra five with the injunction, "Just don't tell anybody." Then he brought the tub over to John and Katie and offered them all what he knew they wanted. John took one, Katie a handful.

"Tucker." Katie grabbed his arm. There wasn't much that affected her. But Tucker touched her every time. "Put your Oreos down for a minute."

"Why?"

"Just do."

He did. Before he could react Katie slid one scarred hand over the burr of his Mohawk, and with the other caught him around the back. Sigourney Weaver couldn't have done it better. She looked in his eyes, gave him a hard squeeze when he started to look away, and waited until she had his full attention. Soot smudged her face and her almond eyes were red from two nights of campfires and she smelled like menstrual blood and sweat, a good smell if raw. Tucker swallowed hard, of course. Then she kissed him on the lips and let him go. "Thanks," she said. She turned and saddled up quickly, sitting back against her giant load. She buckled in and with John's help fought up onto her feet. Pete followed suit, exhaling dry black cookie crumbs onto the snow.

"You ready?" Katie called from beneath her pack.

"It's up there," Pete reiterated to Tucker. "Be careful, man. The living dead."

"See you mañana," said Katie.

"Bye," Tucker said. Nobody'd ever done that to him, nobody that knew how to, anyway. The girls who didn't know how were too shy to try him out in the first place, and the ones who should have known better always tried too fast with too much skill, making him feel dumb and uncoordinated. But Katie. Katie'd gone straight for the heart. He'd never even noticed her before. Now he couldn't put her out of his mind.

"Grab your pack," John broke in.

John was nearly up to the lake when another band of fully loaded climbers appeared. They hey'ed and yo'ed him and picked their way down the hillside. Suddenly one of them, one of the Fuller twins, lost his footing on the wet snow, slammed backward onto his hundred-pound load, and rocketed off into the lower acres. Half a mile down, he skidded to a halt, but like a turtle on its back, couldn't seem to right himself. With great whoops of "Surf's up," the rest of the boys cast themselves down the hill, too. Stoned to the gills. It would be a good idea to patrol the trail just before sunset and make sure no one pulled over to sleep off the THC without a sleeping bag, thought John. Screw that, though. If this was the Boy Scouts, none of them would have been here in the first place.

A few steps higher and John was there. The bent, severed airplane wing marked the entrance to Snake Lake. Saturated marijuana lay drying on the shiny metal, and here and there around the shore other torn panels of metal were seeing the same employment. Close up now, John saw that some of the faces were unfamiliar, but that was to be expected. Something like this was bound to bring out friends and friends of friends and outright strangers. One bellicose longhair in camouflaged hunting pants was toting a lever-action Remington deer rifle as he paced, a one-man anti-fed army. Nobody talked to him and he didn't appear to want any of the score, just some of the audience. Nobody noticed, too busy pushing and pulling at bales or digging holes in the ice or probing the water with sections of copper pipe liberated through the plane's tail. John started to count people, gave up, tried to count the number of holes gouged in the ice, and gave up on that, too. The smell of burning pot was rich and sweet, and twice while he appreciated the lake, wrecked wanderers suddenly plunged one or the other leg hip-deep into the slick round-edged holes. Whether they wore fiberglass Kastingers with super-gaiters for high mountain work, or tennis shoes, moon boots, or rubber galoshes borrowed from a Norman Rockwell painting, everyone's feet stood half buried with a freezing, creamy slush, the result of water splashed from the holes and of sunlight thawing the ice. There had to be a rhyme and reason to the proceedings, but all he could see was chaos and joy. Here was Hieronymus Bosch's paradise, every face stunned with lotus frenzy. They'd found the end of the rainbow. John paused by the erect tail section. The cut had been made with an acetylene torch, the work of the feds unless someone had hiked one in and he doubted it. Tucker joined him.

"It stinks," he said.

"Airplane fuel," said John. He looked down inside the submerged plane. Black water floated inside the cavity like clotted blood. The chain saw roared louder and a cry of admiration swelled. John walked through the slush to a crowd of people, most with empty hands, several bearing tools. The double-bitted Park Service axes in two climbers' hands dwarfed the frail-looking ice axes several others had thought to bring in. In the center of the ring Kresinski gunned the chain saw again, playing to the collective shout from his followers.

"Bitchen," yelled a girl with red cheeks, and her boyfriend in L.L. Bean boots didn't yell any words at all. He simply opened his mouth and generated noise. The babel was contagious. John could feel his pulse racing. Kresinski was all muscle and Ray Bans as he held the chain saw up with one hand and then gripped the handle and lowered the spinning blade into the ice between his feet. It passed like a hot knife through Crisco, spitting ice in a white spume. With fifteen inches of the blade down and in, he made contact with the lake underneath. An abrupt rooster tail of clear blue water shot out of the rear guard. Kresinski gunned the engine and pulled the blade out for a new probe. This time the rooster tail showered out a riot of dark red buds and chopped foliage. Strike. He'd hit a bale. He opened a small nylon hip pack circling his waist and took out a can of spray paint. A moment later the cut in the ice lay in the center of a bright orange X.

"The weed's waterproofed in two layers of plastic underneath burlap." From out of nowhere, Bullseye was by his shoulder explaining things. It was typical that he seemed to have marshaled all the pertinent data. "When the plane hit, some bales got blown out onto the shoreline. That's what Liz and the other rangers and feds must have confiscated. The rest of the bales stayed afloat until the lake froze over. That's what we're confiscating. There's bales frozen to the bottom of the ice"—he gestured in a wide circle—"everywhere." The chain saw sputtered and almost kicked off, but Kresinski accelerated and withdrew the blade in time. Instantly five people converged on the site to begin butchering the ice. Imperiously, even for him, he handed off the chain saw and walked away, and people shouted his name, demanding his cyborg touch. But he ignored them. "He's goin' down," approved Bullseye. Usually he had only bad to say about Kresinski. John looked at his eyes. Stoned. Lucid as a statesman, but wasted.

"Down where?"

"Under the ice. He got Sammy to bring in some diving gear. He's gonna investigate the cargo area and cockpit for real goodies."

"Kreski knows how to dive?"

"Renaissance Californian, man. He knows a little about a lot." Now that sounded more like Bullseye. If there was one thing he disdained, it was poetasting and "life-experience" dabbling. "Come on over here, Johnny. Come see Old Glory." Bullseye knelt by a hole chopped thirty feet from the plane's erect tail. He set his hands on the slick rim and hung his long neck down trying to find whatever it was underwater. "Take a look."

John stepped up, lowered one knee to the slush, and peered through Bullseye's window into the hard, sapphire water. Tilted slightly off the vertical, nose embedded in lake mud, hung the plane's wingless hull. It was pretty much as he'd imagined except for its colors. Striping it from nose to midbay was more red, white, and blue than a Shriner's parade. From a distance, the stars-and-bars job looked so real you could see it waving in the currents.

"Real patriots," said Bullseye.

John grinned. "Points for style, though."

"Tell me these guys didn't have stainless steel balls."

"You know," pondered Tucker, "I thought it was illegal to use the American flag like that."

John kept his eyes firmly on the poor man's Air Force One. Bullseye grunted. He grunted again, struggling to believe his ears. The Kid was a genius on rock, a full-fledged Einstein with his ability to take what wasn't there and conceptualize it into being right where he needed it when he needed it. But God he was dumb. "Guess so," he finally said.

"Those guys still in the plane?"

"Everybody's talking ghosts and zombies and shit."

"We heard."

"There's no way I'd go down there," said Tucker.

"You and me both," said Bullseye. "I hate dead men. Let Kreski fuck with them."

"So you think they're down there," John said.

"I don't know how many are still in the plane. But I can tell you there's one guy that's not."

"How do you know?"

"Up there." And he pointed at a spot on top of the stone ringing the lake. "There's a parachute up there. Nobody's gone up to check it out.

But when the wind blows, the parachute lifts up and moves around and you can see it. What I heard is, last night it freaked out half the brave banditos. They thought a whole gaggle of ghosts was coming for them."

"I'd hate that," said Tucker.

"What?" No idea what he was talking about.

"For the animals to get me."

"Don't sweat it, Tuck," said Bullseye. "We'll keep an eye on ya."

"I'm going up," Tucker said.

"What?" cried Bullseye. "Look. Look here." He pointed at the plane. "That there is a Lodestar. And this here." He fished a handful of pot from the rim of the hole. It looked like spinach. "Lightning. Lodestar Lightning. Wah! Here's the bottom line, Tuck. Those bales they're pullin' up? Twenty kilos each. I'm talkin' dry weight. But wealth. Hunt and gather. Would you walk past a ten-dollar bill in the street?"

"It's okay for you guys," Tucker responded. "I just don't want to."

"Lighten up, Tuck. One bale. One bale buys a year of big-wall climbing for ten guys. One bale buys you a trip to the Himalayas and back plus change. A new tent. Two. A pair of Koflach Extremes, new ropes, all the Gore-Tex and chrome-moly goodies you ever wanted. One bale and you write your own ticket."

"There's other things, that's all."

"Like what?"

Helpless Tucker shook his head at his own simplicity. But there it was. "Tell you what," said John. "If I head for home, I'll come find you. Should be easy to find you in that snow."

"Okay," said Tucker. He slung his pack on and cut north off the lake toward a ramp where the ring of stone dipped low. Higher up the East Face of the peak had turned an ordinary white and gray. When Tucker reached virgin snow on the far shore, his leg sank knee-deep through the crust. His next step landed midthigh. He slogged ahead, forging through the snow like a draft horse, knees high, shins tearing at the crust. Tucker really wanted to be rid of the lake. Postholing is the most tedious labor a climber will endure, especially a rock climber. Rock climbers like to drive to the base, open their door, and step onto righteous stone with the radio playing, no walking, most definitely no slogging.

Someone changed the music in the blaster. The morning got on. The air of loony disbelief hung on as bale after bale was excavated. Ice chips flew. Crews of climbers rotated and sweated, only to be overwhelmed by hordes of scavengers who converged on surfacing bales for a free grab at the pot. There were several near fistfights with these city and country-swing freeloaders, but the climbers clearly outnumbered the others, and that in itself kept the peace. The man with the lever-action Remington kept his lonely vigil against the feds until Kresinski pulled some karate out of his hat and took the rifle away. "You're makin' me nervous," he said and, to scattered applause and whistling, deep-sixed the weapon through a hole. Discarded burlap littered the shore. Every half hour or so, another small caravan departed for the lowlands with their precious cargo. The plundering was fun but eventually uninteresting. Much wealth was trading hands ("See, it works, it works," proselytized Bullseye. "Reagan said trickle down and it trickled down"). Much revamping of the hang-ten Valley ethic came to pass as climbers laid plans for new cars, real estate, vacations, and the latest in climbing gear. People estimated how best to invest, to spend, to hide. But that was boring after the first considerations. Rags to riches is only exciting until you touch the riches, then it's just another way of life. The blaster's batteries started to wear down, and by noon all they had for tunes was the sound of manual labor. There were several minor accidents, lacerations from knives and pieces of plane metal, and one boy cut into his small toe when his ax slipped. The injuries were treated with a variety of home cures, from packing the cuts in snow or binding them with petrol-soaked burlap to liberal infusions of what everyone was now calling Lodestar Lightning. One sweet girl took it upon herself to minister to the wounded with cups of steaming Celestial Seasons herbal tea, but soon found it more rewarding to sell her hot drinks to uninjured Lake Millionaires for ten dollars a cup. Around the time many would have eaten their lunch if they'd brought any in, the chain on the chain saw broke and whipped back and struck Jim Hanson on the arm. The good news was that the chain missed his face. The bad news was that he'd borrowed the chain saw from Kresinski and now their most effective probing device was out of commission. As Kresinski approached with a storm behind his Ray Bans, people expected big trouble. Hanson wasn't much for excuses and just stood there waiting for his medicine.

"Fuck it," Kresinski magnanimously pronounced over the ruined machine, and with no further ado dropped it into the depths after the rifle.

"So help me," Bullseye said a minute later. "I'm startin' to like that guy."

"Spare me," said John.

"He gratifies us with the spectacle of his damnation."

"Whatever you say."

"Hey," a boy neither of them knew called over, ax in hand. "You guys want some of this?" He was a good distance from the crowd.

"Hell, yes," said Bullseye, and they walked over to his freshly cut hole. He and John had spent the morning on the outskirts of everyone else's strikes but always as spectators or referees. To this point they had only one- and two-pound "charity donations" to show for their presence at the lake. This hole and this boy represented their first real chance to score. But when they looked down into the neatly carved hole, there was nothing but water.

"Some of what?" said Bullseye.

Equally baffled, the boy said, "I know. There's nothing there."

"Well, how come you cut here?" You couldn't afford to cut in a hole at random, not at four to six hours a pop.

"Somebody said to." That explained it. He'd been sandbagged, duped into wasting his time on a dry prospect. One less turkey to have to share the lake with.

"You've been had."

"No. Some guy with a chain saw said dig here, he'd found one."

"Sometimes the bales float off while you're chopping," said John. "You got to flop down and do some reaching."

"In the water?" The boy started to kneel.

"Nah," said Bullseye. "You did the grunt work, man. Allow me." He started peeling off the clothing on his upper body, a lumberjack's flannel shirt, suspenders underneath, and under that a turtleneck and a fishnet T-shirt. The end result was a farmer's tan, both arms and his face dark against his white torso. It always surprised John to see Bullseye stripped down like this because you expected a professor's flabby tits and fish belly. Bullseye didn't project an aura of strength, but he was strong and lean. Half naked, he looked capable of those one-arm pull-ups on vertical ice.

"Lights, camera, action," he said and sprawled facedown on the ice. "Oh," he whimpered. "Oh, man, it's cold." He stuck his arm all the way to the shoulder down into the hole. "Cold water. Hope I don't freeze my little nipples."

"Or frostbite your Weinberger," John threw in. Bullseye called it that, partner to his right hand, which he addressed as Ms. Kirkpatrick Sir. Bullseye was having the time of his life. First an impeccable performance on the ice column, now this circus of great apes. Tongue stuck out one corner of his mouth, Bullseye's face translated every sensation he was encountering.

"Ah . . . oh, what this?" He shifted his body around on the ice and slid his arm deeper.

"What?" said the boy.

Bullseye withdrew his arm and knelt back on his heels. "I think we got something down there. Weird shape. A big sucker. Heavy. But my hand's too numb to grab." Frost stood in his chest hair and his arm was bright purple. "I'll try the other one, then it's your turn."

He plopped down again and plunged his arm back into the hole. He had to reach deeper this time. "Oh, yeah." His smile got broader yet. "There he is. This guy's gonna make us millionaires." He pulled the load in closer. "This is the King Kong of bales, gentlemen. You're gonna cream your jeans when you see it." He hauled it in, raised his trunk off the ice, pulled some more. The load had its own momentum now. "*Voilà*," he said.

A dead man's head bobbed up through the hole.

"Fuck!" shouted Bullseye. "Fuck. Fuck." He almost pulled his trick shoulder out of joint rolling away from the terrible sight.

It was a large, sculpted head, hair plastered down, flesh well preserved. As it floated up and down in the hole, the man's face turned toward them. He didn't look dead, just wet and cold. His skin was a darker blue than Bullseye's arms, otherwise the man might have been taking a summer dip mid-hike. He had a drooping mustache and his massive jaw needed a shave. His eyes were blue. Something about him—maybe his size, which was apparent, or the scar like a varicose vein down one side of his face—said mean fucking son of a bitch. Maybe it was just that he was dead and they weren't.

"Fuck!" Bullseye shouted again, stomping around in a circle with his arms stiff and dripping. This time people heard and pointed over and started flocking.

"Ahh, gross."

"Drag him out."

"No way."

As if shy of crowds, the corpse began sinking away. His eyes stared around and then the water was over his forehead. John shoved aside his old Apache bugaboo about touching the dead and dove for the hole. He could have let the man drift back to his bed of undisturbed waters, but for some reason he didn't. His hand slashed into the lake and found the waving scalp lock, and he pulled hard.

It took them half an hour to pull the corpse free. They laid him out on the ice and gathered all around. It was out-and-out voyeurism. "I thought they got all hard and stuff," said a voice.

"The guy's a goddamn giant. Look at him. He could play for the Raiders or something."

"Must be the pilot," shivered Bullseye. "Must be. God, I dragged him out of his fucking grave."

"You thought *this* was a bale of pot?"

"Shit, I didn't know. It felt like . . ." Bullseye gave up and wiped his hands on his knickers.

"Did you see the cuts on his body?" Sammy said to John. "And look at the bottom of his feet! It looks like he walked around barefoot on glass or something." Indeed, he had the scratches and cuts of a mendicant. In Tibet they circumambulate the holy mountains. In California, apparently, they circled lakes filled with pot.

People heard and turned their attention to the implications. "You mean he was alive after the plane crashed?" asked the girl with the tea.

"That would explain the parachute," said Bullseye.

"But why's he in the lake?"

"Hypothermia?" suggested a voice. They grew silent. For the climbers, anyway, that was all the explanation they needed. Hypothermia. Public health brochures about winter dangers always call it the Silent Killer. First you get cold, then crazy, then dead. Everyone had heard the one about the hypothermic camper who stuck the arms of his sunglasses into his eyes and wandered around blind for two days. Lost everything up to his groin and armpits to frostbite. There was the Lightning Man for you.

"What do we do now?"

"Bag it," two climbers said simultaneously.

"Leave the lake?"

"We got what we wanted. It's bad luck now."

"Bury him first," someone recommended. "Then bag it."

"Yeah," came the consensus.

"First take a picture, Delwood."

"Have some class, man." Bullseye was disgusted and fetched a fluorescent green sleeping bag liner from his pack to cover the body over.

"Come on. Let Delwood get a trophy shot." Delwood had done this all before. He prided himself on taking photos of rescue victims *in situ*. It gave him a morbid sort of pedigree. He pulled a small self-focusing Pentax from his parka pocket. He managed to snap one shot before Kresinski hit.

No one saw him join the crowd, but suddenly Kresinski was in the middle of the circle backhanding Delwood. The camera went spinning across the ice. "No camera," snapped Kresinski. "I thought I said no cameras."

"It's just a dead guy," pleaded Delwood.

"You dumb shit. All we need is pictures of this gettin' to the FBI."

A voice whispered in shock, "FBI?"

Kresinski turned from Delwood to the crowd at large. "Don't be simple. This is a federal park, isn't it? Federal property. Federal crime. Federal Bureau of Investigation."

"But officer," one of the city boys mimed, "we was just hikin' around and found it. This shit's just for souvenirs." Bullseye draped the sleeping bag liner over the body.

"Yeah," Kresinski snarled. "Well, my picture's not a souvenir."

"What do we do now?" the question resurfaced.

"Bail out," someone reiterated.

"Why?" challenged Kresinski, and he stepped forward and yanked the liner off the nude body. "Because of him? Big deal. He went too high. He blew it. He cratered. It happens to our guys all the time."

"Matt, don't," John said quietly. Kresinski was starting to grandstand, never a good sign.

"You think covering him up is going to make him go away? Shit!"

"The fun's over," said Bullseye, and he tore the liner from Kresinski's hands. "Have some respect."

"What? You guys want to bury him with honors in a snowbank? Maybe we should build him a Viking ship and burn it? Or, I know, why don't we carry him out and give him to the rangers for a present? They'd appreciate our act of conscience. Let's all say cheese, and Delwood, you take our picture, we'll give them a photo to go with the stiff." He looked down at the body. "Fuck. Look at him." He kicked the corpse's shoulder. "He's been in the freezer for two, three months now. And he looks pretty damn good for it. He was happy enough under the ice. I say put him back where he was. Forget about him."

"It's bad luck," someone repeated.

"Three thousand pounds of smoke is some bad luck, brother," said Kresinski. "And we haven't even gone down for a look inside yet."

"There's nothin' down there," said Sammy. "We cleaned it out."

"Wanna bet?" said Kresinski. "Ask this guy here then." He nudged the corpse with his foot again. "He was safe. He was alive. He landed with his parachute up there, but then he came down here and he took off his clothes and dove in the water. How come?"

"Hypothermia," Bullseye told him.

"Uh-uh. He was lookin' for something."

"Like what?"

Kresinski shrugged. "Ask him. Or you can ask me. 'Cause I'm goin' down and find out. Whatever it was, he paid everything he had trying to get it." He stepped across the blue legs. "Do what you want. I'm here until we empty this gold mine."

"Yeah, me too." Anybody could have said it.

"What about him?" asked Sammy.

"Leave him."

"That's not decent."

"Raise him up then, brother." There were snickers in the crowd.

"You can't throw him back in the water," Sammy persisted. "He ain't a fish."

"We got to do something for him," another voice voted.

"*With* him, not *for* him," growled Kresinski. "Look, you take care of your own. He's not us, though. He's not our dead."

"That's bad luck if you don't . . . do something."

"Something?" challenged Kresinski. He unzipped the little ski pack on his hips and took out one of the aerosal cans of paint they'd been using to mark holes. "How's this?" he said. Before anyone could stop him, Kresinski bent down and sprayed the dead man's face a bright Day-Glo orange.

"What the fuck . . ." said a voice, more startled than outraged. The crowd stirred but not much. Everyone was mesmerized by Kresinski's performance, and that's what it was, pure street theater. He had something to say and they wanted to hear it.

"There's only so much bad luck in the world," Kresinski quickly declared. "And this guy's had it for all of us." Quickly again, he bent over the corpse and with a second can spray-painted "MEAT" in crude hot-pink script. "This guy's done, same as the hamburger in your mom's freezer. It doesn't matter where he is anymore. Besides, what do you think he'd do for one of us? Same thing. Nothing. I say dump him back in the drink. I say let's get on with business before the feds wake up."

"I'm not diggin' around in the water if this sucker's floating around in it, man."

Kresinski was losing his patience. "So tie him off. Put a rope on him and anchor him right here under this hole. Anybody got a rope?"

"Delwood brought a nine-mil," someone volunteered.

"Let's have it, Eddie."

It took Delwood off-balance. "That's not a trash rope. It's brand new. I just started climbing on it."

"Give us the rope, Eddie."

"Come on, *Del*wood."

Kresinski was smiling as he backed away from the crowd. Even when he bumped into John, who'd maneuvered around and placed himself there, the smile stayed bright and full. "John Boy!"

"You're a scumbag," said John.

"A *rich* scumbag," Kresinski qualified. "Just like you. And them. We're all family."

John indicated the body with his chin. "You're wrong. That's all." He moved off.

"That's slick, Johnny. *You* lecturing about the dead?"

"I quit apologizing for that a long time ago."

"Yeah. I noticed."

It felt too much like gunslingers in a spaghetti Western, the two of them glaring at each other, so John walked away. It was time to fetch Tucker and make camp. First thing tomorrow morning he meant to exit the lake. Half a pack of weed came to something like seventeen thousand dollars, and that wasn't too shabby for a three-day romp in the high range. Seventeen thousand dollars would take some of the pout off Liz's anger. That was a year's wages for her, five years' wages for him. He found his pack propped against a piece of weathered driftwood and looked up the mountain. Tucker's footsteps led high and disappeared onto the crest of the stone ring. The boy was nowhere in sight, but he had to return this way.

"Where's my air?" Kresinski yelled over by the plane's tail. He was suited up and ready to go. "It's time for Captain Nemo to find out what's what down there. Come on, where's my air?"

In the center of the ring a climber was genuflecting by the dead man's head. In his hands were an ice screw and an ice hammer. He took a quick notch out of the ice, set the screw to it and, twisting the screw with each hammer blow, drove in a picket stake. Someone else showed up with Delwood's new rope and skillfully tethered the corpse with a doubled figure eight under the arms and, for good measure, with the opposite end of the rope, a hangman's noose around the neck. "Real funny," groused Sammy, but it was beyond his control now. In colorful fluorescent paint, Kresinski's black humor was carrying the tribe back to its festive innocence. Spirits visibly lifted when the body was levered back into its hole and tied off. Bullseye was still too shaken to deliver any funeral invocations, so the unblinking spray-painted pilot of the red, white, and blue Lodestar and its Lightning slipped back under the ice with no memory for the future, no guidance but a climber's rope. Kresinski made his dive and saw what the dead man saw: the bottom of the ice green from the filtered sunlight, bales of pot nudging against the cold lens like seeds ready to break into the upper world, and deeper down the tip of the wonderful spear of an airplane stuck in the still-black silt. People watched Kresinski's progress through various holes, but the light was no longer quite right for viewing, and when he passed too close over the lake's floor—intentionally, some whispered—clouds of sediment puffed upward, obscuring all sight. He was down for a very long time, leading

116

people to believe he was extricating a marvelous treasure from the cockpit. They waited to hear from him that the backside of the moon held ancient, ruined cities, that Prester John would save Europe from the Mongols, that old age had a remedy and they could stay forever in the Valley. But when he surfaced, Kresinski's hands were as empty and blue as the corpse's. Luckily for him, several climbers had built a hot fire with deadwood carried up from three miles away. The girl with the steaming tea asked to sleep with him that night, and before the sun had even gone down he took her to his tent. Shortly after twilight, though, Kresinski dressed and said the moon was keeping him awake. His footsteps squeaked on the cold snow. Had she bothered to look, the girl would have seen there was no moon. It was dark, and dark was the way Kresinski wanted it.

*L*ike a huge, nylon
man-of-war washed onto a
tilted white beach, the parachute's shroud lay limp on top of
the ring of stone that married the lake
to the mountain. Entangled in a comb of
boulders, the shroud lines held it captive,
and though it rustled and bubbled up occasionally, what little breeze there was kept failing
to really give it loft. The jump harness was still attached
to the rigging, sliced neatly open with a knife, one
more shell of the past shed and forgotten. An hour above the
lake, Tucker stood on two nipples of granite poking up through
the snow and tried to read the tragedy even though the evidence was slim and he wasn't Apache.

Winging it, Tucker patched together how the parachutist must have
floated miraculously to the one and only place possible on the mountain
itself, onto this slanted ramp of snow and ice. The man must have cut
free of the chute and said his thanks and took stock and saw his plane
down below in the water. Up here, the slope was steep and slippery but
not impassable, even for a nonclimber. If it was me, thought Tucker, I'd
of tiptoed around on the precarious ramp and descended. But where to?
To the lake to await the rescue that never came, a long, slow starve day
after day casting for fish that probably didn't exist in the lake below?
Maybe he'd tried to walk out and lost his way and his spirit was still wandering in the woods, a limbo man. Or maybe he'd just sat up here with a
broken leg and counted stars until sleep took over. Tucker glanced
around. The deep snow was like a quilt. The man could be dozing right

119

under his feet, a Sierran Rip Van Winkle hibernating until the statute of limitations ran out. One way or another, each of Tucker's versions trailed off peacefully and without any final resolution. He preferred stories without ends. Conclusions frightened him. He hated birthdays and high school graduations and *Life* magazine yearbooks and bicentennial celebrations because they were conclusions. Novels and biographies always made him forlorn, not for their content but for their form: They always came to an end. The dictionary was safer in that sense because you could always cycle back through it. Likewise he avoided summits, shunned them in fact, though the few people who'd noticed had never figured out why it was he always declined the final few steps onto the hard-bought top. He told himself he was simply emulating the British team that climbed to within thirty feet—no further—of Macha Pucchare's summit in Nepal, because Hindu gods lived on top. Tucker didn't believe in Hindu gods though, any more than he believed in MTV. Every climb, every mountain, was part of the same mountain in Tucker's mind. Somewhere along the line he'd decided there was going to be only one summit for him, the last, ultimate, sixty-megawatt touchdown. Then he would descend and take his journey into other terrains, a kayak trip down the longest rivers of the world perhaps, or a walk all the way through the Americas' cordilleras, top to bottom. His book would never run out of pages, and why should it? He didn't have the language for this will to never-endingness, or rather he had the words but not the verbal glue to declare it out loud. His favorite parable was about the man who couldn't decide if he was a man dreaming he was a butterfly, or a butterfly dreaming he was a man. Underneath it all, life as dream just about summed up the whole deal. And so, because he'd missed the resurrection of the giant blue nude of the lake, Tucker had the imaginary smuggler dreaming imaginary dreams. And lest he disturb those dreams, Tucker forbade himself to root around in the crusted snow. Even so, he made a discovery.

First there was a glove jammed into the niche of an exposed boulder ten feet higher up, as if someone's hand had gotten stuck in the mountain and the only thing to do was pull loose and leave the empty glove. It had two significances for Tucker. In the middle of winter his man had lost the covering for that most precious of tools, his hand. And he'd lost it not in descent, but while climbing up the mountain. Tucker scruti-

120

nized the higher way. With hard, compacted snow like now, the climb was child's play up to a certain level. A good, swift kick and the toe of your boot could dent the surface enough to stand on. A staircase of such minimal toeholds would lead straight up to steeper rock where the snow didn't cling, and from there medium-angle slabs culminated at the mouth of a big cave maybe five hundred feet up.

Tucker pulled the glove from the rock and tried it on his own hand. It was enormous. Without really thinking about it he notched the glove back into the rock, a mountaineering habit. You never could tell when the owner might be back and need a stray piece of clothing or gear. The mystery built. Had the man gone up instead of down? He tried to visualize the circumstances behind the reasoning, but came up empty. Climbing up to the cave was one thing, descending the slabs and snow was something else again. Down-climbing is always more difficult because you haven't yet seen and touched your footholds the way you do going up. It would take a climber's eyes and feet to descend, and even then it was chancy. One slip and you'd come plunging down the low-angle stuff and go streaking out over the lip of the stone ring. Then it looked like a good three hundred feet of free-fall to the lake. Maybe one of those Mexican cliff divers could survive it in the late summer, but with a sheath of ice covering the water anyone else would be a goner. Well, maybe that's what had happened then. Tucker kept asking questions of the mountain. Did his man go straight up this gully of snow or had he moved over to the wind pattern snaking along a rocky spine? Would a nonclimber see the subtleties or simply go for it? Was the glove a false scent? Had the man really gone up? And then he saw the heel of a jogging shoe.

Tucker kick-stepped up and across to the shoe and pulled it from the snow. The laces were untied. The man had shucked it on purpose. Connecting the dots, glove to shoe, Tucker calculated the man's path. Now he understood. The man had been crazy. Maybe a concussion had knocked him silly, maybe he'd shot up too much pain drug or smoked too much of his cargo or drunk some liquor to warm up or get brave. However it happened, the man had decided, piece by piece, that clothes were an unnecessary burden. On a vertical beeline for the cave now, Tucker found a green argyle sock and an Oregon Timber cap all locked into the snow. Where the snow met stone, the second glove was frozen under a half-inch coating of ice.

Tucker paused. The sun had slunk around behind the mountain, but it was still early afternoon, plenty of time to make the round trip to the cave and back. It was going to be tricky coming down without a rope, but he had nothing else to do with his time. He'd already given up hopes of returning to the Valley or even leaving the lake by tonight. He shrugged and continued higher. Though steeper, the rock slabs went faster than the snow, and within a half hour Tucker was at the cave.

"Hello," he called, pulling up onto the ledge. Why chance it? he was thinking. After three months alone in a cave, a barefoot crazy man would be crazier than ever. He sniffed for the odor of human dung, any dung for that matter, but smelled nothing. He peered in.

It was a classic cave. An eight-foot-high ceiling curved back to join a flat dirt floor. None too large, the cave was still good enough to break all but a head-on wind. It took a minute to adjust to the darkness. Then Tucker entered the vaulted chamber. To his relief it was empty. Not even a bird's nest or a bone.

So much for the afternoon's diversion, he thought. He'd found a size thirteen running shoe, two giant gloves, a redneck's cap, and an argyle sock. Slim pickings compared to business down on the lake. He didn't regret coming up—he never regretted touching a mountain—but it was a little disappointing to have come all this way for stuff you can find in the back of a closet. The clues had been so . . . eligible for a solution. No loss, anyway. He'd added another cave to his internal compendium of geological nuances, and that counted for something.

He turned to leave. And there, slumped almost invisibly in the corner like one more derelict rock, sat a brown leather flight jacket, the kind hotshot combat jocks wore in war movies. Instantly a shiver passed through Tucker. He wanted to plunder it the way Camp Four was plundering the lake below. But with the masochism of a trained archaeologist he forced himself to stand there trembling, reveling for a minute or two longer in the lonely company of his find. He pretended to himself that maybe he ought to leave it right where it lay, all the time knowing he was going to pick it up. A couple of heartbeats later, he did. It was stuck to the cave floor. On closer examination, he found that the walls of the cave were seeping water and that the bottom of the jacket had frozen in a thin pool of ice. The mountain didn't want to relinquish it to him. Tucker stood up, and with a clean hard jerk yanked it loose. His excitement mounting, he carried the jacket outside, where it wasn't any warmer but at least the light was better.

The leather was brown and pliable with little fissures that spoke of many storms and dry spells. One cuff was torn and sewn up. The collar of white wool was stained from neck dirt. It was an all-American jacket, functional, heavy-duty, well worn, and the smell was like something out of a Hemingway novel—tobacco smoke, blunt bar talk where silence wouldn't do, gunpowder. Tucker checked it front and back, inside and out, for blood marks. Finding none, he tried it on. As he suspected, even over his sweater and Polypro vest, the jacket swallowed him up. The man had carried magnificent shoulders on him, and long arms with thick wrists. It was a warm jacket. Too bad he'd taken it off. Tucker saw it all now. The man had landed, cut free of the chute, and very soon started to freeze. He'd seen this cave and reckoned better up than nowhere, at least get out of the snow and wind. Too bad he hadn't thought to carry the parachute up with him, it would have made good bedding. But then again the man was crazy before he'd even begun the climb. Looking like a ragged barefoot pilgrim, he'd reached the cave and stood on this ledge. He'd shucked the jacket, probably shucked his pants and shirt for good measure, too. And he'd stood on this flat porch. Maybe he'd thought there were wings on his shoulders. Maybe he'd thought there was only one way to find out and had actually tried to fly. Never to be seen again. Tucker looked down at the lake. Just so. It made him sad and yet pleased. An ending without an ending. Out across the range, you could see a scattering of the Tuolumne domes, so many trolls' fannies spanked pink by the sinking sun. Bowie Peak's shadow cut long and cold across the valley. There was the plane's tail, a toy surrounded by animated figurines, and even as he stood there the sky took on bold streaky layers of color like a gaudy finger painting. Suddenly Tucker wished he'd brought up the parachute. It would have been nice to spend the night in this cave overlooking the range. He hadn't, though, and before the light dimmed much more, descent was in order.

Tucker got firm footing on the edge of the ledge and peeked down the steep gully. It always looks worse when you have to climb down, and he took a deep breath to settle down for business. He zipped the jacket shut and pressed its folds against him. There was something hard in the left exterior pocket and something else in an arm pocket. But there was no time to examine the contents now. The alpenglow was about to crest and the mountain was burying itself in blue shadows.

On his knees, then belly, casting all style to the wind, he wrestled over a curl of wind-blasted snow, felt a foothold with one boot, and lowered himself into the gully. The rock was colder, and by the time Tucker made it to the snow slab five hundred feet down, his fingers were like frozen link sausages. There was no sensation left, and he had to look at each hand to make sure its grip was obedient. Down on the snow again, his feet took over. The angle was still severe, but to Tucker it felt flat as a sidewalk. He kicked his toes into the snow and ten minutes later was down at the parachute and his pack again. He paused to stick his hands, one at a time, down into the front of his pants and warm them by his balls. Down by the lake several small fires were winking orange eyes at him, and the ramp was fast disappearing from sight. He was happy. It had been a worthwhile day, full of solved mysteries and well-timed climbing. There was always something very appropriate about getting off a route as night swarmed in.

His belly was empty and his blood sugar low, so he dipped into his Oreo stash, scarfed a half dozen down, and hastily tossed the pack on over the leather jacket. Just then he saw a disembodied pinpoint of white light bobbing around as it neared the base of his ramp. It was a head-lamp. Someone was coming to check on him. John, it had to be John. He couldn't wait to tell John the news. All but blind now, he set off traversing along the top of the cliffs. He found the upper tip of the ramp and slid and skated down toward John's headlamp. Except it wasn't John's.

A voice uncoiled from the dark. "Hey, sport." The light stabbed his eyes. It was Kresinski. "Wow, look at that jacket."

Tucker tried to ward away the light. "What are you doing?" he said.

"Just lookin'," said Kresinski. "Hey, everybody figured you headed home."

"Is John lookin' for me?"

"Nah. Just askin' around. They're down by the fires."

"What are you doing?"

Kresinski shifted in his footsteps and grunted. They were Tucker's footsteps actually. There was only one trail up, and that was the one he'd plowed. Tucker heard the creaking of pack straps like traces on a mule.

Kresinski was heavily loaded. And a heavy load for him could mean two times too heavy for anyone else. Instead of answering, he said, "Where'd you get that cool jacket, Tuck?" He sounded friendly enough.

Now it was Tucker's turn to shift in his footsteps and try to figure a dodge. "Up there," he said.

"Little big, huh?"

"Could you please not shine your light in my face?"

"Whoops. Sorry." Kresinski bent it toward the ground, and now Tucker could see better. In the light's penumbra, Kresinski was leaning into a surprisingly small pack. Tucker had expected a mammoth, towering load of pot.

"It was in that cave," Tucker said.

"No shit. Let's see."

"I'm sort of cold."

"You tryin' to hide something there?"

"I'll show you later."

"Nah, come on. Let's see what you got there." Kresinski hit the release on his belly band and dumped the pack backward into the snow. Reluctantly, Tucker removed his pack and set it down. The smell of wood smoke drifted up.

"Nice leather. Let me try it on."

"Nah."

Kresinski laughed at his suspicion.

Tucker heard the snow crunch and suddenly Kresinski was right there beside him, feeling the leather. He smelled clean, like he'd just washed. Then Tucker remembered his dive.

"You find anything under the water?" he tried.

Kresinski was locked on, though. "Some rusty guns. Nothin' like this." Too late, Tucker realized Kresinski was doing more than feel the fine leather. He was patting the jacket down. By the time the bigger man felt the left pocket, it was too late to stop him. "Wow, what's this?"

Tucker wanted to step away, but that seemed worse than letting Kresinski see inside the pocket. "I don't know."

"Come on. You don't know?"

"I was saving it for down by the fire."

"Why wait, man. Let's see." He didn't wait. His hand curtly rifled the pocket. "God, look at all this shit."

Face up in Kresinski's fingers, illuminated by their globe of light, was a fat rawhide wallet. You could tell by the cheap tooled relief of an Aztec pyramid it was made in Mexico. Kresinski knelt down in the snow and carefully dissected the insides on the sparkling flat whiteness. Paper after paper, he laid out the contents of the whole wallet. "Son of a bitch, Tuck. You know what you got here, don't you? You just ID'ed the body."

"The body?" said Tucker.

"Yeah. You missed it. A fucking giant. In his birthday suit."

"Yeah?" said Tucker. That was his man with wings, all right. Naked to the moonbeams and snowflakes.

"Harold R. Zamora," Kresinski read off a driver's license. "Two hundred and fifty-five pounds, single, eyes blue, hailing from McCall, Idaho. Here, wanna take a look at Harry's face?" He handed the license over to Tucker. "What else we got here? Licensed small-craft pilot. Commercial helicopter pilot . . . oops, no, Harry let that one expire. American Express. Nope, that one's expired, too. Social Security card, book of stamps, Gold Visa card. Ah, darn, expired while he was in the drink. Kind of hard to yup around if your plastic's no good, Harry. Whoa, hey, what's this thing?" He brought a worn dog-eared card closer to his headlamp. "United States Army, one-o-one Airborne, Bronze Star, Purple Heart. So the old fart was a card-carrying combat vet. Must be where he got his color coordination for the Lodestar Art Deco."

Tucker picked up each little document, read it, and then set it back on the snow in a meticulous line.

"You know what I think, Tuck? I think Harry fell on bad times. Things got tight in old McCall. But he knew how to fly. So he gassed up his trusty Lodestar and he went charging off into the unknown. Dadgum it, he was gonna save the old homestead one way or another. Would have made it, too, except for these hills."

"Anything else in there?" he asked the wallet, prying at the flaps and corners. His hands were very clean and white. The persistence paid off. An overlapping fold of leather gave up one last piece of the puzzle, a creased color photo. "Holy shit," whistled Kresinski. "Twins!"

The thing that made Tucker look over was what almost passed for fear in Kresinski's voice. It was an extraordinary intonation for the King.

"Let me see," said Tucker, and he plucked the bent photo from Kresinski's fingers. In front of a sleek khaki needle of a gunship squatted a double image of the same soldier. Both wore their uniforms with the sleeves rolled high above the elbows, both sported the same brushy mustache, the same lofty reserve as if all their lives they'd been marked by Olympian similarities. Between the two of them, you got the sense, very little could not be engaged and won: barroom brawls, a football line of scrimmage, a forest of trees on some Idaho mountain. Paul Bunyan and his brother Sergeant Fury. Tucker laid them down by the other dross. This stuff was all so much driftwood now.

"Now," said Kresinski, reaching for the little red address book. "Let's take a gander at how many girlfriends Harry had." It was bound with a thick rubber band that was too cold to stretch. The rubber broke, the pages fell open. A small, folded pink memo page fluttered loose to the snow, almost escaping from the bright light never to be seen again. Tucker leaned over and snagged it while Kresinski riffled the pages. "This fucker prints like he was still in fourth grade or something."

"Yeah, but he could fly helicopters and airplanes." Tucker defended the dead man. And fight wars and cut down monster trees. And single-handedly deal with Central American gangsters and make it almost home, an hour short that was all. One hour.

"Touchy?" Kresinski grinned.

"He wasn't dumb." Tucker tried to break down his sympatico with the smuggler. Maybe it was as basic as they'd climbed the same mountain, stood in the same cave that no one but them had ever stood in. Why did Kresinski always have to wreck and ruin?

"Didn't say he was, Tuck. At least he knew how to print." Kresinski stopped at the back of the small book. "Hello," he said. "What have we here?"

"What?"

Kresinski showed him. Written on the flip side of the last page were five phone numbers bearing only the names of colors. Blue—546-4733, Red—499-3092, and so on.

"Mafia," Tinkerbell murmured knowingly, not really knowing.

"Mafia?" Kresinski barked with a laugh. "You ever heard of McCall, Idaho, man? Well, I can guarantee no Mafia ever has, either. Nah, this guy was a lone ranger. This was a one-shot deal. Just trying to save the spud farm or some damn thing. I'll bet you he hocked everything he owned in the world, took his grubstake down to wherever, and smashed it all into this lake. A total fucking loser. These numbers, they're probably some fishing buddies. Or secret pussy, hell I don't know."

Tucker shrugged. It had been fun to hang all the clues together and sketch a composite of the man, even if it was overblown and romanticized. Kresinski wouldn't let it be, though, until everyone smelled like dogshit. He looked down and saw the piece of pink paper in his fingers. With little spirit left, he idly unfolded it. And suddenly Kresinski's mean little world opened up and the smuggler was Conan the Barbarian all over again. For neatly ranked in that blocky pencil print marched a vertical row of names and numbers of guns: 150 M16. 350 M14. Uzi, M11, Kalish—any/all. etc. It was a shopping list. Tucker was dumbfounded. It evoked images of an alien, killing world, of guerrillas and tyrannies and midnight knocks on your wood door. All the list lacked was a request for banana-belt berets and mirror sunglasses. His smuggler wasn't just some freak out of *Doonesbury*, he was a full-scale mercenary gunrunner.

"What you got there?" said Kresinski.

"Guns."

Kresinski didn't even ask, he just pulled it from Tucker's fingers. The connection was easy to furnish, especially in Tucker's imagination. Cargo planes are for cargo; if you're coming north, you first have to go south, and it might as well be with a full load of goods each way. Leave no profit unturned. This list was the weak link in the chain. It was evidence.

"Bullshit," muttered Kresinski. "This is make-believe. Why would some farmer be carrying a list of guns around with him when he could get caught?"

"He wasn't a farmer," Tucker replied, confident now that his man had walked with seven-league boots. Obviously the smuggler hadn't intended to fail. Still, Kresinski's question bore merit. If this guy was a professional, then why had he acted like an amateur? Carrying your whole business network in your jacket pocket was the act of either a zealot or a fool.

"How do you know?"

"I found his hat. It said Oregon Timber. He was a lumberjack."

"Oh, great detective work, Tuck." Kresinski waved the pink memo page in the lamplight. "That's like saying this proves he was workin' for the CIA."

"Maybe he was." The thought hadn't occurred to Tucker.

"I don't have time for this," Kresinski said. He started scraping the row of documents into a pile and stuffing the papers into his shirt pocket.

"Hey."

"Forget it." Kresinski stood up.

"That stuff's mine."

"You blew it, man. You should have worked the lake instead of solving riddles. Everybody else got rich. All you got was some hairy-ass fantasies. So we know Harry's name now, big deal. We got a bunch of phone numbers and a list of phony guns. What's that? Nothin'."

"If it's nothing, then give it back."

"Here's the problem, Tucker. Once I leave here I don't want any connection with this lake. When the shit hits, and it's going to once the feds see what happened, nobody's gonna know I so much as dreamed about Snake Lake. Everybody else is getting rid of their pot the minute they hit the trailhead. This stuff, though. I can see you hanging on to it for years to come."

"I didn't do anything."

"You were here. That's enough. And if you were here, maybe I was. You're just a scary little kid. You didn't do anything? Hell, they find these papers on you and push you around a little bit and pretty soon you're telling them who *did* do something."

"That's a lie."

"Yeah, well I'm not taking any chances." He stood up.

"Let me have the wallet anyway."

Kresinski thought it over for a minute. "Sure. Here." The empty wallet hit him in the chest. "Here's how it is, Tucker. We didn't meet. You didn't see me. I wasn't here. There was nothing in that wallet. Got it?"

Tucker was shocked. Kresinski had just robbed him.

The light swung away and Tucker could hear Kresinski saddling up. Once again the pack sounded like it was stressed to the point of ripping. He stood up and found his own pack.

"Promise me, Tuck."

Tucker started walking away. "Go ahead. Brag about your jacket. Brag about your wallet. But you never saw me up here, Tucker, got it?"

129

Tucker didn't answer. He aimed for the closest fire and walked off. The fire was farther away than it looked, and by the time he reached it he was very hungry and tired. John and Bullseye were among the few people surrounding the ebbing flames. There were greetings all around, and someone heated water for a packet of chicken soup for the returning explorer. Everyone admired his leather jacket and asked questions, and Tucker told them about the lost clothing and the cave, and he was about to take his revenge on Kresinski by telling them about the theft, but Bullseye interrupted him.

"You look in the pockets?" he asked. Then Tucker remembered the lump in the arm pocket, and while everyone looked on he unzipped the zipper and pulled out a plastic bag. Inside the plastic bag, stacked neatly and wrapped with a red rubber band, was over six thousand dollars in crisp hundred-dollar bills. Flush with their newfound wealth, everyone congratulated him. They were flush, he knew, because no one even tried to borrow money from him.

*T*here would never
be a party like this one
again, John registered in the
brute din of Airplane, firelight,
and unabashed, punch-drunk, joyful
triumph. It was a rendezvous in the bygone
fur-trapping tradition, no Hawken rifles, no
knives or pelts, but everything else, the
frivolity, drunkenness, and forest bacchanalia was
true and happy and reckless. They were rich, they had
won. And it was spring. A new moon sat pegged on
the points of redwoods and ponderosas, and the bonfire was
rimmed with kegs of beer, and when Grace Slick wasn't war-
bling full-decibel about the white rabbit in wonderland,
then it was Jagger or that most primitive of rock canticles, "Gloria."
As self-delegated Il Duce of the tunes, Bullseye was relentless, and even
though younger climbers were less sentimental about his backward-
looking tastes, still early pagan rock seemed acutely right for this giddy,
acid victory over the feds and dead men and Camp Four's history of feral
poverty. Tucker's attempts to infiltrate the psychedelia with a movement
or two of, say, Ludwig's Fifth had so far been thwarted, and he was being
closely monitored whenever anyone could remember, which was not
often. Around midnight the real huns began fire-jumping, first in their
thongs and blown-out Nikes and Adidas, then barefoot through the
flames. Somebody fell in and was rolled out, smoking, Gore-Tex melted,
but feeling no pain, nor would he until morning. Everywhere there were
boasts, inquiries, and air moves: hands locking off on imaginary holds,
toes twisting, feet torquing. Vicarious flight. Every handshake measured

your grip. John wove stoned through the crowd, buffeted by the language, noise, elbows, excitement.

"Yeah, man, forty feet out on 5.12. No pro. I mean. High, dry, and thirsty." It mattered not at all who was speaking. Words. Sparks off the fire. Arching for the moon.

". . . like glass. Friction city for the last ninety feet. Then mantle off this bashie. I was way gripped. In-*con*-tinent."

"No way." Elsewhere, faceless. "What I heard, he clipped and grabbed, man. Partied on his pieces. That's what I heard."

"That's serious, you know. I yo-yoed once, man, but I never like blew it up for a rep or nothin'."

"I seen it on the Hummingbird, I did . . ."

"The Brooks Range? For sure God made 'em. You'll see. You'll see."

It was a broth of climbing and dreams, talk of Uli Biaho in Pakistan and the North Face of Kwangde up the Khumbu tumbling over Psycho talk and talk of Kresinski's latest or Tucker's newest and the Shield talk and talk of tomorrow's climbs. It had the feel of immortality and would go on until the drugs or liquor put them out or the sun came up, and then they'd be spiders on the walls again. Every syllable made sense to John, nothing was not freighted with obsession. All he wanted was to float in the tide and avoid the undertow. Keep on, keep on. Time and again when someone said hey John, he was deaf and kept on. What made their abandon different and more heedless tonight was the sense of stupendous chance. One week ago they'd been paupers, and here they were millionaires. Evidence of the wealth had flowered everywhere. They wore it on their bodies, in their camp, in their braggadocio. There were new ropes and shiny hardware. A carnival of New Wave-colored tents—neon peach, citrus orange, baby blue—stood fresh and spanking clean among the trees. Many had taken to dining at the exclusive Ahwahnee Hotel with its Edwardian appointments and orange juice in crystal champagne glasses. Thriftier folk could be found in Camp Four cooking up expensive freeze-dried gourmet entrees over brand-new super-lightweight European gas stoves. Even Tucker was affected, having switched to exorbitantly priced Famous Amos chocolate chip cookies. Wherever you ate, at the picnic tables, on a rock, or under the Ahwahnee's chandeliers, there was Dom Perignon and Chivas Regal, and toasts to their own foothold in yuppiedom. And never far away were the other condiments, copious, pungent clouds of Lightning and lines of toot and crystals of crack. Had you told them that Messrs. Gorbachev and Reagan had decided to erase both hemispheres at nine next morning with a push of the button, they wouldn't have escalated their hedonism one bit because they couldn't have. The money was flowing from their fingertips as fast as they could find a target. They had leaped from rags to riches in a week, and were leaping back to rags with a curious, quaint ferocity. One or two had invested in CDs, and someone or other had hied off with his share of the loot as a grubstake for an experimental hydroponic poppy farm in the forests around Bishop. Otherwise their pockets were nearly empty. The Valley had provided. When everything was gone, it would provide again.

As John meandered through the crowd, he saw many faces strange to Camp Four. Most fell neatly into the Hungry, Curious, or Awed categories. The climbers had scored a coup, stolen two tons of pot from under the breathing nostrils of the DEA, Park Service, FBI, and Lord knew what other bureaus, snatched it with the finesse of Larry Bird. Or, hell, Geronimo. Or Mangus Coloradas, John's namesake, lied to by feds of another century, shot, beheaded, displayed. Fuck it, he thought. He detested the politics of being an aborigine, all proper rage and false direction. It was enough that he carried the name and cheekbones. And now revenge. This one's for you, Mangus, and he spit and looked around. Inevitably the noisy celebration had drawn groupies, tourists, bikers, and dopers too late for the Gold Rush, and for this one night they weren't unwelcome. The xenophobia normally reserved for new faces had been relaxed for the occasion, for having an audience confirmed the tribe's cunning and wiles. A general goodwill prevailed, even after one of the bikers chain-whipped a climber and the climber whipped him back with a piece of climbing hardware that opened the man's face and eventually produced a handshake of peace. The bikers were outnumbered and far beyond their own territory, practically timid within this vast natural sanctuary the climbers had colonized. Even liquored up and high, they knew better than to press a retaliation, and so there was lots of hey brother, this and that, you guys are cool, radical. The goodwill held even after the feds showed up to observe and Bullseye cornered one of them against a pitchy ponderosa.

There were an even four of them, and they were with the FBI and Treasury Department. Four days had passed since Snake Lake had been abandoned. No secret, especially one this monumental, could be kept forever, and three days before, "on a hunch," a Park Service helicopter had revisited the chopped, littered, empty lake freshly dusted over from a snow squall in the high country. Ever since, Park HQ had been suffering a flurry of federal agents coming and going, and the Valley walls had been echoing with the popping of helicopter blades, which infuriated more environmental-minded rangers on behalf of their client-wildlife. But their concerns counted for nothing in the high-tech hue and cry. Five thousand pounds of marijuana had crashed at Snake Lake; four thousand of that had vanished in the course of nine days, street value well over a million and a half dollars. The worst part was that in this day and age of drug enforcement, with agents finally gaining an edge in public relations, the theft had gored their pride. This was no curbside rip-off. They'd blown a big one. They knew precisely which group of scofflaws had stolen their contraband, and furthermore knew the names of individuals and which campsites those individuals nonchalantly continued to inhabit. But ice carries no fingerprints and trees don't talk, and what identifying refuse had been left on the lake was entirely circumstantial evidence. From the bottom of the lake, divers had recovered the stolen chain saw, a baker's dozen Park Service axes, a lever-action Remington, and even a lawn chair. The brightly painted smuggler's body with "MEAT" written across its chest had been dragged from the water by its Perlon noose, providing great front-page savagery for national newspapers and magazines. "GANGLAND FUNERAL IN SIERRAS. END OF ROPE FOR SMUGGLER." That climbers had been here was obvious from such signs as runner-slings and carabiners hanging from tree branches and other dead-give-away climbing-related refuse in the snow such as *Mountain* and *Climbing* magazines. But short of some participant turning state's evidence, no one could be prosecuted for anything. Every agency involved was in shock. To date, no one had even bothered to interview any of the climbers. Their silence was presumed.

The agents attending this evening's blowout had apparently agreed beforehand that disguises would only make them more conspicuous among boys who carried crack scars on their hands and knew one another by butts-out reputation. And so, opting for a modicum of dignity, the agents had come dressed as if for a chilly barbecue, the most daring in faded Levi's and an equally faded jeans jacket bearing an old Grateful

Dead logo on the back, a relic of his college days. Singly and in pairs, they worked the crowd. For the most part they seemed like pleasant, bemused family men, aware but not too discomfited by their incongruity in this lawless group. There was a sense in which they even seemed to be on the climbers' side, a clever illusion that appealed to everyone involved because no one wanted the FBI on their ass. Besides, guilt is relative, and all the climbers had done was find—and keep—the detritus of a criminal act, what was so wrong with that? Throughout the evening the agents stayed in attendance, chatting, joshing, laughing, but to a man declining repeated offers of beer and liquor. Whether it was the size of the gathering or the size of their higher priority, the agents had also done a heroic job of ignoring the Havana-size reefers passing back and forth everywhere.

"We take care of our own, by God," Bullseye was impressing upon the federal agent he had collared by a ponderosa sticky with resin. For tonight's activities, the ice climber had imported a kiwi-color T-shirt, pleated white pants, and matching white deck shoes with no socks. He was wearing a lemon-yellow linen sports jacket and a pair of Vuarnet sunglasses perched on top of his head. He'd never watched *Miami Vice* but had seen enough tabloids and magazine covers in the grocery store to understand the look. One hand clenched a bottle of white tequila.

"I'm certain you do," said the agent. He smiled, patrician among these crude outlanders who knew no better. Bullseye knew better and stood his ground.

"So forget your concentration camps," he said. His ship was adrift, rudderless, but he was willing to sample the winds. His remark provoked no retort. "But don't forget Chicago," he threw in with secondary heat. "And don't forget Madison either, bub. Or Huey Newton, yeah. Or Kent State. Or Angela, yeah, Angela . . ." It took another minute for his litany to run low.

The agent waited patiently. "None of that matters now," he finally said.

"Wrong," said Bullseye. "It all counts. Every bit of it." Abruptly he disengaged and went searching for, simply as a destination, the three hookers Kresinski had transplanted from a Carson City cathouse. Renting them had been a masterstroke, putting a high-gloss shine on Kresinski's three-hundred-horsepower legend. They were a dubious gift to his tribe, for so far the three ladies had spent the evening flirting audaciously, getting courted, and otherwise shamelessly exploiting their vestal pretense at being just three more girls at the sock hop. Hookers who would not hook, more illusions in a valley of illusions. For all its raucous, weird, loud texture, the party was innocent. Everyone was savoring the innocence: the whores, the agents, the climbers, the camp followers. They were savoring themselves on a spring night that seemed like it would never end.

"You guys seen Ernie?" Bullseye asked of a knot of climbers. Their faces were drug-struck, totaled by the lake pot. Two of them looked at Bullseye without a word, the other two were stock-still, eyes wide at the bonfire. Zombies. Finally one summoned up recognition. "You mean your *dog?*" He passed a joint across to Bullseye, who in turn passed his tequila. One of the climbers collapsed to the earth. Bullseye retrieved his bottle and headed on, again thinking to find the hookers. A large, densely packed crowd of humanity off to one side of the fire promised the most likely results, so he beelined for that sector. Suddenly Connie, the Four Seasons waitress, burst from the crowd and bumped into him, tears streaking her face. Giving her the benefit of the doubt, Bullseye decided she'd probably looked much better much earlier in the evening. He gently arrested her flight with one hand.

"What's the trouble?"

"He's got *whores* in there," she wailed, and broke away to run off into the woods. Bullseye took a pull at his tequila, then began shouldering his way through the crowd. Lao-tzu, was it, who told a fable about the butcher who never needed to sharpen his knife because he could cut through the spaces between the meat and bone. Neat trick, thought Bullseye, struggling to find the spaces between one body and the next. Maybe it wasn't a Taoist after all, maybe some Zen dude, and he made a mental note to look it up in his van library tomorrow or the day after, whenever he could next focus. Finally he emerged at the inner edge of a ring of onlookers.

Sitting on a thronelike rock, Kresinski dominated the firelit clearing. His powerful arms were draped over the shoulders of two women Bullseye had never seen. Both were dressed in bulky wool sweaters and caps advertising "I Lost Mine at Midnight (ranch)." A third woman sitting against Kresinski's legs was displaying long, lithe legs stemming from a pair of silk gym shorts. All were drunk and bedazzled. In the manner of court entertainers, four climbers were playing Hacky Sack in the center of the ring. With little hops and kicks, they kept the bean bag aloft with their feet, by turns adept and completely barren of motor control. Limbs flailing, one after another lost balance and then gamely struggled back to reenter the competition.

"Waugh!" came a shout. "Look at Bullseye!"

Bullseye staggered forward one step and readjusted his sunglasses. "Man, is he sharp."

"Oh, yeah," someone said. "Now we're goina see some real Hacky Sack." It was true that Bullseye had a keen toe when it came to Hacky Sack, but he wasn't about to play jester to Kresinski's barbarian conqueror. Very public, not giving a shit one way or the other, Kresinski hailed him over. "Threads! And a haircut, too! You trying to steal one of my ladies?"

None too steadily, Bullseye approached. He leaned in toward one of the prostitutes and placed the Vuarnets on his nose and squinted at her. "Where are you from?" he said.

The music was loud, but she heard him. "Minnesota," she said. "How about you, honey?"

"Minnesota?" He cogitated a moment. "Hell, you're from Minnesota? Then tell me what a hooter is."

She batted her eyelashes. "Honey, you want me to show you or tell you?"

"From the rib of man," Kresinski approved. "Amazing, isn't it? You want to dance with her, Bullseye? She's nice and soft."

"I'm looking for my dog."

"Anybody seen Ernie?" Kresinski sarcastically trumpeted. When there was no response, he said, "Guess not. Maybe the bears got him."

"There's bears?" said one of the prostitutes.

"I saw him," said a voice.

Bullseye looked over, and there was good old skinny Tucker. He was nearly engulfed in the smuggler's brown leather flight jacket. Instantly something about Kresinski shifted, the cock of his head, the attitude that all was said and done. Bullseye noticed the change. Suddenly it seemed Kresinski had something more to say and do.

"Hey, Tuck, get your butt over here," he commanded.

"Why the hell should he?" said Bullseye.

"No trespassing," Kresinski snapped back.

"He's not hurtin' anyone."

"What's going on?" said one of the prostitutes. She was too drunk to just shut up.

"See that boy, there?" asked Bullseye. "Well, he freed an A-four pitch, on sight, solo, no chalk, no yo-yoing, no bolts on rappel. And he did it *static,* by God!"

"What?" She had no foothold on the lingo, no idea at all.

"He showed me up," Kresinski translated with a nasty grin. "Once."

Tucker made it over. Some of the strings in his arms and legs had been cut, you could tell. Bullseye diagnosed the probable malady as a madcap stew of every drug and drink he'd been offered tonight, the whole gamut. And yet somehow Tucker was still on his feet and standing before them. It was instances like this that had convinced Bullseye that Descartes was right. The mind and the body *were* separate, otherwise Tucker would be flat on his face out in the forest somewhere. His sole locomotion was willpower.

"Tucker, buddy," said Kresinski. "I hear you're leaving us next fall. Going on a bit of a tour."

"Yep," said Tucker.

Kresinski was patient. "Where to?"

"Nepal." Makalu. His secret. He'd already purchased a plane ticket.

"That takes a lot of bucks. Where'd you get cash like that, Tuck?"

Tucker knew what was coming but didn't care. "Same place everybody else did."

"Funny," smiled Kresinski. "That's not what I heard." Much had to be left unsaid, of course. There was no telling who was listening.

"So."

Kresinski leaned forward and caught the boy by one arm and pulled him close. Quietly now, he muttered, "I thought we were partners, Tuck. You got any more money in there?" He quickly frisked the jacket pockets. Then, as if someone were reminding him, he located the arm pocket and unzipped it.

"No way," Tucker said and strarted to pull away. But Kresinski was faster. He plucked the folded photo from the pocket. The look of amusement evaporated from his face. "What's this?" He was genuinely surprised, Bullseye saw. Whatever was in that photo had the effect of a fist in Kresinski's belly.

"You stole this from me," Kresinski rumbled.

The drugs and alcohol had improved Tucker's confidence, or at least provided him an unexpected defiance. "No way," he shot back. "You stole from me. This belongs to me." He reached for the photo, but missed.

"I thought you were ditching that jacket, man."

Tucker dismissed the loss of his photo. "I never said that."

"What are you guys talking about?" Bullseye asked.

"Nothin'," said Kresinski. "Right, Tuck?"

Tucker didn't answer.

"You seen my dog?" said Bullseye. Time to retreat. Go plug in some Hendrix. These people thought they'd arrived? A little Jimi and they'd see no one had even opened the door.

"That way, out there," said Tucker. "I'm goin' with you."

"Hang on, Tuck," Kresinski ordered. "We're gonna powwow a minute." Tucker glared at Kresinski and snorted. Bullseye threw one arm around the boy's shoulder and the two marched off, disappearing beyond the firelight's corona.

The moon moved. Constellations flattened. Time passed. No one noticed. It was going to be their night forever. The fire stayed high and white and orange, littered with broken glass. More and more, it was just tribe, Camp Four folk, the stayers. People danced. A group joined arms and began stomping in a tight little circle, crooning old Bing Crosby songs as if their very deliverance hinged upon it. A game of pine-cone soccer lifted long, vigorous tunnels of dust toward the stars before finally running out of players. Men and women held hands, kissed, departed into the trees. Katie hunted for Tucker for hours, but never found him. The FBI and Treasury agents called it an evening and left. And John wandered.

He wanted a beer. Cold and wet with a moderate head. And it had to be in a cheap plastic cup. He angled for a dented aluminum keg muddy with dirt and foam and pine needles. Just short of his goal, a pair of iron-hard hands shot out from the shadows and stopped him. John jerked back, but the hands held him tight. It was Bullseye. He was on his last legs.

"All the mountains, Johnny," he said. "They all been climbed."

John looked his friend in the eyes. Bullseye's ambush was a surprise, but the sentiment wasn't. He understood what Bullseye really meant, that there was no longer any proportion worthy of this firelit, hard-core machismo, that the age of giants was dead. They'd had this conversation before and John disagreed. Now that the highest mountains had all been tramped upon, now that the age of colonizing and brute domination had come to a close, it didn't necessarily spell the end. Just because the new hard-core wore Lycra stretch pants and climbed with Sony Walkmans it didn't mean they weren't out on the cutting edge. Risk is risk. Excellence is never reducible. Things had changed, that was all. Now that all the mountains had been climbed, the age of aesthetics could begin. Elegance could take over. Elegance, not sheer muscle, that would be the new ethic. Out of that would sprout a million new mountains on routes and lines never before conceived, mountains that he and Bullseye and Kresinski could never hope to climb because they were too damn old now.

"It's okay," he told Bullseye. But there was no possible way to explain how it was okay. It just was. Part of his certainty that the spirit was alive and well came from being raised by an Indian. "A species of pauper," some general had once promised to make the American savage, and so Geronimo had ended up growing watermelon like a plantation nigger. And the slavery had kept on. His father had been an oil-rig nigger and his brother a big, strapping Marine Corps nigger. Injuns. The general had won. Not all the oil and minerals and ski resorts on all the reservations could revive that demonized soul glaring out from the eyes in century-old photos of Cochise and Naichez and the others. The closest thing to that hungry, egotistical, earth-loving demon that John had managed to find was right here, frolicking all around him in Camp Four. He pulled Bullseye's grip off his shoulders, and Bullseye flung a despairing hand at the shapes twisting and cavorting around the fire. The dancing climbers looked like the ancestors of Vikings or Goths, savages hypnotized by the fire. But they were, most of them, soft. Even though they had corded bellies and feared no evil high on the rock, it was Bullseye's oldest lament that they'd grown up with all the General Electric amenities and couldn't hear the voices in the trees. It was true. They were more domestic than pantheistic and Camp Four was just a phase, and few if any were on for the long haul the way Bullseye was. But John saw in their midst, at their most extreme fringes, that the demon was burning bright. Tuck, for one, you could see the wild god in his eyes. There was someone they could hand off to. Tuck would carry the torch.

"Yeah, but the mountains," sighed Bullseye.

"I know," said John. Bullseye was sinking fast. It wouldn't be the first time he woke up in a pile of pine boughs or limp on the dirt. Best not go pitching headfirst into the fire, though, John thought, and steered him out toward the darkness.

"The walls," Bullseye intoned. "It's just these fucking walls. They're everything." Typical, sloppy, drunk climber talk. Some climbers would actually sob at times like this.

"I know," said John. "You want your van?"

"No," Bullseye declared. "I've got to find . . ." He stopped in his tracks, and it hit John, too. Bullseye had nothing to find. Me either, thought John.

"Go look at the walls," John advised, snapping Bullseye's parka shut so that he could sleep warmly wherever he might drop.

"Right," said Bullseye. "The walls."

They parted, Bullseye charting a black, cool course in search of those beloved cliffs. John was still thirsty, but the thought of beer repelled him now. He wondered where Liz was. In four days of searching, he hadn't managed to track her down. What that meant remained fuzzy, though no news probably meant bad news. Hacked off. More likely in a fury. He wasn't much on regrets, but Liz had made him regret going to the lake. The winterful of petty skirmishes with her had smoothed out so nicely in Reno. And now all their sweet talk of riding off into the sunset was scotched. Even the forty-thousand-dollar nest egg he'd realized from Kresinski's inscrutable Bay Area connection was worth regret because without Liz what was it a nest egg for? Without Liz, there was numero uno, like in the old days of his "singular state" when he'd carried the same condom around in his wallet for two years straight, a very private, very unwanted symbol of his optimism. The bottom line was she was the one woman he'd ever really loved. And he'd betrayed her.

"*Chingado,*" he cursed himself. For an instant Tony Schaller's long, horsey face sprang to mind. Betrayal of a sort. Loss most definitely. Then he cleaned it up and shoved Tony back into deeper recesses and bore in on other losses: a nurse with freckles at the Stockton Hospital emergency ward who'd finally dumped him, unwilling to play widow to his matador in the mountains; his brother, Joe, who just kept re-upping with the Marines and shacking up with his various "brown sugars" at Subic Bay in the Philippines. Realizing there wasn't much to write about, he and Joe had quit writing years ago. Those and a few others like their dad weren't magical losses, though, not like losing Liz. Not like that vein of gold he'd once crossed high on a mountain in the Andes, a rivulet of dull pure Inca mineral that wound through a quartz band near the summit of Aconcagua. John remembered the gold and then he remembered Tony's snaggletoothed grin all over again, because Tony'd seen it, too, scraped a bit loose with his ice hammer and put it in his water bottle where they watched the flakes floating around. Lost. Both of them, Tony and the gold, as they descended. Both still up there. Lost but not forgotten, as if he could forget. John sighed. But Liz wasn't lost. Not yet. He kept looking for her on the dark sides of the trees, hoping maybe she'd slipped loose of her anger and come to join the outlaws. It was a ridiculous hope, though. Of course she was pissed. He'd larked off to Snake Lake and ditched her cold. He kicked a pebble.

"Goddamn it," he rehearsed in a whisper. "I'm sorry, babe." Not even the voices in the trees whispered back, though. So he kept on searching.

Tucker was on the move, too. It was that kind of forest tonight. There were important persons to connect with, rendezvous to meet, potentialities. For one thing, he had to find John and confirm the Visor climb. They'd meant to leave the next morning, but when this party spontaneously generated itself, D-day was postponed one day. Their gear was sorted, food purchased, water bottles filled. He was ready and the weather was perfect. At long last the Visor was going to reach down to them, and then they'd see what was what. He pulled the big leather jacket higher onto his back. He was starting to sober up a little. Good thing they'd decided to wait a day. Katie was somewhere out here, too, he'd heard she was looking for him. It was silly, he knew, but that one kiss at the lake had stuck with him. The taste of her was still on his lips. The feel of her chest against his had bewitched him. He needed to find her and ask, can we talk, can we just go for a walk. What he really needed was another kiss. He needed more water, too. The plastic water bottle in his hand was almost empty, and it was imperative that he flush the poisons out of his system. The six-hour hike in to the base of Half Dome would sweat most of the stuff out, but he had to make sure his blood was pure by the time they reached the Visor roof itself. He was superstitious about virgin routes. What virgin would choose a drunk for her first time? Lots of water had to pass through his system. Lots.

"You ever hear of the Lotus Wall?" Bullseye had quizzed him as they parted an hour before. "Twenty million tons of glacier-polished granite, Tuck, five thousand feet high. And it's got this single crack that runs from bottom to top. Finger jams all the way. How's that sound?"

"Awesome," said Tucker. "Are you kidding?"

"Yeah," said Bullseye. "I'm kidding. I made it up. But that's my point, ya see."

"No."

"What?"

"No, I don't see."

"Illusion, man. Even the big walls. You ever hear of Jim Bridger, the mountain man? He found a mountain made of pure glass. Claimed you could look right through it and see an elk magnified from fifty miles away. What's that tell you?"

"Don't know."

"It means he spent so much time in the mountains, it got so he could see right through them."

"Yeah," said Tucker.

"That's what I'm saying."

"Yeah." Then Tucker was alone and wondering if the mountains would ever open to him like that. There was so much to be true to. So much yet to be found. One thing was sure, he needed more water. A tin cup of icy, milky glacier water would be perfect. Cold and pure. Minus a tin cup or a glacier, the Merced would have to do.

It was on his way to the river that he saw the ghost. For the rest of his short life, anyway, he would believe it was a ghost that rose up from the grape and licorice ferns and called him a little motherfucker. Tucker didn't believe in ghosts, though it was impossible for him not to believe in hauntings. He'd seen climbers take bad falls and never climb again, plagued by the memory of one misstep. He'd seen John after Tony died. But ghosts, that was bullshit.

It began with a noise off to his left, part crackling, part rustle as it kept pace with him. It was too large to be a raccoon or coyote, though for a minute Tucker was sure Ernie was playing wolf with him. A weird dog. Tucker called his name, which never failed to bring the dog in. But Ernie didn't come. The noise halted, then resumed when Tucker did. He stopped again. "Hello," he called. No answer. There were only so many people it could be out there, and he systematically whittled down the real possibilities. Wouldn't be a ranger: too unorthodox, and there was no flashlight. Wouldn't be a tourist or drunken camp follower: too steady on his feet. Wouldn't be Katie. Or would it?

"Katie?" he tried wishfully. No, she would have showed herself by now. But it had to be a climber, fairly tall to judge by the stride, confident on the animal trails leading through the meadow. Bullseye and John wouldn't waste their time plowing around just to scare him. Not that he was scared. He just hated to be out in the open like this, no rock to put your back against. With rock behind you, half your world was always dependable. Ordinarily he could have reached for his palm-size flashlight in the right-hand parka pocket, but tonight he was wearing the smuggler's jacket. He stood still and waited for the moon to hoist itself free of the cloud cover. The noise came closer, and still Tucker couldn't see anyone. It had to be Kresinski or one of Kresinski's droogies. He hated open spaces like this. Tucker crouched down among the ferns and grasses.

Then the voice called to him. "You little motherfucker," it muttered.

At first Tucker thought his name was being called, the words were so soft and the rhyme so exact, and he almost answered back. But the raw black anger in that voice made him hesitate long enough to distinguish the words and keep silent. He'd never heard this voice before. Tucker was shocked. The man was looking for him. Him in particular. If he were bigger, there might have been room to think the man was just looking for a fistfight. But Tucker was wiry and the "little" in motherfucker meant him. Still crouching, he slid back down the animal trail toward the bonfire. There was danger out here. Why and what sort didn't matter. With an intuition that had nothing to do with all the close calls he'd survived, Tucker sensed that if he didn't escape from this black meadow, he would be killed. Slaughtered. It was in that voice.

Moonlight suddenly spilled across the meadow for the space of three fast breaths, then it was gone again. Tucker flattened out on the trail, not daring to exploit the light and look at his pursuer. He prayed the man hadn't seen him. When the meadow went dark again, he continued to retreat, keeping his head lower than the grasses that scratched like whiskers at the leather on his jacket. He was tempted to shuck the jacket and bolt for the trees. What if the man had circled out ahead, though? The noises had ceased or else moved out of his earshot, and there was no way to predict where the man had gone. Could it be one of those bikers? he wondered. Maybe they'd heard about the cash he'd found. Everyone else had cash, too, though, so why pick on him? Also there was something too polished about the man's movement. He was practiced at hunting. At night. Hunting men. Tucker kept a smooth rein on his respiration, easy enough for a climber, and stuck to his strategy of returning to the bonfire. All he lacked was another three minutes of crawling through the ferns and grasses, then a fifty-yard dash through the trees. The fire would save him. Camp Four would rally round. It was a good plan. He almost made it. He was within ten feet of the forest's edge, he could smell the bonfire and hear the music and see the flickering light, when suddenly the clouds pulled back and the ghost reared up in front of him.

It was the dead smuggler. He hadn't seen the body in the lake. But he had seen the photo on page one of both San Francisco papers, the man's thick neck cinched tight with a noose made of climbers' rope. The face was the same as on that body and the same as in his photograph, with a heavy, drooping mustache and wide forehead. Even if he hadn't seen pictures of the smuggler, Tucker could have guessed who it was from the figure's massive size. It would take a man this big to fill the jacket he was wearing.

It was the dead man, all right. The lake was getting its revenge. Tucker barked his horror. He was still on his knees and both hands clenched fistfuls of cold dirt. The silvery face was going to say his name and suddenly he didn't want to hear his name.

Tucker dove sideways and rolled in the ferns wet with chilly dew. He couldn't seem to get his feet under him and his lungs were stuck, no air for yelling, so he rolled some more. The ghost launched a powerful kick that would have dropped Tucker dead, but the meadow grass wrapped around its ankle and shin and it missed.

And suddenly a bass yell issued from the forest, followed by the sounds of pounding feet and crashing as people tripped over tree roots, fire grates, and guy lines in camp. More ghosts? That quickly the smuggler disappeared, and Tucker got to his feet as figures came streaming toward him from the bonfire.

"It's a bust," people were screaming. In the moonlight the forest suddenly looked like the floor of Hell as prone bodies resurrected themselves from the ground and stumbled away. People raced past Tucker and pointed backward yelling, "It's a bust." At the center of light, sparks flew up as a stereo speaker fell into the fire. Tucker had no adrenaline left, though. He could barely walk, much less run. And so it was he alone who saw a cinnamon-color bear and her chubby yearling come ambling from the far trees. The party was over.

9

By the time John
reached the base of Half
Dome's Northwest Face
eight hundred feet above the valley floor, his knees were creaking and
the forest had turned into that obstinate
manzanita brush and rhododendron that
sprouts up in the shatter zone wherever
rock falls off Yosemite's big walls. Early-morning
fog hung in long, torn scarves, and moss grew fluorescent and lime green. The smell this early morning was
primordial, manless. He half expected Himalayan cuckoos to
call in that intermediate fabric, and at one point he caught sight
of a bluejay, all liquid and jewels, flowing between the trees,
the slight beat of wings dampened almost in silence. John kept looking for the wall because he was humping ninety pounds going on, God,
half a ton. So was Tucker, but the boy had shamelessly scampered off on
those pipe-thin legs as if their loads were feathers, not metal and rope and
nine-pounds-per-gallon water. John could hear the water with each step, a
tiny ocean with tiny waves rocking on his back. Atlas with a hangover.

Then the wall was there.

It erupted straight up from the hillside. "Jeez," expelled John, taken
off-guard. One moment the muffled forest slope had him in a glaze, the
next he was just above the cloud layer and this milky stone was rearing
up, hard and cool, the color of a fawn's belly. With both hands he
slapped at the stone and shook his head. It was exquisite, a monument of
black-and-white speckled quartz monzonite. He'd been here before, on
the zebra stripes of Tis-a-ack farther to the right, and twice across and

over the Zigzag Cracks on the standard routes to the left. He loved this formation. Half Dome spun a different beauty than El Cap did. El Cap was all blond, sun-drenched and tawny and sprawled like a coral reef. Half Dome, though, was more like Liz. Here was the soul of a darker woman. The back of her rounded cowl gleamed in the sunshine, but even on the hottest August days the flat north-facing wall presented cool monochromes, contradiction and shadow. For between a few minutes and a few hours each day, depending on the season, the sun would angle in some rays right near the top. Otherwise all was cloistered blue tones up here, mute as an underworld. A half acre of snow clung to the foot of the wall. In the summer you could fill your water bottles with the melt, but as they'd suspected it was still too cold for that luxury. Good thing they'd humped their water in. Across and down the Valley, the low cloud cover paved over the forest floor, leaving John with floating islands of walls across the gap. This was how it looked, he knew, as the final glaciers retreated, a trough full of white quiet.

"Hey, Tuck," he called, though not loudly. No need to break the peace. Tucker was nowhere to be seen along the base. Heavy as the pack was, he didn't want to off-load it yet, not when he could be finished with it at the foot of the route. That way it would be two thousand vertical feet—five, seven, eight days, however long it took—before he had to lug the bastard on his back again. A faint metallic jingling sounded farther along the wall. Running his fingertips across the stone, John walked sixty yards over to a canopy of pungent manzanita.

Tucker was working away in a cave of dark manzanita, each leaf glassy with frozen dew. He was grinning like a mutt outside a Burger King, happier than John had ever seen him, all set to go. Both hands were taped with wide, white adhesive strips to protect against the jam cracks, and his old, ubiquitous pair of British climbing shoes was tied so tight he could barely walk. He had a pair of the new Spanish shoes with sticky rubber soles. But they were expensive and wore out quickly. Moreover, they had the properties of a top-secret weapon—the high-tech quick fix—and Tucker had decided to leave them in the haul bag until, and only if, he needed them. "You seen it?" he asked John.

"Not yet." For weeks now there had been only one It. The Visor. Tucker was horny for the rock, nervous as a kid with his first foldout. Carefully backing up against a stone bench to unsaddle, John gave his camel groan as the weight eased off. He unbuckled the belly band and flipped off the shoulder straps, then stretched his back. A single crack wormed out of the ground, too thin to wedge in so much as a fingernail. Fifteen feet up it gradually opened up to finger and then fist width.

"This the start?" he asked. A typical Tucker selection. Desperate from ground zero.

"Yeah."

John trusted the boy. Tucker had been up here on lone-wolf reconnaissances a dozen times and more. Not even Kresinski could accuse him of not doing his homework. John started pulling gear and old taped Clorox bottles filled with water from his pack. They were starting thin, even for a climb demanding only four days. They'd talked themselves into believing four days because neither wanted to haul more weight. Four days was a lie, though. That would mean covering five hundred feet a day on territory that was unexplored, but that promised some interesting complexities. Still, figuring two quarts per man per day, their four gallons could be stretched to six, max seven days, by stopping down consumption. Water Discipline: No one liked it, everyone practiced it. Hauling it or doing without. One way or another, you suffered for your desires. At least the face was in shade, that was worth an extra day of water in itself.

John eyeballed the crack to where it disappeared two hundred feet higher. He patiently hunted and found a crack that could be pendulumed across to, then lost that one, too, and sniffed. He was scared and excited and happy. They'd find all the answers once they got to the questions. That was the extra high you got in doing a new wall route, the opportunity to prod the unknown with a style all your own. No maps. No preconceptions. The one undeniable certainty was that however they got there, the Visor was waiting two thousand feet overhead. It had been waiting since the last Ice Age for him and Tucker. John bent to the gear, psyching up, psyching down. He was on the verge of adrenaline and didn't want to waste it. They were going to climb, he told himself. Keep it basic.

Tucker had already converted his pack into a haul bag by unbuckling the shoulder straps. Now John made two padded rings on the interior with their foam pads, and on the floor of the haul bag carefully arranged items they would need least, last, or only at night, such things as an extra jumar ascender, some extra bolts, three outsize spring-loaded cams called Friends, and their ground shoes, John's pair of Nikes and Tucker's Reeboks, which they'd hiked up in. They were thin on water, but loaded for bear in the hardware department. Never could tell what you might need in the terra incognita. On top of the miscellaneous extras, he nestled their water bottles. One of the wall climbers' guaranteed ulcers is the water bottle that springs a leak, dooming an otherwise certain ascent to hasty retreat. Therefore John checked the tape sealing shut each of the Clorox bottles, and nested them inside the padding with a prayer. The next layer above the bottles held the hammock that one of them would be sleeping in and the collapsible Porta-ledge the other would use, eight pounds of food, more hardware, and waterproof clothing, and the layer above that their sleeping bags and parkas. John's pack would be carried on the belayer's back and it would contain little more than a snack for lunch, a quart of water, John's big Pentax camera, a *cagoule* each in case of snow, and, bundled in plastic, their roll of precious toilet paper. He hefted the haul bag and grimaced. A hundred pounds, easily.

Tucker was uncoiling their three ropes, two nine-millimeters for leading and one eleven-mil for hauling. The racks of pitons, nuts, Friends, hero loops, hooks, and carabiners were already neatly laid out beside a dozen red, green, and yellow runner-slings on the broken scree. John pulled on the legs of his harness and tied them to his waistband with a water knot, then squatted down to ensure a comfortable fit. Unless they hit a major ledge, the harness wasn't coming off until the summit. You climbed with it on, you slept with it on. It was a trick, but you even shit with it on. He pulled on his French climbing shoes with their bright-green tongue and leather panels, but didn't tie them. They were regulation gangrene-tight for "feeling" the rock with his toes, not exactly meant for leisure wear. Tucker obviously had this first pitch in mind for himself, and depending on the severity of the climbing any single pitch could consume hours. John stood up and exhaled with a whistle.

"How you doin'?" he said.

"I'm about ready," said Tucker. His harness was on, his shoes were tied, and the two nine-mil ropes were knotted at his belly with a figure eight. All he had to do was set the racks on across his chest. But John sensed something was stopping the boy. At last, with a critical glance at

John, Tucker turned around and pulled his sweater off. He was wearing a T-shirt underneath, and when he turned John's mouth almost fell open. Emblazoned across the front of the shirt was Katie's "This Ain't No *#!!** Wienie Roast." Indeed, it *was* Katie's T-shirt. It was tight across Tucker's barrel chest and the sleeves came almost up to his shoulders, but it fit well enough. Tucker defiantly waited for some comment. Obviously he'd lost his cherry, fallen in love, and found a broader biological purpose for his energies, all in one girl in one night. It made John miss Liz all the more.

"Water?" John offered, careful not to bat an eye.

Tucker looked grateful. "Nah," he said. He scooped up one rack of gear, draped it over his head and under one arm, then placed the other rack under his opposite arm. Last of all he hung the orange, blue, gold, and green runner-slings over his right shoulder. The hardware criss-crossed his wide back like thongs of armor. John clapped his fist into his palm and nodded. They were on lock and load. It was time to move.

"Okay?"

"I'm on," said Tucker, meaning on belay.

"You're off," said John, as in off to see the wizard. "Five, four, three, two . . ."

Tucker stepped up to the wall. Right away something changed in his demeanor. Those thoroughbred nerves calmed. His fierce, nervous wanting became thoughtful, more coherent. He scanned the rock and found something he'd probably spied on other forays up here, a tiny polished tab of stone on the outside of the incipient crack. Adjusting his fingertips to the hold—and that required stacking his thumb on the edge of his index finger—he gave a sample pull at it, then had second thoughts and dipped the hand into the chalk bag on his rump. His fingers emerged smoking with white gypsum powder. He found the hold again, located something even smaller for his other hand, and looked down between his outstretched arms for a foothold.

From where John was watching and limply feeding rope ten feet away, there were no holds at all. But Tucker's specialty was walking on water. He wasn't the strongest climber around, even pound for pound, just the least saddled with what was and wasn't reality. Sometimes, if you watched hard enough and had the finger strength and believed, you could duplicate Tucker's imaginary holds. More often, the stone was blank. Tabula rasa. Tucker swiped the inner sole of his left shoe, particularly the inner toe, against his other calf to clean off any mud or moisture, and placed it on a minuscule wrinkle in the granite. One last ritual remained. He glanced over his shoulder at John and grinned and waggled his eyebrows.

"Fire it up," said John. Lift-off.

Tucker left the earth. His right foot released the ground, swiped against the opposite pants leg, and found purchase. He was in flight. Two new holds magically appeared overhead, and then another and another. Tucker exploited the illusion of a ladder and moved higher, fluid, at ease. Half Dome belonged to him this morning, him and his fingertips and go-for-broke imagination. Each move took him closer to where the crack widened. His toes smeared against—John looked—nothing, while his fingers paused, experimented, and pinched at tiny freckles of mineral. Finally with a gentle sweep of his arm, Tucker stretched up and touched the crack. He lodged the first digit of his little finger in the fissure, pulled up, found room for more fingers on his next hand, pulled up again. Forty feet up, he stuffed the toe of one shoe into the crack and stood on it as casually as he stood barefoot on the tops of door hinges for practice. He fished a batch of copperheads from his rack, sized one to the crack, unclipped it, and slotted it with a jerk. Quickly, but not hastily, he clipped a carabiner through the wire loop now sticking out from the rock, turned the "beaner" gate outward, and snapped his lead rope through, effectively attaching himself to the wall so long as John held the rope or the protection didn't pull free.

He climbed higher. The rope slid through the biner. Two hawks drafted across the Valley. The river of clouds lapped at his feet. John listened to his blood and smelled the cold coins of manzanita. The smooth plaited Perlon rippled across the white tape crisscrossing his palm. Here was a day for you. They say forgetting is an art, for unless you forget there can't be room for remembering. For that reason, as Half Dome enclosed them, John did much forgetting.

A week passed and still the Visor hung above them. The wall was elusive and tricked them again and again, sending them up false starts and dead ends or blinding them with too obvious answers or dangling mirror images of wrong choices in front of right choices. Sometimes there were complicated networks of fissures that radiated out from their hands in every direction, each as useful and useless as its neighbor. Other times there was just one crack, but the crack would dodge right and left or shift shapes. It would pinch down to the width of a razor's edge for as far as they could see, then suddenly balloon to off-width dimensions too large for a fist and too small to jam in a shoulder. At the most unlikely and frustrating spots, the crack would flower with wads of thick green and blue moss that the leader had to weed out with the pick on his hammer while hanging by one hand. At times there was no crack at all, and the climber was left staring at profoundly empty granite.

On the fourth afternoon, they came upon a long, guttering, off-vertical tail of decayed sandstone that belonged in the Badlands somewhere, anywhere but here. Even Tucker, at 144 pounds minus the weight they were both losing, was almost too heavy to get them past. For seven delicate hours he coaxed holds from rock that had the substance of raw sugar granules, but he did it, opened the passage, moving them that much closer to the summit.

Elsewhere John led a 165-foot flake so loosely connected to the wall that an old bird's nest got dislodged when he pressed his feet against the wall on a lie-back move. Every time he placed a nut, it fell out when he pulled on the flake. The spring-loaded cams were too large, and he was afraid a piton might pry the whole flake free and kill them both. As a result, he couldn't place any protection, which meant one slip and their connecting ropes would drag them both into the deep just as surely as if the flake detached. It was a harrowing lead, long on testicle, necessarily short on sanity, and all the while John kept imagining what would happen if the whole flake just all of a sudden popped free. A giant surfboard, he decided. And he didn't know how to surf. At the top of the flake, as a reward for his gritted teeth, he found a foot-wide crystal of transparent quartz embedded flush with the wall. He sat in his "butt bag," a triangle of nylon fabric, and enjoyed the rest of the day dangling peacefully beside that beautiful crystal while Tucker took his turn above.

The higher they went, the more sunlight they enjoyed at the end of the day. This was both good and bad. It warmed them for the cold nights, but also it reminded them of how thirsty one quart of water per day can leave you. They got so thirsty it hurt to eat, but they knew better than not to and forced the dry gorp down. The haul bag turned Tucker's

Famous Amos cookies into fine powdery crumbs and the sun melted their chocolate, but that was okay, anything sweet had gotten to be too sweet. Privately Tucker remained unsure if that was a curse or a blessing.

On the fifth day they crept vertically across a sudden border onto enamel-white stone. Since the bottom they'd been handling black-and-gray monzonite speckled with white. Now, suddenly, the world became a region of pure whiteness. It lifted their spirits and John talked about the Carrara marble of Italy he'd once seen. They discussed what it would be like to climb the dome of St. Peter's, and that led to an anecdote about a wild Jewish-American climber who'd been shot by Israeli soldiers when he attempted a spontaneous ascent of the Wailing Wall in Jerusalem. Tucker accepted the fiction as fact, and John accepted Tucker's acceptance. It was on this day that they passed within eighty feet of one of Half Dome's already established routes, the Northwest Direct. Over to the left, they could see a crack and three pitons, and knew that by penduluming across and following the relatively simple line up, they could exit from the wall next morning. A staircase made of cable and wood for tourists led off the rounded back of Half Dome, and there was a stream of clear water not two minutes from the base of the stairs. It was tempting, but they stayed true to the Visor, and soon the crack was far out of reach.

On the sixth day the issue of retreat was raised again. John was "out on the sharp end," leading out, when he inserted his hand into a perfect, fist-size bottleneck and a startled fox bat sank its fangs into him. Without really thinking, already wired with adrenaline from the climbing, John grabbed the bat by one dry wing and smartly brained it against the wall. Then he stuffed the feather-light carcass inside his shirt and finished the pitch. An hour later, after Tucker joined him, they scrutinized the crooked little body and then, unable to decide if it had been rabid or not, tossed the bat off into the abyss. No odyssey can be complete without a monster, John reasoned. This could be his. And besides, they joked, hydrophobia wouldn't be such a hardship since they had next to no water anyhow.

John knew they were adapting to wall life when he started enjoying more than an hour of sleep at a time. The biggest ledge they encountered was a three-inch-wide slat cut into the middle of a pitch where they couldn't really use it. No ledges meant their nights were longer than real time. No ledges meant the hammock and the Porta-ledge. John's was the one-point-suspension hammock, in which sleep ordinarily comes in delirious, half-hour snatches, no longer. No matter how you rig it, a hammock will sling you tight against the cold rock all night long, pressure-bruising your rock-side shoulder and hip. It takes so much wrestling to get into and out of a climber's hammock that a midnight piss requires more misery than it relieves. That problem solved itself with John before long; by midweek one scanty piss was all either one of them could force out daily anyway. John adapted. He began to sleep. To dream. One trick to sleeping better was sleeping less. Each evening, for as long as he could stretch it out, he sat with Tucker on the Porta-ledge. Not much different from a two-by-six-foot trampoline, this lightweight platform could be set up in a matter of minutes to form a springy, comfortable frame for sleeping and sitting. As night chewed away the final light, the two climbers lounged side by side on the platform, backs to the wall, both roped into the anchor, feet dangling over the black void. They kicked around a lot of things—the day's highlights or mistakes; Snake Lake, greed and poverty; TV and the Himalayas; their lives; the origins of the universe—common wall talk.

"Reno," Tucker broached one evening, his voice a dehydrated croak. The plaque of stone at their backs had gone the color of gold and lemons from the setting sun. John passed him their allotted after-dinner pint of water. Tucker sipped a thimbleful from it, smacked his chalky lips, and passed the bottle back. That was part of the game, pretending barely anything was plenty. They were both good at it.

"What about it?" rasped John.

"Reno was okay."

John kept on looking at the thin, magma-bright line of sunlight on the horizon. Already stars were chasing on stage. "Thought you said it sucked."

"I mean," said Tucker, driving to the heart of it. "Liz."

"Yeah."

"Too bad Liz doesn't climb. She belongs here."

"Probably not," sighed John. He had scrupulously eliminated any talk of Liz from his conversations with Tucker. He couldn't get free of her, though. Tucker missed her, too. He missed the chance to even hear her name.

"She'd like it up here."

"Nah. Too scary up here."

"She's scared down there."

John quit talking. Tucker knew something.

"I saw her." The wall was losing its blush. Not long and John would have to swing off the Porta-ledge onto one of the ropes and descend to his hammock underneath. Not yet, though.

"I couldn't find her," said John. "Her cabin's all locked and shuttered up."

"She's in there," said Tucker. "You just got to sit there until after dark. She comes out."

John scored himself for not trying harder. "How's she doing?"

"I wish we didn't go to the lake." Not well.

"I know."

"She ought to cry and get it over with. But, Liz, you know."

"Yeah."

"I make myself sort of sick sometimes."

"It wasn't our fault." But what did blame have to do with Liz suffering? "You tell her we were going up here?"

"I told her I wish it was still Reno. She said me too."

Me too, thought John. Damn. "She's scared?"

"They're kicking her out."

"No way." But that had to be the truth of it, John knew. The thought had never occurred to him before this. But why not? he wondered.

"You think?" Tucker asked hopefully.

"What did Liz do? Nothing."

"I said, you want us to stay with you? She said no. She said go on up there. Touch the moon."

But there was no moon visible, just the Visor rock-steady among the stars.

Regardless of the topic or the pain in his hands from the climbing or his thirst, every evening John forced himself to fill in his topo, the topographical map of their unfolding route. Because this was such a complicated and esoteric route, the Visor topo was especially important, otherwise later climbers would get lost and have to retreat or else damage the wall with bolts to bridge sections not fully explained. An ink line

156

showed where each belay point was, how difficult which sections were, the length of different pitches, the need for which kinds of extraordinary equipment, and the names applied to what and where. On old maps of the Nose of El Cap, for instance, a crack bears the name Stovelegs for the only hardware that could be found back in the 1950's to fit the off-width crack: iron legs sawed off of old stoves. The El Cap maps show Stovelegs as three and a half pitches of 5.10 or A2 climbing, which are entered on pendulum and exited at Dolt Tower. Here, on John's germinating map of the Visor Wall, beside the twelfth pitch, a cryptic addendum declared "Time bomb, 5.12, A4." To a climber it made perfect, chilling sense. A time bomb is made by balling aluminum foil around the head of a wired nut and is used when the rock becomes so barren of features that clean ascent is effectively at a standstill. A last-ditch, kamikaze effort can be made, though few make it, by custom-designing a time bomb from your candy bar foil, setting the aluminum ball against the rock, and then pounding it flat with your hammer. If all goes well, the aluminum will temporarily stick to small crystals or temporarily shape itself to rugosities in the stone. Temporarily. You clip a stirrup on to the wire loop jutting from the aluminum mash, ever so gently stand on it, and instantly begin setting your next higher piece of protection. The device is called a time bomb because you have, at most, twenty to thirty seconds to place your next piece before the aluminum unsticks and you self-destruct. Time bombs shouldn't work, but sometimes they do. On the twelfth pitch, for the first and, he prayed, last time in his life, John fashioned and used a time bomb. Tucker filed the awesome feat as one more example of the primacy of will.

John's Visor Wall map, like all maps, was more than a blueprint for others following in their footsteps, it was also a history of the first ascent and a biography of its pioneers. It was a testament to their courage and imagination and all the other forthright virtues, but also it was a mark of their personality. In the future, climbers who'd never known John and Tucker would have poignant insights into this pair just by reading their map. By the fact that Tucker had named the powdery, rotting sandstone pitch Oreo Crumbs instead of, say, Tucker's Treat or Tiger's Delight, they would know that Tucker had been a modest, gentle man with a sweet tooth. The crack where John was bitten, here designated the Belfry for its bat, would inform climbers that John took his dangers with a grin.

These first climbers on the Visor Wall, the topo would inform people, had humor and poetry and whimsy. And the complete absence of bolts—which require drilling and thereby scarring the rock—meant they had an aesthetics with guts. A first ascent on a big wall that shunned bolts meant you loved the rock almost more than yourself, that you had taken extraordinary risks to keep it pure and clean. And resorting to a time bomb set you square at the high right hand of John Muir.

Each night John worked on his topo map. Each day they explored fresh territory. Before the sun wheeled around to heat them for the final hour or so, the wall with its dark, beetling overhangs reminded John of Anasazi cliff dwellings just before dawn. Now and then, far over to the left, they caught sight of small white handprints like primitive signatures that had survived the elements beneath small roofs of stone. Tattered green and orange slings hanging from pitons and nuts quivered in the breeze like brightly colored snares. Other times the wall reminded John of his oil-rig days. At night, especially, he'd look up at the stars and re-member those tiny islands of artificial light in the barrens of Wyoming and Colorado and New Mexico. He'd feel very small and yet big because to roughneck you have to be obsessed some, like a climber. There wasn't much difference between the effect a big wall has on you and the effect of working a rig. You sleep little, lose weight, bond with your crew, and the ground from high off the deck looks far, far away. Things seem larger than life, what with those Cat and GM motors that can power a subma-rine and those five-hundred-pound block and tackles and giant pipe fit-tings. What with the enormous wall. The difference was that on a rig there is no subtlety. None. But on the wall, your capacity to be delicate, to finesse a move, to perform, is your sole hope. Without that, you might as well stay on the ground and pump iron in front of a mirror. Or jog. Or, as Bullseye put it, "just hang out and beat off with all the other lilliputes."

The Visor Wall was a vast, fantastic landscape, and like fifteenth-century sailors they struggled across places so forbidding the effort came to lose meaning and they were just there, in motion above the still green sea. The wall became their whole world, or half of it anyway, the other half was air. By the end of the week they looked like mere survivors, hard-core fools. Mangy beards, torn clothing, scabs on their elbows and hands. Thirst gnawed at their synapses. Their fingernails had begun to ulcerate, their gums hurt, and their teeth felt loose. Neither one had shit in days. John's tube of cherry Chap Stick was old history, and their lips split and bled anytime a joke got told, even a bad joke. Tongues swelling, their voices corroded into hoarse mutters. "I know it sounds like effeminacy to complain of hardships," an early alpinist once complained. "And I hold that the man who cannot endure hunger and thirst, cold and heat, to have his nose blistered and toes frostbitten, has no business in the high Alps. But you must draw the line somewhere, and I draw it at fleas." There were no fleas, but John and Tucker would have understood. It was the minor discomforts, not the dramatic ones, that were so taxing from minute to minute. John recorded it all. Then, on the seventh day, John's pen ran out of ink.

On the afternoon of the eighth day, taped, dusted with chalk, bruised and raw from two thousand feet of mean endless crack, John stacked two fingers against two others and pulled. He stemmed his feet out on disparate toeholds, rose up, and tossed his free hand overhead, groping for more crack. But there was no more crack. The rock turned to air. John grunted his surprise and nearly slipped while fumbling with the open space. And then he had a handful of crystal-white glacial sand and realized they'd reached a ledge. John levered himself over the curved lip, and there was a whole wide trough of white beach sand, a Hawaiian oasis. It had been so long since he'd stood upright on his feet that his first attempt to walk dumped him flat to his knees. He knelt there, hands clasped in his lap. The sand was soft and yielding. John looked out over the edge to call the good news down to Tucker, but had no voice for it. Tucker was stapled to the blank, infinite stone far below, watching some birds, not even aware that John had disappeared from sight. On every side of the boy the architecture fell away in all directions, up, down, left, right. But now they had their bearings. For just above the ledge hung the Visor.

Eighty feet up, the wall took an abrupt bend and turned into a huge, wide ceiling. A single crack fed thirty feet out across the underbelly. Then it bent sharply upward again along the squared-off front of the Visor and aimed for the summit. John knew from looking that the front of the Visor was another thirty feet high. By the time Tucker arrived at the ledge, John had decided the crack was impossible. He'd begun looking for some other way to exit off the wall, but there was none. None that was quick. None that would slake his thirst by nightfall. They'd either have to retreat all the way to the ground or rappel down and across to the Northwest Direct, then follow the Zigzag Cracks up, and that would take another full day. He didn't say any of this to Tucker. It was better to let the boy come to his own conclusions.

"How you feel?" John asked.

"Good," croaked Tucker, examining the Visor's ceiling.

"Dry?"

"Nah."

"Liar." John dipped into his pack and came out with a pint bottle. There were three swallows of water sloshing around at the bottom. He'd been saving this surprise for two days. "Here," he said. Tucker drank it down, presuming John had taken his share.

"It'll go," said Tucker. John didn't answer. They'd come a long damn way for this ceiling. If Tucker wanted a shot at it, that was what they'd do. "I think I should wear my Fires," he said. John rummaged through the haul bag for Tucker's Spanish shoes and found them. While he tied them on, Tucker was careful to keep the sticky soles off the sand.

"I won't need much pro," he commented. John studied the crack. It was less that Tucker wouldn't need the protection than that he wouldn't be able to use it. The crack was off-width and upside down. He watched Tucker sort through the racks and select the few pieces large enough to possibly fit. Tucker was quick about it and kept his head down. The ceiling pressed down upon them with a strange, oppressive weight.

"Guess that's it," said Tucker, draping a streamlined rack over one shoulder. It held three of the largest spring-loaded cams, two extra-large tubular chocks, and a five-inch bong for hand placement. Along with five or six carabiners, his rack weighed maybe two pounds. That was important. "You're on," said John. Tucker was wasting no time. He was nervous.

The bottom eighty feet were 5.10-ish and presented no difficulty to Tucker. He dispensed with the lower, vertical crack in just a few minutes. And then he was there. His head was bumping up against the ceiling of the Visor itself. Tucker touched the rock overhead, and John heard him clear his throat. He tried to place some protection out behind him in the overhanging crack, but nothing was large enough to stay in place. What

160

that meant was that Tucker's best and possibly only protection was going to be in at the base of the ceiling. And that meant that if he fell, he'd swing down straight into the wall. So be it, thought John.

Tucker dipped his hand into his dusty nylon chalk bag. Chalk dust fluttered earthward, disturbed here and there by soft eddies of breeze. They'd been lucky. The weather had held all week. At dawn they'd awakened to see the western mouth of the Valley choked with storm clouds, and for hours since then the wind had been toying with them, gusting, then hiding. John wiggled his bare toes in the sand and breathed in the height. The trees were small. Mirror Lake was no bigger than a penny. People, if any were down there, were invisible. Only rarely did people come to snap pictures of climbers on Half Dome, because it entailed too much of a walk. El Cap was different. Look down from the Captain's walls on a sunny day and you saw spread beneath your feet a gridlock of cars pulled over for a telephoto shot. The privacy up here all week had been well worth the sunless cold and the extra gruntwork up to the base. More chalk drifted by—Tucker changing hands.

Tucker prodded the crack with bone dry fingers, ferreting out a brief edge that might combine with an opposing knuckle to form a jam. Padding higher with his feet, he felt farther out beneath the roof.

"How're the holds?" John finally said.

"Off-width . . . smooth . . . funny. . . ." The wind gusted and stole the rest of his words away.

At last Tucker was ready to commit himself to the ceiling. He moved his feet up, jammed them to the heels, and moved out. And there he hung, dead parallel to the ground half a mile below, glued to the flat ceiling. John fed him a foot of rope.

Tucker's sorcery had begun. For well over a year now, he'd been training for this roof, imagining it, disciplining his fears. With taut confidence he explored the fissure and wormed the worn toe of his shoe farther along the crack. Not a motion, not even a sideways glance, was wasted. The crack was impassable and dangerous, but Tucker made it look easy. It looked so easy that no sooner had he started the ceiling, than he was almost half finished with it. Upside down, chalk bag and gear rack dangling backward to the ground where he could barely reach them, Tucker flashed the first fifteen feet out under the wild roof. He didn't balk or dally or second-guess his holds, because he couldn't. There wasn't the least hurry in his movements, but there wasn't the least pause, either.

He seemed a little dazed, either by the rock or his performance or the marriage of the two. His green eyes were lit bright, lungs barely working under Katie's T-shirt. Not a quiver in his zebra-striped Lycra legs. No fear. No exhaustion.

John was dazed, too. Not a single other human alive could have repeated what Tucker was doing. Every time a record is shattered, of course, people say never again, only to see a sub-sub-four-minute mile run the next week. A longer jump, a farther throw. And given the Dodge City atmosphere of Camp Four, every other climber would be out gunning for Tucker's latest terror pitch. But John couldn't shake the feeling that something unique was happening up on this ceiling. Maybe someday some trainoid with a clean spirit and transparent eyes would appear on the scene and get it right and smooth and clean like this. Only another Tucker could repeat what Tucker was doing today, though. The Kresinskis and Bullseyes and Johns of the world, possessed of talents and desires each believed were special, would never come close to doing the Visor ceiling. Tucker was separate. Out there. In a sense, once he completed the ceiling, he would have exiled himself from the rest of them. Then halfway across, something happened. The roof began to expel him.

The crack was the same crack. The ceiling didn't take a deeper slant or change the texture of its stone. Nothing was different. But suddenly, fifteen feet across with fifteen more to go, Tucker slowed. He lost his smoothness. One foot slipped from the crack. He replaced it with a short, strong kick. Hoisting himself up, he shoved his hands in tighter. He moved his head between and on the outsides of his arms, for the first time taking notice of the height and gauging the pitfalls of continuing and the possibilities of retreat. What had seemed so casual suddenly seemed desperate. Clearly Tucker was going to fall. Worse, he knew he was going to fall. Other priorities were crowding out his concentration, priorities such as self-defense. Because if he fell now, he was going to be hurt badly. Tucker saw his danger. John saw his fear.

". . . pumped . . ." Tucker groaned.

John stayed calm. "Try some pro," he called up. If Tucker could just get a nut into the crack, falling would lose its teeth.

". . . don't know . . ." Tucker grunted. He looked down at the rack of pro hanging earthward, looked back up at the crack, then down again, estimating which piece to try where. By the movements of Tucker's head, John could tell the crack was oddly shaped. Freeing one hand from the crack, Tucker rapidly pawed through the clinking hardware, spreading the bunched metal and slings with a small slap to see what there was. That innocuous slap, its impatience, further confirmed what John had guessed: Tucker was too wiped to waste muscle on anything but a sure fit, and the crack wasn't going to allow a sure fit. Tucker powered himself farther on, running the rope out another three feet in search of some crack that would take his protection. He pawed at the rack and fished a piece loose, one of the large tubes. He unclipped it and tried to stuff it into the crack. The movement of his hands was slightly too fast, a bad sign. Nerves. A moment later his right knee twitched, no more than a hint of sewing machine leg, but still a hint. He was getting scared.

John spared a glance at the belay anchor. Three solid nuts, one slotted to take an upward pull. If—when—Tucker fell, John was going to get yanked up into the wall. The anchor would hold. John saw that he could catch the fall. But Tucker was going to smash against the wall like a watermelon on a cord. John moved tight against the anchor, bracing for the pull. He was spellbound.

Tucker kept trying, all his effort devoted to inserting the tube and covering his ass. When nothing worked, he did something John had never seen in all his days as a climber: Instead of clipping the piece back on the rack, he simply tossed the useless tube over his shoulder, just cast it away. The tube dropped through the air. Not once did it skip off the lower wall. The overhang was profound and the metal disappeared without a sound. Tucker thrust his hand into the rack again, unclipped the largest spring cam, tried it once, twice, then tossed it, too, into the void. Forty dollars.

"No," wailed Tucker, and he tried to scoot his hands deeper into the crack. He was too tired to rest, and if he rested he'd only get more tired. His hands started slipping. John expelled all his air, clamped his hands tight on the ropes.

Tucker fell.

Tucker's torso dropped and swung. The rack of gear slipped over his head and, clattering like a metal spider, scurried off into the windy depths. The Ray Charles-Oklahoma Sooners sunglasses sprang from his face, following after the rack. A large puff of white chalk emptied from his chalk bag and swirled past John on the wind. But Tucker. Tucker went no farther. His feet stayed wedged in the crack. Upside down, he just hung there, belly naked. Katie's T-shirt draped around his big, rangy rib cage. He shouldn't have been, but he was saved.

"Oh, man," said Tucker, looking up at his feet stuck in the crack. John couldn't believe his eyes, either. "John, look it!"

John couldn't think of any words to say. Tucker had gained a second life. True, the gear had fallen, but now, maybe, Tucker wouldn't need it. With his hand and bicep strength replenished, he could finish. He *would* finish. He had no choice.

"You okay?" John shouted up. Tucker arched backward and looked at John.

"Yeah." He grinned. His fear was gone. He shook his arms, opened and clenched his hands. His arms were like vampires. A little fresh blood and it was a whole new day. The wind hit them. It was about to be cold, John knew. That didn't matter now. You lived between storms. And they'd made it off. Tucker quit shaking his arms. Carefully, so as not to uproot his feet, he twisted to the left and then right, loosening his back, psyching up again. There wasn't much chalk left in his bag, but what remained he dumped out into his palm and rubbed over both hands, from fingertips to the tape ending at his wrists.

"Okay," he said aloud. It was go-for-broke time. No protection. No more chalk. No more adrenaline. One way or the other, all the way up or slam-arcing down, this was the end. He went still. Then he started. Cautiously, slowly, he jackknifed his lower body up beside his zebra-striped legs and met the crack with his fingers.

The rest was anticlimax. Hanging by his hands and feet, Tucker crawled to the outer edge of the ceiling as if there had been no interruption in the climb. He reached around to the front edge of the ceiling and locked his fingers into the crack running vertically along the front of the Visor to the summit. John relaxed his shoulders and thawed his grip on the two lead ropes. His bare toes loosened in the white sand. Tucker located another hold on the front of the Visor for his other hand, and a huge grin crossed his face. Bomber holds. Jugs. And to prove it, he pulled his feet from the crack in the ceiling and let go of one handhold

164

and hung two thousand feet above the earth by his right hand. He was liberated.

"Wooo, woooo," Tucker yelled at the sky and the wall and the abyss. It was a moment of pure ego. He hung at the center of it all. Watching him, John shivered. So primitive. So triumphant. He looked small way up there on the tip of nowhere, and his war cry sounded minute.

"Go plant the flag," John shouted up. The wind tore his words into oblivion, but Tucker heard his voice and looked down. John saluted him with a fist. Tucker nodded his head yes. Yes, me. Then he set to exiting on to the summit. He pulled his feet up, placed them on the front of the Visor, stood high, and hand-jammed the crack. He flowed up the remainder of the crack as fast as John could pay out rope. At the top he flipped a hand over the edge, kicked slightly with one toe, and disappeared onto the summit. For a moment after that there was no tugging on the ropes, and John guessed that Tucker was lying on his back atop the Visor, beaming at God. Then there was some movement in the ropes; Tucker was walking around, looking for a big enough rock to use for an anchor. John listened in vain for the off-belay signal, then gave up for the wind and simply paid out the last ten feet of rope. He busied himself with the haul bag, readying it for Tucker to pull up. It was over.

A few minutes later the haul line came taut. Tucker was ready. John unsnapped the haul bag from the anchor. The rope tightened from above, and suddenly the bag jumped into space. It flew off the ledge and arced fifty feet out, then arced in, then out. In small hops and bounds, it sank upward toward the summit. With all the water gone, the haul bag was much lighter now, and Tucker had it up and out of sight before John had even finished pulling out the anchor pieces. He tried to swallow. Water soon. An hour. Less if the spring was still running. Didn't matter, there was a brook farther downtrail. He was bent over, thinking these thoughts, when a body went streaking past.

John didn't see it, not directly. The flash of color raced down the corner of his vision, followed by a sinuous thread of another color, and then it was gone. John froze. His lungs stopped. Tucker? he thought.

"No," he murmured. He looked over the edge, but it was already night down below, all black and empty.

"Tucker?" he shouted. But it wasn't Tucker. He pulled from his mind's eye the colors of the body. Red. And the trailing thread, yellow.

The haul bag. Tucker had dropped the haul bag and their yellow haul line both. Among other things, the haul bag had their sleeping bags. With that gone, it meant a night in the open with no bags unless they could make it the four hours down to Camp Four in the dark. Luckily John's pack held their headlamps. And his topo. The topo was more important than even their sleeping bags. The topo was history. Irretrievable. It was a dumb mistake, dropping the haul bag, but not really costly. In fact it was a blessing of sorts. It left them sixty pounds lighter, and that meant the descent to the valley floor could be accomplished at jogging speed.

John straightened from his ledge and prepared to "jug" one of the nine-mil ropes. He gave a hard yank on the line, judged it to be anchored, and clipped on both jumars. A set of stirrups hung from each jumar handle. All he had to do was place his feet in the stirrups and "climb" the rope. He set the pack on his back, draped the second heavier rack of gear over his head, and smacked his dry lips. He looked up at the summit rim. And at that moment Tucker reappeared.

Somehow, horribly, Tucker slipped. He slipped headfirst. His black hair flashed, then shivered. Violently, superhumanly, Tucker managed to twist himself around so that he was clinging to the very lip of the Visor. Slightly to the left was the crack he'd just climbed up, and farther over hung the lead ropes, one of which John was clipped onto. He had untied himself from the ropes.

And then, to John's amazement, he saw that Tucker was talking to someone on the summit. He couldn't hear the words, but something about the motions of Tucker's head looked angry. Instinctively, as if the danger were his, John backed away from the edge. He tripped in the sand, and the pack spun him hard, nose first, against the wall. His skull slapped against the granite, and he lay still for a moment, face to the rock, not looking up. He let the ringing subside and tried to think. There was a logic to what was going on up there. He just couldn't figure it out.

Still lying in the sand and hampered by the pack, he looked again. Tucker was hanging to the edge of the summit and he was arguing, the body language left no doubt about that. From this distance, miniaturized as he was, Tucker looked like one of the camp chipmunks scolding an

166

intruder. It wasn't funny, though. It was insane and deadly. Who was he talking to? And why weren't they helping him?

John freed his arms from the pack straps and the extra rack and scooted himself farther away from the edge. Against his will, his eyes darted down at the yawning pit of the floor. A wild, penetrating vertigo punched him. He looked up. Tucker was still holding on, still arguing. Still in need. The thought stabilized him. Tucker needed rescue. He looked around. White sand. The pack. The ropes. The gear. First things first. He considered jumaring up the rope and talking Tucker up and over the summit edge. He didn't dare go up the rope, though. Somehow Tucker's danger had its source at the far end of these ropes.

No, John decided, his place was down here on the ledge, and so he put his mind to securing the area. He remembered taking out the lower anchor, and without it he was dependent on the summit anchor. John mobilized himself. He turned around and knelt facing the wall with the extra rack of gear in his lap. There wasn't time to find the very same nuts he'd pulled from the crack only a few minutes before, not even time to unsnap individual pieces and form a tidy anchor. He just slotted and jammed the first half-dozen nuts that stuck and tied the ends of the ropes and himself in. Immediately the vertigo slackened. His safety was tangible now. Nothing could pull him off the wall with this anchor.

He stood and faced outward to judge Tucker's progress. There was none. From this angle, the summit was barren. A gust of wind nudged John. Tucker kept hanging there.

Because there was nothing else he could do, John vainly tried to whip the one free rope over and across to Tucker. But the line was too tight and the distance was too far. "The rope," he shouted up. He tried again. His voice was a tiny scratch on a record. The rope wouldn't reach. Not even close.

Something got communicated, though, or else Tucker had the same thought himself, for he suddenly scurried hand over hand toward the ropes. John breathed a small prayer of thanks. At least the boy could descend on the ropes and come down to the soft sand, and they could straighten this nightmare out. Whatever it was, they could sort it out and survive.

But the ropes came alive and began trembling in John's hands, then jerking violently, and suddenly they went slack. Tucker howled a fierce, incoherent curse.

The ropes slithered through blank air, disembodied. The first line whipped down and across, pulled by the wind, and sliced into the abyss. It came tight at John's waist with a heavy jerk. The other line, still running through the protection at the start of the ceiling, lashed John's arm, then tamed itself and meekly unthreaded from the pieces above. The two ropes hung from John's hands. He was stunned.

Someone was up there.

Someone had untied the ropes.

Tucker's only hope now was to lift himself over the edge. It was an easy mantle. John had watched him do it only a few minutes before. Instead Tucker started to climb back down the crack, down the front of the Visor.

"Goddamn," spat John. It was too crazy. He looked again; the summit was empty. There was nobody up there. The wind rushed at the wall again, frightening him with its hard, scaly, cold tide.

"Go up," he croaked. But Tucker continued down, plugging his feet and fists into the crack while scouting overhead for whatever it was, his demon, ogre, or dragon. Every motion was supremely sane and controlled; it was his direction that confounded John.

"Up," John yelled again. Half-healed scabs on his hands and around his fingernails ruptured as he clenched the ropes. A thin rivulet of blood ran across the tape on his right hand. The nausea stormed through him, and his knees buckled. His head was drumming. But his vision was crystal clear.

Tucker was frenzied and yet calm. Not once did he glance down at John, only up over and over again. He descended to the front corner of the Visor's ceiling and, to John's greater horror, actually began trying to locate a foothold underneath in the crack. It was completely unthinkable. He found the two handholds that had served him on exiting the ceiling, lowered his legs down into the cold wind, and felt for the crack with the toes of his Spanish shoes. The crack was there, of course, but he'd lost his memory for its precise shape. There was no possible way to reenter the ceiling blindly. It took him only a minute of effort to realize that his bridge was gone. John couldn't see his face, but when Tucker's legs went slack for an instant, he knew the boy had surrendered.

"My arms," John heard him groan. He knew Tucker had to be exhausted. His muscles would be on fire. His lungs would be dragging at the air. He couldn't last.

"Up," John yelled. But Tucker was already on his way up.

This time Tucker's ascent wasn't a nonchalant scamper to the sky. He labored for holds and had to push with his feet to get any pull from his arms. Several times he had to stop and, one by one, shake out his arms. Near the top he slowed further. Hands wedged in the final top inches of the crack, he peeked over the summit lip, then ducked down in a tight ball as if hiding again. At last he turned his eyes toward John. They were far away, but John saw his terror.

Tucker opened his mouth wide and John saw, rather than heard, his name called out. It was Tucker's last rite. With that, the boy straightened from his crouch, grabbed the summit rim, and rose almost to a complete exit. He started to disappear from John's field of view. Then, suddenly, definitely, he exploded backward from the Visor.

Someone had kicked or struck him. There was no other explanation. And yet John saw nothing, only Tucker and how he grabbed for the crack—now five feet away—and started his inevitable plunge to earth. His T-shirt fluttered. As he passed John's ledge, Tucker stared at the last human being on earth. He reached for that fraternity with open hands. John saw his own hands open and reaching. And then Tucker was gone.

A flock of white birds leapt from the void, but by that time John was lying in the sand, face to the wall, clutching the ropes. Later still, as an icy drizzle sprayed the benighted wall, John put on a headlamp. He donned his pack and the extra rack of gear and started back down the wall. It was after all Tucker's choice. Up. Or down. His choice. Just so. Like that, with all language washing clear from his mind, John mechanically followed Tucker's lead. He followed the ropes. He descended.

10

*T*here is a place on
every mountain that climbers must pass through before
their descent is truly complete.
On the bigger mountains, this zone
between earth and summit is distinct and
physical. As a younger man, John once
climbed Aconcagua in Argentina; what
began as a descent through a dead-white landscape
of broken stone that reeked of sulphur fumes had quite
suddenly turned into a green meadow filled with wildflowers. There had been grass to his thighs, bird song, the rich
smell of flowers and animal dung, and a brook. The earth had
softened under his boots, the transition like a dream. Just as
suddenly the meadow had ended. He had awakened from the dream
and the ground had leveled out. A dirt trail bracketed with trash and
rotting potatoes had suddenly led off into the distance where a train
sounded, and he'd found himself on the outskirts of one of those high-
altitude Indian slums with dogs yapping and illiterate barrel-chested men
and doomed children, all the realities he'd left behind. But at least between heaven and earth there had been that meadow. Even on smaller
mountains, even descending from a crag, there is usually a river climbers
cross or a field of blueberries and larks, at least a first sip of water, a moment below the power and the glory, beyond the pain of any injuries or
disappointment or arguing, before renewed responsibilities, a moment
within the moment.

John arrived at Camp Four still walking in this middle zone. It had
taken him nine terrible hours to rope down across the black, stormy face

of Half Dome, mouth open to catch the sweet rain that ran down his cheeks like tears. Had he thought to stop and rest on the wall, he would have died. Lightning would have search-and-destroyed him or the sleet would have glazed him fast against the black-and-white granite. He didn't stop. He didn't think. By the time his foot touched ground, he'd used up all but a few pieces of protection for rappel anchors and the batteries in his headlamp were extinct, leaving him blackness with which to negotiate the steep forest leading down to the Valley floor. With light he might have found the remains of their haul bag somewhere among the trees, maybe even a sleeping bag or parka for warmth. But then he would have risked finding Tucker, and that above all else was unthinkable. He didn't consider the options, didn't regret or thank the dark state in which he touched ground, didn't stop. There was no more use for the ropes, so he simply left them hanging from the first pitch, unclipped himself, and continued fleeing the giant wall.

For the next few hours he ran amok, crazy and yet obedient to the path of least resistance, which was Down. The forest reached out its fingernails and raked his flesh and clothing, but he didn't really feel the insults to his body. Every time a root fouled his stride, he picked himself up. The chili-red headband that kept his long hair out of his face ripped loose on a branch. Part of one sweater arm unraveled like in a cartoon. He should have lost at least one eye to the stabbing tree limbs, but didn't. Luckily his hands were still taped for the climb, so his palms were largely spared. Somehow, without benefit of so much as starlight, he threaded a way down through the complex of cliffs and gullies and brush thickets, and at five in the morning stepped onto the flat floor of the Valley. To this point his escape from Half Dome had for its direction the pull of gravity. Now he let himself be lost on the park trail that led to the paved road winding past campgrounds with well-lit bathrooms and the roar of Yosemite Falls and the Conoco gas station. That he followed the road didn't mean he wasn't lost. Indeed it was the largest proof that he was. He might have kept walking right out of the Valley past El Cap through the vineyards and fields to the ocean, except just then the sun came up and there he halted, stock-still in the middle of Camp Four.

The squall had passed overnight. The ground was damp down here, not flooded like after the serious autumn downpours that swamp tents and drown fires and snakes. People had retired early and were sleeping

172

late. New tents showed everywhere, and only one unfortunate, who had been climbing in south California at Joshua Tree and thereby missed the Gold Rush, was ensconced beneath a plastic-draped picnic table. Through the tent walls you could hear someone snoring, someone turning the pages of a book, someone waking with a moan, and a couple making quiet love. Privacy was an art here, an etiquette built on eyes diverted and ears closed. They might be rock and rollers, dopers, gossipmongers, car thieves, and kamikazes, but they weren't Peeping Toms. A squirrel tap-danced across the metal roof of a van in the parking lot. Here and there, solitary pine cones dropped from high branches. A bluejay floated in on a sunbeam and started exploring around the picnic tables. A minute later three nutcrackers drove the jay away with raucous squawking. A tent door unzipped in the distance, another elsewhere. From one of the ripstop, waterproof nylon caves, a climber crawled upward in wild disarray. His hair was fantastically misshapen from sleep. All he wore was a pair of gray gym trunks and rubber and canvas thongs. The veins on his inner thighs surfaced above the trunks as veins on his stomach and rib cage. He stretched, worked the stiffness out of his back, squatted down at his tent entrance for his toothbrush, and then set off for the bathroom. Five minutes passed. Someone else rose. A van door slid open. The fiery hum of a Bleuet gas stove kicked on: morning tea. It was a while before they found John in their midst.

He was standing there, stunned by the dichotomies. It had been dark and now it was light. The tremendous danger on the wall was now this ordinary dawn. He had fought a storm and the verticality and forest, and here was this amazing calm. Sailors who have been cast ashore in tempests know this daze. Hermann Buhl, the great Austrian alpinist, was like this after his solo of Nanga Parbat. The sum total of John's knowledge just then was that he had survived.

His arms hung limp, clothing shredded, blood everywhere. His scalp had been lacerated by sharp branch tips and his hair was matted with blood and burrs and pine needles. A trickle of blood had forked at the bridge of his nose and run down from his eyes to his sparse black mestizo whiskers. Beneath both eyes, dark circles bruised the sunburn, and his lips looked like something out of a spaghetti Western. As he stood there steaming in the sunlight, a crowd gathered around the deaf, mute, crazed climber. But no one dared to touch him, uncertain what might happen if

173

they did. In whispers and murmurs, people attempted to assemble clues. He was still wearing his climbing shoes, which meant he'd either lost his hike-in tennies or else lacked time to put them on. The pack still on his back looked to be empty, which was odd because surely there'd been gear to carry down from Half Dome. And where was Tucker? John's harness was still tied on, and only immodest rookies parade around with their climbing harnesses on. His hands were still taped. His chalk bag, dangling from his butt loop, was even still open. John looked like he'd stepped straight from the wall directly into Camp Four, and it frightened people more than any novel or movie could have. Something about his state—the smallness of his lapses, their banality—was especially terrible and foreboding. The fact that John wouldn't speak was horrifying.

Kresinski arrived, but he was no bolder than anyone else. John struck everyone still with his stillness and the carelessness of his cuts and blood and torn clothes and his eyes. At last someone thought to get Bullseye.

"Johnny?" said Bullseye when he got there, stepping in closer among the ring of people. "What's wrong? Where's Tuck at?" And then it struck Katie, who was standing near the mouth of the crowd, that Tucker was not coming down. She let out a wail of anguish, and it was that which cut John free from the wall. In that way they laid John down in his tent and found, in his pack, his map of the Visor Wall that traced their route from bottom almost all the way to the top. The one and only blank on his intricate map was that final pitch where Tucker had taken wing and disappeared into the sky.

John came awake later, hungry and sore. His pants and shirt, even his Jockey shorts, were gone, and the tent was hot from the sun. It felt good to lie on his back on the flat ground, listening to the camp's motions and watching motes of dust drift in the rosy light. He wondered whose tent this was, then remembered it was his, he'd bought it right before the big party. It seemed very long ago. He kept his thoughts close and tight and bearable. Over the years, he'd developed a private ritual for depressurizing after a wall climb and reentering the world. It was this that he turned to now. First he needed to wash. A hot shower with Ivory soap. Shave. And in his truck there were a pair of clean blue jeans and a fresh, long-sleeve chamois shirt and clean socks. But his shoes were gone. Gone with the haul bag, he started to panic, gone with . . . but never mind that. Never mind the socks either, he could wear thongs. There were other needs too, mind them, he instructed himself. For one thing it would take lots and lots of water to rehydrate his system. Plain and simple water, no need for vitamins and electrolyte powder now that he was back on the ground. Gradually, at his own pace, he'd get around to a hot meal at the Four Seasons, and without moving he set to imagining that first meal. He would eat slowly. There would be salad with blue cheese and fresh ground pepper. Then he'd have their twelve-ounce steak rare, and a baked potato with sour cream and crumbled bacon. Afterward he might stroll across to the drugstore and pick up a *Time* or one of the San Francisco papers. There were variations on the ritual, but essentially that was it—a shower, shave, and meal. By nightfall his urine might actually be a clear yellow again instead of thick gold. In a couple days he might even shit. Everything else would fall into place. No problem.

John lifted his head. Except for the tape still binding his palms and knuckles, his body was jaybird naked on top of someone else's clean sleeping bag. He was surprised. It looked like someone else's body with all those cuts and bruises and caked dirt and blood. He lifted one arm, and it was so heavy it felt almost tied to the ground. Every muscle was tender. The abrasions and gashes on his hands looked familiar, but the rest was beyond recall. He made a point of not trying to remember. He grunted involuntarily as he sat up. "God," he muttered. There was a big knot on his forehead, some torn muscles on the inside of his right thigh, a cut on one forearm that was still weeping and might want a few stitches. He was a mess. "A fucking mess," he whispered. A tired fucking mess. Maybe it wasn't worth moving quite yet. To the right lay his notebook opened to the Visor map. He closed it shut. Someone had left a pair of white karate pants—Sammy's, no doubt—and a red-and-white-checkered flannel shirt. And a pair of black hightop Keds, Bullseye's college "hoop" shoes. An unopened candy bar poked up from the top of one shoe, and by the door stood a bottle of water and a lukewarm can of Bud. John felt like a flood victim. Bad losses, good neighbors.

He guzzled the water. He pulled the clothes on and unzipped the tent door. Despite every effort not to show his exhaustion and pain, it took a minute for him to climb to his feet. He was sick and tired. Sick and tired of sleeping on the cold, heatless earth like some animal caught out in the open. Sick and tired of worming out of a cocoon and meeting with this three-foot-high ghetto slum of tents and picnic tables. Sick and tired of sticking his fingers and toes and heart and mind to these granite slabs like a leech on pigskin. It was absurd that he couldn't seem to think beyond the reach of his hands, much less the vertical corridors of the Valley. He was sick and tired of Yosemite. Sing your swan song, he silently bitched at himself. Get on. Grumbling and wincing, every joint and muscle balking, he finally managed to straighten up on his stiff knees.

Camp was largely empty. He heard the rattle and tinkling of climbing hardware at another site, someone returning from a day climb. It sounded like goat bells. A guitar was being strummed off in one direction. In the other two boys and a girl were playing Hacky Sack to the sound of Windham Hill—"limp-dick music," Bullseye liked to scorn it. Whoever wasn't off and about was preoccupied. Nobody paid John any attention. It was deliberate, and John knew it. They'd passed the word among themselves—let John be. He was thankful for that and limped over to his table to sit and rest, just for a minute, that's all it would take. His head ached. The rest of him felt like throwing up. He propped his skull against his hands and tried to arrange his next step. Suddenly he knew the post-wall ritual wasn't going to be adequate. He was too hungry to make it to the showers, too fatigued to eat, and too desperate to sleep. When he closed his eyes the Visor was waiting for him. When he opened them, Half Dome was looming in the east. It was hard to breathe. He felt small and lonely. At last he stood up and hobbled over to lower his food sack from a tree pulley. Inside was a bag of roasted peanuts. Back at the table he cracked and shelled and ate peanuts and tried to figure a way out of the brittle present. The sunshine crowded him. Oddly, he remembered Whymper. He discarded the legend as too abstract, but it came back. Every climber can recite the details like a catechism lesson: In the spring of 1865, Edward Whymper conquered the Matterhorn. On the way down, Whymper's team was struck with disaster. Their youngest member slipped and dragged three others off into the abyss. The rope between those unlucky four and Whymper's lucky three miraculously, suspiciously snapped. Europe's most dramatic ascent ended with death and scandal. Instead of knighting the intrepid climber, Queen Victoria considered banning all Englishmen from the sport. The burghers of Zermatt called for an investigation of the tragedy. All eyes turned toward Whymper and that frayed, snapped rope. Now, sitting at the bare picnic table cracking peanut shells, John wondered if this was how Whymper had felt. They were watching him all right, waiting for his story. His answer to the question. Where had Tucker gone? "Fuck you," John muttered at the peanut shells. Hadn't he seen what he'd seen? Tuck arguing with the wind. Losing. Killed. His fingers froze around a peanut. Who would believe Tucker had been killed? Not just that he'd fallen and dropped and died, but that he'd been murdered. By who? And why? You saw it? they'd say. And he'd say no, but I know. And they'd say, how? And he'd say, I just know. And they'd look at him. And why should they believe a wild, sick thing like that? Murder? In their Valley? No way. It would lack the resonance of truth. There'd been rapes and beatings and robbery and even, yes, homicide, in Yosemite, but never among climbers. The Valley as they knew it was a place beyond the world of other people. In this gash of earth fear bought beauty, and beauty was epiphany, a thousand transformations that orbited what was natural and what was human. Like the old Roman poem about metamorphosis—it was no wonder that upon the jutting, serene architecture of El Cap and Half Dome and the Leaning Tower and Sentinel and Mount Watkins and all the other walls, men and women turned into animals and trees and rocks, and that those things in turn took on the aspects of man. No wonder that Tucker had become a bird and soared off. He was gone, maybe forever. That's what they were going to say. Dead, maybe, but not murdered because what did that mean? Now, as the sun shone and animals fed their springtime broods and the Hacky Sack popped back and forth from foot to foot, John brooded at the picnic table that had served him for so many seasons as a writing desk, kitchen counter, and shop table, and suspected that, just so, Whymper too had brooded about the wondrous crossing of man with mountain.

There had been fatalities among the Camp Four tribe before. Not often, but memorably, climbers had returned from their walls and mountains spent and dazed and alone and reeling with visions of their partner's fall, all too ready to equate their own survival as a sort of failure, a fall from grace. Time healed, though. John had seen that. He'd been through it himself after Tony died on Aconcagua. The survivors got what they needed. From Whymper on down, climbers had been dealing with their ghosts. Either they sold their gear off, or else they recomposed a style and attitude toward the rock. Now, all over again, it was his turn. No one was going to bother him for a while. No one was going to visit.

No one would pester him to eat or cry or talk. He'd been closest to the event, and for now it was his to make sense of. John sighed. They would never believe him. He didn't believe himself. This time it was different. No act of God or nature had stolen Tucker. Something indecent had trespassed against the give and take of ascent. Something evil. It made no sense. No, he decided, he was never going to make it over to the showers. All that could wait.

John slept and slept. Camp was quieter than usual. Now and then, when he surfaced from his dreams and lay in the tent, he tried to discern if camp had always been so quiet or if perhaps people were tiptoeing around on his account. As it turned out, the camp was half vacant. On the second twilight, still unshaved, unwashed, bloody, hungry, and thirsty, John struggled out of his tent, more delirious than ever. He felt ill and feverish. His head was throbbing, and all day long, as the sun heated the tent walls, he'd been sweating and mumbling. Whoever the samaritan was kept replacing his empty water bottles with full ones. Small packages of food had begun to appear at his feet, too, but he had little stomach for food. The packages were there throughout the day; then at night, when the bears came out and would rip tents open or push car windows in at the smell of food, the packages would be removed. All this happened while he slept. John noticed, but didn't dwell on the kindness. Some of his cuts, particularly a rope burn along his right thigh, were getting infected. And either his lips and ulcerated fingernails were worsening or else, without the heights to distract him, he was just noticing them more. Individually, his torments were trivial. Taken all together, they were more pain than he ever wanted to feel again.

He hauled himself over to a nearby tree and pissed against the bark. "Son of a bitch," he cussed under his breath. The world became a triangle. There was the tent, the tree, and the picnic table, where he now eased himself down. There was some kind of poison in him, the glands in his armpits and neck were knotty. Somewhere he was going to come out the far end of this, he told himself. The thought made him feel worse yet because here was where he was right now. Up above—and the motion hurt his neck—Jupiter was out, bright and shiny. He looked around. Damn few people around. Where had they all gone off to? Footsteps

178

crunched across the pine needles, and John peered into the dusk. It could have been anyone walking around out there.

"Hey," he called.

The footsteps paused. "Yeah?"

It was not a voice he recognized. Nor did it sound like they knew him. "Where'd everybody go?"

The footsteps shifted. "Gone looking for some climber." Of course, they'd gone after Tuck. The voice was unfamiliar. Probably some climber from out of state.

"When was that?"

"Tuesday, I guess."

"What's today?"

"Thursday."

John groaned. He was getting sicker. He had to lie down.

"You want some help?"

They'd been gone two days. Something wasn't right. It was half a day up, half a day down. "When are they coming back in?"

"Dunno. I guess they can't find him. Somebody said so." The figure stood still in the gloom. "Man, I wonder what two thousand feet puts on a body."

John didn't answer. If he didn't get into the tent and onto his back and soon, he was going to end up flat on the dirt. A sudden chill shook him, and his teeth clicked comically.

"Glad I'm not up there," the shape continued. "Can't imagine being the first guy to find him. Not after all that fucking air time. Not after the animals are done with him."

John remembered what Tucker once said about animals getting him. It put a wild panic in him for a minute. Body evacs were always bad, especially after the birds and insects and predators had exacted their tax. First thing gone was usually the eyes. Those electric green eyes. John clenched his jaw against the chill. "Who told them where to look?"

"I dunno the dude's name. It was his buddy. They said he showed up in camp babbling weird shit about boogeymen." John wondered what else he'd said. More than enough, no doubt. "They said he flipped out 'cause he keeps killing partners."

"Who are you?"

"Who are *you?*"

"You're no climber."

"Fuck no. I came here to score some smoke. You got any?"

"Go away."

"What?"

"Leave me alone. I don't want to talk to you anymore."

"No problem, asshole." Like a nighmare receding, the stranger's footsteps moved off. John pressed on the tabletop with his open palms. So he'd been talking and they knew. But if they knew, then why hadn't they found Tucker? And if they were calling Tucker's killer a boogeyman, then they hadn't found him, either. Nor, probably, had they looked. Looked for what? Footprints on the summit of Half Dome? After that storm, it would be like looking for traces of John's imagination. He'd talked but they hadn't listened, or they'd listened and blamed his words on guilt and fever and illusion. What they were searching for then was proof of their own illusions. Still, Half Dome wasn't so large that a boy's life could completely disappear upon it, regardless of whose reality was dominant. They'd find Tucker, bag him, strap him in a Stokes litter, and carry him down to the floor. Somehow Tucker would speak to them. His death would instruct them. John's horror would redeem them. The Valley's normal rhythm would be restored and they could get on with their climbing.

But they didn't find Tucker.

The following night, hearing the sounds of the evacuation team entering camp, John stayed burrowed in his tent for as long as he could. It was dark, though he could tell by listening that it wasn't very late because the coyotes weren't yipping and screaming and the bears and raccoons hadn't begun roaming among the sites, tipping over loose cans and snuffling at tent walls. There was still some loose acoustic guitar floating in the air and the drone of distant climber talk. When the evac boys came in, you could hear their weariness and excitement and sorrow as they dumped their packs and tripped over fire grates and guy lines and fanned out for their individual sites. Someone was wearing a tape deck, John caught the tinny sounds of country western. He heard several people doff heavy packs on the picnic table thirty feet over in the neighboring site. Headlamps bobbed against his tent wall. Huge silhouettes eclipsed the light. Then someone brought over a big kerosene lantern, and John felt caged in the tent, foolish and cowardly. Instantly he regretted his sloth of the past few days. He was filthy and his hair was greasy and he stank. They were going to wait for him at the table. More and more people were congregating outside, and when he crawled from his tent they were going to see him like this. The longer he stayed in here, the worse his spectacle would be. He had to sit still for a minute because the fever had gutted his strength. Pack straps whipped free, and he heard the metallic jingle of hardware on the tabletop.

"Whoa," a voice admired. "Copper RDs, man. A whole set. Look at all these toys."

"Somebody bring over the rest of his shit?"

"Yeah. It's all here."

"Check how heavy this steel biner is. The old-timers must have been animals to carry these antiques around up there."

Unable to fathom why they had chosen to gather here rather than go to bed, John simply tried to sort out all the voices. He stared woodenly at the monstrous shapes playing against the tent fabric.

"Tuck found that up on Lost Arrow Spire." It was Bullseye's voice. All the animation was gone out of it. "That one's not up for grabs. Maybe his dad and mom'll want it."

"Shit, they're not gonna know. They're sure not gonna care. I mean that old biner's got history in it. It oughta go to somebody who can appreciate it." That was why they were here then. To sort out John's gear and divide up Tucker's. Someone had broken open Tucker's footlocker, and now it was all subject to *ad hoc* disposal. Among Camp Four climbers, this was the way it was done. In that way, Tucker would be absorbed into the tribe. By using his gear in their climbing, Tucker would be climbing, too.

"Like hell," Bullseye snapped.

"All right already," the other voice backpedaled. John heard the heavy steel carabiner plop back onto the pile.

"Maybe we ought to wait," someone suggested.

"Wait for what?"

"I mean they haven't even found him yet. It seems like not very decent to . . ."

John was stunned. They hadn't found Tucker. But that was impossible. There must have been twenty or thirty people up there for the last

181

three days, and Half Dome was no more than half a mile across. If they hadn't found him, where had he gone?

"He cratered, man. He's not gonna use this stuff again. It's spoils."

Then a darker, angrier voice stopped the hubbub. "Where's Coloradas?" it demanded. Kresinki had arrived. "Time to get us some answers."

"Hey, Johnny," someone called at the tent.

John was terrified. Trapped. But he had to face them. He reached for the door zipper and pulled it down. The shapes quit dancing on his tent wall. The silence felt like a deep, deep pit. He hauled himself free of the tent and, with some difficulty because of the infected leg, pushed to his feet. Over at the neighboring site the lantern hung from a tree branch, casting a brilliant white glow and making everyone's face stark and morbid. The table was heaped high with gear, among which John detected the ragged shreds of his and Tuck's old haul bag. Some of the climbers had pieces of equipment or magazines in their hands, examining or arranging it all on the table. The magazines, John noted with a glance, were from Tucker's Silver Surfer comic book collection. Everyone paused to watch John gimp from the tent to his table where Kresinski and Bullseye were sitting with a pot of water on a cooker, waiting for him. Bullseye had evidently already taken his choice of Tucker's effects. He was wearing the big leather jacket that Tucker had found in his cave high above the lake.

Now John understood why no park rangers had visited over the last few days to question him and file a report on the incident: No one had informed the rangers. In typical fashion, Camp Four had decided to take care of one of its own its own way, only this time around the process had gone sour. The idea was to retrieve and honor Tucker, and only then make an accounting to the Park Service. *They,* not the rangers, would bring him out to the world. In the past, such voluntary body evacs had served to show that the climbers took their tragedies seriously. It also emphasized that the walls were their turf. But the search had failed. An ordinary tragedy had turned extraordinary, and the climbers wanted to know what had gone so wrong that they couldn't even track down a body. Trusting John, they'd swarmed off to find Tucker, but hadn't. Now the park cops would get involved. The rangers would trespass on territory that wasn't theirs, and that made the climbers angry. John sensed their hostility. This was no wake. It was an inquisition. No one helped him stand up. No one offered a hand when he limped over to the table. Even Bullseye looked stern and distant.

"Should have done this to start with," Kresinski growled at him. "But Bullseye said cut you slack. Let you sleep. So I did. You were talkin' crazy and Bullseye said let's check it out. Fuck of a lot of good that did us. Hoppin' round through the bush up there. Checkin' treetops. Pickin' up your gear. Now you've slept, Johnny. Now where's Tucker at?" He paused for emphasis. "You ditched him on the wall, didn't you?"

John sat down with his right leg thrust out stiffly. He felt faint, but forced himself to keep his head up. The truth was, he repulsed himself. He'd done nothing wrong, and yet he felt like he must have. This gauntlet, the shame of his filth, the pain of his cuts and fever—he welcomed the punishments. He welcomed Kresinski's questions because John wanted to know what had happened, too, and maybe the blond, blue-eyed son of a bitch could free him from his ignorance and confusion. He wanted nothing more than to confess, for he'd lost Tucker. "I don't even know what I told you," he said.

Kresinski looked over at Bullseye, who was studying the dirt. "Exactly what your buddy said you'd say. Poor old John's out of his head. Cut you slack."

Bullseye broke in. "You said Tucker fell off the Visor. He finished the Visor. And then he"—Bullseye trailed off indecisively—"died."

"Died?" Kresinski fumed. "Shit. You said the Kid got pushed. Got killed. You said somebody killed Tucker."

"That's what I said?" breathed John. He prepared for the onslaught. "Well, that's what happened."

"Somebody pushed the Kid off the Visor," Kresinski reiterated.

"Pushed. Kicked. Threw. I don't know. But Tuck didn't fall." John frowned. "He didn't."

Kresinski looked at him hard, but John couldn't read behind the loathing. Kresinski knew something, it seemed. But maybe that was a bluff. Or a pretension. Ultimately, what did it matter? Everyone was in search of something. Finally Kresinski let go of his eyes. "Ah, come on, man. The little shit barely threw a shadow. Why would anyone go shove him off a mountain?"

"You talk too much," snapped Bullseye. "Just shut up."

183

"Sure. Sure thing. Tell me you believe this crap, I'll shut up."

Bullseye fell silent. There was a curious, defeated resignation on his face. A complicity with his old enemy Kresinski. The two of them had obviously done a lot of talking during the search for Tucker.

"It doesn't make sense to me, either," said John.

Kresinski bent in closer. "That's because you're a goddamn liar." Bullseye seemed angry and embarrassed but didn't interrupt. *Et tu,* John thought sadly. You couldn't blame him, though. Over at the other table, climbers were chattering away, neatly lining up the gear for the final pick-and-choose.

"Doesn't much matter what I say then," said John.

"How come we can't find your little buddy?" Kresinski pressed. "We found every other damn thing down under the wall. The ropes you left. What was left of your haul bag. Your last crap. We even found stuff climbers dropped twenty years ago. But no Tuck."

"It's the truth," Bullseye confirmed.

"I don't know." John was sick at heart. The animals had gotten to the boy. The thought disgusted him, most of all because the thought had always disgusted Tucker.

"But *I* know," said Kresinski. "While everyone else had their noses down rootin' through the trees and bushes, you know where I kept lookin'? Up. At that big mother of a wall. And you know why, don't you? Because you ditched Tucker up there. He's up there on a ledge, and I'm gonna climb your fucking wall and find him. You ditched him just the way you ditched Tony."

John snorted his reply. But he'd expected this, too. John examined Kresinski's face. There was an interior to the man's words and his hate, something that went far beyond personal dislike. John had seen it before, though never this distinctly. As in the past, he pushed away the mystery of Kresinski's hatred. He didn't care. But for all Kresinski's venom, John still wanted to talk about it. Otherwise it would remain a cipher. "I saw Tucker climb all the way to the top," he said. "He went around the summit lip. It was windy and I couldn't hear anything. But I felt him tug on the ropes and untie from them. Then I got ready to go up. He was safe. He was off. One hundred percent done."

"If you couldn't hear anything," asked Bullseye, "how do you know he was finished?"

"Because he took the haul bag. He brought it all the way up and off." No one challenged that proof because it was self-evident. If Tucker had hauled up the haul bag, then he'd been anchored in and secure. "Next thing, the haul bag goes flying by. Next thing, Tucker came flying over the edge. But he caught himself." John could see it all again. He'd been saving the image until now, when someone else could make sense of it for him. He wanted to talk fast, but kept it slow and monotone. "He hung on to the rim and kept edging around up there. And he was talking. Arguing. I couldn't hear a word. But somebody was on top arguing back. And then Tuck started back down the crack, but he was untied and there was no pro, nothing. He tried to down-climb the roof but it was hard 13, hell 14, I don't know."

Kresinski spit. Even dead, Tucker and his magic hands galled him.

"You can't down-climb something that hard," said Bullseye.

"He tried."

"Bull," said Kresinski, but he was really disputing John's estimation of the difficulty. Next to no one in the world could climb 5.13. And 5.14 didn't even exist.

"And no pro," John reminded him, just to twist the knife. Tucker would have enjoyed the bitter expression on Kresinski's face.

"John," said Bullseye with a voice full of sudden revelation. "That's not where he fell, is it, there on the ceiling?"

John saw what Bullseye was getting at, that perhaps Tucker had fallen on the Visor ceiling, gotten injured or killed. And that John had abandoned him just as Kresinski was insisting. John shook his head. "Tuck climbed back up to the top. He was pumped. He was scared."

"The ropes were tied off?" said Bullseye. "Then how come he didn't just grab one and batman up or down?" To batman was to climb the rope hand over hand.

"The ropes came untied," said John.

"What, the knots fell apart?" scoffed Kresinski.

"I keep saying, somebody was up there."

Bullseye was staring at him, judging the improbabilities. "But you didn't see anybody?"

"Didn't see. Didn't hear."

"And Tucker didn't shout down, like, this guy's trying to get me or something?"

"He was scared. And there was that damn wind."

"What wind?" asked Kresinski. "It's been like banana land down here all week."

"There was a storm," said John.

Bullseye kept staring.

"The ground was wet when I got here."

"Maybe," said Bullseye. "Maybe it stormed up higher. At night."

"Maybe not," said Kresinski, then waved the question away. "Screw that. Motive. Try motive. Why Tucker? Why up there? And why let you go? How come you keep surviving and your partners don't?"

John leaned against the table. Those were the questions he'd slept through for three days now, the questions Bullseye and Kresinski were supposed to help him answer. But they hadn't come down with answers.

"I hiked around and went up the stairs to the top, John," Bullseye said. "There wasn't anybody up there."

John raised his head. "You didn't find Tucker's anchor?"

"I looked."

Then he remembered. "But Tucker dropped his rack halfway across the ceiling. When he got to the top he didn't have gear. So there wasn't any anchor to find."

"So what'd he tie off to?"

"A rock? A tree?"

"There's no fucking trees up there," Kresinski said.

"I don't know," said John. "Maybe a rock."

"What about tracks?"

Bullseye shrugged.

"Ah, you're not going to pull that redskin horseshit on us, are you?" groaned Kresinski. "Come on, man. Why would anybody go all the way up there to boot the little fart over?"

"I don't know." Then he had a thought. It was remote, but at least something. "The lake. Maybe it had to do with the lake?"

"Woo! You're reachin', Johnny. We were all at the lake. Why pick on Tucker?"

"Maybe Tucker found something we didn't, I don't know."

"Fuck that," Kresinski exploded, all patience gone. "I think you're a fucking psycho, man." It came out as a terrible hiss. Something rang

186

false, though. He was too angry too suddenly. Even Bullseye detected it and looked over. "Next thing, you're gonna tell us the dead man rose up out of the waters and came looking for . . . what?" Kresinski looked around, saw the jacket on Bullseye. "For his jacket? What, or his airplane?" He hit the table with his open hand. "Psycho garbage. Lies."

"That's real useful," Bullseye said to Kresinski.

Kresinski hit the table again. "What, you buy his line? This thing keeps getting more twisted by the second. First he comes down— alone—looking like a junkie, babbling about how Tucker's gone. Tucker got shoved. We look around and come up empty. Then we find out from the horse's fucking asshole here that he didn't see anything in the first place. And then he tries out Tucker got assassinated."

Bullseye reflected a moment. "He's right, John. Something's off. Pick a smuggler. Put yourself in his shoes. The feds already have his plane, his pilot, his dope. Everything's gone. What's left to get? Much less kill for?"

"Blood?" John tried.

"Goddamn it," swore Kresinski.

"Uh-uh, John, I don't think so. It's too weird that way. Too spooky and screwy."

"I don't know." John lowered his head into his folded arms.

The water was boiling. Catching one sleeve in his hand for a pot holder, Bullseye lifted the pan off the fire and poured it into a big plastic mug. With a twig he stirred in a packet of soup mix. "Here." He pushed the mug against John's arm. "Drink this."

"We've got to do—something," said John.

"Tell the rangers?" said Kresinski. "Go ahead. They'll file that one and you know where. Or the FBI? Maybe Communists did it. Or the ghostbusters. Hell, maybe Bigfoot punted old Tuck off the top."

"Leave it," said Bullseye. He sounded weary and disgusted, all the trust gone from his voice.

"He keeps acting like he's got to figure something out," Kresinski went on. "But it's already all figured out. Tucker crashed somewhere up on the wall. You panicked. You ditched him. Just like with Tony. But at least you told us half the truth about Tony." He paused, furious. "Still moving. Still talking. You son of a bitch. Alive and kicking when you left him up there. But Tucker? All I'm getting are fairy tales. And self-pity. Tell me something, Johnny. How come you're still alive? How come you keep coming back down?" The invitation was as malicious as it was clear. Every five or ten years someone went up high and "slipped." People didn't mourn. To the contrary, the suicides were a point of pride because they were so true to the Jack London formula: Go in flames, not embers. Like Norsemen who cursed the "straw death" of ending in your bed with no teeth and a soft cock.

Suddenly Bullseye did an astonishing thing. He reached across the wood table and hit Kresinski. "Why don't you just shut the hell up," he said. It wasn't much of a blow, more like punching a bull on the shoulder. By clenching his fist speckled with warts and scars and swinging blindly at the King, though, Bullseye reasserted his faith in John.

"You stupid bastard," Kresinski barked in surprise. Over at the other table people stopped and looked. Even from a distance they didn't like to see Kresinski mad, because there was no guarantee his fury wouldn't still be whirling destructively days down the pike. He started around toward Bullseye.

John levered himself to his feet to block Kresinski's advance. They were, all of them, descending. Someone needed to say enough before the whole balance disintegrated and the tribe with it. But even as he got his leg out from under the table and squinted through his headache, the thought wouldn't go away that something about Kresinski was false. Too much talk, too little destruction. Beneath all the gutting, goring harangue about abandoned partners and sanity lost, something was not quite authentic. Maybe later there would be time to put his finger on it. For now just standing up to intercept Kresinski took a hundred percent. On another day, John might have won. Tonight it was child's play for Kresinski to swipe him out of the way. John stumbled. The corner of the table knocked against his infected thigh. John clutched his leg and fell down.

For years Camp Four had been waiting for this battle. Three seconds of nothing and already it was over. Even if they'd known about the infection in John's leg, it wouldn't have mattered. You are where you are in the world, and what they saw was defeat. John had crumpled at a touch and now he lay at their feet. Only Kresinski, because he was the one who touched him, understood that John was debilitated and that

188

another night it could have been different. The victory disappointed him, but still it was victory. From now on, the Apache would be mortal and common in the eyes of Camp Four. His power was gone. For that reason, Kresinski suddenly lost interest in Bullseye. He could now afford just to walk off into the darkness, leaving Bullseye to help John back to his tent. And so he did.

11

*A*nother smaller team went up to scour the base of Half Dome for Tucker's remains. But Kresinski didn't go this time. In another week or two, word had it, he was going up on the Visor Wall for "the final look." By repeating the climb, he meant to find out what had really happened. Thanks to Kresinski and a few other wild imaginations, the grapevine flourished with rumors of a tunnel halfway up the wall into which John might have dropped the body. According to one version, this tunnel shaft sank a thousand feet deep within Half Dome, and Tucker was permanently entombed at the heart of the mountain. Someone countered with a story that Kresinski was really going to climb just to climb, but that he was waiting a week or two or more—his departure date remained fuzzy—so that the wind would have a chance to sweep away Tucker's chalky handprints on the underside of the Visor ceiling. That way, Kresinski could call into question one last time Tucker's magical abilities. He could try his hand at the ceiling, and if it proved beyond his talents, he could claim that the route had never been finished anyway, that no one, *including* Tuck, had broken the back of impossibility. Among the other stories, rumors, and outright lies making the rounds, what could be classified as "middle explanations" had it that Tucker had simply slipped, or that the wind had knocked him overboard, or that he had wandered off into the woods and that John may have been so delirious from thirst and hunger that he'd imagined the whole disaster. Remembering Tucker's nightmares, some people harbored opinions that the boy had freaked out and jumped for no reason at all. It was also suggested that Tucker and John had spent their week camping, not climbing, and that this was all a ruse to test Camp Four's affections and grief, that Tucker was hiding somewhere, spying on his own funeral in the manner of Huckleberry Finn. The obvious rebuttal was that if it were so, the joke was really on Tucker, for all his equipment had been given away. His dictionary now belonged to Katie, his comic book collection had been dispersed among a dozen readers, Bullseye wore his giant leather jacket, and most of the tapes in his library of classical music had been recorded over with U2, Talking Heads, and Johnny Paycheck.

But the most favored rumor was, perhaps out of habit, the most esoteric one. It took John's strange suspicions and festooned them with Katie's insistence that Tucker had told her about seeing the ghost of the smuggler on the night of Camp Four's blowout. While the idea of a huge, bloody ghost seeking vengeance was gory and superstitious, it was far less frightening than the alternative explanation that John had marooned his partner, dead or injured, on the wall. The Valley climbers were fundamentally peaceful folk, and it came naturally to them to give John the benefit of the doubt even if it meant lying to each other with impossible ghost stories no one really believed. For some reason this particular rumor angered Kresinski more than anything else. He would get quieter as the various details were told, until finally it got too much and he'd erupt, cursing their naïveté and paranoia. Why he should get so hot over the absurd ghost story, no one really knew. But one result was that people took to steering clear of Kresinski's campsite and knitting their gossip around other fires. Everyone did his best to pretend the war was over, that the matter was buried and it was the old days again when you could smile and tell jokes while racking up for your day climb. Big-wall season, when the dark nights were short and the weather mild, was right around the corner, and everyone had begun thinking of this or that route and training for another bright, hard-core summer.

Only eleven climbers volunteered to hike up to the base of Half Dome for the second look. At Bullseye's suggestion, three people jogged up the tourist route to the top of Half Dome and snaked out to the edge of the Visor on their bellies and examined the entire face from above with binoculars. Not only had they found no body, they'd found no ledges except for that last one with the white sand, and Tucker definitely wasn't there. Empty-handed, they were back in camp before twilight. Already people were forgetting what Tucker looked like, and the rangers hadn't even been told about his disappearance yet.

On his third morning down, John quit hiding. Hobbling across the road to the pay showers, he cut the filthy hand tape off with a pocket-knife, washed away the sweat, blood, mud, and wall dirt, shaved, and poured a small brown bottle of hydrogen peroxide over his cuts and blisters, astonished at how much the foaming solution burned. Wearing a clean pair of jeans and a brilliant white oxford shirt with the sleeves rolled up, he returned to Camp Four and grabbed his climbing shoes, a pair of green cotton shorts, a last can of tuna, and his notebook with the hand-drawn topo of the Visor inside. He passed through camp to the parking lot. The fact that his truck's engine started right up gave him confidence. Maybe things would start going his way again. He pulled out of the lot and headed west toward the park exits. It was a warm day and he had some decisions to make. If nothing else, maybe he could get some bouldering in up near Tuolumne Meadows. As El Cap soared in his windshield, John couldn't resist pulling over to sightsee and check the obvious lines for climbers. It was still early enough in the morning so that the Nose was highlit beside the Dawn Wall, and west of the prow the Heart, Salathe, Excalibur, the Shield, the Diagonal, and all the other routes hung cool in the shadows. To the right of the Nose, John's eye traced up Mosquito Wall. It was closed and off limits for the next six months so the falcons could breed and nest, and there were no climbers on it. That was a rule the rangers didn't have to enforce. For the local climbers, the animals—the real animals like falcons, not the caricatures like the sugar-stupefied bears—came first in the Valley. In close second came the climbers themselves. And way behind them came everyone else. Any "outside" climber stupid or brash enough to trespass on the nesting grounds would be met at the top by a posse of Valley boys. If they were lucky and pleaded dumb and their ignorance was halfway credible, they only lost their equipment. If they acted righteous, though, as a pair from Santa Cruz once had, they got a beating and their fingers broken—climbing privileges revoked. John and Tucker's risky ascent of Mosquito Wall last Christmas, with all its dangers and off-season suffering, had exemplified the sincerity behind Camp Four's aesthetics. It was the Golden Rule backward: Do as we do, or fuck you, die. John let the truck idle while he squinted up at the Captain. Sometimes climbers blended in with the stone, so he spent an extra minute looking for stationary dots of color that would signify haul bags. But there was no one up on the wall yet. Almost May, and the walls were empty. We got distracted, thought John. The lake had blinded them to their purpose. In that sense, they'd lost far more than they'd gained these past few weeks. Soon, though, people would be back on track. The rock would be teeming with minuscule creatures inching high. How strange, the old thought suddenly hit him. To gamble everything and only end up where you started. Each climber carries a landscape in his mind, a place of very private mountains and seas. For some, Everest or the Eiger Nordwand or the Visor or Tucker's Makalu West Face had to be wrestled with and suffered and touched before they had a place in this landscape. For other people, just driving through the Valley was enough to connect them with their interior mountains. And in the end, the mountains were all inside your mind anyway.

John had begun to let Tucker fade. It was hard to let go. But then again, it was hard to hang on. As with Tony, his last image of Tucker was of a breathing, moving, vital person square in the middle of life. As with Tony, there was no body—yet—to say good-bye to. So it went. One minute they were so present you could smell what they'd eaten for breakfast and touch them and hear their exertion under heavy labor. And the next minute, the other end of the rope was suddenly simply empty. After years of carrying Tony around inside him, John had found a place to leave his memory. By now he could barely remember the shape of Tony's long face. Likewise, Tucker was fresh today, but in six months? In two years?

"Goddamn it, Tuck," John whispered. His heart was heavy. It shouldn't have been like this. He wanted Tucker here beside him so they could pass the binoculars back and forth while they lounged in the meadow dreaming up new routes on El Cap, pointing, wondering, fearing. No more. John clenched his teeth at those two words. No more. He limped up to the cab and worked his right leg in, purposely milking some hurt out of the leg in order to blanket the hurt in his chest. Tucker's equipment had been absorbed into the tribe. His body was nowhere to be found. The boy had been erased. And still his parents didn't know any more than the rangers knew, which was nothing. The thought put John in a spin. Yesterday Katie had asked him to go over to Yosemite Lodge with her and make the phone call to Tucker's parents. It took him a few minutes to say yes, and then once they were there at the bank of pay phones he'd almost bolted for the door in search of air. The operator put them through to Norman, Oklahoma, but as chance had it, all they'd gotten was a woman's voice on a recording machine, and of course they'd immediately hung up. The Valley climbers truly lived in a separate world. If they chose to, Tucker's death could be kept a secret for months, maybe forever. The rest of the world would believe he was deep in a Sierran maw, playing out his teenage destiny, safe with himself. At peace. And he was. All of those things. The only difference was that Tucker couldn't sit in the meadow anymore. He couldn't brush his teeth in the river. He couldn't dumbfound Bullseye with his mispronunciations, and he couldn't stand in stirrups at a belay anchor listening to Beethoven on his Walkman. John was going to miss that. He already did. Badly. He pulled out onto the one-way road and continued along, turning right toward Mantica, and twenty minutes later turning right again on Highway 120 toward Tioga Pass and Tuolumne.

As he tooled east and north, domes started surfacing from the earth like white and gold whales taking air. Their humped backs gleamed with glacier polish and sunlight, and water streaks showed black where erosion had fleshed away the granite and left behind dark feldspar crystals and spurs. John had spent many summers up here high above the Valley's heat and tourists, and the domes spoke to him with an old familiarity. He knew his way around up here, and that was a comfort. On his left stately Pleasure Dome faced Tenaya Lake and faded into Harlequin Dome and The Shark. He passed cracks and smooth face-climbs sporting titles like Get Slick, Aztec Two-Step, Vicious Thing, Shit Hooks, Luke Skywalker, Pencil-Necked Geek, The Whore That Ate Chicago, and Tales From The Crypt. There was still a good amount of snow up here. The snowplows had given up just short of the sweeping flanks of The Lamb, and their circular turnaround had become a convenient parking lot for weekend cross-country skiers. The plows would begin chewing away at the snow in a couple of weeks, opening the highway pass for summer tourists. Today the cul-de-sac was empty. Half a dozen wispy, melting ski tracks led off into the woods in different directions. John parked. Ahead stood Daff Dome with its 5.11a Bearded Clam, and to the left jutted the glossy tit of Doda Dome. He enjoyed it here in the Meadows, but though he was alone this morning, the terrain felt overpopulated, too public. He suddenly felt impatient to get where he was going.

Grabbing his rucksack, he mounted the snowbank and followed a hard-packed ski track on foot. The snow was firm but melting. From the looks of it, touring season was finished. The ski track was at least two weeks old, and in less than a quarter mile the snow was interrupted by a vast disk of green field. The snow picked up at the far edge of the field, then petered out altogether where the tree line stopped and the sun could attack the snow without interference. He cut between Hammer Dome with its Low Budget, Barbary Coast, and Motor Home for Midgets, and North Whizz Dome with its classic Handbook. By the second mile, John's leg had loosened up. The slope began to decline, though gently enough not to hurt his knee. He unbuttoned his shirt, then took it off and tied it around his waist. The heat worked like a massage on the big muscles along his spine, unknotting some of the nightmare. The bird song was thinner up here because the birds had only begun their annual settlement. John paused to search out animal sign and found some mouse prints, a rabbit run, and, under a tree, the fresh bones and scattered feathers of an owl kill. He tried jogging and only ended up winded and limping. Ten years ago, he'd have felt fresh from the morning after a climb like the Visor Wall. His body was slowing down, though. "Recovery time" had crept into his vocabulary. Never blatantly, but with a keen eye just the same, he'd taken to noting that Kresinski didn't go storming up new routes the day after coming down from a wall anymore, either. Bullseye, himself losing hair and flexibility, cattily insisted that Kresinski was getting a lease on life with injections of celestone-40 for the arthritis and tendonitis they each suffered. But that was no lease on life. It was the cry of an atheist. Forget it, Kreski, John thought. We're citizens. Not gods.

Still heading north, he skirted the circular base of a small nameless dome, pulled up through a notch, and faced a thick patch of budding oak saplings. The saplings were so thickly spaced, and a block of stone behind them so obviously a dead end, that anyone else would have retreated back down the notch and continued on around the dome in search of passage. But John knew what lay beyond the barrier of foliage and granite. He pushed into the thicket and squeezed behind the stone block. It was a tight fit between the stone and the dome, but the sound of falling water drew him on, and a moment later he was on the inside of a tiny, separate cove. Many of the Valley climbers had private tree boles or caves or cracks in the rock, bank vaults and safe-deposit boxes essentially, in which they hid their "possibles." What money and drugs remained from the lake adventure, for instance, were salted away in these small, secret places. But only John had an entire south-facing half acre with a twelve-foot waterfall to himself. The cove was special for more than its privacy and size and sunlight, however. Turning around, John faced the wall and felt the breath catch in his lungs. For he was at the bottom of an ancient sea.

It was always like this when he entered. The way he had the first time here, he reached out and gently pinched the foot-long spine of a fossil trilobite. It was perfectly intact, practically alive on the rock, with its broad mushroom head and the ribs right down to the spiky tail polished to a dull green gleam. Stretching on for another twenty yards, the wall blossomed with old fossil life, whole remains mingling with bits and pieces, some tipped, some flat, some actually swimming headfirst into the eroding elements. Somehow this marvelously encrusted limestone slab had surfaced in an area so hidden that no one, not even the Ahwaneechee so far as John could tell, had ever found it. He'd never seen such a mass of creatures in one place, much less tilted up on a vertical surface. Here was how it looked on the floor of the ocean millions of years ago. A necklace of tiny pods, petrified seaweed leaves, hung beside the vertebrae of more trilobites and brachiopod shells and bony creatures. John walked along the wall.

At the end of twenty footsteps the limestone dove back into the granite capstone, and John stood by the waterfall. Its thin tube of water poured musically into a granite bowl, which then emptied into the earth through a hole. By July the higher snow would have vanished. The cove would be silent and dry. John tipped his head back and drank some of the cold water. He took his pants off and washed the still-weeping cut on his right thigh. Then he found a spot in the sun and scooted his back against a boulder opposite the wall, buck naked, to enjoy the frieze of life-forms that had paused for eons. To think. Over the years he'd studied the walls so lovingly that some of the fossils seemed like old friends. There was a lot of comfort here, in part because it was his, in part because God had made this place so calm. Here death was a lie. Here you could live forever. It made him feel a little decadent, keeping the cove to himself, not unlike hoarding artworks. But then again, remembering that his father had showed him how to look for fossils, it felt like the end of a long hunt. Besides, he'd never exploited the fossils, never broken any away for gifts. Just once, he'd climbed on the limestone fossils. Ropeless, shoeless, savoring the fragility with his bare toes and fingers, he'd got high enough to hurt himself when his holds turned to limestone powder and he fell to the ground, spraining one wrist. Nowadays he respected the wall for what it was, a window on time, and never climbed on it. Here he could feel small but not lost. Tony's face had lodged in among the swimming, teeming forms and quit pursuing him in his sleep. John lay back and closed his eyes, inviting in whatever thoughts wanted to come. Soon he fell into a deep sleep.

Hours later, a woman's voice startled him awake.

"My God," it barked. John jerked up from the slab, groping for his pants, groggy and alarmed by the discovery. It was Liz. She was shocked not by his nudity, but by the wall of remarkable fossils.

"Liz!" he said. It had been two, almost three weeks since he'd last seen her. Everything had happened in between. Almost everything had been lost to him, including her. She was taller than he remembered, and also heavier, her breasts bigger, her legs thicker, butt wider. Under both eyes there were dark cricles, and her nose was red from crying. She looked miserable.

He'd never even mentioned this place to her, it was to have been a surprise someday. Right away John knew that she'd followed his tracks. It would have been easy. Over the winter he'd taught her some of his tricks, plus she had a few of her own from park work. One morning they'd played a tracking game in the woods and snow. But that was then, and how had she found his truck to start with? No one knew where he'd gone. He'd thought no one knew he'd even left. Not much happened in Camp Four that someone didn't see, though. Anyone seeing him leave with a pair of climbing shoes and gym trunks would have known he'd be back by nightfall, and that limited the range of his journey. And there were precious few roads in the park. If he wasn't up one dead end, he'd be up another. It was good to see her. She'd gone to a lot of trouble to find him, and that made him feel good. Maybe they could put things behind them. He pulled his pants on and buttoned up the fly.

"I missed you," he said. It seemed like a good beginning. One of them had to say it. He even opened his arms, further exposing his gladness. But she was mad.

"Who gave you the right?" she stammered, unable to keep her eyes off the wall. At first he thought she was talking about his hoarding the fossils.

"It was going to be a surprise."

"What? Are you crazy?" Her anger stung him. "A surprise?"

Then he realized. "Liz, wait—"

"That was Tucker. *Tucker*."

Someone had told her then. Katie? Bullseye? What did it matter?

"Who gave you that right?" The shock was fresh, that was easy to read. She was wild. Heartbroken. At least he'd had the whole length of the Visor on which to exhaust his confusion and fury.

"I know."

"You know what?" she shouted.

He had so much to say, and he wanted to keep it so simple. No words came to him.

"Goddamn you, John. He was mine, too." She stabbed her fingertips to her chest. "I loved him."

"I know."

With her hollowed-out eyes and red nose she was ugly, which amazed John because he'd never imagined her ugly. It went beyond plain grief. She was in ruins. Too much food, no sunlight, no company. She looked like a prisoner. "You didn't even tell me," she repeated.

"I didn't think."

"No. You were punishing me. Well, it worked, John. You hurt me."

"It wasn't that."

"You know who told me? Little Katie. She said you haven't even told his parents. And I know you haven't told the office."

He had no answer.

"People aren't furniture. They aren't things. You can't lose one and not tell anybody."

"Liz." He bit the inside of his lip, but it didn't work. "He's gone."

He didn't say it like information. It was a plea. A question. How could he be gone?

"You had no right," she said more softly.

"He's gone," John repeated. It was that simple. Suddenly he wasn't so sure Tucker could ever be let go of any more than he could be found again. Tears ran down his sunburned cheeks onto his chest. They trickled onto his belly. He kept his head up for a minute so that she could see his sorrow and believe in him again. Then, realizing that he was using Tucker's death to try to unlock her, he turned his face to one side.

"She came to my cabin. Did you know it was Katie who took care of you when everyone else went up to look for him? Because that's what Tucker would have done. She slept by your tent and listened to you at night. She brought you water."

"Katie? I thought maybe it was you."

"I didn't even know."

"She could have told you sooner."

Liz shook her head no, shielding Katie from blame. "This morning she came to my cabin because you drove off with your climbing shoes. But no rope. She said John's gone off to jump. Could I help? Because she couldn't anymore."

"I wouldn't do that."

"I told Katie, yes, I'll go find John," she continued. "Because John's not a strong man."

"What?"

"You're weak. You're selfish. You wouldn't even come tell me Tucker died."

John traced the unhappiness written on her face. It was like graffiti, the hollows and bloodshot eyes and greasy hair. Something more had happened, and he hadn't been there for her. Now she was striking back on her own terms. She'd found him hiding. Cowering, he told himself, no different from cowering in his tent and cowering in his silence. She meant to be insulting, but not shrill or poisonous. Angry but not hateful. That wasn't Liz. It was the sorrow and . . . whatever else had gone wrong. So he didn't say anything to hit back.

"In camp I saw Tucker's things . . . all over the place." She stopped, upset. "Vultures. There's nothing left of the poor boy."

"It works that way," said John.

200

"It works that way because that's how you live it," she bluntly returned. Something was shouting to John between her words, a collapse in her dreams, a surrender, or maybe just heartache. It was all shout, no enunciation. She was bitter, that's all John could say for sure. He waited a moment so they could hear the waterfall.

Then he asked, "What happened, Liz?"

She chose to play it dumb. "What happened? I drove up the Glacier Point road and down to Cascade Creek and to Tamarack Flat. I went all over looking for your truck. And here you are."

"Liz. What happened?"

"I told headquarters."

"Told them what?"

"Tucker's gone."

That wasn't what he meant. By being literal she was playing dumb. She was dodging him. He was afraid, with that, that Liz was closed to him forever. "Just please tell me what happened," he tried again.

Liz glared at him.

"Please."

"You really want to know? They shit-canned me."

"I know," said John.

She looked at him.

"Tucker told me."

"Did he tell you I'm going to jail? While I was sitting there in the office, they arrested me."

"No."

"Conspiracy. Racketeering. Aiding and abetting in the sale of controlled substances. You want me to go on?"

"They can't do that."

"No? There's going to be a grand jury. Until then, it's 'desirable' for me to continue residing in the ranger compound. In the same cabin. I'm free on bail, John. Two hundred thousand dollars. My parents put up the ranch as a guarantee. They're loving it."

"I didn't know."

"Don't you read newspapers?"

"I'm not your enemy, Liz."

"Yeah," she snorted.

It was on his tongue to say, I would have helped, but it was him

201

who'd harmed. He *was* the enemy. Because that's the way he'd lived it. Sorry wasn't even a Band-Aid this time around.

"Besides," she confessed, "I did come looking. But you were gone. You were already up on Half Dome." John sighed. No wonder she looked like shit. They both looked like shit. They'd done a whole lot of fucking up their lives in the last few weeks.

"What did they say about Tuck?"

"The rangers? They said, pretty early to be breaking out the body bags, isn't it? They sent someone over to Camp Four to take statements and find out what the hell's going on. Where do you guys get off, not telling anybody? All you get is more scum on your name. Drug freaks. Bums. Thieves. Liars."

"Liz," he stopped her. "Tucker didn't fall. He fell, but he didn't slip." John said it impetuously, just to sidetrack her. In fact, he wasn't sure he believed his own story anymore.

"Yeah." Her voice was flat. "Katie told me."

"Somebody was up there with him," said John.

"I also heard you pushed him," she said.

"Katie said that?"

"Katie said everything. We talked for a couple hours. We had our cry. Blew our noses. Now I know what Katie knows. A whole bunch of not much."

"What if I'm right?"

Liz shrugged. "Katie believes you."

"You don't."

"Nope."

He blinked. His headache was returning.

"You think this is some horror movie? Nasty psychos with steel hooks? It's not that easy."

John blinked again. She was going to dice him into pieces with her coldness and cynicism and walk away. She was going to abandon him. There was justice in that, and yet he felt wronged. "You came all this way to call me a liar?"

She paused. "No. The truth is I came to save you."

"Save me from what?"

"Your own revenge."

"What?" Then he saw the thrust. They were back to suicide.

"Nobody likes empty spaces," she said.

"You sound like Bullseye. A whole lot of hot air."

"I've got empty spaces, too," she went on. "But yours are bigger. And worse. Maybe it's all right for you to see it all as murder."

"Hey. Thanks." At last she'd made him mad. He shook his head in disgust. They'd reached the ultimate impasse, pity.

"No," she murmured. "That's not what I came to say. I didn't come to say anything, John."

"Someone pushed him."

Liz hesitated. "It's done, John. They'll find him now. They'll bring him down and we can say good-bye."

"Too late. The animals took him off. You know what Tuck said once? Don't let the animals get me. Well, they got him." He was losing control again. There was flat ground under his feet, and here the vertigo was, killing him.

Liz stepped closer, none too confident that John wouldn't push her away, nor certain either that she even wanted to approach. But she did anyway, and John watched. He watched himself watch. He couldn't move. "Don't worry, they'll find him."

Before she got any closer he confessed. "I ditched him, Liz. You don't know."

So he was going to push her away. Liz stopped.

"He was sitting there. Just gotta rest, he said. But then he wouldn't stand up. And the last thing he said was fuck yeah, John. That's it. And then I had to go or I'd still be there."

It took a minute, but then she recognized the bones of the Andes disaster. "You're not talking about Tucker," she said.

"Forget it," he said.

"You," said Liz. "You forget."

He drew a breath.

"Forget Tony. Forget Tuck."

He quit pushing her away. His arms just hung there.

"Bury them," she said.

"I can't."

"You can."

"Do you know how much I hate them?" he asked.

She frowned.

"I was sick. I was dying. Just like him." Sometimes he could see it so vividly. "Torn to shit by the mountain. And the storm, it was like a Veg-o-Matic, ripping us down. We were getting shredded." Immense, beautiful avalanches had blossomed on either side of their ridge. Until the sun disappeared you could even see rainbows in the hovering avalanche powder. "There was no hope. And he knew it. There was no reason for him to say fuck yeah, John. What's that mean, fuck yeah, John? That's *my* name. John." If he stared at the fossils hard enough, Tony's face appeared sometimes, lips working over and over at John's name. Now there were two of them to answer to. He'd begun hearing Tucker call to him on the long swim down.

"John," said Liz.

He was desperate.

"I forgive you, John," she said.

"You can't."

"But I do."

She took the chance and collected him against her chest. There was a moment of pushing away, but she held on. In the end she was right. He was not a strong man. Holding his scratched, brown body against hers, Liz wondered if she had any love left for him, but that wasn't the point right now. She had forgiven him. That was paramount. Having said it, now she had to find ways to be true to it.

When they ended up making love beneath that strange wall of fossils, Liz felt little passion. Neither of them climaxed, which embarrassed them both because impotence seemed like a bad way to start things all over again, if that's what this really was. Instead of trying the sex with more energy, they fell asleep cushioned against one another. In that way, each wordlessly hoped, when they woke up the bad times could seem like a dream.

As it turned out, Liz had packed in gear and supplies for an overnight. The sleeping bag and food and gas stove had nothing to do with spontaneity, even less to do with expectation. She hadn't really expected to find John. But even cashiered and disgraced, she was a professional, and no professional would enter the backcountry on a search without the basics. Unable to sleep for long, she squeezed out through the entranceway and then manhandled her pack back through. John woke up, and they shared some food and kept their talk small while the horizon burned out and dusk fell. The hike out would be simple and flat, unimpeded by trees or streams, and they could be back on the valley floor before midnight. All the same, seeing her sleeping bag, John asked Liz to stay the night. "There's some sort of mineral in the wall," he said. "It makes the fossils glow in the dark."

"We could," she answered dubiously.

"I want to sleep with you is what I'm saying." Because of Kresinski, Liz had always refused to stay overnight with John in Camp Four: "Too incestuous," she'd say. And now, because of her trouble with the law, John guessed Liz wouldn't want him at her cabin.

"Are you cold?" They had dressed again, and she was nestled under his arm.

"Keep me warm is all."

John had never built a fire in the cove, and he didn't offer to now. For one thing you could never be sure who might see the glow and try to investigate. Also, he was afraid the smoke might blacken the olive-color limestone and mute its fluorescence.

"You know," he said, "I have some money."

To his surprise, Liz smiled in the failing light. "I'll bet you do."

"A lot of money." Her good humor warmed him. "And none of it's spent."

"And you want me to run away with you."

John decided she wasn't being sarcastic. "Yeah. I do."

"Leave the Valley?"

"We already talked about it."

"I know."

"I'm not part of it anymore. You aren't, either."

"Amen. But what about my grand jury?"

"Screw it."

"Jump bail?"

"Screw it."

"You have enough money to buy my parents a new ranch?"

He stopped. Even turning it into a game had hidden snags. His spirits sank. "I'm just saying—"

"What?"

"Are we that stuck, Liz?"

"I am."

"But afterward, we can go, Liz."

"Afterward? You can see the future?"

"It's all bullshit. They're not going to do anything to you. You didn't do anything."

"You're going to make a great character witness, John. Camp Four Bum. Drug pirate." She was trying to keep it light. Trying to dodge his intent.

John plowed ahead. "I want you to go with me. Now or later. Whenever you say."

"That's a switch," Liz said. Her voice was guardedly wooden. To John's ear, she sounded the way he felt about Tucker. As if he were tip-toeing beneath a levee that was about to break.

"Not really. It just took a little time, you know."

"John," she sighed. "I don't know if I can do that with you any-more."

He tried misunderstanding her. "Anywhere you want," he said.

"It might be you and I've gone everywhere we need to. Maybe it's just too late anymore."

"No," he reacted. But of course he would react. It was a climber's mind-set. Wherever there was a challenge, there was a fight. Wherever there was a mountain, there was assault. Once upon a time, Liz had found that contrariness charming. Now it was tiresome. John sensed her annoyance and tried to back away.

"What I mean is, all of a sudden, lately, everything seems too late," he said. "And I just don't want it to be too late for you and me."

"Uh-huh," she said. Even the "you and me" annoyed her.

I'm losing her, thought John. But maybe it had been too late to start with. With distaste, he suddenly saw in himself his father's pattern. Drift. See the sights. Beat the bitch, there was always some bitch: your latest pussy, the rig chief, the worn-out clutch, the road, the sun, the wind. And there was always some way to beat it. Cuss it. Hit it. Quit. Move on. It was a curse, and John could see a future in which there was no way free of it. There seemed not a single thing to say that would change things.

The night got chillier. Liz's Thermolite pad and sleeping bag were designed for one person, so they kept their clothes on and clung together for warmth. Her head pillowed on John's shoulder, Liz dropped into a deep, still sleep that suggested need. She needed sleep. And she needs me, John decided. Her breath was warm and smelled a little of garlic from the supper cheese. For John, there wasn't much sleep. The night was like a big-wall night. Through the first half, he catnapped. Around midnight, though, the stars and the glowing fossil wall and the silence kept him awake. The water's source froze up and the waterfall quit splashing into its granite bowl. High above, the constellations moved. He felt a rock poking his ribs through the pad, but shifting would have meant waking Liz, so the ribs stayed on the rock. He breathed her smells gratefully and waited for the eastern sky to darken into the cobalt that precedes dawn. The sunlight would turn Liz's hair into a golden nest. He remembered other mornings, lying in the cabin or out in a tent or on the ground, watching the way her hair caught the light while she went on sleeping, oblivious to how central she was to the sun's purpose. John waited and thought a few thoughts, drifting halfway between yesterday and tomorrow.

12

*I*t might have been another night as Bullseye knelt on the edge of the abyss with his hands and arms wired together behind his back, slightly stoned and yet sharp as a laser. But it wasn't. It was the same sky twisting overhead, the same star groups, the same rising moon that elsewhere was lighting up Liz's golden hair in John's secret cove. He found Sagittarius, his birth sign, and connected the dots and shot the arrow. Cross-valley, Sentinel gleamed like a vast slick cock. The trees were like candles guttering silver in the moonlight. And beneath his knees spread the floor of a small amphitheater, but he couldn't see it, didn't look. Forever hung in that inky pool. It was only a hundred feet or so of free-fall, but that was about eighty feet more than he wanted to go. *Nada* was *nada*. It was that kind of a night, Manichaean with lots of dark, but lots of light, too. He even saw a white owl leap from its roost, utterly transcendent, and wing off into the nether hunting critters. Taxman's comin', thought Bullseye. Always got to pay them taxes. His mind was racing. Logically he knew that a rock dropped from this cliff would strike ground in, what, about five seconds. But that was the trouble with logic. Because he also knew that if you dropped Bullseye into the pit, he'd never land. No problem, though. He wasn't going to take off in the first place. He had a plan.

His face was pulpy from the beating. The beating, Bullseye had decided by now, was for shock value. The stranger had simply yanked him out of z-land and administered his fists without a word. Too bad Ernie was off courting coyote bitches or taking rabbit or just checking it out, wherever he was, because this bastard would have gone down in a pile of screaming meat. You got the wrong guy, Bullseye had meant to shout in the first few minutes. But the man had already thought of that with a blow to his belly, which kept Bullseye occupied searching for air. Besides, there wasn't any right guy for middle-of-the-night gestapo crap like this. It was like the man had wandered in from a Nicaragua death squad or something. And yet there was nothing sadistic about those big methodical knuckles. They did their job, no more or less. It took probably three minutes to flatten his nose and seriously scare him. He'd been allowed to vomit, then his arms got pulled behind him and he felt the wire whipping tight around his wrists. Right away his hands went dead. The man knew exactly what he was doing as he bound higher up Bullseye's arms. With a final tug, he got Bullseye's elbows to touch and wrapped them tight that way, an impossible position that created impossible pain. Bullseye heard his sternum pop and he wanted to bellow his hurt, but that was the whole idea of getting trussed this way, shallow breathing, minimal protest. A shorter strand of wire bound around his neck formed a leash that got wired to the van's door handle. The man had actually patted him on the shoulder, like relax, this'll only take a minute. It took a bit longer than that, though not much.

First he ransacked the van, throwing books and gear and his spider collection and some potted cacti around. The damage could have been worse, but the man appeared to be searching for something fairly large, and Bullseye had figured, screw it. Once the son of a bitch realized his mistake, he'd untie him and Bullseye could put his house back in order and let his face heal up. No real harm done. No teeth broken. And the nose had never been much to look at in the first place. He wouldn't even report the incident to the rangers. Strange, violent things happened when outsiders came into the Valley. Sometimes you got in their way was all. Mostly they just disappeared like evil genies back to their nether lands and you never saw them again. Living alone out in the woods carried certain vulnerabilities. As Bullseye stood in his Fruit of the Looms next to his van tied with baling wire smelling Ernie's musky piss on the bumper, he actually wondered why something like this hadn't happened before.

In a word, he was pacific. His water was calm, no tempest in sight.

Once or twice, he let himself wonder where the hell his dog had hied off to, and God, the weeping and gnashing of teeth when this motherfucker met the bloody wrath of a kick-ass halfbreed. But, seeing as how Ernie was nowhere on the horizon and his only alternative was to choke in the wire leash, Bullseye kept it sweet and cool. His various efforts to see his assailant's face were in vain, for one eye was puffed shut, and the darkness among all his trees was profound. All he could say for sure was that the man had the strength of—he paused—a garage mechanic? A sumo wrestler? A robot? The residual THC of his earlier pot helped a bit, but mainly he kept his anger down by keeping his intellectual composure up. There were, for instance, the five journalistic W's that needed answering: who, what, why, where, when. None of it was coming together, though. Was this one of the duped bikers from his past? Some L.A. chemical freak? A highway psycho? Strange thing was, the man acted more like a cop than a stalker, certain of himself, unfrenzied, every motion a study in economy. But what had he done that everyone else hadn't? And say this *was* a cop. What kind? And why alone? And what was he looking for? DEA? One of those FBI dudes he'd harangued at the blowout? But even at the height of his revolutionary fever in the ripe hot days of Vietnam and Chicago, Bullseye wouldn't have dreamed up a lone agent working this far beyond the pale. Weirder things had happened, he reckoned, and just wished it could be over soon. At last the man backed through the van's sliding door. Stabbing his flashlight beam here and there around the clearing, he started to circle the van to where Bullseye waited.

Suddenly, his light picked up Bullseye's food bag hanging like a giant blue plum in the treetops, and the man stopped cold. The way he looked from the bag to Bullseye and back up, you could tell he was thinking bingo. He lowered the bag and eagerly yanked open the drawstring on top and jammed his light inside. From where he stood, all Bullseye could see was a yard-wide set of shoulders slumped in disappointment, which was enough. Whatever the man thought was in there wasn't. Perch on it, Bullseye grinned with deep satisfaction. Now it was over. The bastard would leave. Fuck you, thought Bullseye, and started to plot how he'd cut the man off in the woods and hamstring him with his Swiss army knife or call a strike in with his dog or sound a hue and cry in Camp Four, not that they'd hear. But, still being wired to the van, Bullseye kept his cards close to the vest. The sucker was crazy, but even a crazy man's not going to let a hornet loose. And that's what Bullseye figured he was: a mad fucking hornet. So Bullseye was surprised when the man came over and unwired the leash from the door handle. He was even more surprised when, incredibly, the man pushed the van shell over on its side. It was like being at the mercy of a bad drug.

"What the fuck do you want?" Bullseye finally dared to ask.

"That's not even close to good enough," the man replied.

"Serious, man. I don't know what you want."

The dark shape sighed. "That's your elective," he said. "Let's go." He started to lead Bullseye off into the woods by the wire leash.

"Tell me what it is," Bullseye pleaded. "I don't know."

"Here's what it is, Mr. Broomis." The use of his real name seemed as calculated as the rise-'n'-shine beating. Again Bullseye tried to see his assailant's face, and again glimpsed only a huge dark figure in the night, like a black hole in the blackness. "All you need to know is that you're doing this to yourself. I'm not really against you."

The thought hit Bullseye harder than a fist. "Can I think a minute?" he begged. He needed to slow down, sort through, orient. It was a mistake. But the man knew his name. There had to be options. Compromise. Already Bullseye was prepared to capitulate on almost any terms, if only he could grasp the terms. A minute and he could find his bearings and communicate. He could network with the motherfucker. All he needed was a minute.

"No," the man said and yanked on the wire around his neck. Stage by rapid stage, Bullseye learned how quickly the human spirit shuns chaos. He was at the man's mercy, and yet there was no hint of mercy in this man. This was Bullseye's Valley, and yet this stranger knew the path better than he did. The assault made no sense, and yet Bullseye had always believed that ignorance was your own responsibility.

He kept begging for a minute, just a minute, first to think, finally just to breathe. And he kept not getting it. By the time they had climbed the hillside stretching high above Bullseye's hole in the forest and threaded between piles of old, rotting slash left over from a fire ignited by lightning in 1958, by the time Bullseye was led to the edge of this circular cliff and had knelt down on the cold earth to observe the quicksilver trees and the quicksilver owl, he knew his captor was exactly right, that ignorance is a form of knowledge, too. There are no accidents. There is no coincidence. The goofy fog he'd spent a lifetime weaving for himself . . . lifted. He suddenly understood that John had warned them all, but they'd made themselves deaf. They'd made themselves blind with doubt, mute with gossip. Tucker hadn't slipped, because Tucker wouldn't have. Because there are no accidents. There is will. Bullseye stared off over the trees, marveling at how much we pretend to ourselves not to see. Now he realized that from his very first perception, he'd known this giant was Tucker's killer. The other connections escaped him, the whys and now-whats, but at least he was clear now. He was in tremendous pain and fear. But at least the confusion was gone. As it always does, if only to affect the next cause, the chaos took on a purpose. That was the foothold he needed. He began crafting a plan.

"Mr. Broomis?" The man was pacing behind him, but his voice was patient.

"Not much scares me," said Bullseye. "But you got me scared. Honest-to-fucking-God scared." That empty black pit terrified him. He was nose to nose with nothing. It was sniffing at his balls, teeth bared.

The footsteps padded on the gravel.

"Where'd you get my name?" asked Bullseye, trying to feather in. If only he could get a dialogue going.

"A whore."

"A whore?" Then he remembered the party, the three whores. "You killed Tucker, didn't you?"

"The boy." He said it like an old memory.

"But why?"

The man snorted.

"The lake?"

"Good."

Bullseye felt the nausea crawling up again and fought it. "Well, you fucked up," he said. "Tucker was the wrong guy."

"I know."

"I'm the wrong guy, too."

"Maybe. But you've got the college education. I'm counting on that to help us out here."

"What happened to Tuck?"

For an answer, the dark silhouette darted in close and grabbed Bullseye by the scruff of the jacket. Arms pinned behind by the wire, Bullseye felt his upper body dip forward over the abyss. The stranger held him there and shook him like a doll. "I'm not trading with you, asshole," he snarled.

"Please," whispered Bullseye. "Please. Please." But even as he begged and pissed in his pants, part of him was sorting out the pain and fear and terror. What's going on is what's going on, he instructed himself. The wire hurts you. The pit scares you. In that way part of him still held control. That was the part of him that was still crafting the plan.

"Please," he hissed. His head and torso jerked up from the blackness, and once again he was kneeling square on the hard ground. The fresh adrenaline nailed him hard. He was going to puke unless he somehow shunted the adrenaline into what it was meant for, fight or flight, and fight was out.

"You dumb cocksucker," he tried to roar. It came out as three sad small coughs of noise. But the man heard. He laughed. It was a single deep bark filled with approval of Bullseye's defiance. It was a bullfighter's laugh, the kind Hemingway used to draw for his hammerheaded, tiger-by-the-tail machos. And Bullseye despised Hemingway. With a sudden twist of his head, he chanced that the moonlight would reveal more than just a silhouette. It did this time. What he saw froze him.

It was the smuggler. The ghost. Standing up, he was even taller than when they'd dragged him from the lake, beefier, too, with a hooded sweatshirt under a down vest. His shoulders and chest and face were enormous, like statuary that is a scale larger than life. For a moment Bullseye relinquished his carefully hoarded control to sheer confusion. There was an explanation, but he had none. The smuggler's grin faded under his mustache. Back to business.

"You must have known I'd be coming," the man said.

Still shocked, Bullseye stared. You're right, he was thinking. I knew you'd be coming. It was one of those backward-looking foresights that hit him as unnaturally profound. For how many years had he been waiting for the voice of the night? And here it was, the reckoning. The ice that moved quicker than the Iceman could climb it. "Guess so," he murmured. The plan. Where was his plan? Where were his footholds?

"You go out into the world, Mr. Broomis," the smuggler said. "And pretty soon you learn that innocence is the bottom line. The virgins don't want to be virgin. The boys want to be men. And the ones that are all growed up like you and me, we waste time dreaming about how it would be to be innocent all over again. There's second chances on some things. But not on that. So let's not fuck around with innocence, okay? You were there."

"Okay."

"I want my cargo."

"It's gone. It's all gone."

"You know it's not, friend."

"Yes it is. It's all sold. The money's all spent."

For a minute the smuggler sucked his teeth beneath the black mustache. Finally he said, "I've talked to your buyers."

Bullseye wondered if he'd talked to them the way they were talking now, close to death. "So?"

The smuggler tsk'ed. "You and your wild bunch cashed in approximately one and a half tons of marijuana worth between one and one point five million dollars."

"People just spent it all," said Bullseye. "It's gone."

"Shit, you boys earned it. Matter of fact, I salute you. The one and only way to get that stuff out was the way you did, on your backs. And you did it with style."

Bullseye didn't answer.

"Oh, I heard the stories. I heard about the chain saw and the axes. I heard about Mr. Kresinski's dive to locate the buried treasure. I heard about it all."

"Yeah."

"But that was only half the shipment. My sources inform me that you never cashed in the other half. And now I want it."

"There's nothing left."

"That jacket," said the smuggler. It seemed like a throwaway remark, nothing else to say. But that was only if you weren't listening. "That jacket's left." Bullseye heard the ominous concern.

"It's not mine," said Bullseye.

"You're right."

"Take it."

"It's not even yours to give."

"Look, I don't have anything else that belongs to you."

"Of course I wouldn't be here if I believed that, would I?"

"I don't give a fuck what you believe," Bullseye suddenly snapped. "Get this goddamn wire off me."

"Not yet."

"Then tell me what you're looking for."

"I don't really care, Mr. Broomis. You can give me the cash. Or the coke."

Bullseye reacted with disgust. "You're nuts," he mocked. "What coke?" He was here suffering for that myth? The three great lake fictions: gold, diamonds, and blow. When all there was to be had was fuel-soaked weed.

The smuggler's voice dropped to a new sobriety. "Do you realize how much my information has cost, Mr. Broomis?" he said. "It has cost me a lot. It has cost certain of my sources everything."

Bullseye accepted the rebuke. He wet his lips and smelled new fear. He wanted to give in and slide, just slide with the knowledge. But it was becoming more and more apparent that he had nothing to give. "I'm having trouble keeping up is all," he said. "Serious. I don't know what coke."

"All right," the smuggler allowed. "We'll trade. Your buyers assured me there was no transaction involving cocaine. And I learned that when the government went back up to Snake Lake to appraise the damage you boys did, there was nothing of any value remaining in the cockpit or under the lake. They found your tools, your garbage, your footprints, and a bale or two of marijuana that escaped your attention. But the most expensive item on board was missing. And remains missing. That package is easily worth twice what the marijuana was. If you gentlemen want to sit on it, that's your business. But the money you stand to realize, that's my business."

Bullseye shut up. Pot was hippie action. But coke. The legends of casual murder in the jungles of Colombia and Peru and Bolivia, of Communist guerrillas and corrupt army and failed interdiction and double and triple dealings and wild-man pilots and smugglers without conscience, none at all, all of it came tumbling in at once. Some of it was TV and Hollywood pyrotechnics, some of it was U.S. scare propaganda aimed at yuppie consumers, some of it was just toot talk. But even discounting all the lies and bullshit, there was an apocalyptic zone right beneath the veneer. There was evil. It was pacing in the dirt behind him.

A tremendous weariness settled on him. Kneeling on the cliff's edge like this was sapping every bit of his attention. Each moment the abyss had to be resisted, and each moment he fought became yet another moment that it was right there in front of him, sucking and calling. Singing. Give me just a piece of your heart. He was weakening. His balance was off, and the pain all over was edging toward unbearable. He had to think. He had to trade, and yet what was there to trade? How could he think properly with all that music heat-seeking him from the blackness? He remembered the list of guns in the leather jacket Tucker had brought down from the cave. "Guns," he tried feebly. "There was a list of, like M16s and shit."

"You can get that coke for me."

"Yes." He still didn't believe there was any cocaine, and yet he did believe. There was one too many realities going on, which ordinarily was no problem for Bullseye. The more the merrier. Right now, though, with the wire cinched around his arms unjointing both shoulders and his knees breaking down on the stone rim and the songs reaching up out of that syrupy darkness, it was like trying to decide if you should climb a melting waterfall. The ice looks blue and plastic and majestic, but you can hear the water falling behind the ice, wearing it away. Which one do you obey, which one do you ignore—what you see or what you know? "Fuck, yes," he said.

"Where is it?"

"I have to get it. We hid it." It wasn't going to work, though, he could tell.

"That's what I thought," said the smuggler, the disappointment thick in his voice. Bullseye even felt disappointed in himself. He'd failed them both, and failure is never free.

"Look," he surrendered, "I'd tell you if I knew. I would."

"I know," said the smuggler. And, amazingly, he started to unwind the wire from Bullseye's arms. He took his time and kept talking. "No one hasn't lost something out of this whole deal. Painful losses, some of them." He paused, and Bullseye felt a tug somewhere at the lower end of his arms. "Snare wire bit you there," the smuggler remarked. "Nothing bad. A few more scars for the collection, right?"

Bullseye was full of relief. He'd lost sight of hope, but now there was a chance, a miraculous, championship, go-for-broke chance. "I don't know you," he said, and then groaned as his shoulders came forward and his lungs filled. His hands were completely dead. Even staring at his fingers and commanding them, they wouldn't move. That changed nothing. "I can't go to the cops anyway. They'd nail me for the pot. Besides, we don't have cops." He was just chattering, filling time. Whatever came to mind he spoke. "I stay put for a while and just pretend I'm in church, right?"

"You're right. You don't know me. You never even asked who I am."

"I don't want to know."

"You've seen me before, though."

Bullseye licked his lips and stared at his fingers. Still no blood in them. "No."

"Yes," the smuggler contradicted him. "You were there. You saw the body."

Bullseye could hear his heart drumming. He started to hyperventilate, but quietly so the man couldn't hear him.

"That was me."

"Bullshit."

"Right again. But God, it worked on the boy."

Bullseye pressed his rubbery hands against the gravel. Time to boogie. A word or two more, and there was going to be a wholesale collision, and he had none of the momentum.

"I saw the pictures in the newspaper," the man said. "All decorated like a subway car or a shantytown wall. Hauled him out of the water by a rope around his neck. Sort of made me sick, you know."

Bullseye waited and watched, and there it was, a window between the syllables. But when he made his move, his body was different, heavier than he'd ever felt, and his legs had lost their spring. His arms half collapsed at the joints like soggy puzzle weed. His calculations were all wrong, but somehow he got all the way up on his feet and managed a full step sideways along the rim, making for the forest.

He was too slow, of course. It felt like a feather, the hand that nudged him. He started to twist his balance back toward the solid ground, but then cool reason took over and he knew it was just more of the same. So while there was still earth to relinquish, he shoved with his feet and launched. He didn't even say anything. In the original Sanskrit, *nirvana* means "blowing out," as in signing out as John Doe, hello cosmos. Bullseye had never thought it entirely coincidental that climbers apply the term "blowout" to a fall, though the connection had never appeared so literal as right now at this moment. He felt his toe let go of the world. And he blew out with a whisper.

13

*I*t was like treading along the scales of a sleeping dragon. Each footstep planted on rocks that vibrated and shifted and rocked. Steep and loose with scree, the hillside looked safe, even innocuous. But the climbers knew how mercurial such terrain can be. The entire slope was ripe to slide. They'd considered going up through the neighboring thickets, pines, and underbrush, but short of sending Sammy up with the machete he'd brought back from his Amazon trek three years before, they'd never be able to bring Bullseye down through the dense woods. Cutting a path would have taken forever, and besides, Sammy was already up there with Bullseye.

No, it had to be a direct approach and a direct descent with the litter. They had taken what precautions they could to secure the slope, though only a climber could have seen them. Some of the worst rocks and most threatening windfall had either been tumbled down or stabilized with makeshift chocks picked up from the forest floor. At two of the steepest points a braking system lay ready to lower the litter and rescuers, and someone had contributed a retired "trash" rope as a hand line across a span of slick gravel. Kresinski stood just outside the mouth of the Amphitheater containing Bullseye. He surveyed the precautions and backups primitively installed on the hillside below him. He watched the string of five climbers slowly snaking upward across the long, nerve-racking slope of granite rubble.

They were in a hurry, but there was no hurry in their ginger plodding. Those who'd slogged at high altitudes recognized a familiar pace. You take your time. Keep your eyes down. Copy the feet in front of you. Find the rhythm. Eventually you get where you need to. Besides ropes, water, and hardware, they were loaded with the two halves of a litter so old there was rust on the chicken wire between its metal ribs. Also they were carrying two twenty-pound bottles of oxygen that Tavini had brought back from one expedition and had been saving for another. There was no breeze and the sun was hot. Dust hung in the air. It was going to be a while before they reached Kresinski. Someone had Robin Trower on a tape deck, so the cloudless sky held strings of electronic riff, a dark, bass, lashing dirge.

They were just starting on side two of the heavy metal when John appeared at the edge of the trees far below and started upslope. Whereas the rescue team was zigzagging on informal switchbacks, John surged up the scree in a straight exhausting line, loping from stone to stone, limping but dogged. Unburdened by a pack and spurred by alarm, he caught the rescue party after only ten minutes.

"John," greeted Pete, holding to his snail's pace. "Where ya been?"

"That John?" said a voice up front, face obscured by his pack. The line kept moving.

"Hey, man." The music humped their skulls. Victims of the fury, sang the blaster.

"What happened?" said John. He slowed to match their pace and tried not to breathe so they could hear him. One more conceit of the aging.

"I don't think I want to see this one," said Pete.

"It's that bad?" said John.

"It's Bullseye," Pete declared, as if that explained it all.

"I know."

"He's fucked. Blew his guts down into his balls. His spine's busted. His legs. His arms. He's fucked."

"Is he going to make it?"

"You tell me."

"He must have gone out again," remarked the forward voice. "I haven't heard him for a while."

"What do you mean?" said John.

The rock under Pete's boot suddenly skated loose and almost took him for a ride. John grabbed the ax strap on the back of Pete's big pack and steadied him. Pete grunted thanks and they rejoined the line.

"He was like a fucking banshee," the forward man said. "Want to make you throw up just hearin' him. Like, what, three o'clock? Four? All the way until dawn. Then the sun came up and he got quiet. Wouldn't never have found him if he didn't start up again."

"He was screaming?"

"Oh, man," the forward voice admired. "The Amphitheater's got awesome acoustics."

"When did you find him?"

"Hour, hour and a half ago," said Pete. "There was a bunch of 'em, but Kreski was the only one who'd go in and look at first. He sent Tavini and everybody else down to get people and rig the slope. Sammy came up half an hour ago. He's playing doctor." Sammy was an ex-Rocky Mountain Rescue man. He knew as much about real medicine as a frontier doctor. But that was more than the rest of them combined. "Everything's ready," Pete said. "Soon as we get up there, we're gonna scoop him and run."

John looked upslope and appraised the rigging job. So long as the hill didn't slide on them, things looked about as stable as you could get. "What happened, though? What was he doing up here?" There were so many questions to ask.

"It's Bullseye," Pete said again, and again presumed that explained it all.

"He picked a fuck of a place to do it," said another voice. "Who ever goes up to the Amphitheater? He had a tomb in mind."

There was the suicide talk again. John bit his teeth together. People were getting pretty damn free slinging it around. First Tuck, now the Iceman. "Bullshit," snapped John, and everyone knew what he meant by it. For a minute they listened to the Trower music and the rocks toc-tocking hollowly under their feet.

"Yeah?" someone sullenly challenged. "Well, how come he slashed his wrists before he jumped?"

"You seen it?" said Pete, siding with John.

"You?" the voice retorted.

"Fuck it," Pete cursed.

"His wrists are slashed?" John asked more quietly.

"All we got is assholes talking. Kreski started it."

"It's the ghost," someone digressed.

"Bad karma," someone else posted.

"Karma. What's that?" Pete ridiculed. "It's nothing." John listened. They'd been talking. Or at least formulating explanations. What was in the air was fear, not anger.

"Kreski said it was bad karma, too."

"Great," snorted Pete. "The latest bozo theory. Bad karma. If you went to the lake and scored some smoke, you're fucking doomed. People are even collecting proof. Tucker got wiped out. Some dude from Sacramento totaled his brand new Z on 101. One of those Santa Cruz dudes drowned surfing. Hank Jones slipped in the john last night and snapped his ankle. And now Bullseye. So that makes it final. Bad karma."

"Yeah," added one of the front voices, mistaking Pete's intent. "And you didn't say about Katie stepped on a cactus down in Joshua Tree and about died from allergies."

"Katie went down to Joshua Tree?" said John. He'd seen her only a couple of days earlier, and Joshua Tree was an eight-hour drive south.

"She said we were full of shit and kissed us off," said Pete.

"She'll be back, though," a voice asserted.

"And what about Hoag?" They were fired up now. "He popped out both knees stemming on Outer Limits. Grody."

"Wasn't Outer Limits," someone corrected. "It was Juicy Fruit."

"See," said Pete. "Fact is, you didn't even have to be at the lake to be doomed. Remember that guy with the van at the roadhead, the guy everybody was selling to? Kresinski's candy man. His apartment caught on fire in Berkeley. He went up in flames. All you have to do is touch the stuff and you die. Or break. Or step on cactus." He paused. "Bullshit."

"Explain it, then," a forward voice growled.

"We're gettin' killed and hurt. We're takin' a beating. That's all I know."

"Karma."

Suddenly a terrible, echoing shriek cut into the music and speculation and silenced them.

"No," breathed John. He'd never heard such pain.

"Bullseye," said Pete.

John looked high upslope and saw the mouth of the Amphitheater.

It was a small black crevice in what appeared to be a solid hundred-foot-high wall of stone. Few visited up here, but everyone knew that on the inside of the formation was a natural amphitheater open to the sky. From down here, the entrance looked like the front of an Egyptian tomb with massive, toppled lintels on either side of the doorway. Then John saw Kresinski watching him from the corner of the entrance. They were too far apart for him to distinguish any expression, but the moment their eyes met, Kresinski turned and disappeared through the crevice. It never failed to astonish John how the man's very manner spoke possession. The screaming kept on, then abruptly quit. Next to that agony, the heavy metal music seemed silly and pretentious. There was nothing more to be learned down here, John decided.

"Want me to take some of your load?" he offered to Pete.

Pete heard the urgency in John's voice. "Guess not," he said. "We're about there." They weren't, not by a half hour or so, and the load was heavy. But at least John had offered.

John waited until the group picked its way diagonally to the edge of the scree field and then resumed his steady loping trot up the middle. Rocks teetered underfoot. Goat, his father used to call him. Joe, you and the goat, go show us how to run in them mountains. And he and his brother would tear off racing for the top of a mesa, hopping from rock to rock, drawn by the mountain and powered by the wind and their father's pride. See, he'd tell snaggletoothed roughneck *compañeros* over for a Bud, that there's how Apaches used to do it. After about ten minutes he reached the entrance. There was a small flat ledge like a porch at the mouth of the crevice. Delwood was sitting there in the cool shade, dejected.

John didn't bother hiding his respirations this time. "Where is he?" he panted.

"In there," said Delwood. "I can't go back in again. I don't want to. Sammy kicked me out." More quietly, he added, "I barfed."

"The rangers inside?" John asked. He tried to think who would have come up. Several of the younger rangers could always be counted on in emergencies. Besides Liz, two were trained paramedics, and that came in very handy for packaging and stabilizing fallen climbers.

"What rangers?"

"Nobody told the rangers?" said John. He was surprised, then angry.

The pain he'd heard was begging for morphine, and if the injuries were half of what Pete had described, then it was going to take trained hands just to hold the pieces together.

"No. Kreski said we take care of our own. The rangers would just kill him."

"They'd do what?"

"You know, like bang the litter around. Or try a chopper extraction like that Teton rescue." The Teton rescue had entered local lore when an injured Wyoming teenager was plucked from the saddle on the Grand, then got accidentally dropped. "It makes sense. The rangers don't give a shit. They can't even find Tuck. And after the lake . . . maybe they just might kill him."

John looked out across the Valley. His thoughts were spinning. The center was no longer holding. They were out of control. Could people really be believing in ghosts and karma and killer rangers? The Valley was a place of illusions. With its gigantic curtains of stone and sunlight, it fostered illusions. Here you could believe life was a poem. You could close your hands on the rocky walls of the world and say, here is everything. But the illusions had come unfastened from their moorings and were crashing against common sense. Why should a ranger kill a climber? They were practically the same species. Just another tribe.

"Yeah, well we need some rangers," he said.

Delwood looked up from the shadows. "Kreski said—"

"Get some rangers," John commanded. "Find Tip. Or Stammberger. They'll come."

"It's too late," said Delwood. "We'll have him down before—"

"Get the rangers," said John.

"Delwood clambered stiffly to his feet. "Okay, already. I got to get my pack first. It's—in there."

"Don't bother. I'll bring it down."

"Okay." Delwood was not relishing the thought of having to descend quite yet. "Are those guys bringing water? I could use some water."

"Tell them Bullseye's dying," he said.

"Okay," said Delwood. None too vigorously, he moved to the edge of the porch. It took your breath away to look down the long, steep slope. It wasn't much different from standing on top of a Mayan pyramid and dreading the staircase down. Delwood's hesitation made John realize how intimidating the hillside was going to prove, especially with six people and a litter.

"Tell someone we need more ropes," said John. "Lots more. And tell them bring the cable." There was a five-hundred-foot spool of half-inch braided cable down in Camp Four that they sometimes used on big-wall rescues. Sideways, Delwood reached down with his left foot and tentatively found a rock. John debated racing down himself, but there was too much that needed doing up here. Among other things someone had to curb Kresinki's bird-brained tyranny and his "We take care of our own."

Delwood picked his way down another few yards. He was cowed by the loose rocks. He looked back up and grinned his embarrassment. "Downhill always kills me," he said.

John nodded indifferently. Chagrined, Delwood pushed himself to go faster. It was a mistake. His foot released a stone. The stone triggered a small cascade of rocks that gathered size and power. In slow motion the effects immediately began to fan out, creeping wider the farther down the rock slide progressed. He froze, stupefied by his error. Dust shot into the air. The mass of rocks snowballed larger and wider, and suddenly it appeared to be so sluggish that it would slow and even stop. But individual rocks had begun spitting loose of the slide, skipping downhill like big rubber balls. Two hundred yards lower, the rescue group was blithely unaware of any danger. They had their heads down and music loud.

"Rock," shouted John. He plundered a resonance that came up from the bottom of his rib cage and cast it across the Valley. "Rock," he shouted. He gave the syllable a moment to form, then released it again. "Rock."

One of the group stopped and looked up. An instant later the rest of the group halted, too. Dozens of rocks were ricocheting toward them. Each rock had its own trajectory. Several preliminary missiles whistled past them, and you could read their panic in the ways they ducked and gesticulated and tried to escape. Through the cloud of dust, John saw two climbers hit the release on their belly bands and dump their packs and hop toward the forest's edge. Another of the climbers lay down and covered his head with his hands. The fourth man ponderously turned his back to the hillside and sat down, his pack effectively a shield.

Pete was the last in the line. He dumped his pack and simply faced the upper hillside. It was classic balls-to-the-wall Petey. He crouched down in a high school wrestling stance and stared up into the face of disaster. He ducked one rock, then dodged a pair, then fended away one more with his open palm. Mouth open, John watched the bravura performance. He'd been in rockfalls before, every mountaineer has. The rocks buzz by like handsaw blades. The sole impulse is to ball up and close your eyes and ears until the sky quits falling. By not hiding, Pete pulled it off without a scratch. Nearby the boy who had thrust his back to the danger like an armadillo wasn't so lucky. A volleyball-size rock struck him square in the middle of his pack and kicked him forward and down the hill.

Then the rockfall was over. John tried to account for everyone. Two of the climbers had reached the forest. Pete was threading downward to his stricken partner. The boy struggled to his elbows with the pack still on, then lay back down. Pete reached him, carefully lifted off the pack, and hunkered down at his head to determine the extent of injury. A minute later the boy was able to stand up. He left his pack where it lay and very slowly started back down to the floor, badly shaken.

"God," said Delwood. "I didn't mean to."

"I know," said John.

Voices raggedly drifted up to them.

"Fuck!"

"Is that Delwood? It is."

"Use a gun, Eddie. It's quicker."

"Stupid a-hole."

"I'm leavin' the Valley," Delwood muttered. "Everything's fucked. Everything."

"It's not your fault," John soothed him. They needed rangers up here. They needed rope and more manpower. "Just be careful." He pointed to another part of the slope. "Try it over there." Delwood angled over and started down again.

"See how it is?"

John turned. Kresinski was standing at the entrance to the tunnel. Behind him, on the other side of the tube of darkness, sunlight was streaming down. It looked like another world back in there, lush and green. With Delwood gone, John was alone with Kresinski.

228

"Somebody's got to stand up to him," Kresinski said. His tone was casual and yet conspiratorial, as if the two of them had been sharing this conversation for a long time.

"What are you talking about?" John decided it was just more of the man's manipulation. "Move," he said. "I want to see him."

"Don't worry, Bullseye's not goin' anywhere. Besides—"

"Besides, what?"

"I know who did it."

"Did what?"

"Booted Tuck."

John stopped and gaped. "Damn," he said. He was relieved and stunned in equal proportions.

"He's smart," Kresinski continued. "He's using us against ourselves." He gestured at the little figures on the slope below. "Shit like this. Chain reactions. He's hiding behind our own carelessness. He's there, but we just can't see him."

"What are you talking about? That rockfall was an accident." John wanted what he was saying to be true because it answered . . . much. Everything. And yet he felt compelled to call liar on him. Even as Kresinski spoke, he disqualified his own words. Above all, why had he waited until now to reveal what he knew?

"We're scared. We're fucking up. That's what he wants," said Kresinski. "We're down. Any more down and there won't be anything left of us."

"Quit talking around," John snapped. "Say what you mean."

"Simple. What would you do if we had the motherfucker? Here. Now."

John didn't answer.

"You'd kill his ass," Kresinski snarled.

John kept staring at him, wary and still shocked.

Disgusted by the silence, Kresinski sniffed. He flicked a rock at the wall. "You been wandering around lost ever since Tucker smoked. Your problem is you don't know what you're looking for. I do." He ducked and started back into the crevice.

"Wait," said John.

"I *been* waitin'. It's time to move. Tonight. Before he gets to us."

"What are you talking about?"

"You smell like pussy, sport. While your buddy's up here gettin' trashed, you were off dippin' your stinger, weren't you?"

"Move," said John.

"After you." Kresinski moved to one side. "While you're looking, take a good look at the cuts on his wrists."

"I don't believe that. Bullseye wouldn't cut himself."

Kresinski shook his head and smiled. "He didn't. That's what I'm saying. It was no knife that cut his arms. It was rope. Or wire."

"Wire?" John saw no significance in it.

"Come on, Johnny. Keep up with me." Kresinski crossed his wrists in front of him. "His arms were tied together. He didn't jump. He didn't fall. Bullseye got trashed. Just like Tucker."

"What?"

"I thought that's how you wanted it. A boogeyman on the prowl." John peered through the tunnel at the far sunlight.

"God's truth, man. It's the way you said."

"How do you know?"

"I don't know his name. I don't know where he is right this minute. But he's out there." Kresinski paused. "I don't know why he's out there. But he is."

"What do you want, Kreski?"

"The question is what does *he* want?"

"All right—"

"I don't know."

"Come on."

"Remember that leather jacket Tuck brought down from the lake?"

"So?"

"There was some things in it."

"I saw."

"No." Kresinski's bleached-blue eyes didn't blink. "You didn't see it all. Because Tuck and me ran into each other the last night at the lake. He'd just come down from the cave. Before anyone else even knew he'd found the jacket, he gave me something." He paused. "You want to know what the boogeyman really looks like?"

"Quit screwing around."

Kresinski lifted a folded photograph from his shirt pocket and opened it with the fingers of one hand. John started to reach for it, but Kresinski pulled back. "Ah, ah. Look. No touch."

Fed up, John snatched the photo from Kresinski's fingers.

It was the dead smuggler and his mirror image in jungle fatigues. Behind them sat a military helicopter. The truth was too obvious. John had seen that singular face. But seeing it duplicated side by side this way, he registered blank. "Who are these guys?"

Kresinski grinned. "Dead men."

There was the clue. "Oh, no," breathed John, digesting the implications and spinning out further implications. "His brother?"

"Yep."

John was fascinated by their similarity. What kind of a bond would you form with a person who looked exactly like yourself? In how many ways would the world seem that much more like a game of coincidences?

"What does he want?"

"His pot?" Kresinski shrugged.

"No." Something about that answer was too pat. Too explanatory. It had to be something else. Perhaps, John considered, he wanted something as simple as revenge. Given the desecration of his brother's body with spray paint, that carried a fundamental logic. But why target Tucker? And why Bullseye? Neither of them had violated the corpse. His mind churned on, shuffling pieces and shadows of pieces. There was so much to assemble. Suddenly he dropped his hand and looked at Kresinski.

"You've got something that belongs to him."

To his surprise, Kresinski didn't deny it. "Tell me who among us doesn't."

"Tuck. Tuck didn't."

"Fuck, John. We're all sinners. Even little Tuck. It was him who swiped the jacket and started this whole thing."

"You've got something," John repeated. He went back in his mind to their days on the lake and tried to think what Kresinski might have taken that the rest of them hadn't also. Then he remembered the dive. "You found something in the lake," he said.

"Come on, John. I came up empty. Everybody saw me. Cold. And empty."

It was true. John recalled how they'd pulled Kresinski from the freezing water and stripped his dry suit off and exposed his naked body to the fire. Some girl with black hair had given him hot tea, he remembered that now. And teeth chattering, flesh blue, Kreski had regaled them with tales of the deep, painting a fabulous underwater land of cold fishes and the barren coffinlike interior of the cockpit. Except for his bullshit, he had indeed come up empty.

"Then what's he after?"

"Unfinished business."

"What, damn it?"

Only then did it catch up to John. If Kresinski knew the answers now, he would have known them yesterday. And a week ago. There was only one place such knowledge could have come from, and that was the lake. He'd known from the beginning and yet warned none of them. The enormity of that wrong stopped John's breath for a moment. Kresinski was watching his eyes carefully. When he saw John's realization, he flinched and backed against the rock, and he raised his big arms in front of him.

"The lake. It's something at the lake, John. I don't know what. I wish I did."

John's voice pinned him against the wall. "You knew."

"No, I swear." He went on. "You want him, though. And I can give him to you. But I'm in. That's part of it."

"No way."

"I want to stake this fucker to the earth. Same as you. That's it. I swear."

John stared at Kresinski. It was like looking at a stand of dead trees. He was lying his ass off, you could hear the dead words scratching against each other.

"The lake." Kresinski trailed off.

"He's up there?"

"Not yet. But he's gonna be. He's gonna follow us."

"Why?"

"He'll go where we go. He's watching us. Call it a hunch."

"So we're bait," said John. "Is that what Tucker was? And Bullseye?"

"They were in the way. Now they're not." Kresinski said it in a careless way that meant he'd lost his fear. John could see that he thought he was back in the saddle.

"Why go to the lake then? Why not Modesto or San Francisco? Why not wait for him here?"

"Might as well make it our high ground for a change."

Just then the rescue party began mounting the porch of stone. Pete was the first. Sweat was cutting lines down his dirty face. "Gonna be a long day," he said, and pointed at the dark crevice mouth. "Through there?"

. Kresinski nodded and eyed the oxygen bottles. "You guys bring a mask, too?"

"Yeah," said Pete. He kept working on a piece of gum. "That hill's gonna be a bitch to carry him down. You sure we wouldn't be better off with a chopper?"

"We got it under control," said Kresinski.

"Liz should be coming soon," John quietly added. Kresinski snapped a look at him. "And some extra rangers. We don't move Bullseye until they get here."

"Fine with me," said Pete.

"You trying to kill him?" Kresinski challenged.

"I told Delwood bring more rope and people," John went on. "The evac cable. And the trauma kit. And we'll see about the chopper."

"There's no room for a chopper to land up here," Kresinski spat.

"Maybe not."

"A long day," Pete reiterated for himself.

As other rescuers arrived and dumped their loads, John said, "Might as well rig it for the cable." He told them Delwood was bringing the heavy spool of cable and more hands.

"Fucking Delwood," one boy muttered.

"We better get in there," said Pete. "Somebody want to bring the O-two in? And the mask."

"I got it," said another climber.

The rescue team squeezed single file into the crevice, leaving John alone again with Kresinski. John opened one of the rescuer's packs and rummaged around for some hardware to make an anchor. Even if the litter was ultimately lifted out by helicopter, it made good sense to rig the cable and have it ready just in case. He found a rack of nuts, angles, and knife blades, and a rock hammer. In another pack he found a half dozen weathered slings. He scanned the wall and, finding two separate seams to work with, knelt in front of the rock and began hammering in the metal.

"You owe me, John. For Tony."

"Shit."

There was a desperation to Kresinski, an apprehension, that John found curious. That he would keep ramming his head against John's "no" was almost mystifying.

"He's trying to spring it all loose. All."

"There's more," said John. "What is it he's really after?"

"Nothing. And everything. All at the same time," Kresinski said. "He's like a force of nature. Like gravity. I mean, what's gravity all about?" It sounded like a dodge, and yet Kresinski's performance seemed genuine. If not genuine, then at least energetic. He was putting every last milli-amp into the persuasion. But why me? wondered John. "Entropy," Kresinski went on. "That's what he wants. Total fucking entropy. Flat. Still. Silent."

John looked at him. "Screw that," he finally said. "What's he want? What do *you* want? In plain English."

Kresinski made himself dark. He loosened the scowl on his face and the ferocity in his eyes and, like that, he took on further, darker guile. "Maybe we want the same damn thing," he said with an honesty so complete that John suddenly despised him. He despised him because the man had reached a point where the truth was intricate enough to actually include deceptions and lies and evil. He wasn't telling the truth. But he was.

"What's that?"

"Nothing. And everything."

"Well," John said. "That's not good enough."

"Good enough isn't the point anymore."

John recovered himself. "You're on your own. You always were."

Then Kresinski smiled, confirming that his reasoning was all just a ploy. "Too late, Johnny." He winked. "All our choices got made a long, long time ago."

"Yours maybe," John tried. But it was strangely difficult to deny him. "Forget it."

234

"We're almost there," Kresinski declared brightly. The way he said it, you could almost see the lake shimmering in the distance. You could sense their lost purpose restored.

John turned his head away. As wrong as Kresinski was, he was also right. They'd spent a lifetime getting to this moment, this ledge, this purchase in the world. And now they were almost there. He matched one of the baby angles with a half-inch crack in the wall, snugged in the tip, and hit the metal with the hammer. And hit it again. But Kresinski wouldn't go away.

"What about it, man?"

Far below, at the base of the scree slope, several figures appeared from the trees. "There's Liz," said John.

"All for one," Kresinski said.

14

There was no good reason for Bullseye not to die that long, dusty day. Everybody said so. From wings to wheelchair—or the vegetable farm— that was the bleak devolution he stood to gain. "If it of been me," Sammy murmured to John as they knelt on either side of the body, waiting for help, "just finish it. Drop a rock on my brainpan. Just let me go." John passed it off to too much Rambo until he saw the dried tears striping Sammy's cheeks. Everything tasted of salt that day—their sweat, the blood on the backs of their hands, and, when the sight hit them one by one with their own mortality, the tears. It was almost as if Bullseye were already dead. Liz brought with her Michael Stammberger and Tip Escuela, two well-liked rangers with paramedic skills, both in their twenties, both indifferent to her and the climbers' outlaw reputation.

The first thing they did was replace the climbers' Himalayan oxygen mask with a clear plastic re-breather, crank up the flow from the classic high-altitude rate of four liters per minute to a more liberal twelve, and start an IV. While they worked to stabilize the body, Liz took Escuela's walkie-talkie out through the crevice and ordered a helicopter to meet them in the meadow down the hillside and across the road. John held the glucose bag while the two rangers and Sammy and Pete got a plywood backboard under Bullseye and a cervical collar around his neck, and taped his forehead and chin to the board to prevent further cord damage. Then they straightened and air-splinted Bullseye's twisted limbs—the traction splints for femur breaks were out of the question because you could feel the shattered pelvic bones—and gradually packaged him for transport in the now-assembled litter. There was internal injury, though in the field you can rarely say which organs have been affected. His abdomen was swollen with hemorrhage and sounded like a liquidy drumhead when they palpated it. Even more gruesome than his broken limbs was his scrotum. Bullseye's boxer shorts had been ripped away by the landing, and it was plain for all to see that some of his organs had blown down and now rested with his testicles. Much of the skin on his buttocks and upper legs had been flayed loose by the rocks, and he looked like a sacrificial victim badly sacrificed. But worst by far was the cord damage. It was nothing you could see or feel along his spine, but it was there. No amount of scratching his bare, cut feet elicited a response, and he was breathing with his stomach, not his chest, suggesting damage near the neck level. They were quick and thorough, but even so it was a full hour before Bullseye was strapped into the litter with a bottle of oxygen tied between his knees and ready for descent to the helicopter, which had yet to arrive in the flat meadow. He looked so peaceful and rescued lying in the litter as they carefully handed him through the crevice and attached the cable to a rung above his balding head, pinioned between two rolled-up towels and crisscrossed with tape. He looked so saved. A short spell in the hospital . . . a long spell of physical therapy. And then Bullseye would be back in the Valley to keep their flame bright and their pillars of ice humble. So long as he was covered up this way, you could at least wish that.

John didn't tell Liz or Sammy or Pete about the dead smuggler's violent twin. The rangers remarked on the odd lacerations girdling Bullseye's wrists and forearms, but when they asked about his drug consumption and any history of depression, it was plain what they made of the marks.

"Anybody check up there?" one of the rangers asked John, nodding toward the top of the cliff that hung overhead. "You know, for notes. Messages. Good-bye."

"No," said John, and that was the end of their curiosity. But once the litter was clipped to the cable and it was plain there were plenty of hands for a smooth carry-down, John made an excuse about his infected leg and lingered behind. When no one was looking, he slipped back inside the

Amphitheater and combed the ground for further clues. Finding nothing of use, he climbed a corner of the Amphitheater wall to the top and scoured the earth for whatever story it might tell. In his heart he knew that Kresinski was right, the mayhem was man-made and at the same time larger than life. The smuggler had killed Tucker, crushed Bullseye, decimated their tribe. And yet John found it difficult to hate the man because he was, after all, just a concept. But then he found two imprints on the edge of the cliff that confused him.

They looked like no prints he'd ever seen, rounded and long and deep. Careful not to disturb the sign bracketing these strange, somehow precious prints, he backtracked a hundred feet down through the thick forest slope and then followed the trail forward chronologically. There were two principal sets of tracks, one made by Bullseye's bare feet, the other by a pair of enormous Vibram-lugged boots. Here, John saw, Bullseye staggered. Here he fell down and raised himself, but without benefit of his hands—there was no palm print in the forest loam under the pine needles, John checked. Mimicking the tracks, John replicated the event. Why no palm print? he asked himself, and tried to raise himself without his hands. In that way he understood that Bullseye's arms had been tied not in front the way Kresinski had signified, but behind him. He remembered the faint marks around Bullseye's neck and understood that his friend had been led to his slaughter by a cord or wire around his throat.

Arriving back at the strange prints on the edge of the cliff, John was again consumed with curiosity. How had they been made? From the right and the left and above and then with his head down at ground level for a side view, he studied the two rounded tracks. Only when he lifted himself from his knees and saw the imprint left in the dirt did he feel any real hate for the smuggler. For now he saw it all. Here, two inches from the edge of the abyss, hands tied behind him, Bullseye had been forced to kneel and contemplate his execution. There, a few feet behind him, the smuggler had paced back and forth, tormenting him with questions and demands. John looked out across the Valley. Out there stood Sentinel rock. Closer, an ancient tree broke the skyline. Bullseye must have attached his soul to these and other things in the last moments. And then his hands were untied—John found two sets of knuckle prints on either side of the knee prints—and Bullseye had stood up and tried to escape.

He found the footstep where the smuggler had broken his pace to parallel the break for freedom. Here was Bullseye's final purchase with the
edge, a gouge in the earth one toe wide. "Fuck," said John.

He started to follow the smuggler's tracks back down through the
forest, but what was the use? It would take hours to track him back to
the floor, and eventually the big ugly boot prints would turn into tire
marks and the tire marks would lead onto asphalt and that would be the
end of it. Returning to the lip of the Amphitheater, John searched for
another five minutes. He opened his mind to anything out of the ordinary—the string or wire used to tie Bullseye, bits of torn clothing, a
splash of blood, maybe a piece of paper dropped by accident or a last
message scrawled in the dirt. The killer was almost what Kresinski had
said, a force of nature. His violence borrowed ingeniously from what the
climbers already risked their lives on: the void. By simply tipping the balance in favor of the abyss, who but a climber could say the killer wasn't
that same gravity and ego that always had and always would plague ascent? Except for some footprints and a few trivial marks on Bullseye's
racked, flayed body, what evidence was there he hadn't wandered up here
in a psilocybin haze and jumped?

Crouched, knees bent Apache-style, John hound-dogged the entire
area, intent on the ground. Aside from the tracks, there was nothing left,
though. He was almost ready to down-climb the corner and exit the Amphitheater and descend the scree slope to help with Bullseye, when his
eyes lifted from the ground and he saw the rag. Almost out of reach, it
was hanging stiff and pink from a branch, like a tattered flag. It should
have been the first thing to catch his eye, not the last; indeed, it was intended to be seen. But John had been so focused on what was at his feet
instead of the whole picture that he'd walked underneath it at least four
times. It had been tied to the branch not far from Bullseye's knee prints
and was obviously meant to be found. John had to stand on his toes to
reach the knot. Excited that here, at last, was a deliberate communication
from the smuggler, possibly a key to finding the barbarian, certainly
proof of an external, real malice, he opened the crusty rag. It was all that
remained of a T-shirt. Originally white, the shreds had been dyed pink
with blood and snow. Before John's mind could catch up with the possibilities, he turned the rag over. Printed across what was left of the chest
shouted the slogan, "This Ain't No *%&*!! Wienie Roast." Even then

it took him a moment, for this was more than a message from the killer. This was Tucker.

Suddenly John knew where Tucker's body had gone. It hadn't whisked off into the heavens or limbo or been dragged away by the animals. The smuggler had taken it. The climbers had desecrated the body of the dead pilot in the lake, and now Tucker's body belonged to the darkness. In a way the idea relieved John because now Tucker was partly found, even if more fully lost. Now he knew the boy's disappearance had nothing to do with all those venial gods in the trees and rocks and animals. Tucker's disappearance had nothing to do with sin, none that he had committed anyway. The smuggler had killed Tuck and then descended around to the base of Half Dome and laid hands on the thin, innocent, broken body and stolen from it the ultimate decency—a place with a name.

Oddly, the thought of Tucker's spirit wandering forever without definition relieved John because it fired his hatred, and the hatred felt good. Its hot, certain existence was what counted. He hated the smuggler. He hated the smuggler's boot print and Polaroid image. He hated the man's dead brother and the lake and their ridiculous foolish plundering of the airplane's cargo. He hated Kresinski, too, because in this world of illusions there are always the magicians who point less clever people toward false gold. He even hated himself, and that was all right, too, because he recognized how that was one last chance to be true to himself. No one is your friend, not even your brother. The echoes poured over him. Only your legs are your friends, only your brain, your eyesight, your hair, and your hands. John resisted the solipsism of that wisdom, but he listened, too, and knew that, yes, he would do something, but wondered what it was he *could* do.

By the time John descended to the valley floor, Bullseye had been carried off into the meadow and the helicopter had fled with him into the sunset. Climbers and tourists were standing around in loose clusters, still dazed by the spectacle, and John could see where the rotor wash had fanned the early blooming wildflowers flat. An elderly couple with a Winnebago had pulled over to the side of the road and were now dispensing fresh, red strawberries to the thirsty rescuers. Someone had brought a couple of six-packs of icy Mexican beer from the store. Kresinski's smoke screen—the notion of bad karma—was on everyone's lips.

People were somber, which they often are after bad accidents like this. But they were also scared, and John could tell that tonight the fires would burn very late while Camp Four searched its heart. Their climbing would go on, of course, but death—and Bullseye was effectively dead—always wanted pause. When expeditions on big mountains lose a member to storm or avalanche, there is a period of intense doubt. The mission of ascent, which is simply to ascend, becomes trivial, hardly worth a life. Everyone takes a deep breath. And then next morning the climbing resumes. John heard the melancholy and fear in the babble of voices as he threaded his way through the loose crowd, but he didn't tell anyone of his discoveries on top of the Amphitheater or about the Polaroid picture Kresinski had showed him. He found Liz all alone beyond the gossiping, shocked spectators. When she saw him, she kept her hands in her pockets and began to cry.

"I know where we can go," John told her and folded his arms around her. Kresinski was drinking one of the beers and looked over at them. He smiled, but without humor.

"Where?" she asked without much hope.

"Just for tonight," he said.

"Not Camp Four," she said.

"No," said John. "Bullseye's van. He wouldn't mind."

Liz loosened her embrace. "We can't do that."

"There's food and water there. And we can use his mattress and bag."

"But . . ." She searched for words to object and looked at her hands. "His blood's on me. It's not right."

"You need to wash?"

She hesitated. "Isn't there someplace else?"

"We can't go to your cabin. Or Camp Four. It's too late to go back up to Tuolumne." Suddenly the Valley felt small and constricted, like one of those Appalachian hollows where nobody leaves and naïveté breeds itself into bucktoothed ignorance.

"I'm so tired of hiding," she said.

"I know," said John. "But it's just for tonight." Also, going to the van would give him a chance to read the beginning of Bullseye's end. It would constitute part of a crime scene, if only he could bring himself to share what he now knew. But he couldn't. Whatever sign remained at the van belonged to Camp Four and him, not them, the outsiders and disbelievers. Kresinski was right. There was an inside and an outside, an "us" and "them." There was a tribe.

"Come on," he said, and started to lead her away.

"What's happening, John?" she asked, exhausted and dazed. For the first time John heard her vulnerability, and it shocked him that this was only the first time, that she had been so strong or he had been so deaf. He wanted to protect her. Protection was the wrong word, though. They were being driven from the Valley by a rapid, unbeatable erosion of all that had brought and kept them there. Protecting Liz would mean somehow halting the flood, and he had barely enough energy to flee.

"We have to leave the Valley," he said. "As soon as we can."

The birds were full of evening song, and although it was twilight, the squirrels were celebrating the approach of summer by scampering around on the still-warm earth, chasing pedestrian jays and nutcrackers. John half expected Ernie to hook up with them before they reached the van, but the yellow mutt never appeared. Holding hands, something they ordinarily never did while walking in the woods, John and Liz neared the clearing. High overhead the trees opened to a deep blue sky. No stars yet, but it was going to be another clear night. They felt the relief of a man and woman that yet another day had passed in good labor and, no matter the rest of the world, that each was still whole and well. Their sense of fragility was so keen that they clung to each other as the forest paled. Much darker and they would need a light to guide them.

"Ernie," John called into the trees, in part so they would be greeted with a wagging tail, in part so they wouldn't be attacked.

All that met them in the clearing was emptiness and further chaos. Bullseye's possessions were scattered on the ground, and the shell of his van lay tipped on its side.

"My God," Liz gasped and pulled on his hand. They stepped over books and papers and trinkets.

"I can't believe this," said Liz. "How could anybody be this low?"

John looked at her sharply in the midst of the pitiful, devastated collection of things Bullseye had called home. "What?" he said, equally shaken.

"Thieves," hissed Liz. "They must have heard about the accident and come while we were up there bringing him out."

John found a big boxy flashlight on the ground and cast around with it. "It wasn't thieves," he said, gathering evidence by the second. "Too fresh. See"—he pointed out a pile of spilled brown rice and oatmeal and other grains—"that food got spread around by bears and coyotes. And that couldn't have happened in just a few hours. And look, his camera's still here. And all his climbing gear. If it was thieves, that's the kind of stuff they would have snatched." Even as he spoke, John was finding more of the same huge boot prints left on top of the Amphitheater cliff. He resisted showing Liz, telling himself it was unnecessary, what needed to be done would be done. And there was Kresinski's xenophobic little truth once again: We take care of our own. Tribe, the bottom line.

"But if it wasn't . . ."

"I don't know," said John. "I'm not sure."

Suddenly she halted as some other thought dawned on her. "Oh, God," she groaned. "Did he really do this?"

"Who?"

"Bullseye," Liz said. "Out here all alone." Sadly, John understood she'd accepted what everyone else was accepting, that Bullseye had flipped out and gone for broke. Destroying his odd little pack rat's nest in a last-ditch frenzy would fit perfectly with the theory. Dust to maniac dust. "How could we not see his demons?" John let her believe what she wanted. He saw how simple it had been for Kresinki to point everyone in the wrong direction. By calling the violence suicide, or in Tucker's case a moment's imbalance, people were able to go on believing in the primacy of will. Suicide was an act of will. And slipping on the edge of the Visor was somehow willful, too. It was at least close enough to holding your fate in your own cupped, callused palms. That was the religion they practiced. The very idea of a larger force shaping your destiny was tantamount to heresy. It violated all that they risked their lives for: control.

"Now what?" said Liz. She was very near her limit. Her despair pained him.

"In the morning," John decided with haphazard authority, "we'll gather his things. For now"—he looked around—"let's try to tip the van upright. We should sleep." He bent and picked up a granola bar in an undamaged sheath. "Here. Eat this. I'll find some water."

The van shell was lighter than he'd guessed. Working together, they managed to lever it back onto the flat stone foundation Bullseye had pieced together years ago. As they worked, John's hatred for the killer mounted. Everywhere he turned, there was evidence of the giant intruder. His boot prints, his irreverence for Bullseye's books and records, his clear intent to maim. John found drops of blood on some pine needles and by the front door, on a tiny green seedling. The rearview mirror mounted on the driver's door was smeared with blood. Bullseye's suffering had started down here and lasted much longer than John had thought. The clearing, so peaceful and separate, had been violated. Like a wolverine, the smuggler had fouled the place with his presence. John swept the light through the trees, searching for other morbid signatures like the ones he'd found on top of the Amphitheater. There were no more ghastly souvenirs hanging from boughs, though. While Liz pushed the mattress back onto the plywood shelf in the rear of the van, John raced the light across the ground, demanding but not receiving more infomation. Questions kept leading to other questions. If the bastard was only after revenge, why trash the van? If it was revenge, why the long, torturous trek up to the top of the Amphitheater? Why not simply execute Bullseye down here? There was a distinct logic at play, but it was as inscrutable as it was malevolent. The mind and power behind all this random havoc had a purpose and direction. It had to. But what was it? Again John doubted Kresinski and his conspiratorial insights. But by stages, Kresinski's revelations were bearing out. There *was* a ghost, of sorts. In his twin brother, the gigantic pilot had been resurrected from the lake and was methodically, supernaturally hunting them down.

Suddenly John realized that Ernie was gone. Aced. The dog's absence aside, it made sense that the smuggler would have poisoned or shot him ahead of time. Bit by bit, they were all being erased. But why? John wondered. Revenge needs to be particular and coherent, otherwise it turns into blood lust. Blood lust has no honor. Revenge does. It was one or the other. Or something else. Something Kresinski knew but wasn't telling. Something at the lake. That was the extent of John's understanding. The longer he stood in the gathering night, illuminating this and that piece of Bullseye's past on the ground, the more he felt compelled to go ahead and trace all the scents, read all the clues. From experience, though, he knew more signs would be destroyed than found at night. There was much to sort out, and it would be far better to wait until morning. A taped Clorox bottle for big-wall climbing lay on the ground, and in stooping to check for water, John saw a three-inch-high potted cactus Bullseye had brought in from Nevada last summer. It had survived the winter inside his van. Now, surrounded by scattered potting soil, its green carcass had begun to shrivel.

"John, I'm cold," Liz called from the van. John hefted the Clorox bottle—half full—and climbed in through the sliding door.

"Some water," he offered. In taking off his gray gym trunks, he remembered putting them on early in the morning in his cove of fossils. Liz had lain in the sleeping bag and teased him about his hard-on, observing that "men even brag about having full bladders." There'd been goose bumps on his thighs until the sun rushed in. On the drive back down from Tuolumne, John had impulsively pulled his truck over and Liz, behind him in a borrowed car, had pulled over, too. "I just wanted to kiss you," he said. Her face lit up with surprise, and she smiled and promised to meet for dinner at the Four Seasons. And here they were, grubbing food off the forest floor, fugitives in a ransacked metal hut. The morning's light simplicity hung surreal against the rest of the day's gut-wrenching drop. John wondered if there could ever be a morning like that again.

He started to close the door, but Liz said, "Leave it open. For Ernie when he comes back home."

John closed it anyway. "He's not coming home."

"How do you know?"

John sighed. "Not now." He could see his breath in the flashlight beam.

"What's this?" Liz asked, lifting one bare arm toward the ceiling. John looked at the picture Bullseye had taped above his bed. It was a black-and-white NASA photo of Mons Olympus.

"That's Mars." He put his finger on what looked like a lunar volcano. "This here is Olympus. It's the highest known mountain in the universe. Bullseye used to talk about climbing it."

Liz was quiet for a minute, then she said "Jesus" as if there could be no more sadness. John's shoulders slumped.

"Take off your shirt," Liz told him. She switched the flashlight off. "I want your skin against me while we sleep." Under the sleeping bag, which smelled like Bullseye's solitude—a hint of sweat, the smell of garlic and peanut butter, and a strong overlay of the Lodestar Lightning sin-semilla—Liz pressed her breasts against the side of John's hard rib cage. With a sweep of her hand, she draped her long hair up over his shoulder and nestled into the hollow of his arm. Tomorrow was a new day; both were holding on to the refuge it would surely offer. Neither spoke. John cradled Liz in his arms and smelled her golden hair. She kissed his neck. They fell asleep.

It was black and cold. They were dreaming. Suddenly the sliding door swept open with a terrifying slash, and the entire van shivered from the impact. A beam of light stabbed in, and John reared up from sleep. Liz stifled the start of a scream.

"Rise and shine," mocked a voice. Liz recognized it before John did.

"Matt," she said and pulled the edge of the sleeping bag up to her neck to cover her nakedness.

John unclenched his fist and shielded his eyes from the light. "Kreski?" he said. "Son of a bitch."

"That's okay," Kresinski said, lowering the light. "I don't mind makin' the wakeup call. Not for my favorite couple."

"You're a prick, Matt," Liz cursed him. "You're the whole reason we're out here hiding."

"I'm flattered. But I'm not all you're hiding from. Let's go, Johnny. Cage your snake. Let's boogie. We got a scalp to take."

"Go away," Liz said.

"Go back to sleep, Liz. I'm just collectin' your man here. Then we'll be out of here."

"What are you talking about?" she said.

"Change of plans," John addressed Kresinski.

Kresinski's voice dropped its cheeriness for menace. "No you don't."

"What's going on?" Liz demanded. They ignored her.

"I'm not going to the lake," said John, prolonging what he really had in mind. He wanted to punish Kresinski. Just for being Kresinski, the bastard deserved punishing. As he'd hoped, his declaration stung.

"You fucker. You said you were in."

"The lake?" said Liz.

"So you're ditching me." Kresinski grinned. "Just as well now than up where I might need you."

"I'll go halfway," John finished. "Halfway's far enough if you're telling the truth."

"Quit talking around me," Liz said.

"Shut up," said Kresinski.

Liz turned her anger on John. "What is this?"

"Johnny didn't tell you?" said Kresinski. You could hear the pleasure in his voice, for in keeping silent about the lake, John had betrayed Liz. John saw his mistake and tried to tell himself the silence had been for Liz's benefit. There had been too much to digest yesterday without this. And besides, he'd still been deciding. The lake. The damn lake. It spelled trouble every time. "We're goin' on a snipe hunt," Kresinski baited Liz. "Wanna go?"

"John," she said.

"Kreski thinks he knows who—"

"Shut up, Johnny," Kresinski warned him.

"—who killed Tucker and dumped Bullseye."

Now Liz saw the full breadth of the betrayal. She edged backward away from John, who looked out the window. All there was to see was blackness. That and the tapestry of frost their breathing had shaped on the inside of the glass. "But John," she said. "We talked about it. Nobody killed Tucker. And Bullseye . . ." She paused, not wanting to slander him in his own home. "Bullseye got lost. He got lost out here alone." Choosing to see a parable in that, she continued. "You're not alone, John. You're not lost. Not if you have me."

Kresinski searched his bowels and found some gas. Grinning, he squeezed out a fart. "How come you never tried to save me, Lizzie?"

"You belong by yourself," she said. "Out on some island."

"I'd agree with that." Kresinski smiled. "Thing is, I'm already there."

"What the hell time is it?" John said.

"Four-thirty, dude."

"Forget it," said John. "Tell you what, I'll find you."

"Uh-uh. Now's it. I wanna be *far* in front of this sucker."

John squinted at Kresinski and his rude light. "Get out."

"I'll wait for you right over by that tree, man. We got to haul ass, though." He left the door open. John slid it closed and ducked under the sleeping bag again. He was shivering.

"This isn't right," Liz was muttering to herself. "I deserve better than this."

"Liz, I'm not going to the lake. Only partway. Kreski said the man would follow us in. If that's true, partway is far enough."

"What man? There is no man."

"There was a photograph. Tucker found it in that big leather jacket. Kreski took the photo away from him before anybody else could see it, but yesterday he showed it to me. Remember that body in the lake?"

Liz didn't reply. Of course she remembered it.

"Well, he had a twin brother. The photo shows them both."

"And that's got you running off with Matt? A face in a photo?" She shook her head. "No, John. This is too selfish. You're being paranoid and abusive. You're abusing yourself and you're abusing me."

"There's more, Liz. I just haven't told you."

"Don't bother."

"Up at the Amphitheater there were tracks. The same tracks are down here. You really think someone just came out of the blue and vandalized the van? This was no chance encounter."

"Stop. Just stop. You've created a monster out of all your fears. You want him to exist. You want a simple answer. A scapegoat."

"I found part of Tucker up there, too."

He felt Liz freeze in his arms. "You what?"

"His T-shirt. It was hanging from a tree on top of the Amphitheater."

"What are you talking about?" she said.

"Nothing," John said.

"I thought you were different," she said in a sad, dying voice. "I hoped. But you and Matt, you're both the same." When John couldn't find anything to say, she turned her back to him and curled up. "I deserve better," she murmured. "I do."

John ran his fingers down the hard, silky ridge of her spine, counting. "You're wrong," he said. "Kresinski." And suddenly the thought came out more forcefully. "He thinks all that glues us to the world is this, this much." He held up the fingertips on one hand. He reached around so that Liz could see them even though it was dark. "But he doesn't know. It's this." And he set his hand over her heart. "This."

After a minute, John felt her chest heaving. She was crying. Even so, she kept her back to him. Then they heard Kresinski whistling off in the distance.

"I have to go," said John. He found his clothes and quickly pulled them on. His hand touched the Clorox bottle and he took a drink of water, then groped for his tennis shoes. "Tomorrow. Maybe the day after. I'll be back." He leaned back and touched her leg. "It's almost over."

She stayed curled under the sleeping bag, inert and silent. If she was still crying, he couldn't hear it.

"I'm coming back for you, Liz."

John muffled a groan as he straightened up outside the van. Fucking knees, he thought. His back was stiff. His hands ached. He was starved and sore and weary from too much laboring and too little sleep. But soon it would be over. A brisk hike halfway to the lake, then they could lay their ambush and wait. John had no idea how to lay an ambush or if that was even the best thing to do. All he could say with certainty was that the Merced River was muddy with runoff, and that meant the back-country snows were melting. That meant the avalanche hazard up Bullseye's Valley of Death would probably be minimal now. The sun would have triggered most of the slides. The pillar of ice that Bullseye had climbed would be gone. The lake might even be melted. He couldn't imagine what was drawing Kresinski up there, or why the smuggler should follow them all the way in.

Again he wondered why he was going in with Kresinski, and again he accepted that there was simply a momentum. A day in. Maybe a night spent waiting. By tomorrow night he could be back in the Valley. And then his obligation to the dead would be done as far as he could person-ally do it. Either the smuggler would follow or he wouldn't. If not, then John would pay a visit to park headquarters and share his findings with the rangers. He would show them the boot prints at the Amphitheater and here in the clearing. He'd show them Tucker's bloody T-shirt and explain its significance. Somehow he would get that photo Kresinski was hoarding. And, of course, if Bullseye recovered enough to speak, they could all hear the story from a victim firsthand. If he and Kresinski came up empty on this "snipe hunt," then John would surrender vengeance to the state. But if along the trail John turned around and the ghost was actually there, then what? Feeling like he did—hung over from too much wilderness—he couldn't summon up the rage of yesterday. Not at this hour on this stomach in this dark. As gently as he could, John slid the metal door shut and closed Liz safely away. Kresinski quit whistling. John could feel him smiling in the dark.

They'd come close, Liz thought curled beneath the sleeping bag. She listened to John's and Matthew's footsteps recede and kept her eyes shut. No one had traveled quite so far with her, and together she and John had almost reached the house. The house was both an image and a ruins, one of her greatest secrets. When she closed her eyes like this, she could sometimes draw it from the well in the backyard, a perfect oval in which the house stood reflected. It was her grandfather's place on the original homestead in Oregon, a squat, beetle-browed cabin with a chimney made of stone and stacked, rust-eaten flour tins for flues. Though it had fallen into disrepair and the roof would have caved in if not for the intertwined roots of grass growing on top, still the river mud packed between its peeled logs was hard as cement. The Oregon desert wind had cured the logs, and the house was close to ageless. The waxed-paper windows had torn, naturally, and the front door was off its steel hinges so that horses and cattle had learned to huddle in it during storms. Coyote and rabbit and mice and birds lived in burrows or nests built into the rafters or under the walls. It was a hundred miles from anywhere, and Liz knew of it only because her brothers would bring her there for picnics. They'd set up cans and bottles and practice with Ken's lever-action 30-ought. It became a faraway rendezvous for the sons and daughters of the sons and daughters of homesteaders whose names they all carried. Sometimes you'd drive up and find a condom outside one of the windows or someone would have forgotten a piece of their clothing. Because she'd always associated the cabin with love, and also because her grandpa had deeded it to her, Liz had decided this house was going to be her house. She was going to fill it with light and inhabit it with children. One day she would bring her husband out onto the sweet, musky desert, and they would unpiece the massive log beams. Onto each timber they would nail a metal plate stamped with a consecutive number, and then they'd truck the whole kit up off the desert onto a mountain slope. Montana, California, Colorado. It didn't matter so long as there was a thick stand of aspens outside the bedroom window so that the leaves would rattle like gold coins in the autumn. They'd build a new roof for it and trim the gables with copper flashing. The copper would slowly go to verdigris. They would be happy.

John had come close. She'd almost invited him to drive north the afternoon after her Wild Horse interview, but Tucker had been waiting in Reno for them. And then yesterday as they departed from John's secret hole in the wall, she'd almost said on a whim to hell with the Valley, I have this dream to show you. Half the proposition still stood anyway. Precisely half. To hell with the Valley. In a way she resented him more than any other man in her life. At least Kresinski had been treacherous up front. John. John got your trust and faith. Even when he was a son of a bitch, you wanted to believe in him because he wanted you to. It felt safe and proper in his arms, but in the end all he was was another wild man full of visions and lies. She felt deeply disappointed in herself. There had to be something all tangled up for her to keep abusing herself with men like that. Fuck them. Maybe it was time to go to her house after all, but leave it on the high Sonoran flats out with the cutting wind and to hell with a friend and a lover. She could do it all herself.

Maybe a quarter hour passed, she was unsure. She might have drifted into sleep. Then she heard a single set of footseps returning to the van. It was John, she knew. It had to be. He had changed his mind and ditched Matthew. Her heart filled with gratitude, and she started to rise up and look out the window into the darkness.

But suddenly the door ripped open and her legs were gripped by two enormously powerful hands. Naked, she felt herself pulled out into the cold and dumped belly down on the ground. She started to fight, but one of those hands clapped the left side of her head with amazing force, deafening her. Even though it was too dark, she tried to look up, but her head was yanked violently backward by her hair. For a minute she was paralyzed with the thought of her neck breaking. She went perfectly still on her hands and knees as her head bent back further yet. Her breasts hung down and her cunt felt wide open. The vulnerability of her sex and breasts alarmed her, convincing her this was a rape. That blunt. That simple. Then a thin cold edge of metal traced across her exposed throat, and she quit breathing. Her eyes stared at the cup of sky high above.

"Please," she said.

In the next instant she felt the knife change its mind. Instead it cut through her long, perfect hair. Indifferent to her flesh, the knife turned hot as it sliced part of her scalp. That suddenly her head was released, and her severed hair dropped in a bundle across her hands.

"Now tell me," said a man's voice. "Where did they go?"

*I*t was slow, muddy
going. Nothing was straightforward, and the detours
were so numerous John began to
feel like a rat in a maze. Except for
where trees and rocks shaded it, the snow
had melted, and their trail—Kresinski's idea
of a trail—lay choked with young rubble
and fallen timber. The Great Yosemite earthquake
had occurred several years before, a six-pointer on the
Richter, but John had largely forgotten about it because the lower Valley had consumed the marks of devastation.
The Park Service had quickly restored ruined footpaths and
bucked tipped pines and oaks into firewood and otherwise
adjusted the necessary cosmetics. Where they had suddenly jutted up,
shear lines had turned into conventional features and landmarks. Climbers new to the Valley never even suspected that certain cracks on the
walls had shifted, closing tight or widening into difficulties they now
took for granted. But here above the Valley where park rangers seldom
came, the land was almost impenetrably tangled, and John was reminded
of the earthquake all over again. Just a month earlier, with deep snow
covering the trail and visions of gold dancing in their heads, it had been
easy for the raiders from Camp Four to blithely ignore the buckled land.
Now it was impossible. The trail was a bald, muddy, choked puzzle, and
John was not pleased.

"Hump the bitch raw," was Kresinski's parting advice, and their wis-
est act yet was to part almost as soon as the trek began and keep a good
mile or two between them. Now John picked his way through the deso-

lation. Trees had been uprooted where they stood or else piled down like Lincoln Logs by wide torrents of landslide. Higher up, John saw, big granite spires along the skyline had snapped off like old telegraph poles. With great patience, not always following Kresinski's footprints, he picked his way across a field of tenuous scree, then caught the remains of the trail for a short while before it disappeared altogether. Rather than posthole across a field of wet snow, he outmaneuvered it along a wind-polished drift. The path cut toward Mount Lyell and Electra Peak, then crossed a minor pass. Kresinski, the trickster, stayed far ahead. He had lured John into coming to the lake, then fooled him by insisting they take the longer, conventional trail instead of the shortcut John, Bullseye, and Tucker had used on their entrance. The other way would have been shorter and certainly less tortuous. But Kresinski had reasoned that the smuggler might get lost on the shortcut or might suspect a trap. So the trek was on Kresinski's terms, his trail. John's foul mood wasn't helped much by the turning weather. The sky was dark and leaden, mottled with gangrenous patches like in one of Albert Bierstadt's stormy, moral-istic landscapes. It reminded John of the "warts, tumors, boils, and blis-ters" and other invectives that Europeans had once heaped upon their mountains. The Christian opinion back then had held that mountains were mineral wreckage left piled after the Great Flood, and had reviled them as a terrible, chaotic region like the soul of man. Full of deceptions. Full of illusions. It was the same reason Apaches called the earth a shadow world.

John shifted his pack. He grunted a prayer against the storm. His heart wasn't in this bullshit vigilante trek. Not for the first time this morning he sensed that Kresinski was bluffing. He was annoyed with himself, most of all for his petulant uncertainty, but kept moving along. He felt unanchored. He had a USGS topo map for the region, but it was no help at all in this strange and rapid territory. Like the land through which they were moving, events were just too masculine and large, too jungled and wild and fast. The day's sole bright point was that the pissy sky wasn't pissing on them yet, though now and then a solitary snow-flake streaked by. He couldn't decide which would be worse: getting snowed in or getting snowed in with Kresinski.

At noon or so—the sun was deeply buried—John shucked his pack and scampered up the butt of a small, smooth dome for a look around.

He scanned the trail they were laying, but there was no motion back where there should have been, no smuggler. He recognized Mount Florence, but that didn't prevent his feeling lost. His old claustrophobic feelings of the labyrinth were closing in on him. The longer he stayed in here, the more the walls were going to spring up and lock him in. After a few minutes of concentration, he located Kresinski a mile or more ahead, a tiny reed receding on the long, steep plain whiskered with tufts of green spring grass. Not far from here, down on the Nevada piedmont, Paiutes used to quarry obsidian for arrowheads, and magnesium was being mined in huge sci-fi concrete tombs lit with eerie green vapor lights. In the far distance a handful of Sierra peaks bragged along the horizon. There was Mount Florence and the back of Unicorn Peak. But where was he really? What was he really doing here? He felt like he was soaring high above the earth and yet at the same time trapped in the cold mud. Christ, he cursed. I'm just an ape flapping my wings. He'd come such a long, long way to find the source of the Nile, to reach the South Pole, to track Friday's footprint on the beach. And this was where he'd gotten. A country ravaged by the hand of God. We're running and we're scared, he thought, watching Kresinski. But what were they fleeing? A creature, to be sure, but a creature that was invisible, monstrous, and irrational. The smuggler had become their dragon. Slaying it would never restore the Valley's innocence, though. Nothing would. Nothing could. They themselves had violated the pact.

Descending from the dome, he slipped on his pack straps and continued along the trail. Several times he fixed on a certain rock or tree in the distance and swore that would be his end point. He would go that far, no farther, then turn around and find Liz and leave the Valley forever. But each time he reached his landmark, he went farther. It was a habit. Climbers always need to see where the crack will lead. Another few feet, another pitch. Pretty soon you're standing on the summit. In a way he was just climbing another mountain by following this trail. In his mind, anyway, it felt the same: You reach, you grab.

Moving steadily along a high, narrowing ridge, he followed a rocky tongue to where it abruptly ended and dropped away. Below, some hundred feet down, a sharp igneous spine led off into the distance. On either side the spine gave way for another five hundred feet to open space and wind. His first reaction was to be annoyed and blame his own inattention. Very obviously he'd taken a wrong turn somewhere. And yet Kresinski's footsteps led right up to the edge. Then John saw a faded-green rope dangling over the left-hand corner and remembered the stories told in Camp Four about a steep, frightening bottleneck on what they'd dubbed the Great Spice Road. This rope on this cliff had cut miles off the regular trail, but it had also cost much time, for thousands of pounds of marijuana had needed to be hauled up by hand. The wind was picking up a little, swinging the rope like a lazy cat's tail, and individual pellets of snow spun past. One of John's fingers throbbed from old frostbite, and he pulled his headband down over the tips of his ears. Enough. This had to be halfway. Now he could turn around and return to the Valley. They'd offered themselves as bait, but the dragon hadn't budged. Aloud, he said, "Adios," in part to Kresinski, in part to the voyage, the lake, and the revenge. He backed away from the edge. But his pride complained. He was reluctant to turn back because it would confirm his legend of abandonment. Two went up; one came down.

As if on cue, he heard a scant ounce of noise on the forward horizon, a faint "pip" too bass for a marmot. He inspected the skyline, and there, ridiculously, was Kresinski's tiny figure flapping its arms. "Jackass." John frowned. A moment later he heard the minuscule peep again and shook his head at it. Had the King been trying, he couldn't have seemed more trivial. The whole venture was deteriorating into a nasty little cartoon. Time to bag it and haul on out of here before the day turned him into a stick figure, too. But John hesitated anyway. He took stock. They'd covered at least fourteen miles since dawn, and the lake was supposedly twenty miles in by this route. Doing some hasty math, he calculated that it would actually be quicker to go up to the lake and descend by his shortcut than to double back along the path already covered. The day brightened for him. By going to the lake he would actually be accelerating his departure from it. Also, he now admitted, there was something undeniably magnetic about the lake. That little scoop of water had given birth to much legend, both good and bad. One more look and he could really say good-bye. He'd done too many climbs to expect any sort of punctuation at the lake, of course. There was no end to the circle any more than there was a one and only summit. From every summit, you always saw other summits, that was in the topography of ascent. Indeed, climbers take their bearings off other mountains and past ascents and future summits the way sailors once did off the stars. One last look at the lake, John told himself, and his compass would be set. He would know there was nothing else to be pulled from the lake, or from the walls or the Valley itself. He could be at peace with his escape into the future, wherever else it lay. So he didn't turn and leave. Plowed by the wind, he stepped up to the edge and looped the rope between his legs and across one shoulder and decisively lowered himself down to the thin spine of igneous rock. The spine was so narrow he had to straddle it, a leg on each side. Hastily he pulled the rope free of his body and inched himself forward with dwarf evergreens whistling far below. It was hard enough to move along the spine with twenty pounds of down and food in his pack, and he wondered what it must have been like for all those people carrying sixty-, seventy-, and ninety-pound packs. At last the extrusion widened, and he was able to stand and carefully balance across the remaining hundred yards to less threatening ground. He picked up Kresinski's tracks again and headed upslope across ragged, stubby grasses that had no smell because the wind was so hungry.

It took him another half hour to reach Kresinski. At the top of the vast, inclined grassy plain, hiding from the wind behind a solitary boulder, Kresinski was sitting inside his pack. It was a mountaineer's bivouac. He'd taken all the things out of his pack and stuck his legs inside it. For a pad, he was sitting on a coil of yellow rope. For a moment John thought he meant to spend the night here. "This the bivy?" he asked.

"You must be kidding," Kresinski said. "I'm just keepin' warm." John turned and searched the horizon and middle ground behind and below them. There wasn't a single motion out there. Even the stunted pines, deformed by the elements, weren't moving in the wind. John's black hair whipped across his eyes. He kept looking for any part of the landscape to shift and become a tiny animal that would become a man, their man. Or ghost. "Don't worry about it, man," Kresinski shouted up to him. "He's coming."

John backed up and squatted down beside him. Something about the flat light made Kresinski's eyes even lighter. It was like looking into the sky when there was nothing to see up there. Kresinski smiled. "Want some strawberry Kool Aid?" he said, offering a plastic water bottle.

"We'd see him from here," said John.

"Don't crap out on me now, dude."

259

"There's no one out there, Kreski."

"Don't give me that redskin crap," Kresinski retorted, losing his smile. More heatedly, he said, "You can't see everything. Besides, I got a feeling he don't want to be seen." And then he smiled again.

John pried a pebble loose from the tundra and flicked it in the air with his thumb. "I'm thinking I'll head back now," he said, even though he wasn't. "This is a drag."

"Yeah?" Kresinski appraised with a glance. "I think you're going the distance. You look pretty beat, though. You tired?" When John didn't reply, he fished inside his parka and pulled out a small jar that said D. Marie's Olives on the label. "Time to punch on the overdrive." He unfolded a blade from his Swiss army knife, unscrewed the jar's lid, and then hunched against the boulder, away from the wind. His back lifted once, then twice with separate inhalations. It was cocaine. "Here you go, bud," Kresinski offered. "Put you over the hump."

John almost accepted the jar of powder and the knife. It would indeed put him over the hump. He could pack his nose and race to the lake, and there wouldn't have to be a downside to the high. Not for a day or two at any rate. There was enough coke in the jar to last them to the lake and back. But it was Kresinski's high. Bad enough this was Kresinski's trail on Kresinski's time schedule. "Where'd you get that?" John asked, not that it mattered. It was just something to say.

Kresinski screwed the lid back on and tucked it inside his parka. He wiped the blade between his fingers and smeared the residue on his gums. "It's just leftovers, man. Come on, you sure you don't want to catch up?" When there was no response, he snapped the blade shut.

"He's not out there," said John.

"No problem. He'll come."

John stood up into the wind. It tore at his long black hair. "We'll see," he said. He saddled up and walked on. The lake couldn't be more than a few hours deeper in, and he'd grown tired of having Kresinski out front like a guide. By dusk they'd be on the shore of the lake; by dawn tomorrow, John would be hustling down the Valley of Death toward exit and Liz. He wondered if Bullseye's rope was still attached at the top of the ice pillar or if the feds had cut it loose or confiscated it as evidence. Either way, descent was no problem. Like Kresinski, he was carrying a coil of rope.

It was ironic, he thought. He had more in common with Kresinski than any other person alive. Not quite side by side, but at least simultaneously, they had survived hundreds of walls and mountains and seen things people had never seen. They had seen tiny spiders clambering across snow on twenty-six-thousand-foot mountains and solitary blue flowers in the Antarctic. They had seen that where life was possible, it persisted. Especially on the brink. In their vertical wilderness, that was the measure. It was more honest than right or wrong, sin or justice. Survival itself was right and just. The fact that each of them was still on his feet with air in his lungs on a day like today made it so. They should have been friends.

John moved quickly, a prizefighter's ache in his bare hands. Closer to the lake, he started coming across refuse left by the Gold Rush crowd. Smaller trash like candy and food wrappers had blown east with the jet stream, but the heavier stuff like abandoned sleeping bags and flattened tents were either pegged to the ground or tied off to rocks or plastered into the trees and brush. People had jettisoned everything they owned to make room for the marijuana. Closer still, John found torn, slashed burlap sacking fluttering from branches. He passed sorry roofless shelters made of stone with blackened circles staining this or that corner: cavemen's fire pits. Well, the fire had gone out. There were no Young Turks in search of booty this time around. They'd come all this way just to find the ruins of Stone Age rock and rollers. The place looked more like an archaeological dig, like the disintegrating remains of a long-lost tribe.

The temperature continued dropping and snowflakes streaked past. Up ahead the land hit sky in a solid horizontal line. That would be the lake, John knew. He hurried on, anxious to get it over with. The mud was freezing up; his footing got slicker but also more solid. Hell, he thought, why bother even staying the night? He could tag the lake, descend what was left of the ice pillar, and be partway home before Kresinski even got here. With the headlamp in his pack he could even pick his way back to the valley floor and Liz by dawn. When all was said and done, he'd accomplished nothing by coming up here except to put more wear and tear on his knees and more hurt in Liz's heart. Certainly he didn't feel noble for having come. He didn't feel particularly true to Tucker's spirit. To the contrary, Tucker had never wanted to come up here in the first place. The smuggler, if there was a smuggler, had declined their invitation to follow them. The closer he got, the more reasons John counted for not being where he was. Spurning the lake was a luxury he could indulge in now that the lake was so close. A true ascetic at heart, John believed in pacing his self-indulgences, and for him emotions were as much an indulgence as sex, food, or climbing. Only now did he allow himself to be angry at being led off to tilt Kresinski's windmills. He had too many of his own to tilt.

Nevertheless, for all the negatives, it was a fine, brusque day. He looked around and sniffed the wind. A touch of ozone in the air, and that could mean lightning among the snowflakes, always a sight to see. The wilderness swelled lyrically on every side. John breathed in the power. It was a fucked day, but a fine, very fine day, too. And since even his aesthetics were subject to pacing, his pleasure with the lake steadily mounted along with his repulsion of it. A few steps higher, and John reached the object of his ambivalence.

He was shocked. The lake looked like a scavenged battlefield. John hadn't expected the sunny carnival scene of the Gold Rush, but he'd figured that over almost a month's time nature would somehow have improved upon the rape of Snake Lake. But what lay before him was a ravaged, forgotten corpse. It was completely untransfigured. The ice had not thawed. The holes chopped in its surface could have been shotgun wounds, raw and ugly. Slinging around the rocky, looming cirque, the wind was faster and colder as it howled across the lake. None of the Lodestar's metal had been airlifted out, none of the crash cleaned up. The hacked, spray-painted, cruciform tail section jutted vertically. Bowie's East Face soared overhead like a massive gravestone. John had been in inhospitable places, but this beat them all. The sky and his mood didn't help. He took a step out onto the ice, but it creaked and groaned, forcing him back to the shore. Even as he watched, Bowie unleashed a small powder avalanche down its lower face. When it hit the top of the ring of stone, the snow rocketed up and out, forming a cloud that descended slowly to the lake below. A few minutes later the sound came rumbling across to John. The lake, the whole area, was in cold decay. It looked like the far end of a lost civilization.

The wind mashed against John in a steady tide. Its roar formed a continuous, thundering ceiling. Despite that, he heard a low, repeating pop-pop sound in the distance. He turned his head and opened his mouth slightly to locate the sound. It was off to the right somewhere. Only as an afterthought did he consider it might be muffled gunfire. It wasn't anyway. Following his ears, he crossed over a hummock of glacier debris and found the parachute Tucker had found. It had detached from the ramp above and blown down. The shroud lines were tangled around a rock and the fabric was snapping and popping in the wind, flapping hopelessly like a bird with one broken wing. It reminded John of Buddhist prayer flags deep in the Himalayas: not a human in sight, their muslin turned to rags, their inked message faded with every passing breeze. Whatever ambitions the pilot and his brother had written into this flight and its cargo, however high-minded or money-grubbing their hopes had been, the details were gone now. All that was left was this parachute punctuating the elements. From above, John watched the shroud arch up, then lose its volume of air with a pop.

A sudden idea carried him down the slope of glacier debris to the parachute. He needed a new shoelace for his left shoe, and the shroud cord looked perfect for the job. With his pocketknife he cut off a long, ten-foot length, and from that cut a piece for his shoe. He pulled the wispy nylon strands out from the cord's sheath and sat down. With one slice of the knife he dispensed with the old lace, and then threaded his shoe with the new cord.

The sight of his knife and an old story about parachutes set John to thinking about a weapon, not that he believed the smuggler was coming. He recalled how aviators downed in jungles and deserts fashioned primitive slingshots from the elastic band in the parachute's vent hole. John had never examined a parachute this close, but sure enough the vent hole contained a twelve-inch circle of elastic rubber. More to test the theory than compose a weapon, John carefully cut the vent band free and slotted a speckled granite pebble into the crook of elastic. He drew it back and fired off a shot of moderate velocity and miserable accuracy. He tried a few more pebbles. The slingshot was distinctly nonlethal, at least against anything larger than a rabbit or squirrel. Mainly it was a curio. He decided to keep the elastic and experiment with his marksmanship. With a sense of self-satisfaction at having derived two uses from the parachute's carcass, a shoelace and a slingshot, he backed away from the flapping, bucking shroud. It was time to break out of this hinterland. Kresinski could find his own way home, and if he couldn't who would miss him?

John started to leave, but then a sentiment drew him back for one final act. He opened his knife and, thinking this was the sort of thing Tucker might have done, sawed through the remaining shroud cords, freeing the parachute. The strings tore loose from his hand, and the shroud ballooned diagonally with the wind. It stayed aloft for nearly a minute before dipping out of sight.

"That was cute," said Kresinski. John took his time closing the knife. He looked down at the makeshift slingshot and saw how ridiculous it was and threw it away. Kresinski was standing overhead, shaking his head in amusement. "God, this place looks like hell. Did we tear the shit out of it or what?"

"You were wrong," said John.

"Not yet, I'm not. He'll show."

"Best of luck, Kreski. I'm gone."

"He wants us too bad. He's comin'. For all I know he's already here."

"He's not here," John stated decisively. He hadn't checked more than a portion of the lakeshore, but chances were pretty good he would have cut any sign by now. The smuggler absolutely had not beaten them in along their trail, and the shortcut was far too obscure for him to find. There wasn't a map in existence that showed the shortcut; it belonged exclusively to climbers' oral literature.

"See that cave up there?" Kresinski pointed at Tucker's cave on the East Face. "He doesn't know it, but he's waitin' for us to go up there. And come down."

Now it was John's turn to smile. He smiled his pity-the-mad smile. Kresinski recognized the deference and his eyes hardened, but he kept his temper. "I was up there not so long ago," he said. "Nobody knows it except Tuck." He watched John's face for a reaction, and John was careful not to show any. But he was surprised. Tucker had said nothing about this. Then again he'd said nothing about giving the Polaroid picture of the twins to Kresinski, either. For some reason he'd kept his encounter on Bowie Peak a secret. "See that col?" It was Tucker's col, or couloir, a gully that was very nearly vertical from this head-on view. The bottom part was full of hard snow that probably wouldn't thaw until August, just in time for a new plastering. The col funneled straight up to the cave from the tall, circular walls ringing the lake. Over to their right lay the ramp that Tucker had used to gain the top of the stone ring. "For people like me and you, Johnny, that col's a sidewalk. For people like our friend out there . . ."

John snorted his dismay. Kresinski was actually trying to entice him up to the cave. Step by step, this was a seduction. But it wasn't going to work. "You're crazy," he said.

"Let's cruise, sport. We got an hour to make the cave before it gets dark. It's dry and it's out of this fucking wind."

"I told you, I'm out of here. See ya."

"And miss out on me and Tuck's big secret? I don't think so. I don't think you're goin' anywhere 'til you've seen the whole tamale."

Again John kept his face impassive. "Fuck your secrets," he said.

"Ah, ah. Bad attitude." Kresinski paused. "No wonder you keep ending up with the sloppy seconds." A gust punched Kresinski's back. His hair guttered sideways with the blast, and his clothing smeared against his arms and legs. But he was solid. Immovable.

I can take you, John scowled. No one would miss you, asshole. No one would ask.

Kresinski chuckled. "He's comin', man, believe it or not. And when he gets here, you're gonna be a whole lot safer with me. And me with you. All for one."

And one for one, John finished in his head. Kresinski turned toward the face and started threading up the fan of glacier debris. John looked over his shoulder in the direction of the ice pillar. He still didn't know if the rope was hanging down where Bullseye had fixed it, and although it was only a few hundred yards away, he suddenly didn't care. If the rope was there now, it would be there later. If there was any foothold left for him in Liz's life, it would still be there tomorrow night or the next day or the next. Of course he was going up on the mountain, just as, of course, he'd come up here to the lake. You can't go halfway or you never reach the end. That's just the way it was. Suddenly he was tired. Tired of thinking. Tired of wondering. Way too tired to bluff the night and try for the valley floor. The night promised to be eternal the way bad, cold nights in the open always are. The cave would at least break the wind and keep him dry. In the morning, regenerated, he could descend from the mountain. Or maybe he wouldn't descend. Why not wake up and finish climbing the face to the very top? It was uncharted territory up there. Maybe there were fossils to find. Maybe he'd even find that cowboy's

Bowie knife still jammed in a crack on the back shoulder. Pull it loose and show up in Camp Four, and he could become the new King. The sun would shine. The climbers would thrive. There would be peace. He grimaced at his own bullshit.

Aiming for the mountain, he started walking. The shattered rock turned to hard, crusted snow as he started up the ramp. He followed Kresinski's footsteps, which followed earlier eroded tracks—Tucker's, John guessed. With plenty of space buffering them and no rope connecting them, the two climbers moved swiftly and separately. The ramp was easy. It led to a ledge atop the stone wall ringing the lake, and a five-minute traverse on the ledge led to the col that led to the cave. The ledge was steeply pitched with snow, and John was careful as he looked over the edge down at the lake. From this height, the holes in the ice reminded him dismally of pockmarks, his own. It was a good three pitches down to the ice from here, four hundred vertical feet of air. Like Tucker before him, John tried to imagine the pilot standing here overlooking his crashed plane and ruined dreams with winter stropping its claws on his face and hands and the mountain wall resounding with sheer presence. He turned from the lake and started up toward the cave.

Just as Tucker had, John read the pilot's mental deterioration on the climb to the col. He passed first one discarded shoe, then the other, and a glove, all frozen into the snow and ice. He read the madness brought on by hypothermia. The col was tricky, but not overly difficult. John found some of the holds thin and greasy, especially when it was just tennis shoe rubber on slick, icy verglas. But even with a pack on, the climbing was smooth and unexposed. Because he was a climber, John admired the pilot's insane decision to tackle the gully. It had been a very wrong decision, but at least it had been ascent. Several hundred feet higher, as the mountain was darkening for the night, John's hand touched the bottom tip of a rope. It was Kresinski's yellow nine-mil and, John saw, it extended right up to the cave. He grabbed it and batmanned up to the cave. A rocky ledge jutted from the cave like a cat's rough tongue.

"Kreski?" said John.

"How's this for real estate?" Kresinski's voice answered from inside the cave. John paused to take in the panorama. The landscape was all gothic peaks and ghastly, Dantesque shadows. Sprawled before him was a profoundly humbling wilderness. The horizon was jagged and impossibly low, meaning this cave was impossibly high. The sight stuffed John full of the same sense of grandeur that once led explorers like Zebulon Pike and Robert Brown, the botanist, to calculate their mountains five and ten thousand feet higher than they really were. Up here, fiction was equal to fact. Here things could be what you said they were. It was the wilderness of antiquity, the devouring, relentless wilderness in which Kresinski's savage faith in himself made perfect sense. You divided the universe into night and day, black and white, tribe, taboo, and trespass—the simple brutality of a species under way.

"Come on in."

John tried to see inside the cave. In the darkness all he could make out was the tiny blue flame of a propane cookstove. Kresinski already had a pot of water on for soup. The exterior rock was speckled with garnets. John ran his fingers over the ruby-color buds as he stepped inside. Instantly he felt lighter and realized how hard he'd been fighting the wind all day long.

"Cocoa?" Kresinski offered without much enthusiasm. After a minute John adjusted to the darkness and saw that Kresinski was hunkered down on his heels, pouring chocolate powder into a tin cup. He set his pack against one wall, too weary to refuse. "Hot," snapped Kresinski at the handle on the metal pot. He blew on his fingertips. John drank some of the cocoa, then contributed a pint of his water into the pot and started it boiling for a packet of soup. Cooking, even over a fire this trivial, was one of those rituals that climbers appreciate with atavistic pleasure. Slowly the two men settled in for the night, each taking turns over the pot, concocting whatever hot foods and drinks they'd brought in with them. On a big mountain at high altitude, the ritual could go on for many hours and served practically to replenish their body fluids. Here, in this cave, the ritual was little more than a form of truce. They squatted by the cookstove as if it provided real heat or protection from the night. The flame cast a mineral-blue illumination on the curved walls while they plucked chill peach halves from a can and sucked the juice from their filthy fingers. Outside, the wind thundered monstrously.

Once their bellies were full, they pulled out the sleeping bags and pads. Each visited the cave's mouth for a final piss and came back in wiping urine from his hands and face and muttering about the blowing gale. With another partner, it might have been funny. With Kresinski, it was just another thing. John stripped and bunched his clothing inside an empty stuff sack to make a pillow, then zipped the bag up around his body, lay back, and plunged toward sleep. Kresinski wanted to talk, though.

"You ever wonder what it must have been like to be the first guy into, like, King Tut's tomb?" he contemplated out loud. John focused on the howling wind. He tried to ignore Kresinski. "Or one of those guys that found Spanish gold on the bottom of the sea?"

"You want to be quiet?" John said.

Kresinski didn't. "You know what? You're the only guy who didn't come up and say, hey man, what'd you find down under the ice? And you know what? You're the only guy I'm gonna tell. The truth, I mean."

"I'm asleep. Shut up."

"It was spooky down there," Kresinski said. He was talking fast. It was aggressive, speedy coke talk. "That dead pilot was floating around, I could see him not so far away. And you could hear our guys beating away on the ice, like boom, boom, boom. And there was that old Lodestar, nose down. You're the only guy who didn't ask me, hey Kreski, what the fuck *was* in there? Everybody else, I just said it was all smashed to hell, you couldn't get in." John let him ramble. "But it wasn't."

Suddenly Kresinski flicked his headlamp on and painted its light across the ceiling. With a sigh John looked over at him. Kresinski was staring at the ceiling's sparkling red garnets, a whole vaulted mosaic of them twinkling like a galaxy of dwarf stars. His long, aquiline nose and jutting brow showed a brute silhouette. Beneath the funnel of light, zipped into his bag, he looked like a sleek, beached nylon shark, long and streamlined and menacing.

"I had this hunch, you know. So I told Pete to bring in my wet suit."

"It was Sammy who brought it in."

"Whoever. The thing is I had this hunch. Pot's one thing. But there's better cargo for my money. That's what I was thinking. And I figured, where would *I* stash it? In the cockpit where it was real handy. Hell. It's worth more than the whole load of weed *plus* the airplane. I'd want it real close to me."

Now John was fully awake, despising the Neanderthal profile beside him because there was very little else Kresinski could be doing but confessing, and he didn't want to hear it. Even in confession, Kresinski wouldn't be hunting penance. It would just be business as usual, annihilation, his own and everyone else's.

"That pilot wasn't crazy like everybody thinks, man. He might of come up here. But then he went back down to the lake to get his cargo. He knew what he was doing. It was just like finding treasure, Johnny."

"Bullshit," said John. "He was crazy. He came up here. He was out of his mind."

"Nah." Kresinski already had it down in his mind the way he wanted it.

"The only reason he ended up down in the lake was because he fell," said John. "Fell. Or jumped."

"It was just like finding treasure," Kresinski went on. He wanted an audience, not a dialogue. So what else is new, thought John. "He didn't quite make it. But I did. I found it. First I sitrred up lots of lake mud for cover. Then I got inside the cockpit. And there it was in a steel trunk."

"What?" said John.

But Kresinski was going to unfold it at his own pace. "After that it was just a matter of swimming it down the lake to where we tied the pilot. It was a safe hole. Nobody was going to go pulling that fucker out again. Remember how scared everybody was? Nobody was even digging inside of fifty yards of that hole."

"What are you talking about?"

"Man, you should have seen the guy underwater all naked and decorated with Day-Glo. He looked like somebody's bad dream swimming around down there. He looked like he was waiting for his trunk. So I tied the trunk to a rope that was floating loose beside him. He kept bumping into me. He kept putting his arms around me." Kresinski's skull kept on chattering.

John was barely breathing. He already knew the punch line. Suddenly everything already made sense. It wasn't much consolation. But at least things made sense.

"I came up through that hole by the plane and got the hero's welcome. I dried out. I warmed up. Ate. Got laid. Took a nap. I got ready for the night. And then just when it started gettin' nice and dark, I went out on the ice and fetched up the trunk. I still didn't know what was in the trunk for sure because if it was what I thought it was, you couldn't open it underwater without ruining everything. I was just guessin', but all my guesses were right on that far."

Kresinski's excitement had been building with each sentence. Now, unable to lie still anymore, he swept the light down into a corner of the cave, set the headlamp on the floor, and unzipped his sleeping bag. He hopped to his bare feet, and frost poured from his mouth. John followed his beam of light and for the first time saw Kresinski's old black Lowe Alpine pack nestled in the farthest corner. It was completely encased in an inch of transparent ice.

"I pulled up the ropes. First I got the dead guy. But on the other rope was my trunk. And once I got it hauled out and layin' there on the ice, that's when I knew I'd scored."

He advanced on the pack and struck the ice with the edge of his hand. "Bingo. Heavy, heavy score."

The ice shattered with a crunch. He yanked the straps open, flipped the top up, and dumped the pack on its belly. Plastic bags of cocaine spilled around his ankles onto the cave floor. He stood there with the treasure piled on his feet, ankle-deep in white gold.

"Sometimes you know things, man. You just do. And I did. The trunk was waterproof and airtight. Not even one key got wet. All I had to do was wait for the right time. Right then was the wrong time. Everybody and his grandma would have been lining up for a share. And why should I share?

"So I packed it all up and humped it up to here. It was the perfect place. Everybody else had their noses down to the ice, they weren't comin' up here. And Tuck had broken a great trail for me. In the morning people were gonna wake up and see tracks up the ramp toward this cave, and they'd just say, Tucker's tracks. They'd never even know I left the lake. So I loaded up and humped it. Ninety, a hundred pounds. You ever try to climb wearing that kind of load? Shit, I've fucked women that weighed less than that.

"There was no problem. No problem at all. Nobody even knew I was gone. Then I ran into old Tuck. My timing was off. I thought he was already down and he wasn't. We ran into each other at the base of the ramp, and he gave me that picture. And here we are. You and me."

John listened to the wind. Part of him wanted to find the evil in this. Another part was in love with Kresinski's audacity and power. Here was the essence of soloing, and soloing is the essence of climbing. But still something was missing in the story.

"Why'd you bring me in?" he said.

"What do old climbers do when their fingers start going on them, Johnny? You've got years to go, but fuck-all little future 'cause you wasted it on the rock. No job. No education. No family. Nowhere to go. No real nothing. You got too much pride to be a peon, but that's exactly what you've trained yourself to be. So what do you do? You ever ask yourself that? I do." He didn't wait for the reply that wouldn't have come anyway. "But then it came to me." Shuffling gently among the fat plastic bags, he turned around in the light. "You retire."

"Why me?" John said.

"Because I have a problem, man. From the picture it looks like he's about six foot eight, two hundred sixty pounds. That's about eight inches and eighty pounds more than I want to deal with alone. And of all the people I know, you're the one who'd appreciate the solution most."

The solution. John intended to get back to what Kresinski meant, though he already knew. But there were other questions, too. "How'd he know to come looking for you, though? How'd he know anyone found the coke in the first place?"

"Easy. He asked. He asked Tuck and Bullseye, and all they could do was shrug and drop like bird shit. And he knew the feds didn't find it, because they would have splashed 'COCAINE DISCOVERED' all over the newspapers. Which they didn't. In the face of all that ignorance and silence, he did what I did. He guessed."

John's black eyes fastened on Kresinski. He felt empty and cheated, not by Kresinski but by himself. He felt beguiled and had nothing to blame but his own will to innocence. Well, here was a crash course in the geopolitics of the human spirit. Not trusting himself to remain thoughtful, he remained prone. He listened with the probing attention of a philosophy student. Something was still missing. Less the truth than a proper question with a proper answer. "How'd he know it wasn't on the bottom of the lake, Kreski? Or in the trees. How'd he know?"

271

"How does anyone know anything?" Kresinski volleyed back.

The evasion alerted John. It could only mean he was closing on the problem. "Uh-uh," he grunted. "He knew. How?"

Kresinski surrendered with a shrug. "The aluminum trunk," he said. "I ditched it in the trees. The feds didn't find it. But he did. He must have."

On the face of it, Kresinski's answer was inane. By itself it had no value. But Kresinski's manner implied a special gravity. He'd screwed up and had somehow led the smuggler on to the tribe. If it were anyone else but him you could write it off as a mistake. But with Kresinski there were too damn few mistakes that could be called honest ones.

"Why'd he go after Tucker and Bullseye?" John asked. "Why didn't he pick on you? You were the one that went down in the lake."

"Who knows? Maybe it was that leather jacket. Maybe he figured Tuck found it with the coke. Maybe he thought Tuck stripped it off his brother's body, and he just wanted a pound of flesh back."

And then, bitterly, John recalled how Kresinski had manipulated Camp Four to believe Tucker's murder was John's doing. He scanned backward and saw that damn near every response Kresinski had made over the past few weeks had been part of a charade. "You knew Tucker got killed, didn't you?" he said. "You knew he didn't fall."

Like a vampire, Kresinski withdrew into his own darkness. "What do you think?" he answered.

Now the implications came tumbling together. It had taken a while despite all the clues, but now John knew. "You used us," he said.

"Ah. Yeah," said Kresinski. "Don't worry. You got a share coming. How's twenty percent?"

"You killed us," said John, groping for the full scope of when Kresinski had known what. But the man had worked his way with them to such an extent that it almost made no difference anymore.

"Get a grip, man. The boogeyman's out yonder. Down there. He's comin' to git ya. You'll get your crack at him." He tossed a kilo packet across to John. It landed on his chest. "You get another nine of those for your trouble. Nobody's even had a chance to step on it. Pure unadulterated handmade Third World folk craft. That's a quarter-million bucks just for you."

Arms still enclosed in the sleeping bag, John lifted his head and examined the packet. He didn't think of white sand, turquoise waters, pink coral, and margaritas. He didn't calculate the quarter million in terms of real estate, cars, MX missiles, hamburgers, or Picassos. He didn't gawk or doubt. He didn't bother considering that for this Kresinski had cheated and lied to them. All he did was look. There was nothing moral or immoral about it, nothing bizarre or significant. It rested on his chest like so much baby powder or processed sugar. Finally he tilted his body and the packet slid to the cave floor. He closed his eyes and obeyed the wind. He went to sleep.

16

Morning came in
thick plasmic waves. The
wind was shrieking. They
could have been stranded on
Bullseye's Martian volcano, it was so
cold and alien. The parachute saved them.
Her, anyway. Without it, and him, she
would have perished overnight in the
freezing hurricane. She stared dully at the flat white
shroud in front of her face. It was too close or far away
to properly focus the parts of its fabric. No stitching.
No warp and woof. The world was just blank white. She was
remembering how the color white had driven a group of Ger-
man terrorists to suicide. The prison staff had painted everything in their individual cells white. A few months later, the prisoners
lost their minds. She stared at the white. She could smell his breath
against her neck, feel his gigantic arms under her shoulder and across her
chest. Thank God for his warmth, she thought. Thank God for the cold,
too. It had been too cold for rape. In a way it wouldn't have been rape.
Last night she would gladly have traded the use of her cunt for his body
heat. Last night as the sun sank and the wind jugulated the land, she'd
even offered to lower her pants if he would just hold her. "You must be
kidding," he said. But he wrapped her in his arms just the same, tenderly,
like a lover. The wire wound tightly around her wrists conducted the
cold like refrigerator coils. All night her head ached from the rapid hike
to higher altitude and from the times he cuffed her skull to goad more
speed. Sleep never got there for her, so she just lay still and kept warm
counting his pulse. All night the minutes masqueraded as days. Thank

275

God for the darkness, she thought. Darkness meant rest. But please God, where's the sun? she also prayed. John had told her the formula, the one monks use before dawn. *Fiat lux.* Let there be light. Let there be order. Coherence. Life. Let there be . . . white.

The strange thing was he was religious. She'd figured that out on the march in. Several times she'd fallen or he'd tugged too hard on the wire around her neck and she'd expelled a hardy "fucking Jesus" or "Christ" like some muscle-tongued cowboy. He hadn't punished the blasphemy, hadn't said a word. But she knew it constituted blasphemy from the way he got quiet and looked at her. Once his displeasure became clear, she quit using those words to cuss with.

In hope of achieving such insipid cowlike mediocrity that her captor would eventually turn her loose, Liz made up a few guidelines as the miles passed beneath their feet. Do whatever he wants, she instructed herself. Shut your mouth. Keep up. Be nice. Don't look him in the eye. Some instinct informed her that this man was different. He wasn't wantonly cruel, and there wasn't a shred of paranoia in him. Beating her, cutting her hair with a swipe of his sheath knife, wiring her hands together, kidnapping her—these were completely impersonal acts, cost-effective, timesaving means to an end. He had purchased her fear for the lowest price obtainable. In that context, eye contact would be utterly futile. Her real reason for avoiding his eyes was more spiritual. Very simply, she didn't want to lose her faith in man. Right up to the instant he might take her life, she wanted to believe.

Quite suddenly he woke up. He didn't grunt or jerk. His breathing didn't change, and he didn't say anything. But his presence altered. Liz swallowed her fear. One moment he was a vast scoop of heat shielding her from the Martian winds. And then, suddenly, his eyes were open. She sensed it. Her destiny was once again in rapid, uncontrollable motion. She lay inanimate in his arms, but knew there was no way he could not feel her breath pumping quick like a hummingbird's. There was no way to stop him from doing what was begun. If only he would leave her in this whiteness. If only the day would pass her by. But the Valley had finished harboring her. The arms released her. The heat and solidity against her back vanished. It felt like half the world just swept away. With an arc of his arm, the giant stripped the parachute canopy from over them, and

276

there it was, the harsh, rocky, stock-still earth. The sky was like cold stained pewter, clouds on clouds. No sun today.

By their heads was a frozen stalk of waterfall ice. Rising well over a hundred feet, it carried in its glass every color of blue Liz had ever imagined. She had guided them here yesterday, acutely uncertain if here was where they really wanted to be. All she could say with confidence was that whatever he wanted, she wanted. His will was her god. "There's a shortcut to the lake," he'd told her. "Show me." Based on foggy memories of John's description, she'd led her captor through a miserable gauntlet of avalanche debris and mud straight into this cul-de-sac. The dead end was so bluntly barren of any exits that Liz had started crying, though silently and without theater because she didn't want to annoy the man. But he didn't lose his temper. He didn't kill her. There were two reasons why. A weathered rope lay draped down the side of the ice shaft, and that was a declaration of progress. Secondly, this parachute had lain rustling behind a rock. The giant man recognized it. "Congratulations," he'd said. "We made it." Then night fell, and they pulled the parachute over them.

"Morning," he greeted her from high upon his legs. It was a mistake to brand his flashes of courtesy and affection and cheeriness as aberrant schizophrenic touches. Nor were his demonstrations of violence a symptom of monstrosity. Liz had never encountered a more genuine person. You could tell he knew himself well. He knew the weight of his hand, the length of his shadow. He kept his vanities simple—a mustache, a silver belt buckle—and his risks slight. He had no use whatsoever for hesitation. For all she knew, he was married. He might be a splendid, demanding lover. A father his children could brag on at school. For all she knew he could have been her Adam. Could have been.

Her golden hair mutilated, old blood from the scalp wound crusted down the left side of her neck, Liz remained curled in a ball on one corner of the parachute and didn't plague him with her gray eyes. She was in conflict with herself. She was his instrument, a compass for his guidance. But she was also the daughter and granddaughter of men who would have gutted and castrated the son of a bitch for his sins against her, who would have made him lost forever. She was passive and even, inescapably, worshipful of his Old Testament certainty. But she was also alive to the possibilities of escape. The man was hunting John and Matt for reasons that were unclear. So be it. It had to do with the lake. She hated John for not anticipating this savagery, or anticipating it and yet not telling her. She hated him for his weak, gentle ignorance. If only he'd been more like this giant stranger, she would have been safe. But at the same time, she feared for his life the way she feared for her own.

"Well," the man decided. "We'll go up now."

Liz was relieved and yet terrified. He wasn't finished with her yet. Against reason, she was still feeding the tiny fire of hope that any minute now he would unwire her hands, spank her ass, and send her galloping down-valley, hurt and ugly but at least alive. Not only was that hope illogical given what had happened to Tucker and Bullseye—and she had revised all her doubts that they had been murdered by this man—it was also an act of intellectual cowardice. Without even knowing it, she had taken sanctuary in her womanhood. In her mind this torrent of events was a masculine storm. It was a bad accident that she was a victim. That she could lose what Tucker and Bullseye had lost and what John and Matt were in danger of losing was unthinkable. She was free. She was safe. It was only a matter of time before her captor realized the truth of it.

She stood up. She left the white folds of nylon and staggered back onto the dirt of the world. "You hungry?" the man said. He had a big army-surplus rucksack that was empty except for some nuts and fruit. Sticking his arm shoulder-deep inside the rucksack, he pulled out some apples and a can of beer nuts. The apple was sweet and cold, the first liquid Liz had tasted since chewing dirty avalanche snow the previous afternoon. The beer nuts were almost too sugary, but she forced herself to eat everything that was offered. That was another of her guidelines for survival. Take what's offered. Say thanks. "Thanks," she whispered.

"You're sturdy," the man praised. He walked over to the rope and gave a hard yank on it, then tied a loop near the ground and put his foot in it. He tried his weight on the rope, then hopped up and down in the loop to really stress the anchor above. They couldn't see around the edge where the rope was anchored, but it seemed secure enough for the man. "How close are we?" he asked.

"Close," said Liz. She didn't really know. But that's what he'd want to hear.

The man worked the loop of rope off his foot. "Here's how we'll do this," he said. "I'll go up first. Then you'll come."

At first the plan seemed absurd to Liz, not much different from trying to get the fox, the hen, and the peasant across the river in a boat that only carries two. There was no way she could climb the rope, even if her hands were untied. And the moment the giant reached the top of the ice shaft, she could run away. She'd be like the wind back down across the avalanche debris. Back to the Valley.

"Okay," she said, cloaking her excitement. Then he removed another ten feet of wire from his rucksack.

"I'd like your help when I pull you up," he said. "Try and use your feet while I pull, okay?" With the wire he hobbled her ankles, leaving maybe ten inches in between. By the time she got the wire unbound—if she even could with fingers this numb—he would spot her escape attempt and slide down the rope. He unknotted the loop in the rope and with some slack tied a tight coil around her chest and gave the knot a good extra tug, the way you do with a packhorse. "Ready?" he asked, though it didn't matter. She nodded yes.

"Would you sit over here, Liz?" he asked, patting a rock. When she sat down, he draped the parachute over her shoulders. "Keep you warm," he said. "I'll call down when it's time for you, all right?"

He grabbed the rope with his bare hands and planted one foot against the ice. The muscles bunched under his flannel sleeves when he pulled. Smooth and steady, he walked his feet up the slippery surface. Halfway up his boot slipped and he cracked against the ice, showering Liz with crystals and shards.

"Are you okay?" she called up. It seemed important to ask that. She wondered why.

The slip didn't faze him. He hung on. He hammered a few powerful kicks against the ice and regained his footing. Every few feet he looked down to check that Liz was still in place. Though her body was covered by the parachute and she could have been working invisibly at the wire bonds, she didn't. The man was omnipotent. Her obedience disappointed her. But that's the way it is, she told herself. The end was near. Above all the end was something that couldn't be disobeyed. All the patterns of action were set, and it was practically her duty to be what she was. The feeling shocked her, but she was almost happy. It went beyond resignation. Her own history was being written, and she was right there to read it.

The giant man was not graceful. More ice came clattering down, though nothing big hit her. His mechanical power looked all the more clumsy to Liz, who had the likes of John and Tucker and Matt as examples of how ascent ought to look. Where this man pounded the ice and thrust himself higher and higher along the rope, they would have glided. They would have whispered across the ice. Just the same, measured against this huge juggernaut of a man who was pursuing each climber to his doom, it made very little difference how beautiful their climbing was to watch. Art is a delicate thing. Unless you've provided for its safety, the painting fades, the sculpture melts away.

The man pulled himself over the edge of the ice shaft and disappeared from sight. Once again, Liz imagined that her freedom was about to be granted. The rope would collapse in a heap around her shoulders and feet. She would untie the wire from her ankles and wrists and the rope from her chest and leave the harsh violence behind to those who'd bought into it. Take the parachute with you, she reminded herself. Weakened like she was, it might be another night in the open before she reached the valley floor, and the canopy would keep her warm.

Abruptly the rope jerked her from the rock, cinching tight around her chest. It notched into her chest and squeezed the air from her lungs. "Ready?" she heard distantly. There was no chance to answer. The rope hauled her a yard off the ground. Desperately trying to relieve the suffocating tightness, Liz scrambled with her feet against the ice. She almost found an edge to stand on when the rope hoisted her higher. With her bound hands, she tried to grab hold of the rope, but the wire deadened her grip. She rose another three feet, banging against the ice. For pity's sake, she thought, the sun isn't even showing. Every breath was a struggle. The thought occurred to her that if he wanted, the man could simply tie the rope off and walk away. It might take a half hour, but eventually the effect would equal dropping her. She considered it all without alarm. The rope hurt too much.

At last it was over. Barely conscious, Liz felt herself arrive on a bank of flat ice. "Get up," the giant told her. Liz tried. Her arms had gone numb. She lay on the ice panting.

"Okay," the man said. Patiently he picked her up and walked over to a thin rock sticking up through the frozen streamlet. He deposited her sitting on the ice and began wrapping the rope around her and the rock.

"It's almost over, Elizabeth," he said. His voice carried a tenderness that told her this was it. She was going to freeze here. Then he would fetch his rope and wires, and by the time the animals and the elements finished with her, all people would wonder was what on earth she'd come up here to see. They would wonder about the other two bodies, too, John's and Matt's. Some would call it a love triangle smashed.

"Sleep," the man murmured by her ear.

Liz felt tears flickering down her windburned cheeks.

Then he was gone.

CHAPTER

17

*F*or centuries drag-
ons infested the Alps. They
bullied the imagination and
held men at bay from the mountains. They represented risk, but a very
peculiar species of risk. Like dragons themselves, the risk was composed of squat, dangerous, brute acts that soared in the sky
for no good reason, unlikely ascents above the flat
landscape of correctness and ordinary possibility. The
great climbers were those who chased after dragons,
not to kill them or banish them, but to cavort with them, to
celebrate the light. How many times had he and Tucker talked
this through and elected worthy names and sterling climbs?
Edward Whymper, Walter Bonatti, Paul Preuss, Hermann Buhl, Lay-
ton Kor, Dougal Haston . . . the Eiger, Nanga Parbat, Annapurna, Cerro
Torre. Lounging by the Merced River or perched on bivouac ledges high
above the trees, he and Tucker had wondered if they would ever encounter a dragon of their own. Once, just once, in a moment of extreme confidence, Tucker had reckoned how the West Face of Makalu might be his
great ascent, and the singularity of that remark had saddened and also
thrilled John. It was easy to see, given Tucker's secrecy about Makalu,
that what the boy had in mind was a solo of the immense eight-
thousand-foot face. And despite all his talents, John knew Tucker would
never make it. Like George Mallory in 1924 on Everest, Tucker might
get to the top, but he'd never come down alive. Of course, John hadn't
tried to talk him out of it. You don't snuff another man's fire. From that
time on, John had figured that Tucker's days were numbered. Just as pri-

vately, he'd also figured that of the two of them, at least Tucker would meet his dragon, and that was fine. For the handful of visionaries like Mallory and Whymper, that was the very point.

But then Half Dome had cheated them of Tucker. Half Dome and the smuggler. The smuggler and Kresinski. John saw that now. Now, with the wind pouring past their shattered citadel of rock, John also saw that he had come face to face with a dragon of his own. His was a different kind of dragon, though. It had nothing to do with going higher or meeting darker risks. Very simply, he'd come all this way to learn that he could turn around and go back. And that's what he was going to do. Turn back. Back away. Quit. Lying there on the floor of the cave, John realized—for the first time really accepted—that descent was valid. For all these years it had been the thing he dreaded most. But now, faced with the chance to touch top, to loot the gold and buy his own kingdom by the sea, his own beach on which he and Liz could count sunsets and race the surf and mount the world and never come down—now he was turning away. He was turning his back on Kresinski, on the coke, on the song of glory. Whatever it was up top—Oz, Shangri-la, Eden—he was bagging it.

He unzipped his sleeping bag and stood up. There was no telling what time it was; the gray light tunneling in from outside was absolutely generic. It was day. That was all John needed to know. He dressed quickly, stuffed his bag in its stuff sack, and reached for his coil of red rope. In the pall of gray light, the cave looked like a tomb. Kresinski looked dead. The coke had wiped him out. But when John stepped across him and moved toward the entrance, Kresinski's eyes opened automatically.

"What you doing, Johnny?" he asked.

"Going down," said John. It would be faster rappeling than downclimbing the uppermost section of the col, faster still if he didn't have to uncoil his own rope. Outside, snowflakes flashed diagonally like sword cuts. There were more flakes than yesterday, though none were landing. The wind seemed, if anything, stronger and louder.

"I knew you'd split, man," said Kresinski. "Do your famous fast fade."

John ducked his head out the cave. There was Kresinski's yellow rope. And far below, barely visible through the light snowfall, lay the lake. John felt strangely light. It was an ecstatic feeling. All the gross, vulgar reaching was behind. One step, the sensation told him, and he would fly. The lake would sink below. The mountains would fall away. The sun would grow warm. He stepped back into the cave.

"I'm going to rap down your rope," John said. "You mind?" He hefted his pack and slugged it onto his back. This was easy.

"You're not going to make it," Kresinski hectored him. He sat up, fully clothed, half out of his bag. "He's down there. He's waiting for us. We got to go two-on-one on him, John. It's the only way."

John didn't answer. He was ready. "You mind?" he said.

Kresinski was scowling at him. Fatigue had hollowed out his face. "Nah, I don't mind," he decided. "Do me a favor, though. Leave me your rope." John understood. With John's rope and his own tied together, Kresinski could double the length of his rappels when he finally descended. He'd be needing to rappel, what with all that weight to carry. The longer the rappels, the fewer anchors he'd need to set on the way down. The fewer the anchors, the quicker he could get down and away. "I'll buy your damn rope," Kresinski growled. "Take one of those keys with you."

John didn't take any of the cargo. "Just bring my rope back," he said, knowing that was the end of the rope. He tossed the red coil down by the entrance.

There was nothing else left to say, not even good luck, so he left the cave. The wind broke against his body and tore at his hair. Quickly now, he stepped into position and arranged the rope over his body.

Kresinski came to the cave's entrance. "You're gonna lose, John," he shouted.

John tugged on the rope, testing the anchor. A rappel is only as safe as its anchor. It wasn't much of an anchor, two nuts in parallel fissures, but he didn't need much. He leaned out against the rope and fed some slack over his shoulder. He edged across the snowy cornice and entered the col. Smooth and gentle, he continued down. The feeling of lightness magnified. Part of it was the act of rappeling, which is basically an act of zero-gravity motion. But part of it was descent itself.

"You lose, man," Kresinski yelled down at him. John looked up the gully walls, and there was Kreski's savage head jutting over the cornice. "I knew you would." Then his head was gone.

Twisting to look over his shoulder, John continued tiptoeing down the col. The wind was freaky and unnerving, but twenty feet lower and the angle would diminish. From there on down, he could climb. Once his hands and feet were firmly attached to the mountain again, he'd feel less exposed. Some people enjoy rappeling precisely because it frees them from holding on to the world. John hated rappeling. During the time you hang on the rope, you're essentially out of control. Your life depends on the anchor, the rope, and the friction of a braking device. If any one of those elements fails, you die.

He was still lowering himself when the rope suddenly quivered. Then it quivered again. He could feel the vibrations in his hands. His first reaction was that the wind was playing against the taut line between him and the anchor. His second reaction—too late—was that Kresinski was pulling the rope. John poised one toe on a ledge and darted a glance upward. But it was too late.

The rope suddenly collapsed in his hands. For an instant he managed to balance over his toe. Then his pack tipped him backward and he pitched down the col. He'd fallen before and always come out okay. But this was different. There was no chance for survival this time. This time there was no rope to catch him. This time the advantages of free space were null and void.

He hit the gully wall and bounced and hit the opposite wall. Like a pinball, he ricocheted from wall to wall. Here and there he was intercepted by a rock poking out from the mountain and flung into the air. He was tossed and beaten on the long descent that was neither air nor rock, just the physics of an angel stripped of its wings. Even if the brutal fall didn't kill him on the way down, the lake would. There was no escaping the lake. Once he hit the snowy ledge below and launched out into space toward the lake, nothing more needed doing except impact, and that was guaranteed.

He had no time to think. No time to feel. Each blunt, wracking blow from the mountain registered as a change in direction. That was about it. After the first hundred feet or so, he quit trying to ward off the blows with his hands and feet. He belonged to the mountain now. He belonged to the lake. All the same, he kept his eyes open. This was the big ride and he was paying admission, and there was no sense closing his eyes for the finale. It seemed to take a long time. Fast and slow, the assault on his flesh was nearly over. He bounced a final time.

Then it was all air. He was riding the wind. He *was* the wind. All that was present was the vast gray sky. It went on forever, the cold, the roar, the gray. He lay in the palm of air, astonished by the never-ending journey. This was how terminal velocity felt. There was no reason not to accept it. This was how it had been for Tucker. Zeno was right. The arrow never reaches its mark. In order to go all the way you have to go halfway, and in order to go halfway you have to get halfway to halfway, *ad infinitum*. No wonder they'd never found Tuck. He'd simply never hit the ground. That was okay with John. He savored the chill air.

After a while he tentatively tried moving his arms, but they wouldn't. His legs were locked down, too. It wasn't what he'd expected. He felt encumbered. Heavy. And all at once the adrenaline high flushed out and there was a rush of pain that had no center because it was everywhere at the same time. He needed oxygen to scream with and he drew at the air, but his ribs ignited with a sharp fire. Like that, his pain brought him back to reality. He wasn't in perpetual flight, not even remotely so. His infinity of halfways hadn't even spanned a single respiration. The second breath was no better than the first. The sense of peace was a lie, as was the sense of being airborne.

Lifting his head, John saw that he'd lodged head up in the snow on the ledge crowning the cirque. The lake was spread beneath his feet, and he was half sitting, half lying on the precipitous rim. Kresinski's yellow rope lay in tangles all around him. He saw these things, but not really. Not well. His focus was shot and his head hurt badly. What he saw was a gray hollow overhead and a gray hollow underfoot. As for the rope, he identified that with his hands. He was nearly blind.

John nested his head back on the pillow of snow. The sky had quit calling to him. The languid sense of grace was gone. He kept his breathing shallow. Ribs were broken. He allowed himself to be lazy. His body terrified him. It was an injured animal, and there was going to be pain, a whole lot of pain, when he finally got around to exploring himself. For a minute he thought about how much easier it would be just to give his mind to other matters. The sky was wonderfully blank and the wind was so elaborate. Rest up. Close your eyes. Hypothermia wouldn't be far off, not with this wind. It would replace the adrenaline. He considered how he'd always loved the cold. There was an interior beauty to the cold. A sexuality. Like a queen in a legend. She'd come hump him slow. No need to move for her. Didn't even have to strip the way that pilot had. Together they'd manage it fine just the way he was, flat on his butt. She could take her time. Take his pain. Give him grace.

He forgot all about Kresinski. For a while he catnapped, though that, too, might have been something imagined. Time was evasive. The rapid snowflakes were hard and nipped at his face like tiny piranhas, so maybe he didn't sleep at all. His eyes opened and closed and opened, always to the same dull, soupy sky. Here was how limbo would look: a bleak monochrome, no focus, no color, no light. He heard a whispering. It was his own. *"Padre nuestro,"* it went. *"Que estás en los cielos . . ."* He was surprised by the beautiful prayer. Years had sunk since he'd last prayed. It was so beautiful that he started it all over again, louder, to hear its music. *"Padre nuestro, que estás en los cielos . . ."* God he didn't need. Nor heaven. Didn't need shit so long as he had his hands and eyesight and mind. But those weren't always enough. Right now a little color, a little focus, a little light would go a long long way. Anything to contradict this blank, vaulting sky.

Then there was a motion. Above and behind him, a shape slowly rounded the corner of rock. John didn't exactly hear it. And he couldn't have seen it because his eyes were closed. But suddenly he was aware of that second presence. The literature of Himalayan mountaineering is checkered with accounts of a nonexistent man who joins hypoxic climbers near their summits. There was something similarly phantom about this other presence, but also something different. Tangible.

Like a yeti, it shifted across the snow, stealing toward the base of the col. John tilted his head backward in the snow, trying to see above him. Upon his movement, the shape halted, as if John were a surprise. All John could discern was more mountain. When the shape moved again, a leg appeared in the corner of his vision. Holding his ribs and grunting for air, he craned further for a view above. He dug the heel of one foot into the snow and pressed upward and sideways, but the pocket holding him onto the steep ledge complained with a peculiar ripping noise. He froze. He looked into the wild maw between his knees and took several shallow breaths. The wind stripped the frost from his lips.

"Kreski?" he said, but the wind drowned his word.

The shape moved closer toward the mouth of the col, but slowly and cautiously. It hugged the rock wall and stamped its feet over and over with each step as if the snow might collapse or the ledge might avalanche. Just might, too, thought John. Man, animal, or phantom, it seemed horrified by the height. The thought of Kresinski lurking behind and overhead caused John to chance another twist in place. He had damn little to lose. Plowing both heels into the crust, he folded his arms across his ribs and lurched upward and to his left. The pain sucked him empty for a moment, and when he could breathe again, the shape was gone.

Now sideways to the face, one leg stretched long, the other bent, John could at least appreciate the miracle of his survival. Half from memory, he assembled from the hazy blur how the col's throat reared in a steep complex of outcrops and bends. The chute should have propelled him far out onto the lake. Rearranged now, he could also better survey his landing spot. The col had bucked him high in the air and, with the weird mercy of a mountain, deposited him square upon the only bit of ledge that could have saved him. The snow was pink with blood where his head had rested, and that helped explain the throbbing in the back of his skull and his virtual blindness. Besides that and his ribs, he seemed to have beaten the odds, at least for the moment.

"That was a nasty spill," a deep voice observed from the other side of the col. In the wind it could have been Kresinski's voice. John jerked his head around, too violently as it was, and his vision blurred from the pain. Where was the bastard? He didn't dare move again. If only the rope were anchored to the wall, he could have pulled himself from the edge. The limp, tangled shanks of rope were useless. "Careful," said the man. There was a sympathetic fear in that voice, the gut reaction of one person watching another on the brink.

Casting backward, John appealed to that fear. "Help," he said. Not that he expected help, not from Kresinski. It was the old college try, that's all. He wanted, very simply, to see Kresinski's face because now it would be his real face. There was no fight left in John. None at all. He was scared and hurt and blind. Also he was resigned. Even if he managed to get across the ledge and descend the ramp, there was no way he'd ever make it back all those miles to the trailhead alone. And he was very alone.

"Is that my coke down there?" asked the voice.

The question made no sense. But it identified the shape. It wasn't Kresinski. It was the smuggler. The smuggler had followed them up.

"What?" said John. He was not particularly shocked.

"Down there. That pack, boy." John obligingly bent his head and looked into the abyss. He couldn't see a thing. Nevertheless, he was able to imagine his pack as a tiny blue dot flattened on the lake. It must have been plucked from his back during the fall.

"Is that my coke?" the man repeated. There was no bullshit to the man. He was direct. It wasn't "goods," "merchandise," or "snow." It was "my coke." "Or is it still up there?" said the smuggler.

"I can't see you," said John. This was it. He was dead fucked now. His one regret was that the finish couldn't have been on his own terms, sleepy, caressed by the cold. Another few hours and she would have had him stiff and blue, locked to the mountain. "Let me see you." He didn't have a plan. He just wanted to see the man's face, even though he couldn't.

"It's still up there, isn't it?" said the smuggler. "With your friend."

John gently rested his neck back on the snow. His black hair fanned out upon the white snow. "You know what you did?" he asked the smuggler. The smuggler couldn't hear him.

"Call him. Call your buddy."

Lifting his voice against the wind, John said. "He wouldn't come even if I did." He was indifferent.

"Call him, damn it."

"He pulled my anchor. He dumped me."

Suddenly he felt his shoulder nudged by something hard. The toe of the man's boot. "Loud. Get him down here. Now." His shoulder dipped under another nudge of the boot.

Holding his ribs, John attempted a yell. The bones actually grated under his hand, and he fought against vomiting in pain.

"We'll wait then," said the smuggler. They listened to the wind for a minute. "So which one are you?" he asked conversationally. "John or Matthew?"

John's eyes were closed tight against the stinging snow and the sear in his chest. One thing about the broken ribs, they kept his concentration in a nice tight tunnel. No room for anything but the next tiny breath. Hardly room to even hear what the man had to say. But then the implication of the man's words hit him, and John's eyes opened in alarm. There was only one person who had the kindness to call Kresinski by his full first name. Liz.

The smuggler detected his alarm. He'd been waiting for it. "You thought this was all for free?" he said.

"What have you done?" said John. He tried, but couldn't catch up with the possible branchings of fate. Keep it simple, he told himself. The man had talked to Liz.

"I took something that was yours."

John tried again to look over one shoulder, then the other. The smuggler was just out of view and, most definitely, out of reach. He was taking no chances, not that John was an adversary. Then John was tired again. He laid his head on the snow. "We didn't even know," he said.

"Ignorance is a hell of a reason for dying," said the smuggler.

"Goddamn you," John cursed. It was an old-style curse, sincere and final. But because he couldn't see his enemy, it was like hexing the wind.

The smuggler was full of patience. "I know," he said. "I know." After a moment he added, "Hell of a place for a Mexican standoff, ain't it?" The man was terrified of the mountain. John could tell by the bonhomie in his voice. It was an artificial camaraderie.

"What did you do with her?" John demanded.

"With Elizabeth? The real question is what did *you* do to her? In a month some hiker will find her. Then they'll find you two boys. They'll wonder about it all."

John squinted blindly into the wind. There was a sense in which the smuggler didn't even exist. He operated in their interstices, between their daily mechanisms. Their risks became his weapons. Their motives and dreams and jealousies and petty entanglements became his explanations—and he didn't even have to explain. All he had to do was tip their forward motion into terminal velocity.

"She came in with you?"

"She's down there, John-or-Matthew. Somewhere out in your wilderness there. Waiting for you."

Still alive, John decided. How alive was another problem. And he couldn't even fight to save her, or see to track her.

"It's time, friend. You going to jump? Or do you need some help?"

His kindness was obscene and yet comforting. John went on sitting sideways in the snow, clutching his ribs. "Can you stand up?" the smuggler asked.

John didn't even attempt to stand.

"That's okay."

The smuggler kicked him in the back. It wasn't much of a kick, too high, oblique, and tenuous. The man was too scared to descend for a really good swing. The second swipe caught John on the shoulder. He grunted. Then the smuggler had a better idea. He changed position and lowered his boot to John's inside shoulder and shoved down. John budged. The extra weight forced him six inches lower. Grimacing, John replanted his feet. The boot nestled against his neck and shoved down again. John lost another few inches. He was afraid to resist the boot because the snow was barely glued to the ledge as it was. The boot shoved him down again.

"Fuck you," he said.

"I know," said the smuggler. And he did know, John reflected. He'd practiced. First with Tucker. Then with Bullseye. Now with him. One thing the bastard must have learned: Climbers stick. You have to shove and kick and beat them before gravity gets her due. He couldn't fight back, but he could sure let the man work for his conclusions. The boot jarred him again, pushing the abyss that much closer. John grunted.

And suddenly the smuggler grunted, too.

John heard the snap of bone. It was distinct, a sharp cracking noise, like a baseball bat rapping a stone. There was only one thing it could have been. A rock had hit the smuggler. It had hit him square on the skull, the sound of cracking bone was unmuffled by clothing. He heard a body drop against the snow. Then the smuggler was lying there, upside down by John's side.

The man's face was indistinct, but John could see the black outline of a mustache. A dark pinkness was leaking in a widening patch from inside his dark hair. The man had fallen headfirst, faceup. One of his huge arms was lying off the ledge. If not for his enormous size, he would have slid off the ledge. But his weight had broken the crust, and just beyond reach he'd stuck the way John had stuck.

"See, man. There really *is* a boogeyman."

Kresinski was standing twenty feet overhead on a rocky shelf. John could just make him out. He'd rappeled all the way down from the cave. Now he finished coming down to the ledge. His movements were ponderous, and that meant he was carrying the cocaine. The gigantic black pack on his back came into focus. He solidly rooted his feet in the snow with two powerful stomps. He stayed on the upper rim of the ledge.

"Sort of like a party, huh, John? Everybody showed up." With broad, careful motions, Kresinski off-loaded the heavy pack. John wiped his eyes, but the image stayed blurry. Kresinski sank the heavy pack into the snow by his legs and prodded it with a slap. It was firmly socketed and going nowhere. Ever the careful mountaineer, Kresinski started pulling one end of his rope through the final anchor in the col. John kept looking back and forth from the motionless smuggler to Kresinski's pumping arms. At least the other half of the rope pulled free, and the line came whipping down on top of them all.

Kresinski attached one end to his pack, then took his time looking for a crack to anchor into. What John couldn't actually see he was still able to perceive with common sense. Of course Kresinski would try to anchor the rope. He would use it to secure the pack to the wall. Also, once anchored, the rope would eliminate Kresinski's risks. He could tie himself into the rope and safely tidy up the ledge. But he couldn't find any adequate cracks for an anchor. Finally he gave up on setting an anchor. "Well, anyway, guys," he said and straightened up.

John knew what was coming. One finality was equal to another. But Kresinski's appearance offered one hope. "Kreski," said John.

"Yo." Kresinski had begun coiling John's red rope, the one he'd rappeled down with. John wondered what Kresinski would have done if he'd refused to lend him the extra rope. Without the extra rope he couldn't have afforded to cut the yellow one.

"Liz is down there. He brought her in with him."

"Bullshit." Kresinski stopped coiling. Then he said, "Where?"

"I don't know. But we have to find her."

"We?"

John expected that. He didn't argue. At least Kresinski knew she was in need now. Maybe his evil had a limit. Maybe he'd find her and save her. Probably not, though. The coke was a demon riding him into the deep. He'd already sacrificed Tucker and Bullseye for the treasure. Liz was just as cheap. But maybe not.

"It's time to rodeo, John," he said. He finished coiling the rope and slapped it hard against the snow. It stuck there for a minute. Then the wind started hounding it loose. Snaky shanks started creeping down and across the ledge. Kresinski didn't bother recoiling it. "Tell you what, though," Kresinski said. "You did me a favor by helping me catch this sucker. I'll do you one. You want to watch? How's that?"

Kresinski kick-stepped down from the wall and his pack. It was only ten feet or so to the smuggler. Since dropping by John's side, he hadn't moved. His bare hand hung over the ledge in the wind. Kresinski's rock must have killed him, thought John. There was little left to do. All Kresinski had to do was shove on the man's boots and set him loose. The smuggler's head was only inches from the edge. It would take a few seconds. Then it would be John's turn.

Instead, Kresinski took a handful of the tangled yellow rope, his rope, and doubled a section. He bent down and lashed the rope across the man's face. "Wake up, asshole," he said.

John closed his eyes. He hunted for peace inside his mind. But even if the wind had permitted it, Kresinski wouldn't. He whipped the smuggler's face again. There was no reaction. The man was dead. If he wasn't yet, he would be in a minute or two. In an hour's time Kresinski would be down the ramp and traversing the lakeshore, homeward bound. The rest of the players would already be arranged down there, John and Liz and the smuggler, like mannequins on a stage. It would be a quiet stroll past the lake.

"Okay, sport," Kresinski mocked the smuggler's motionless body. "You want to jump? Or you want some help? Can you stand up?"

So, thought John. Kresinski had stood above and watched the smuggler invite him over the edge. Kresinski even had the man's odd, courteous tone down.

"Get it over with," John said with disgust.

"Be with you in a sec," said Kresinski.

Kresinski stepped in closer to the body, careful to jam his feet deep into the snow. He bent to the task. With one hand bracing him above, he grabbed the smuggler's pant leg and tried to throw his leg up and over. The leg was enormous, though, and he barely managed to lift it.

"This sucker's even heavier than his brother was," he said. He sat against the slope of snow and placed one foot against the man's huge rib cage. He shoved once, got some downward movement from the body, and shoved again. The smuggler's head slid halfway over the edge. "There he goes," Kresinski puffed. "You watching, Johnny?" He pushed again. And again.

You must do something, thought John. Do something. It was an instruction. Now. It had the feel of a new thought. But it was an old thought, ancient. Your legs are your friends. Your eyes. Your hair. Your hands. Do something.

John filled his lungs twice, mainly to fathom the coming pain. He hugged his ribs and inhaled. Then rocked forward over his legs. Behind him, Kresinski was busy with the smuggler. Following through with the arc, John managed to stand up. The blood rushed from his head. The sky jumped from gray to black, but he forced himself to brush the rope from his legs. He touched the snow with his left hand and took a step away from the edge. Kresinski noticed him.

"No good, man," he said, unconcerned with John's attempt. He was winded from kicking at the body. Doggedly he kicked at it again anyway. John wavered in place. He looked around, afraid Kresinski might come after him before he'd even had a chance. All he needed was a chance, he told himself. Disgusted with the slow labor of dislodging the giant smuggler, Kresinski stood up to catch some lighter prey. "Say good night, John," he said.

It was then that the smuggler came alive. Maybe he knew what he was doing. Maybe he just grabbed the first thing he felt. His hand closed on Kresinski's leg.

"Shit," barked Kresinski.

John saw what was happening and took another step away. But it was a feeble grip. Kresinski pulled his leg from the grappling hand. He backed up, then decided to get it over with, and landed a terrific blow on the man's hip with his foot.

John took another step up and away from the execution. The horror of what Kresinski was doing—of what he had already done—flooded John with repulsion. He panicked. His next step was too high, his next breath too deep. His body couldn't keep up with his will, and the injuries felled him. By wrenching his torso to the right, he barely managed to land against the steep bank of snow with his good side. As he did, he saw Kresinski hammer the smuggler one last time with his foot.

There was no frenzy to the fall. Where there had been a man, there was now an empty trough of torn snow. John blinked. Snowflakes crashed down on his eyes. He gasped for air. Kresinski looked up at him. Even as they hung there, wordless, a gigantic rag doll was careening toward the lake. John gave it a few more seconds. Then the image hit. It broke the ice, surely it would do that. It hung in the water, head floating among the shattered plates of ice. Then it sank.

In waves, between nausea and the curtains of storm, John watched Kresinski's shape collect itself to resume the slaughter. There was no shame or doubt or pleasure on that approaching face, though the truth was John couldn't really see Kresinski's face. He just read the story it had to tell, belonging to who it did. A new strength had cut into Kresinski's features. I chose, his eyes bragged. My will be done. John tried to dispel the perception, but Kresinski's desolation was radiant.

John pawed at the snow's crust. His bare hand touched a strand of rope. Instinctively he clutched at it and reached for more, rifling through the slack in search of rope that was taut and anchored. He discarded yards and yards of coiled and serpentine line. He flung the useless slack away from him into the wind. At last the rope came taut. It led upward. He pulled on it. The muscles of his back and chest snapped across his broken ribs, but he kept on pulling.

There was no thought of where the rope led to or what it was anchored to. Up was good. Always had been. It lifted him. His legs pulled free of the snow. He kicked a step, stood, pulled. Down and across the ledge Kresinski bellowed. John looked. Lunging powerfully up and across the tilted ledge, Kresinski plowed through the snow and scattered rope.

"No," Kresinski howled. His voice should have rung with the mandate of his power. Instead it sounded desperate and unbelieving. But what was there not to believe? It was all his. All their rare, streamlined desires and sunburned ambitions reduced to now. Every mountain they'd ever climbed on or dreamed of reduced to this mountain. Every dragon was this dragon. Too bad, thought John. All their collective ascents should have arrived on top of an almighty mountain, something grand and radically mythical like Bullseye's Martian Olympus. And yet here the struggle ended. Beneath a backpack filled with nose candy. Kresinski had won. He was king of the mountain. It should have been John bellowing that Shakespearean "no" into the storm, but he had no air to yell with because he couldn't believe it was over, not so low, not so impoverished. He hauled down on the rope and kicked one higher footstep, scrambling to escape to nowhere. He was too slow, too fat with gravity. There was no way this time around. The Lightning Man had got him.

At that moment the rope failed. Hope stopped. The mountain was coming apart in his very hands. He looked up just in time to see the dark angel spread its wings. Like a gargoyle, death took off from its white roost. It didn't leap grandly into space and gouge him from the wall with its talons. Rather it leaned out and lazily nodded off its perch and fell toward him like a fat, ungainly reptile.

"No!" echoed Kresinski's howl.

Entranced, John watched as the gargoyle became Kresinski's huge black pack. In another part of his mind it registered that the rope had been anchored to the pack and the pack had been anchored to nothing. John let go of the rope. He plunged his arms into the snow. His hands struck the rock wall beneath the snow, and his fingers scraped for purchase. He embraced the mountain with his whole body.

The pack dropped from its roost in the snow. It glided with a hiss. A hundred pounds of deadweight fell and punched John like a fist. It struck him high on the back and drove his legs groin-deep into the snow. The buckles and straps clawed at him, wrestling for possession. The wind sucked to loosen him. His fingers lost touch of the rock. He dug at the crust and embedded himself all over again. He shrugged at the clawing weight.

Then the pack was past him. He heard the hiss of its glissade down the remaining few yards of ledge. Abruptly the hiss stopped. Still clutching two armfuls of snow, John cast a look over one shoulder. The immense black pack was gone. Less than a dozen feet away, Kresinski was standing stock-still on the empty white ledge.

Again John heard the sound of hissing. But this time it was a more delicate, slithering noise, barely audible beneath the wind. Snakes make that shimmering sound crossing silvery deserts at midnight. In the morning you find their beautiful sinuous signatures in the sand. John couldn't see it, but he knew the sound. It was the whisper of rope across snow. As the pack sailed toward the lake, it was carrying behind it a long, thin comet-tail of rope.

"Matt," warned John. Kresinski was standing in the rope.

"You're dead," said Kresinski. Then he gave a strangled, shocked bleat as the rope coiled fast around his legs. John heard the pop of bone unhinging. He caught a blurred, hangman's flash of color, and Kresinski was gone. The void plucked him away. There was no more drama than that.

John was alone.

Once more it was simple.

The world was his to create again. Memory would guide him through some of it, his failing knees through the rest. He picked his way across the ledge. Resting often, he descended the ramp. The lake spread to his right. It would hang in his mind forever, cupped at the chin of a mountain two cowboys climbed once upon a time using a knife and a lasso. He couldn't see very well, so he didn't look. But ghosts swam in the dark blue waters under the ice. And as he limped and crawled down the ramp, John thought he smelled cocaine in the wind, and that confirmed how the pack stood on top of the ice, leaking its white contents into the raging sky. There was bound to be a great calm behind this storm, there always is. The trick is somehow weathering the storm.

John had no sleeping bag or food. He had no shelter except for the primitive rock walls his tribe had once stacked against the wind. He had no weapon except for a pocketknife. It was cold and he hurt, and it was going to be a long journey out. He wanted to curl up and sleep and wake up in the Valley among thick beams of sunlight. But that was impossible, of course. Somewhere out there in a wilderness of dead ends and wrong turns and circles without end, Liz was waiting for him. Somewhere out there he had a descent to honor. And stories to tell. He had much to do before night came on.